The Other Side of Dare

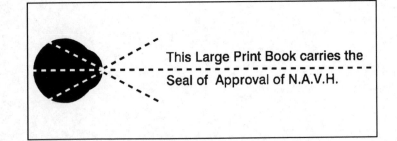

THE OTHER SIDE OF DARE

VANESSA DAVIS GRIGGS

THORNDIKE PRESS
A part of Gale, Cengage Learning

GALE
CENGAGE Learning®

Detroit • New York • San Francisco • New Haven, Conn • Waterville, Maine • London

GALE
CENGAGE Learning

A Blessed Trinity Novel Series.
Thorndike Press, a part of Gale, Cengage Learning.

Thorndike Press® Large Print African-American.
The text of this Large Print edition is unabridged.
Other aspects of the book may vary from the original edition.
Set in 16 pt. Plantin.

LIBRARY OF CONGRESS CATALOGING-IN-PUBLICATION DATA

Griggs, Vanessa Davis.
The other side of dare / by Vanessa Davis Griggs. — Large Print edition.
pages cm. — (A Blessed Trinity Novel Series) (Thorndike Press Large Print African-American)
ISBN 978-1-4104-5851-3 (hardcover) — ISBN 1-4104-5851-2 (hardcover)
1. Childlessness—Fiction. 2. Adopted children—Fiction. 3. African Americans—Fiction. 4. Domestic fiction. 5. Large type books. I. Title.
PS3557.R48954O83 2013
813'.54—dc23 2013011353

Published in 2013 by arrangement with Dafina Books, an imprint of Kensington Publishing Corp.

Printed in Mexico
1 2 3 4 5 6 7 17 16 15 14 13

To
My mother, Josephine Davis,
and father, James Davis Jr.

ACKNOWLEDGMENTS

Thank you, Lord, the author and finisher of my faith. I'm forever grateful and in awe of Your exceedingly, abundantly, above-all-I-can-ever-ask-or-think blessings. To my loving mother, Josephine Davis, and father, James Davis Jr.: You introduced me to the Lord and brought me up knowing that no matter where I was or what in life I did, I would never be alone because the Lord would always be with me. Thank you for making me believe that I really *can* do all things through Christ who strengthens me. I love you both more than words can ever express!

Thanks to my husband Jeffery for walking this journey with me. We've stood together, and no matter what the devil may have tried to throw our way, with God on our side, we've come through it. To my children: Jeffery, you have so much love, it truly blesses my heart seeing you bless those whose lives you touch. Jeremy, I remember the time you found a baby bird that had fallen out of its nest and had broken its neck. Your father and I watched you try to save him, to the point where your father took the bird to a person who confirmed he wouldn't make it. But you wouldn't give up. You cared for and nursed that bird. No, it didn't live, but I knew that anyone who was blessed enough to cross your path would always know true love and care. As an adult, you've shown that and so much more. I thank God for you. I'm also excited to welcome to our family my new daughter-in-law, Sonceria Griggs. Congratulations, you two! Johnathan, my talented artist and from-the-heart chef: You need to come home and visit your family. We miss seeing you terribly. LOL. Love you and I'm happy that you're walking in your gift. Asia and Ashlynn, just thinking of the both of you causes me to smile. My arms stretch deep and wide so I can wrap them around you! You're my vacation when we do things together, even if all we do is hang out, play games, blow bubbles, play around in the kitchen, or eat fruits and vegetables picnic-style on the bedroom floor. I am blessed to be your "Nana!"

Loving my family so much! My sisters,

brothers, their spouses: Danette Brown and husband, Herbert; Terence Davis and wife, Cameron (who ALWAYS reads every single book I write and lets me know what she thinks — thank you so much for that, Cameron!); Arlinda Davis; Emmanuel Davis and wife, Cumberlan; my aunts, uncles, cousins, in-laws, nieces, and nephews — I thank each of you for all the loving memories we've made and for those that are surely to come.

I give my sincere thanks and appreciation to Kensington senior editor Selena James, and all of the personnel at Kensington/Dafina who work diligently to make things happen. To Bonita Chaney, Rosetta Moore, Vanessa L. Rice, Zelda Oliver-Miles, Linda H. Jones, Vina Lavendar, and Shirley Walker: I thank God for being blessed to have people like you in my life that I can also call my friends. To Pastor Michael D. McClure Sr.: You made me laugh when I showed you the cover and title of this book and you said, "I'm scared of that title!" Thank you for letting folks know what I do (believe me, not all pastors are so generous).

Thanks to author Kimberla Lawson Roby for those kind words on my novel, *The Other Side of Goodness.* I appreciate you so much for that! Also to authors Lutishia Lovely, Pat G'orge-Walker, Linda F. Beed, Maurice Gray Jr., Shelia Goss, and Margaret Johnson-Hodge: It's been such fun interacting with each of you in some way, whether by phone, in person, or via Facebook. People may not know this, but when the "Spirit" hits us, Lutishia Lovely and I will start a praise/song service on Facebook if you're not careful. Yes, Lord!

I'd like to give a shout-out to a few folks who participated in a Facebook post where I asked which of my books you liked the best or you posted a message about me and my books that blessed me. Thank you to: Kimyatta Angola, Felicia Toni Garrett, Trinita Ford, Mia Danielle, Val McGhee, Phillis Adams, Deborah Frazier, JeaNida Luckie-Weatherall, Juwana Harris Roberts, Shanae Collins, Stephanie Holston Shelton, Patrice M. Harlson, Alicia Thomas, Le'Tanya Berry Mitchell, Sharon Hunter Barrow, Princetta PJ Williams, Angiel Jackson-Washington, Rhonda McIntyre Gilbert, NaTasha Hargress, Bethany Jackson, Kim Albritton Thompson, La Trese Moore, Paulette Griffin Sabree, Cassandra N. Johnson, Deborah James Murray, Fearfullymade Holman, Ruthie Wilson, Kimberly Ivory Graves, Melissa Louis-Juste,

Karen Gray-Bullock, Deirdre Davis, Chenel Choice, Tara Cunningham, Betty Bailey Brown, Faith James, Michelle Tootsie Bell, Doris Chenier, Gregg De'Vincent Pelt, Sabrina Collins, Lanee DeShawn, Tracey Turner Peebles, Alvetta Rolle, Gretta McFarland, Tiffani J. Showell, Shon Garner Cole, Portia Lang, Jonnie Williams Young, Lisa A. Truss, Pamela Brown, Yvonne Griffin-Jackson, Anthony R. Sanders, Myra Walker Williams, Jami Taylor, Nikeya Brumfield Avery, Nakeisha Brumfield, Kim Knight, Hannah Black, Yarnetta Sellers.

Anthony and Denise Thomas, Tamara Davis, Nicole Davis, NaSonya K., Shawna Bynum, Jessica Ann Goodman, Yolanda Gore, Anthony Conley, Stacey Saunders, Eden Carlton, Mornesia Beal, Ninette E. Patterson, Melva Jackson, Melvin Smith Jr., Crystal Roberts, George W. Stewart, Pastor Byron Woods, Laneta Fullenwiley, Kimberly Miller, Pamela Perkins Lewis, Sarah Morris, Sally R. Clem, Lorraine Mungo, Tracey Yvonne Smith, Cheryl Sloan Wray, Joanne Sloan, Tori Dorsett, Rita Hester-Pompey, Ja Woods, Shiela Toby, Chandra Lee Thomas, Belinda Alexander-Walker, Sharon Jordan, Zsa Zsa Rambeau, Sheila Williams (Roll Tide), Kathryn Lang, Billie Scales, Eric M. Felton, Jeanette Hill, Milbourne Biddy

Stafford, Norma J. Robinson, Maria Bailey, Carla McKinney, Trina Banks, and Adrienna Turner.

To the book clubs that let me know you chose my book(s) as your book club pick, I thank you so much. There's E.S.T.H.E.R. Book Club, Agape Ministry Book Club in Richmond, VA, Purpose 2 Read Book Club, WBRT Book Club, D.I.V.A.S. On the Move for Christ Book Club, Narrative Expressions Book Club, Belle Noir Societe, The LADIES of Mt. Calvary of Leeds, AL Book Club, In the Spirit Book Club in Knightdale, NC, Butterfly Book Club in Dolomite, AL, Sistaz Society in Savannah, GA, Ladies of Distinction (LOD) Book Club in Columbus, GA, and Sisters Sippin' Tea Book Club. I would also like to thank: RAWSISTAZ Book Club, Troy Johnson and AALBC.com, Cydney Rax and Book-Remarks.com, URBAN Reviews, ChristianFiction.blogspot.com, OOSA Book Club, and Carol Mackey and Black Expressions Book Club. If your book club has ever chosen one of my books and your name was not listed here, please know that I thank and appreciate you SO MUCH, more than you'll ever know!

I thank you for picking this novel. It is because of wonderful people like you and the favor of God that I'm able to keep doing what I do. As always, I love hearing from you. You can find me on the Web at: www.VanessaDavisGriggs.com and on Facebook at: www.Facebook.com/vanessadavisgriggs.

Until next time . . .

Chapter 1

> Thus saith the king, Let not Hezekiah deceive you: for he shall not be able to deliver you.
>
> — Isaiah 36:14

"The devil sure *is* busy. That's really a lot going on." Tiffany Connors paced from one end of the couch to the other as she talked on the phone. "Yes, I definitely know that God is busier. Pastor Landris reminds us of that enough. But in my thirty years on this earth, I don't believe I've ever seen the devil as busy as he seems to be right now. It's like he's messing with pretty much everyone we know, all at the same time. Poor Gabrielle. She's dealing with some stuff these days, that's for sure."

Thirty-three-year-old Darius Connors sat in the den at his computer listening intently to his wife's conversation about Gabrielle Mercedes while trying to pretend that he wasn't. She was talking to Fatima Adams, a fellow dancer in the church's dance ministry. Oddly, he wasn't listening so closely because he'd once had a three-year-long affair with the now thirty-six-year-old Fatima that consequently ended about five years ago. He thought for a second. Today was April 29, 2010. He counted back to 2005, the year Fatima ended things. Yes, May 14, her birthday, it would be five years.

He felt pretty confident Fatima wouldn't tell his wife about them, not at this point anyway. Not since Tiffany and Fatima had become friends through the dance ministry. If Fatima was going to spill the Kool-Aid, he figured she would have done it already. Telling Tiffany now would most certainly put their friendship in jeopardy with questions like why Fatima didn't tell her in the beginning, and why she'd gone a whole year with them knowing each other on a friendly basis and she still hadn't said anything. It would cause more than just mere tension and not just in the dance ministry, but in church. Knowing Fatima like he had, he knew she wouldn't want to be responsible for anything like that. Not little pristine Fatima.

Tiffany glanced over at him and flashed him a big smile, then winked. He quickly realized he must have been staring harder than he'd intended. He really wanted her to think he wasn't listening at all. Generally, that's what she accused him of: not listening to her at all. He quickly began to tap on the keys on the computer to give the impression he hadn't been staring down her throat, trying to capture every word that was coming out of her mouth, but instead purely absentmindedly thinking.

"Well, it's now the end of April, and I know you were looking forward to Gabrielle's return from her leave of absence and fully taking back her position as the director over the dance ministry. But you've been doing a fabulous job in her absence these past few months. Fabulous. You have. Everybody in the ministry is saying so. And I've told you that if you need my help with anything, I'm merely a phone call away." Tiffany walked over to the end table where the base of the phone resided.

"All right, Fatima. Well, keep me informed. You know how much I love Gabrielle. Yes, we all love her. And we've all been praying for her and that precious little girl. You know what they say: If it's not one thing, it's another." Tiffany shook her head. "I don't know why things happen to good people, either. But one thing we do know, and that is that God is *still* on the throne. What Satan may mean for bad, God will use it for good. Yes, He will."

Tiffany listened, then nodded. "Okay. I'll talk to you later. Call me if you need me now. All right. Bye now." Tiffany carefully placed the cordless phone back into its base.

Darius continued to type as he looked out of the side of his eye. He didn't want to give Tiffany the impression that he was waiting for her to get off the phone to pounce on her. But he was definitely anxious to find out what had been said on the other end of his wife's conversation.

Tiffany walked over to Darius and placed her hand on his shoulder. "What'cha doing?" There was a touch of sweetness in the low register of her voice.

Darius stopped and turned fully toward his wife whose straight, jet-black hair was hanging down to her shoulders. "What I've been doing for the past seven months now: looking for a job. You know I need to hurry up and find something. I need a job so I can take care of my family." Darius got up from the computer, grabbed Tiffany's hand, led her over to the couch, and pulled her down onto his lap.

Tiffany let out a quick yelp, then giggled like a schoolgirl. "*Now* what are you doing?"

Darius smiled. "Well, according to Pastor Landris: If you have to ask, then that means I haven't been properly taking care of my business at home."

"We've both been so busy, especially lately. Me working all the time at my job, coming home and taking care of the children, cooking and taking care of our house; and you searching hard for a job. So how's the job hunt coming?"

Darius wrinkled his nose, then smiled. "About the same. But don't you worry your pretty little head about it. I'm working on something that, if I play my cards just right, I believe is going to come through. I can feel it. If it does, then financially we'll be sitting pretty, maybe even finally able to catch up on these past-due bills that are dogging us like pit bulls. And at least we *can* be thankful that I get an unemployment check. I know some folks who can't even get that. For now, there's *something* coming into our household from my end to help out so I'm not completely hating. Looking for a job these days is no joke though. It's hard out here; I ain't gonna lie."

"Darius, your unemployment check *is* a blessing, but we both know it's not close to being enough. We were barely making it when you were bringing in a full check *with* overtime." She wrapped her arms around his neck. "Listen and hear me out: I saw an ad for a part-time job I'd be perfect for. It would take some doing, with me working full-time already, but if you would take care of the children while I'm not here, I could —"

Darius placed his index finger over her lips, effectively quieting her. "Woman, what have I told you already about that? Didn't I just tell you not to worry? I'm going to take care of us. Haven't I been hitting the streets almost every single day trying to secure something? I'm applying for jobs over the Internet, which apparently is the new way of putting in applications no matter who's hiring. I've been networking when and where I can, which is still fashionable no matter how high tech the world gets. There's nothing like getting out there mingling with folks, meeting someone who knows someone who *knows* someone who can hook you up. I'm working on it. Okay? I got this." He smiled and nodded his head with the words, "I *got* this."

Tiffany smiled back, her lips going from what looked like a line drawn slightly downward to an upturned curve. "If you're sure? Because you *are* good at getting people to do what you want. I do have to give you that much."

"Oooh! Ouch! I'm not sure if that was an openhanded front slap or a backhanded compliment."

Tiffany placed her hand on his chest. "Don't try to play me, Darius. You and I both know you can be a little slickster when you want to be. You have a gift of luring folks over to your side before they even know what hit them. If there's something locked in your targeted scope, you're going to keep at it until you bag it."

"So, was that Fatima you were talking to on the phone?" Darius wanted to get around to what he really wanted to know. Talking about job hunting was depressing, to say the least.

"Yeah." Tiffany slid out of his lap, sitting beside him now.

"So, what is she talking about? Besides, of course, dance stuff."

"Like you really care about what we talk about," Tiffany said with a sideways, playful glance.

"I care," Darius said with a full grin and true conviction. "You know I care. What matters to you, matters to me. That's why I'm out there doing whatever it takes to ensure you and our kids are taken care of. You and I are a team. We roll like that."

"Is that right? So we roll like that, huh? And here I was thinking you were merely looking for any old excuse you can find to get out of the house and away from us as *much* and as often as is permissible and possible."

Darius didn't care for that remark, mostly because it hit so close to home. He wasn't going to holler though. His grandmother used to say when you throw a rock into a pack of dogs, the one that hollers is usually the one that was hit. No, he *wasn't* a homebody sort of guy. He didn't like much being cooped up in the house. But he didn't want to get off the subject at hand to argue the point and convince her otherwise. "Okay, so back to Fatima and you: What were the two of you talking about? Seriously."

Tiffany sighed. "You remember I told you about our dance director, Gabrielle Mercedes, taking a leave of absence several months back when she was helping that woman whose child had that bone marrow transplant?"

"Yeah. You're talking about Jessica Noble and her daughter, Jasmine."

"Yes." Tiffany smiled as she pulled back her head a little. "Wow, I'm impressed. You remember both of their names. Well, when the mother died last month, her nine-year-old little girl, Jasmine, effectively became an orphan. I told you all about that and how Gabrielle took her into her home with fast-track plans to adopt her." Tiffany looked at Darius.

"You know, I still don't get that. I mean: I don't get how Gabrielle ended up so deep in all of that in the first place. Did Gabrielle know them before all of this took place or something? I'm talking about even before the little girl needed the bone marrow transplant. I just can't see a mother turning over her child to a complete stranger the way she seemed to have done with Gabrielle. Especially with some of the things we know about Gabrielle and her past. I'm not gossiping, just stating a fact."

"Darius, you of all people know that God works in mysterious ways. God knows what's ahead for us before we ever get there. I believe He places people in our paths even when we don't know the purpose or the reason. But God knows. He's omniscient — all knowing. And if we'll just follow His lead, He'll order our steps every single time."

Darius shook his head. "There you go again: spouting off something Pastor Landris has said. But I don't know that I'd say God is really the one working here, not in this case. Not that I'm trying to tell God how to handle His business. But the best thing, if you ask me, would have been to not let the mother die in the first place, especially with the father having died earlier. Then the child wouldn't be orphaned. But when it comes to Gabrielle, it just feels like there's more to this story than what we're privy to. I keep telling you that you should talk to Gabrielle yourself and see what more she might tell you. She likes you. I'm sure she'd tell you, especially if you were to ask."

Tiffany chuckled. "You're such a cynic when it comes to things. It's obvious that you don't care much for Gabrielle at all."

"I'm not trying to be cynical. And I don't *dis*like Gabrielle; I don't really know the woman. She used to be a stripper, she gave her life to Christ, and now she's not a stripper. But come on, Tiff, you have to admit: It feels like there's a lot more to this story. There's a lot being left out that apparently no one knows, or if they know, they're not saying." Darius looked at Tiffany. "So what did Fatima tell you?"

"She was just telling me that even though Gabrielle had planned and even told us last week that she'd be returning as director this week from her leave, she's not going to right now. Fatima didn't fill me in on everything, but it appears Gabrielle is running into some obstacles in gaining complete custody of little Jasmine. Gabrielle has decided to direct her energies toward that fight, for now. So she'll continue to be on leave until further notice."

"Obstacles?" Darius tried to set his face just right. He didn't want to overplay his hand and appear *too* interested. Tiffany would definitely know something was up if he seemed *too* anxious to know. "Obstacles like what?"

"She didn't tell me much. Just that someone was threatening to challenge or is already challenging her rights to adopt the little girl, even though that was the mother's expressed dying wish."

"Did Fatima say who that someone is or why that person might be doing something like that?"

Tiffany shook her head. "No. I don't know if Fatima didn't tell me because she doesn't know, or if she didn't want to feel like she was gossiping — basically divulging too much of Gabrielle's business. Fatima and Gabrielle are really sort of close. She was merely calling to let me know, as well as the others in the dance ministry, that Gabrielle wasn't coming back full time yet as she'd said. Fatima was also soliciting prayers for them. According to her, Gabrielle has vowed she's not going to let anyone take Jasmine from her, not without a fight. And I'm telling you, Darius: I feel sorry for anyone who tries to get in Gabrielle's way when it comes to that child. There's a bond there for sure. Anybody with eyes can see that. And I believe Gabrielle will fight with all that she has if she's forced to."

"I can't believe someone would be doing something like that," Darius said. "Trying to stop her from the adoption, I mean. Unless there's something in Gabrielle's life, past or present, that's causing someone in a higher position to give pause. Like I said, we *do* know that Gabrielle was once a stripper. I'm just saying. Maybe that's where the problem's arising."

"I don't know. I just know it looks like everyone we know is dealing with something these days. You lost your job when they shipped the company's operation overseas. We were already struggling financially before all of this. And now —"

"And now, baby, I told you we're going to be all right." Darius took his hand and lifted Tiffany's chin higher. "You trust me, don't you?"

"I suppose."

Darius drew back in a dramatic way and

cocked his head to the side. "You *suppose*?" He smiled and squinted his eyes halfway. "What do you mean, you suppose?"

Tiffany twisted her mouth. "Okay, I guess I do." She smiled. "All right, I do."

"Now, *that's* my baby." He made a smacking sound. "Listen, I need to go out for a little while."

Tiffany looked down at her wristwatch. "Now? You have to go somewhere now? But it's already after six."

"Yes, now. Didn't I just tell you that I have to network? Well, I have a lead on this job I'd love to get. There's someone I need to hook up with to prove just how interested I am in getting it, *and* that I'm the perfect man for the job." Darius kissed his wife on her slightly pouted out lips. "When it comes to my family, I'm going to do whatever I have to do. If it means going outside of the norm, then so be it. And if I can't get something here in Alabama, well, I hear things are booming in North Dakota. Something called fracking, which has to do with oil, has companies *begging* for workers. If you don't want me to have to go there to get a job, then you need to work with me here. All right?"

"Okay. Because I definitely don't want to move. And I sure don't want to move to someplace like North Dakota. Are there any black folks even in North Dakota?"

He ignored her question about North Dakota. "Believe me: I don't really want to leave you right now. You know I'd rather be here with you and the kids instead of out there sucking up to a bunch of bougie folks, begging someone to give me a shot. But a man's got to do what a man's got to do." He tapped her on the nose.

Tiffany stood up. "How long do you think you'll be this time? I have dinner cooking; it will be ready in about an hour. You know I like for you to be able to eat while it's hot and fresh out of the oven."

Darius stood and wrapped Tiffany up in his arms. "I promise I won't stay one minute longer than I have to. But don't worry about me. I'll just heat mine up in the microwave when I get back. No biggie. And if I get this job, that means I can take you out to dinner and make up for all our lost time together. You know I love you, don't you?"

Tiffany frowned.

"What's the frown about?"

"I don't know, Darius. I want to believe you love me, but —"

"But you're still tripping about that nonsense of me having gone to that strip joint those times." Darius turned his head away from Tiffany before turning back with slightly moistened eyes. "Clarence Walker had no business ever letting you know that. But that's all water under the bridge. I told you I was sorry. I told you I didn't even want to go there in the first place. I was merely trying to hang with some of the fellows from work so I could move up on the job. That was all there was to it. You know how it is. It was dumb of me, but it wasn't even something I wanted to do." He wrapped his arms even tighter around Tiffany. "Do you really think I care about other women when I have all of this" — he leaned back a little and slowly scanned her body, mainly for dramatic effect, then back up to her eyes — "at home waiting on me? Do you?" He broke into a huge grin.

Tiffany pulled out of his embrace. "Apparently you did. You went there for, ever how many times you did. And if Brother Clarence hadn't spilled it, who knows: You might still be doing it, and I would *still* be in the dark about it."

Darius grabbed her and pulled her close to him again. "I made a mistake. Okay?" He squatted his six-foot-six body down a little so his eyes were even with hers. "Baby, it was a mistake. One stupid mistake, but a mistake nonetheless. I am a man. You know how we are. I was merely going along to get along. I asked you to forgive me. You said that you did. But if you're going to keep throwing it in my face every chance you get, then I don't know what else to say or do. But I do know that's not true forgiveness. And not that I want to bring this up myself, but it's not like you've been perfect all of your life . . . like you've never done anything wrong, even when it comes to you and me. Come on now; stop fronting."

Tiffany looked into his eyes. "I know, Darius. And I want to let it go. I do. It's just so hard. I can forgive; it's just a lot harder to forget."

"I know it's hard." Darius stood tall and hugged her, then looked down into her eyes. "I know that. But I'm trying, Tiff. I'm doing the best that I can. I'm under a lot of pressure here. I don't want to be worried about you while I'm out there trying to be the man you deserve, a man who takes care of his own. I'm trying. I just need you to meet me halfway. Can you do that? Can you meet me halfway?"

Tiffany looked down, then back up at him. "I know. And I'm not trying to add to your stress."

Darius glanced at his watch. "Look, I've got to go. I promise I'll be back as quickly as I can. I'm going to go meet this person, do what I have to do, and if things go the way I hope, I'll have some good news soon. Real soon. Okay?" He smiled.

Tiffany smiled back. "Okay. Blessings."

Darius kissed Tiffany on her forehead and held his lips there a few seconds. Tiffany used to say "good luck." But after Pastor Landris preached last year that as Christians they didn't put faith in luck, she immediately stopped saying that and began doing as Pastor Landris taught by saying blessings. She left and went to the kitchen.

After he was sure Tiffany was gone, Darius pulled out his cell phone and texted. Can u meet me n 20 @ our normal spot? Need to c u. Important. He pressed SEND.

A few seconds later a reply came back. Dare I us?

Darius grinned. He loved the way she was making a play on his name: Dare I us. He texted back, Dare u us. It's worth it. He pressed SEND, grinned a little more, then left, hoping — unlike the last time she'd said she'd meet him — this time, she would actually show up.

CHAPTER 2

And the Lord said unto me, Say unto them, Go not up, neither fight; for I am not among you; lest ye be smitten before your enemies.

— Deuteronomy 1:42

"You came," Darius said as he stood and greeted her thirty minutes after sending the text. He pulled out her chair for her. "I was starting to think you might have stood me up like the last time."

Twenty-seven-year-old Paris Elizabeth Simmons-Holyfield gave a half grin. "I almost didn't come."

"Well, I'm glad you did." Darius flashed her one of his signature full grins, showing off his pearly whites straightened by early years of braces. "You look good. Look at your hair all perfect; that one side laid with that feathery cut going on everywhere else. Your face is all made up; I like the eye shadow." He nodded. "Yeah, it looks good. That's hot. Got on red lipstick. And that cyan blue dress is fitting you to the T." Darius tilted his head slightly as he continued to nod, visibly scanning her from her head down to her painted red toenails. "Those shoes are saying something. Sexy, momma, sexy *momma.*" He looked back up and into her brown eyes.

Paris rolled her eyes as she swung her top crossed leg. "So you like my Miu Miu, huh?"

"Excuse me your what? Your moo who?"

Paris laughed. "My shoes." She held one foot in the air. "Miu Miu. It's the name brand of my shoes." She twirled her foot in a circle in sync as she spelled, "M-I-U M-I-U." She put her foot firmly on the floor.

"So . . . do you always dress to the max or did you do all of this just for little ole me?"

"For you?" She waved him off. "Please. Don't be silly. I never step out of my house without full makeup on and me looking my best. Not ever. You never know who you'll run into. And for whatever reason, people seem to think that famous folks are always supposed to look their best, even if they're merely running to the grocery store to pick up something. It can be a hassle, but I handle my business." She relaxed her body and leaned in, putting her arms on the table.

"Oh, so you consider yourself famous."

"Not really. But my father is an Alabama congressman, so that means, by proxy, his family becomes a target for the media. All it takes is for one crazy-looking photo to get out and people will start accusing you of either being on drugs or possibly in the throes of a mental breakdown. I just save everybody the trouble by always looking my best when I step out of my house." Paris leaned back against her chair and again began to swing the top leg of her now crossed legs.

"Would you care for something to drink?"

She shook her head. "I really don't drink coffee this late in the day. It keeps me up at night if I do."

Darius leaned in. "It's not even seven yet. Don't tell me you're one of those folks who goes to bed with the chickens."

Paris smiled slightly before adjusting her back against her chair. "Listen, Dare, I don't have a lot of time to be playing around. I told my husband I was going to get us something for dinner. So —"

Darius nodded. "Dare. I like that. Dare. Yeah, I like that."

"Oh, you do, do you?"

"Yeah. It has a certain badness to it. You

remember back in school when someone would draw a line in the dirt with their feet and dare you to cross it? Or someone would put a stick on a person's shoulder and dare the other person to knock it off to get a fight started."

Paris looked around the coffeehouse. "No, actually I don't. I'm not familiar with any of those barbaric antics. I didn't grow up with folks who were all the time trying to start fights. The people I was exposed to were more civilized."

Following her lead, Darius glanced around the sparsely filled coffeehouse. "Are you looking for someone?" Darius asked.

"No. But my father is not very happy with me right now. He's upset about my plans to challenge Gabrielle for custody of Jasmine Noble. I wouldn't put anything past him at this point, including having me followed and spied on."

"Your father?" Darius said. "We're talking about Congressman Lawrence Simmons? Don't you think you're being a tad bit paranoid?"

"No. My father is really upset. And he's told me, in no uncertain terms, that if I don't let this go, I'll regret it. My father may love me, but he doesn't play when it comes to things he feels may hurt him. He's a fighter, and it doesn't matter even when the opposition turns out to be family. If you dare defy him, you're the enemy. You then get to experience the other side of dare. What can I say? That's my daddy."

"I know he told me the time he and I had dinner together that he could chew me up and spit me out whenever he wants."

"And yet," Paris said, "here you are, doing what you can to help me. Or what you believe will advance your own agenda. I've not quite figured out your angle yet."

"You're *definitely* your father's child. Just like he's a fighter, it looks like so are you."

"Well, no one can ever accuse me of not getting mine honestly. My daddy taught me that if you want something bad enough, you go for it. And if you want it and another person has it to give and won't, then you fight for it with all that you have, if that's what it takes." Paris looked toward the counter. "Maybe we *should* buy something. That girl at the counter keeps looking over here while talking to the girl working behind the counter. And neither of them is looking over here in a good way."

Darius turned around and looked. The woman at the counter was indeed looking at them. But not for the reason Paris was thinking. Darius recognized her immediately. "Then I guess I'll go buy something and put a stop to the gawking."

Darius got up and went to the counter. "Hi," he said to the woman standing at the counter.

"So who's that you're with?" the woman with her brown hair in a ponytail at the counter said.

Darius turned and looked back at the table where he'd been sitting. "I suppose you can say she's somewhat of a client. She's someone I'm working with on a project."

"Uh-huh. I *bet* she is."

"What's with the ponytail? I almost didn't recognize you. And when did you start drinking coffee? I invited you to come do this, and you told me you'd never pay this much for a cup of joe."

She shrugged. "I just decided to stop in and give it a try, see what the hype's all about. That's the answer to the ponytail question, too. It's a weave."

"What can I get you?" the woman working behind the counter asked Darius, interrupting their conversation.

"Yeah, what can she get you and your" — the woman at the counter nodded Paris's way — "client."

"Look, Gigi, it sounds like you're upset

with me. But this isn't what it looks like at all."

"Oh, I'm not upset with you. Just because you were coming on to me not that long ago, trying to make me think I was all that and a bag of chips. And now you're here apparently doing the same thing with someone else," Gigi said. "I have eyes. I've been watching the two of you. And believe me, the way you're acting with her, she's not just some 'client.' Unless, of course, you're in the escort business or something. Trust me when I tell you: That woman is *definitely* into you."

Darius laughed. "Gigi, you're reading it all wrong. I confess: She and I have become somewhat friends. Maybe that's all you're picking up on."

"Sir, what can I get you?" the woman behind the counter asked again.

"Just give me a cup of regular black coffee and one of those pastries," Darius said, pointing his head toward the glass case. "The strawberry one looks good."

"Oh, look at you, Mr. Big Spender," Gigi said as the woman behind the counter went to fill his order. Gigi picked up her cup of coffee and went and sat down at a nearby table.

The woman behind the counter handed

Darius a tray with his coffee and the strawberry pastry on it and collected his money, which took the last of the dollar bills that remained in his wallet. All he had left now was the money that made noise.

Darius strolled back to the table. "I got you a pastry." He set the white plate with the pastry down in front of her. "It's strawberry." He sat down with his cup of coffee, leaned over, and slid the empty brown tray onto the vacant table next to them.

"How do you happen to know that I like strawberry pastries?" Paris asked.

"I didn't. It was just a lucky guess. Oops! I forgot. Our pastor has admonished us not to use the word 'luck' or 'lucky.' So we'll say instead that I took a blessed guess."

Paris smiled. "I enjoyed Pastor Landris that one time I visited. I'll have to visit the church again maybe after things settle down. But strawberry is my favorite. So I'm impressed." Paris pulled off a piece of the pastry and placed it in her mouth. "This is *so* good." She nodded. "So . . . what were you and that woman at the counter talking about?" Paris looked where Gigi now sat.

"Who? Me and her?" Darius casually glanced back over his shoulder. "Well, I *could* lie and say we were merely chatting about the weather."

"But you're not going to lie to me. Not now; not ever." Paris pulled another piece from her pastry and placed it in her mouth.

Darius broke into a slow grin. He took a sip of coffee and sat the cup down as he nodded. "Not now, not ever. Her name is Gigi Thornton. I met her about two months ago at some event she and I both attended. She was turning around and almost knocked me down. We started talking . . . and that's about it. She's cool."

"Gigi, huh? What's the Gigi a nickname for?"

"You mean her real name? I think it's Gigi."

"Most of the time Gigi is not the name a person is given at birth. I'm sure she has another name."

"I don't know about that. All she told me was that her name was Gigi Thornton. I assumed that was her real name. But I can go over and ask her if you want me to." Darius made a gesture like he was about to get up.

Paris grabbed him by the wrist. "Don't you dare. I don't care enough to know for you to do that." Paris let his wrist go. "So . . . do you ever call her?"

Darius twisted his mouth and sat back comfortably in his chair. "I've called her a few times. That's about it." He smiled and leaned in. "Nothing really serious. She was just asking me what I was doing here with you."

"I take that to mean then that she knows you're married with three children?"

"Yes, she knows that I'm married. I don't lie about my family or my marital status. I even wear my wedding band when I'm out." He held up the back of his left hand and wiggled his ring finger. "See."

"I assume then that she knows I'm not your wife since she asked you what you were doing here with me. She knows that I'm not your wife, right?"

"Yes, she knows you're not my wife. I showed her a picture of my family, which included Tiffany."

"And knowing all of this, she still wants to talk to you?" Paris shook her head as she primped her mouth. "You'd better be careful," she said in a singsong voice. "I'm sure you're aware that there are lots of crazies out there."

Darius took another sip of his black coffee. "I'm not interested in her that way."

Paris grinned. "Sure you're not. But you can't speak for her. It's funny: We've been reacquainted for a little over two months now and you've not bothered to show *me* a picture of your family."

Darius chuckled as he pulled out his wallet. "That's because I don't have a problem introducing you to my family in person. But here you go." He flipped to a picture and held out his wallet to Paris. "That's my family."

Paris took the wallet and looked at the photo. "Very nice." She handed his wallet back. "You have a beautiful family. Your wife looks almost the same as she did when you brought her to that party a decade ago when we were in college."

He put his wallet back up. "That picture is a year old. And, yes, my wife looks pretty much the same. I'm also telling you that I'm not interested in Gigi other than as a friend. She's in between jobs. I've been doing my part to encourage her. She was a little down about where she was in her life. I encouraged her to find what she wants to do and to go for it." He picked up his cup of coffee and took another sip.

Paris smiled as she nodded. "So you're Mr. Encourager. I have to give it to you: You sure do know how to pick them." She cast her eyes in Gigi's direction.

Darius set his cup down on the table and leaned in. "You'd think you would have figured out that, when it comes to the women I give my time to, I'm really picky.

I'm not drawn to just any old body."

Paris sat back against her chair. "Is that right?" She pulled another piece from the pastry and slowly placed it on her tongue. "Then I see that makes two of us."

"Sounds like you and I make a great team."

"A team, huh? You're still pushing that line?"

"Yes. You want to get that little girl from Gabrielle Mercedes. And I just happen to have eyes and ears on the ground that can help you, at least, have a heads-up."

Paris leaned in closer to Darius. "So does this mean you're going to help me any way that you can?"

"Yes." He smiled. "But I need you to help me get a job with your father. If I'm going to keep my wife happy and feeding me with information about what's going on with Gabrielle to help you, I need a job. And I don't want a crappy position, either. I'd prefer a job working on his campaign. That's probably a good place for me to start and prove myself. It would also give me some flexibility."

Paris slowly shook her head. "I don't know what I can do to help you there. I guess you weren't listening when I told you that my father is upset with me. After he learned I was serious about going after custody of Jasmine, he literally went over to the other side. He wants me to stop my crusade of rescuing Jasmine from Gabrielle. Under any other circumstance, I probably *would* have some influence with him. But right now, crossing him like I am, I'm on the outs with both him and Andrew."

"I take it then that your husband is not for you pursuing this?"

"Nope. He was fine when I mentioned adopting a child. But when he discovered the child I had my sights on was the one Gabrielle had already, he almost blew a gasket. But I can handle Andrew. He'll come around and see things my way."

"Well, then I guess I'll have to take care of your father. I'll convince him to give me a job. I'll make him see that it's in his best interest to hire me. But you need to know that Gabrielle is gearing up to fight you with everything she's got. I don't know what you said to her that Wednesday night when you saw her at Bible study —"

"I told her I was going to petition the courts to get Jasmine."

Darius nodded. "Well, she was planning to return to her job as director of the dance ministry, but she's postponing that now. My wife just told me a little while ago that she's gearing up to fight whoever is trying to get in her way of her keeping that little girl. I don't think Gabrielle is going to be an easy battle for you to overcome."

"Oh, I'm sure of that. People think she's this nice person. But the person I knew was one who saw what she wanted and went after it no matter who was in her way. She may have given her life to the Lord, but I assure you she's not the good girl everybody probably believes that she is. Well, I'm not going to sit back and let her ruin that little girl's life. If no one else is willing to step up and fight for Jasmine, then I guess it will have to be left on me. And if my husband and father won't go along with what I'm doing and I have to do it alone, then so be it."

Darius placed his hand on Paris's free hand, completely covering it. "You're not going to be alone. I'm here. If you need me, day or night, you call or you text me. And if I'm not available, I promise that I'll get back with you as soon as I can."

Paris looked down at Darius's hand on hers. "I'll see what I can do to get Daddy to give you a job or at least help you to get one. Daddy has connections. That will at least make things a *little* easier for you. I appreciate you, Dare. I really do. You're the only one who seems to be on my side on this. I told my husband when we were discussing this the other day that I've only just begun to fight. He has it in his head that he can talk me out of this 'notion,' as he calls it, or that him refusing to be a part of this will deter me. But he's wrong. I'm in this for the long haul."

"Well, Pare, if I know —"

Paris pulled her hand away from his. "Pare?" She shook her head. "Uh-uh. Nope. Don't call me that."

"What? You don't like Pare? We could be Dare and Pare." He laughed. "I think it's kind of cute myself."

"No, I don't *like* it. It's not cute. Yuck! So don't ever call me that again, do you hear me? It's Paris. Paris. No variation of it. Simply Paris."

"Okay. If you feel that strongly about it. But it's all right for you to call me Dare?"

She smiled, put the last piece of strawberry pastry in her mouth, and said, "Yeah. Because *dare* I say, you like it when I call you that."

He nodded as he smiled. "Yeah. I *dare* say that I do."

CHAPTER 3

> My heart was hot within me; while I was musing the fire burned: then spake I with my tongue.
>
> — Psalm 39:3

The following day, Darius called Lawrence Simmons and made an appointment to see him. He knew Lawrence wasn't interested in meeting with him, not after their last time two months ago. But he also knew Lawrence was a smart man who knew it was best to keep his friends close and possible enemies even closer.

Not that Darius considered himself an enemy of the representative. In fact, his greatest desire was to work on the man's reelection campaign. And when Lawrence was reelected, he'd like a job working in his administration or something. That wasn't too much to ask. And in exchange, Lawrence would have his undying loyalty.

Darius sat down in the chair across from Representative Simmons.

"What do you want?" Lawrence said, not bothering to hide his impatience or displeasure with Darius.

Darius held his six-foot-six-inch frame upright in his chair. Although he was only thirty-three years old, he wasn't going to allow this fifty-year-old man to intimidate him. "What I told you I wanted the last time we talked. I'd like a job. I *need* a job."

"Well, you should be down at the unemployment office and not here taking up my valuable time."

"I told you: I want to work for you. I feel like I have some valuable assets that will serve you well. I'm loyal, a self-starter, self-motivated, confident, and most of all, a hard worker. Did I mention I was loyal?"

"Well, if you're such a great asset, then why are you unemployed right now?"

"The company I worked for moved its operations overseas. But if we want to get to the real reason I — and many others — are unemployed, that blame can be traced back to politicians such as yourself. If I'm not mistaken, it's the politicians who pass these laws that have gotten us in the mess America is in. Laws that seem to be stacked more toward the rich and against the little people and even small businesses. Laws that amazingly reward companies with tax breaks when they send our jobs overseas."

"Sounds to me like you're *just* the kind of person I'm trying to reach in my campaign," Lawrence said. "People who are tired of big government and the government getting in their way."

"No. I'm likely one of the people who would never vote for you. And especially not with some of the stuff you've been spouting off lately."

Lawrence chuckled. "And yet, here you are up in my face begging me for a job to work on my reelection campaign. I don't know who taught you the skills of landing a job. But if you happened to have paid for it, you should request a refund. In fact, I'd consider suing them for malpractice."

"I know how to interview for a job. But right now, there aren't many jobs available. I'd like to work for you because you need to know how to talk to folks like me and get our votes while you attempt this little black-Republican-trying-to-get-elected-in-Alabama experiment you've decided to embark upon." Darius shook his head. "I don't know who's advising you these days, but I'd say there *should* be a job opening right there. I couldn't believe it when I heard it. You, pretty much the face of Mr. Liberal, now running as a Republican in the state of Alabama. Alabama? Seriously?"

"For your information, there are more black Republicans in Alabama than you know. And this election cycle is dictating that I do this. In two years, it may very well swing back. But for now, if you want to be in the game, then this is where the action is being played."

"So if you get reelected, are you planning to flip back to being a Democrat when the tide turns? Because you know 2012 is coming, and I have a feeling it will behoove a lot of folks to look at where they are then. I'm just saying."

"Well, in politics, you have to be flexible and keep your finger to the wind."

Darius pulled a small notepad out of his dark blue suit coat pocket and began to write.

"What are you doing?" Lawrence asked.

"Taking notes. If I'm going to work for you, I need to know what you want."

Lawrence visibly frowned before starting to laugh. "I'm *not* hiring you."

Darius closed his notepad. "Yes . . . you are. And do you want to know why you are?"

Lawrence smirked and leaned forward, resting on his forearms. "Oh, please. Don't keep me in suspense. *Why* am I going to hire you? Give me one reason."

"For one, because I know too much about you and your personal business, that's one."

"You know nothing you can prove."

"I know enough to cause you trouble. And I know enough to keep trouble at bay. Guess who I had coffee with last night. Go on . . . guess. You'll never guess."

"Mr. Connors —"

"Oh, please, Lawrence. Let's not be so formal. We're about to be working together. Call me Darius. Or if you want to use the little nickname your daughter is using for me these days, you can call me Dare. Isn't that clever? Darius . . . Dare."

"Dare?" Lawrence sprang to his feet. "Listen. You need to leave my daughter alone."

"No, sir. I think you need to be asking me to get as close to your daughter as I can." Darius also stood. "You see, Lawrence. It looks like at this point I may be the one person able to help control your daughter. You need me on your payroll, Lawrence, if nothing more than to keep your daughter from totally wrecking your campaign at this juncture. And she's on track to do it. It's now April thirtieth. November is the election. You and I both know that in politics, that can be a lifetime. Paris is determined to go after Gabrielle Mercedes and take that little girl that she's convinced is your daughter, albeit illegitimate one. Paris has no intentions of waiting until after your election is over, which by then, would be too late."

Lawrence leaned on his desk. "And what exactly do you think you can do when it comes to my daughter? No one can control that child of mine. Not me, not her mother, not even her husband, Andrew."

Darius leaned on the desk, putting his face up close to him. "Paris trusts me. Or at least, she's learning to trust me. She believes — unlike you and her husband — that I'm on her side."

Lawrence stood straight, folding his arms across his chest. "Well, how do you think she'll feel when I tell her that you were here in my office trying to sell her out?"

"She already knows that if I'm here, I'm likely trying to get a job with you."

"Is that right?" Lawrence grinned. "So if I were to call her right now and tell her you're here, she would be okay with that?"

Darius pulled out his cell phone and pressed one number. "Hi there, Paris. It's me . . . Dare. Listen, I'm here with your father. Would you please say hello to him?"

Darius handed his phone to Lawrence. "It's your daughter. She wants to say hello."

Lawrence took the phone. "Hi, sweetheart." He nodded. "Yes, I hear you. But I can't say that I have anything for Mr. Connors in the way of a position. Yes, Paris. Listen, dear, we'll talk more on this later. Here's Mr. Connors back." Lawrence handed the phone back to Darius.

Darius smiled. "Thanks, friend," he said to Paris, then winked at Lawrence. "Yes, I'll let you know if I get something. Send up a prayer for me. Bye now." He pressed the END button and put his phone away. "Told you."

"I'd like you to leave my daughter alone. In fact, I'd like for you to leave *me* alone. I don't have a job for you, and my daughter doesn't need anyone egging her on this ridiculous quest she's embarking upon to try and take that child away from that woman. It's none of Paris's business nor is it any of yours." Lawrence's voice steadily escalated as he spoke.

"But I happen to agree with your daughter. I don't think that child should be with Gabrielle Mercedes, regardless of whether you're really her father or not."

"So do you know Ms. Mercedes or something?"

"Let's just say I don't know her in the way I would have *liked,* not in the biblical way of 'knew,' if you catch my drift. But I've come as close to it as one legally can. I've seen her live dance performances before, and I'm not talking about at our church, either. Although I confess that the first time I saw her dancing in that club, she had a lot of us calling out the Lord's name, if you know what I mean." He chuckled.

"So you've actually seen her perform on stage at that club where she reportedly worked?"

"Yep. I see you've done your homework. But she's a different woman now. She really is. A lot of folks I know who say they've changed, most times, are putting on an act to impress other folks. But Gabrielle . . . she's the real deal."

Lawrence sat back down. "So why don't you think that little girl should be with her?"

Darius mirrored the actions of his host and sat down as well. "For one thing she's not married."

"So. The world is full of single parents, many not by choice. They've turned out some pretty amazing children. Dr. Ben Carson for one. And, of course, Bill Clinton and Barack Obama were both raised by single mothers and they've done okay for themselves. Besides, a person's status can change at any time. I know for a fact that Miss Mercedes has a boyfriend. Some doctor."

"You are *quite* resourceful. Nothing gets by you," Darius said. "Okay. Let me be straight up with you. I want your daughter to be happy. And if she doesn't like Gabrielle or if she thinks *she* should have this child, then I'm going to be on her side. That's it in a nutshell."

Lawrence nodded. "You're just trying to get my daughter in bed with you like you've done with countless others."

"I'm not going to lie: Your daughter is fine now. And if I wasn't married —"

"Which you are, as is she," Lawrence said.

"Yeah, I was just about to say that if I *wasn't* married and she wasn't married, I'd definitely be trying my best to get with her. But for now, your daughter just needs someone who will listen and who understands her. She needs a real friend."

"She has a husband for that. And she has plenty of girlfriends. She and her mother are also quite close and I know they talk and share pretty much everything."

Darius nodded. "Yeah. But from what I'm gathering, her husband is not supporting her, not on this, anyway. She said when she told him of her plans about wanting to adopt Jasmine that he blew a fuse or a gasket or something."

"Not that it's any of your business, but they're trying to start their own family. Andrew is like me: We don't care for unnecessary drama, not if it can at all be avoided."

"That's great," Darius said. "I'm all for family. I just want to be there for Paris during this time. If I worked for you, I could possibly keep her mind away from this Gabrielle and Jasmine situation. Right now, it's hard to do. You've had me investigated. You know that I'm married. You know I have three children. If I worked for you, I could be your eyes and ears, alerting you to potential problems and scandals brewing. I would also have a reason to be around your daughter, thereby keeping her under control for you. At least until after you win the election."

Lawrence nodded. "So you're asking for a job that would include keeping my daughter occupied and in check during this remaining election period?"

"See, we're speaking the same language here. So what do you say about that job? I work for you on the election and as a bonus I keep your daughter in check."

Lawrence rubbed his chin, then scratched his cheek. "Let me talk this over with my campaign manager. We *might* have something for you. I'll get back with you."

Darius stood to his feet. "Just don't take too long. I promise: If you hire me, you won't regret it." He held his hand out to shake Lawrence's.

Lawrence stood up and shook Darius's hand. "I hope not. But I haven't said it's a definite *go* yet."

"Well, a *maybe* is good enough for now." Darius nodded. "But if you could hurry up with a yes, I'd appreciate it. You know how these doggone bills are: They wait for no one. And my bills are stacking up." Darius left.

Lawrence called his right-hand man, chief of staff, campaign manager, and best friend, William Threadgill. "William, I need to see you in my office. Pronto."

Chapter 4

And lest I should be exalted above measure through the abundance of the revelations, there was given to me a thorn in the flesh, the messenger of Satan to buffet me, lest I should be exalted above measure.

— 2 Corinthians 12:7

William came into Lawrence's office. "What's up?"

Lawrence sat back against his high back leather chair. "Darius Connors just left my office."

"That boy doesn't give up, does he?"

"No, he doesn't."

William sat down. "You want me to shut him down? We have enough on him to wreak havoc in that boy's life, give him a good old-fashioned home whooping. He's unemployed with a wife and three children. His credit is bad, a FICO score of about three-eighty-five. And he has a good amount of past affairs stashed away in his closet that I'm sure opening that door will keep him busy trying to explain to his wife for a few months."

"He still wants to work for me."

William laughed. "Well, *that* ain't never going to happen."

"Yes, William. It *is* going to happen. Find him a place in our campaign."

"I thought you told me we weren't going to be blackmailed into doing anything by anyone . . . ever. What's up with this now?"

Lawrence leaned in toward William. "He and Paris are getting closer. Apparently, he met with her last night. She just asked me to give him a job."

William began to shake his head slowly. "I don't know about this, Lawrence. That's playing with fire. This is your daughter we're talking about, your *married* daughter. This is Paris."

"You mean my daughter who is determined to push full steam ahead on trying to take that child from Gabrielle Mercedes even though I specifically asked her to leave it alone? *That* daughter?"

"It's because she thinks that little girl is her half sister. You know how deep you've drilled the importance of family into your children's heads. She's doing what she thinks is the right thing to do."

"Since when did you become head cheerleader of Paris's cheering squad?" Lawrence asked.

"I'm not her head cheerleader. I'm just trying to see things from both perspectives. Listen, Lawrence, I got this gift for you to give to Paris that I believe just *might* make all of this go away. They're bringing the gift here today before we leave. You can drop it off at Paris's house. I promise with this, Paris will forget all about that little girl *and* Gabrielle. Then things can go back to being the normal abnormal we're accustomed to around here."

Lawrence nodded. "I know one thing: I have *too* much going on to be dealing with Paris and her attention-getting antics and drama-queen drama."

"Well, I think this little surprise will be *just* the thing you're looking for. You just wait and see. I'm telling you." William snickered.

Lawrence rang Paris's doorbell. He'd called and told her he was stopping by. It was evident from her chilly reception over the phone that she wasn't all that happy about his impending plans to visit.

Paris slowly and nonchalantly opened the front door. “Hi, Daddy.”

He gave her one quick nod. “Paris.”

“If you’ve come here to fight with me again, then let’s just save us both the trouble —”

“I come in peace.” He stepped over to the side, picked up the carrier purse he’d hidden from view, and held it out to her.

“What’s this?” Paris asked, to which, almost on cue, a small head with white hair, black button eyes, and a black button nose poked forth. Paris let out a squeal and quickly, but carefully, took the puppy out of the carrier, essentially leaving her father holding the bag. “Oh, my goodness! Oh . . . my . . . goodness! It’s a Maltese! A girl?”

“Yes, on both accounts.”

Paris held the puppy up to her face, snuggling up to her. “Oh, Daddy! She’s beautiful! Oh, my goodness! Look at how beautiful she is.” Paris stepped into the house and went straight to the den.

Lawrence followed after closing the front door. He laughed as he watched his daughter hugging the puppy. “I take it you like the gift?”

“Like?” Paris said, cradling the puppy. “I love her! Does she already have a name?”

Lawrence shook his head. “No. She’s all

yours to name as you please. She's a purebred, complete with her papers." He sat the pink carrier purse down on the floor.

Paris held the puppy up in the air and looked into her eyes. "Ambrosia."

"Ambrosia?" Lawrence said with a frown. "You're going to name her Ambrosia?" He laughed. "I thought for sure you'd go with a name like Snowball . . . Snowcap . . . Snowflake, maybe. I sure wasn't expecting Ambrosia."

"A snow name would be much too easy . . . too predictable. My baby needs her own special name. One of my friends named her Maltese Gucci. When I saw her" — Paris held the puppy and looked into her eyes — "Ambrosia was the first thing that came to my mind. So I'm going with Ambrosia." She lowered the puppy.

"Well, she's yours, so whatever name you give her is perfectly fine with me."

"Thank you, Daddy. You know I've always wanted a Maltese." Paris got up and kissed her father on the cheek. "Give Granddaddy a kiss, Ambrosia." Paris held the puppy up to Lawrence, pushing her toward his cheek.

Lawrence pulled back quickly before the puppy's mouth could touch him. "No, you don't. And don't be calling me Granddaddy, either."

"Well, you might as well get used to it," Paris said. "One way or the other, you're going to be a grandfather and soon."

"Listen, Paris. I'm the first person who's hoping . . . praying actually, that you get pregnant soon. In fact, I pray that you're already pregnant. More than you'll ever know. Your mother and I make that part of our nightly prayers now. Maybe a baby of your own will take your mind off Gabrielle and that little girl."

"Well, so far your prayers haven't worked because I'm not pregnant. And, Daddy, I don't want to ruin this wonderful time we're having now, so let's not discuss my intentions of challenging Gabrielle for custody of Jasmine. I know you keep saying that Jasmine is not your child, but I don't believe you." She shrugged. "I just don't."

"Paris, I've told you: I never had an affair with Jessica Noble. I never slept with that woman. I didn't know that lady prior to that day we had that news conference. I don't know what else I can do to convince you. I only met her when she was in need of a bone marrow transplant for her daughter. That was the first and only time I've ever lain eyes her. You're making something out of nothing. And frankly, I have enough folks to battle without having to fight with my own flesh and blood. So can you please, *please* just drop all of this nonsense of you trying to take that child from Gabrielle? Just let it go. Leave the two of them alone. *Please.*"

"Okay, Daddy. I'm going to say this one more time. Even if that child is *not* yours, she doesn't need to be with someone like Gabrielle. I stand on that truth alone."

"And I'm going to tell you one more time: It's none of your business nor is it your concern," Lawrence said. "Why don't you just concentrate on making your own baby while you get used to this new addition you now have before you. I was told that these little puppies require quite a bit of attention, especially at this stage."

Paris held the puppy up in the air as she looked into her eyes again. "She is so beautiful."

"Well, I'm going to get on down this road. Your mother is going to freak when she hears I got you this puppy. She's been telling me forever how much you've wanted one."

"I have," Paris said. "And I love you so much for getting Ambrosia for me. Thank you, Daddy. Andrew is out of town on business for the weekend. I can't wait until he gets back on Monday and sees her. He's going to be the one to freak."

Lawrence leaned down and kissed his daughter on the cheek. "Just think about what I've said. Okay? Work on making your own baby, and in the meantime, take care of Ambrosia."

Paris walked Lawrence to the door. He smiled, then left for home.

Chapter 5

> Out of the south cometh the whirlwind: and cold out of the north.
>
> — Job 37:9

"How are you, Gabrielle?" Darius asked when he saw her in the church's vestibule following Sunday morning's service.

"Blessed," Gabrielle said, holding tightly to little Jasmine's nine-year-old hand.

Darius bent down to Jasmine's level. "Well, hello there, Jasmine."

Jasmine swiveled back and forth a few times. "Hi."

"My name is Darius Connors. I don't think you and I have had the pleasure of meeting."

Jasmine merely smiled, then looked up at Gabrielle.

Gabrielle moved Jasmine over to her other side away from Darius. "I'm sorry. We really need to be going."

Darius stood up. "Why the hurry, Gabrielle? I just wanted to show some love to the two of you. Just being a good Christian, you know?"

Gabrielle forced a smile. "Yes, I'm sure. But I'm trying to catch up with Fatima."

"Well, you're in luck. I mean, you must be blessed. She's right over there." He pointed toward Fatima, who began to wave near the staircase when Gabrielle looked her way.

Gabrielle left and greeted Fatima with a hug. Darius watched as the two stepped away from the constant flow of foot traffic over to the side next to the glass bulletin case. At that moment, he wished he could read lips. From the look on Fatima's face, it didn't appear to be a fun conversation for either of them. He watched Gabrielle and Jasmine leave, then hurriedly made his way over to Fatima.

"Fatima! Hold up!" he said, trotting slightly to catch up to her. The two of them hadn't talked in a while.

Fatima didn't look too happy to see him. She made a loud sigh before she spoke. "What do you want, Darius?"

"Wow, that's certainly not a real Christian way to greet your brother in Christ. In fact, I think I've heard or read somewhere in the Bible that we're supposed to greet one another with a holy kiss."

Fatima cocked her head to the side. "What do you want?"

"I hear you and Trent Howard are tying the knot. Good old nerdy Trent Howard landed him a woman. I just wanted to give my heartfelt congratulations."

"Thanks," Fatima said dryly.

"I hope he knows what he's getting and what a lucky man he is," Darius said with a grin.

"We don't subscribe to luck."

Darius smirked. "Yeah, that's right. I keep forgetting. I suppose old habits are hard to break." He scanned from her face down to her neck and back up to her eyes in a purposely dramatic fashion, then smiled. "Pastor Landris and his teaching that we're not lucky, we're blessed. Okay, then allow me to correct myself. I hope Trent knows what a blessed man he is in snagging somebody like you."

"Thanks."

"So when is the big day?"

Fatima shifted her weight to her other side. "May fifteenth; two weeks from today."

"And one day after your birthday." He smiled. "Yes." He nodded. "I remember that May fourteenth is your birthday."

"Well, it's going to be a small ceremony.

Nothing big or fancy and mostly family and a fair number of friends."

"In other words you're trying to politely relay to me that I'm not invited."

"I gave your wife an invitation. So I suppose if you'd like to come with her, nothing's stopping you."

"That's something isn't it? How you and my wife have become such close friends the way that you have. I suppose life can be funny that way. Just one big barrel of laughs after the other, wouldn't you say?"

Fatima lifted up her arm and, with a certain flair, looked at her watch. "Oh, my! Look at the time. I've really got to be going."

"Of course. Well, it was great seeing you. Maybe you and I could get together for a celebratory dinner or something . . . maybe coffee before you become an old married woman. You know: One more time for old times' sake. It could end up being a double celebration. I think I'm about to land a new job any day now. I'm sure you've heard I got caught in this economic downturn and my job was shipped overseas."

Fatima shook her head. "I don't think so. Not unless you're planning on inviting your whole family." She tilted her head and smiled.

He laughed. "Now why would I want to go and do something like that?"

Fatima straightened her head back right. "Then I guess the answer is a definite no."

He reached out and grabbed Fatima's hand as though he was merely trying to shake it. "I miss you." He took his index finger and rubbed the inside of her palm, an unspoken signal men used to let a woman know he was interested in getting with her.

Fatima snatched her hand out of his, then leaned in close to his ear. "Well, I don't miss you. And don't you ever . . . *ever* put your hand on me again. Have I made myself perfectly clear?"

He chortled. "Wow, getting touchy in our old age, huh? I remember when you used to melt just hearing my voice. Now you're so cold. You don't have to worry, Miss Adams; I'm a happily married man now. Yes, that Tiffany of mine is something special, something special indeed."

"I hope so, because whether you realize it or not, you really have a wonderful wife. And she deserves an equally wonderful husband."

He smiled wide. "Will you just look at how much things have changed? Oh, and you're doing a great job with the dance ministry.

How much longer are you going to be in charge now?"

"As long as I'm needed," Fatima said. "I've got to go now." She turned and started walking away.

"See you later," Darius said mostly to her back since she was gone as soon as the last word left her mouth. Darius quickly turned to leave and bumped smack into a woman. "Oh, excuse me." He grabbed her and helped her maintain her footing.

"Darius?"

He looked in her face. "Gigi?"

Gigi Thornton frowned at first, then smiled as she straightened her white ruffled blouse. "You go to this church? I didn't realize you went here."

"Yes. I'm a member here. I thought I told you that." Darius frowned a little.

"Oh, you very well may have. I'm sure if you did, I just forgot," Gigi said. "Sometimes I think I might forget my head if it wasn't screwed on to my body. It appears we keep running into each other everywhere. You're not following me, are you?"

"Yeah, we do. Maybe God is trying to tell us something," Darius said.

"That's a nice suit you have on, the man in black. You're looking open-casket sharp. But then, every time I see you, you're fashionably dressed." She laughed as she scanned him from his freshly cut hair down to his ECCO Windsor slip-on shoes, then back up again. "How's the job hunt going? Have you landed anything yet?"

"Not yet. But I think I'm close. Maybe you should send up a prayer for me that the job I desire comes through." He rubbed his bottom lip as he smiled at her.

"I can do that, although I'm not sure how much my prayers will help you. I'm not exactly the best Christian out there. In fact, I'm not certain that God is even taking my calls, at least these days," Gigi said.

"Well, if you stay around this church and Pastor Landris too long, you'll find yourself having a personal relationship with God. You'll be talking about how God walks and talks with you on a daily basis."

"Really now?" Gigi said. "I can believe that. I really enjoyed Pastor Landris's sermon. He has a way of taking scriptures and breaking them down to what's really going on in real lives. I like that. In fact, I hope to come back again. So I suppose that means we may run into each other some more."

"Well, we'll be more than happy to have you." Darius scanned the area to see if he saw Tiffany anywhere around. "Look, I hate to bump and run, but I need to catch up with my family. I enjoyed seeing you again."

"Same here," Gigi said.

Darius turned back to her. "Oh, I meant to ask: Is Gigi your real name?"

She laughed. "You mean real as opposed to fake?" she joked. "Don't tell anyone, but my birth name is Georgina."

Darius nodded a few times. "Georgina. Okay."

"But I prefer Gigi. That's what everyone calls me."

"All right, Gigi. It was good seeing you again. And you are rocking that short cut. I like your hair like that better." Darius winked at her, then hurried over to Tiffany, who was huddled together near the information desk with their three children.

"Who was that you were talking to?" Tiffany asked Darius as soon as he stepped up to her.

"Oh, just someone I bumped into who's visiting here. You know how crowded this place is when church is over. You can't turn without bumping into somebody."

"So do you know her?" Tiffany asked.

"That's what she and I were trying to figure out. I met her at one of those networking functions a month or two ago. This was her first time visiting here. She said she really enjoyed Pastor Landris. I don't know what it is about you women drooling all over Pastor Landris and his preaching. He's all right, but y'all act like he's Moses bringing down the Ten Commandments from the mount or something."

"Daddy, Moses is old," four-year-old Junior said. "I saw a picture of him in that book Mommy reads to me and he had a really long white beard. Pastor Landris's beard is not long or even white like Moses's."

Darius placed his hand on his son's head and gently wiggled it. "I know, Son. I was merely making a point to Mommy here."

"Well, Mommy knows Pastor Landris isn't Moses." Junior turned to Tiffany. "Ain't that right, Mommy?"

"*Isn't* that right?" Tiffany said, correcting him. "It's 'isn't that right.' Not 'ain't.' "

"Isn't that right?" Junior looked up at his mother and smiled.

"Yes, Junior," Tiffany said. "We know that Pastor Landris isn't Moses. But he *is* someone God uses to bring the Word to His people, just like God used Moses."

"I like Pastor Landris's preaching," nine-year-old Jade said. "He makes it so interesting and plain. I remember that time he told the story about the people in the cave who'd never seen fire before and were afraid of what they didn't know."

Tiffany placed her hand on Jade's hair, which she'd allowed her to wear hanging down, and brushed it down. "Oh, you remember that one?"

"Yes. It was so good," Jade said.

"I remember that one, too," seven-year-old Dana said. "The people didn't realize that the fire would not only warm them, but give them light and help them to see what they'd never been able to see before while they were in the dark."

Junior jumped up in the air twice. "I like fire!"

"Yeah," Darius said. "You like fire a little *too* much. And I'd better not ever *hear* of you trying to start one on your own again, either. You hear me? Not until you have children of your own."

Junior laughed. "Daddy, you funny!"

"I ain't being funny. I mean it."

"Ooooh," Junior said. He turned to his mother. "Daddy said 'ain't.' " He turned back to his father. "It's 'isn't.' I *isn't* being funny. Oops!" He clamped both hands over his mouth and giggled. "I'm *not* being funny."

Tiffany nodded, then looked at Darius with a scowl.

"You ready to go home?" Darius asked Tiffany.

"We're ready," Tiffany said.

They started toward the set of glass doors. For some reason, Darius felt prompted to turn around and looked where he'd left Gigi standing. She was still there, looking quite intensely his way. He couldn't quite explain it, but there was something that bothered him about that.

The questions were: what and why?

CHAPTER 6

> And he brought me to the door of the court; and when I looked, behold a hole in the wall.
>
> — Ezekiel 8:7

"Why didn't you tell me Fatima Adams invited us to her wedding?" Darius casually asked Tiffany as they were preparing for bed.

Bent over, Tiffany was brushing her straight hair to the side, wrapping it, and pinning it in place with large bobby pins. "Because I knew you weren't interested in going, that's why." She stood up straight and finished, gathering the ends of her hair together and pinning them down.

"I'd go."

Tiffany placed one hand on her hip. "Yeah, right. I've asked you about attending weddings before. You never go."

"Well, I'd go to hers. She's your friend

and fellow dancer in the ministry, right? She's over the dance ministry right now, at least until Gabrielle returns full time. I'd support you and go."

"Darius, do you know the last wedding you attended?"

Darius grinned. "Yeah, I know. In fact, I even remember how bad I felt for that beautiful bride. In my mind I was screaming, 'Run, girl, run. He ain't no good! Run while you can!' "

"Boy, you're crazy."

Darius wrapped his arms around her waist and reeled her in to him. "I know I'm crazy . . . about you." He gave her a quick peck on her lips. "So, yes, I *do* remember the last wedding I attended — it was ours."

On vibrate, his phone made a buzzing sound. He pulled out his phone and looked at it. "I need to take this," he said with a coolness he'd perfected over years of practice.

"Who is it?" Playfully, Tiffany reached for his phone.

He maneuvered the phone up and out of her reach, giving her a quick peck on the lips when she reached upward. She laughed and sauntered to the bathroom.

Darius quickly left the bedroom, trotting down the steps. "Hey," he said, hoping she hadn't hung up.

"Hi," Paris said. "I was just about to hang up. I hope it's okay that I'm calling you this late. I didn't want to, but I don't have anyone else to turn to at the moment."

"It's not late. It's only, what?" He glanced at his watch. "Nine thirty. So what's going on? What do you need?"

"I need some help. Andrew is out of town on business and I can't find anyone to help me. I know this is asking a lot, but would it be possible for you to come here to my house?"

"To your house? You mean right now?"

"I know it really *is* asking a lot. And believe me: If I had any other option at this point, other than calling nine-one-one, I would. I promise I wouldn't be imposing on you like this. I wouldn't."

"So you want me to come to your house? Right now? Tonight?" Darius asked again.

"You know what? On second thought, don't worry about it," Paris said. "I don't know what I was thinking. I'll find some other way to take care of this. Forget I even called. Okay?"

"Hold on. It's not a problem. You can't call somebody up for help, then say that's okay. I was just making sure you were serious. Give me your address, and I'll be right over."

"That's okay. Let's just forget it. I shouldn't have even called you. I don't know what I was thinking. I'll just try to find someone else —"

"Girl, quit playing and give me your address. I told you it's not a problem. I'll be right there." Darius quickly tore a page off the shopping list pad being held to the side of the refrigerator with a magnet and grabbed a pen out of a nearby holder. It was apparent she needed help with *something.*

"Are you sure?"

"I'm ready. Now give me your address, and I'll be there in a few." Darius wrote down her address as she gave it.

He then went back upstairs and hollered at the closed bathroom door. "Tiff, I have to run out for a few minutes. I'll be back shortly." He went to the garage, got in his car, put Paris's address in his GPS, and found his way to her house.

Paris was waiting at the door, opening it before he even rang the doorbell.

"Thank you so much for coming. This way. Hurry!" She walked quickly up the stairs. Darius followed close behind her into her wine-color-scheme bedroom. Paris kneeled down, practically placing the side of her face on the rose-colored carpet. "She's either stuck or she's just refusing to come out on her own," she said.

"She?" Darius said. "She who?"

Paris looked up at Darius from the floor. "Ambrosia. She's under this armoire entertainment center here. She went in through that decorative opening, and she either *can't* or *won't* come out. She's probably scared, poor baby. The thing is too big and heavy to move to get her out of the hole she's gotten herself into."

"I'm sorry. Apparently, I'm missing something. Who, or should I say *what,* is Ambrosia?"

Paris sat on the floor and looked up at Darius. "I'm sorry. I'm just babbling without telling you everything. My father came by Friday and brought me a puppy."

"A puppy?" He began to chuckle as he realized what this was all about.

"Yes. She's a cute little Maltese I named Ambrosia."

Darius chuckled some more. "Oh, so you got one of those little toy dogs instead of a real dog."

"Ambrosia is a real dog. Or she will be a dog when she grows up. Right now she's just a baby . . . my baby," Paris said.

Darius was fully laughing now. "Please. You're going to make me gag." Darius reached down and grabbed her hand, helping her up off the floor. "Bring me a saucer of warm milk."

"Milk? Why, of course," Paris said, softly slapping the heel of her palm against her forehead. She swished out of the bedroom, returning shortly with a saucer of heated milk. "Here you are." She carefully handed the saucer of milk to Darius.

Darius put the saucer on the floor close to the entertainment center opening, but far enough away for the puppy to have to fully come out to get to it. "Come on, girl. Come on. Come and get some nice, warm milk. Here, girl, here."

"Ambrosia, baby. Come to Mama. Come and get you something to eat. It's milk, baby."

The puppy poked her head out of the opening and slowly walked over to the saucer of milk. Paris quickly grabbed her up along with the saucer of milk, allowing the puppy to lap it as she carried her over to the bed, carefully sitting so as not to spill the milk.

"Thank you so much, Darius," she said. "I don't know why I didn't think of that on my own. I tried using a stick to help guide her out to no avail. I didn't want to hurt her. But I didn't even *think* about offering her some milk."

"So what's Daddy dearest trying to do? Buy you off."

"Most likely."

"Well, is it working?"

"Nah," Paris said, shaking her head. "But before I can move forward with my plans, I have to convince my husband he and I need to unite on this front. I can't very well go into court petitioning to get a child from a woman claiming that I'd be better for her because I'm married when my own husband is not standing by my side. To the court, it will look like we're both single."

"If you can't convince your husband, and you need me to stand in as his double, just let me know."

Paris laughed. "I doubt that will work. If Gabrielle sees you, she'll bust us on it for sure. And even if Gabrielle didn't know you, I've told you before that I don't want to cause any problems between you and your wife. I hope my little dumb call tonight hasn't messed up things."

"Don't worry about it. My wife is probably already in bed now."

"So where did you tell her you were going at this time of the night?"

"I didn't. I just told her I had to run out for a few minutes."

"And she just let you leave without asking a million and one questions? Oh, she's a good one."

Darius walked over to the bed and snatched up the decorative roll pillow with gold fringes hanging on it. "Tiffany is pretty cool. She trusts me, most of the time anyway. As long as I'm not gone for too long, it'll be okay." He stuffed the pillow into the opening where the puppy had originally made her way in. "You might want to find something to cover up this hole so Ambrosia can't do that again. At least until she gets bigger."

"Sure." Paris set the now empty saucer on the nightstand. "Ambrosia has her own bed. I was going to put her in her own room, but I was keeping her in here with me these past few days until she gets used to being away from her mother. Poor baby. I set her down on the floor and was only gone about ten minutes. When I came back, I couldn't find her anywhere. I was looking everywhere for her. I then heard her whimpering. And like I told you: I tried everything I knew to get her out."

"So your husband's out of town?" Darius sat down at the bottom of the bed away from Paris. She didn't object nor appear bothered by him doing that.

"Yeah. Some kind of conference in Dallas. They left Friday morning. He's due back home tomorrow."

"So he hasn't gotten to meet the newest addition to the family yet, huh? You said your father brought her by Friday evening."

"Not yet. In fact, I haven't even told Andrew about her. Andrew didn't really want me getting a dog, at least not one like this one. He's not crazy about house dogs. Don't get me wrong; he likes dogs. He'd just prefer we have something like an Alaskan Husky or a German shepherd. That's why we hadn't gotten a dog before now; we couldn't reach a consensus. My mother and father have known I've wanted one of these little doggies for years." Paris snuggled Ambrosia up to her face.

"So your father, being the caring and loving man that he is, got you one."

"Yeah. I suppose he thinks getting me this puppy will distract me from trying to get Jasmine. Like somehow the two are remotely equal." She shook her head.

"I don't mean to appear mean or overstep my boundary, but it doesn't sound like your father really knows the real you."

Paris tilted her head slightly. "Thank you

for that. He really doesn't. I believe everybody thinks I'm a little shallow. They say I'm self-centered, like it's impossible for me to care about anything or anybody unless it somehow benefits me. But I *do* care." Her eyes became soft. "I do."

"Believe me: I understand how that can be. Personally, I think you wanting to get that little girl is a noble thing. It takes a lot to raise a child. I can attest to that. And anyone who puts him or herself out there to take on parenting responsibility is *definitely* not self-centered. Not in the least."

"I enjoy talking to you. You really seem to get me," Paris said. "I don't understand how my father can sit back and let someone like Gabrielle just take that child and he not do anything to stop it."

"So you still believe that little girl is your father's? Even though he's repeatedly denied it?"

"I do. I don't know why I can't shake it, but there's something deep down inside of me telling me that Jasmine is my father's child. I'm sure, if it's true, Daddy doesn't want my mother to know anything about it, which is probably why he's allowing things to go on as he's doing."

"Maybe that's something you should be thinking about as well," Darius said. "Your mother and how something like this might affect her. How will she feel if what you're doing, whether it's actually true or not, backfires?"

Paris frowned. "You know, I didn't really think about that part."

Darius stood up. "Well, maybe you should. You need to count the full cost of what you're doing before you proceed. It sounds like your husband isn't for this. Your daddy certainly isn't. And if you push it, you may end up hurting a lot of innocent people, including your mother. It *is* something to consider."

"Yeah." Paris stood up as well. "Thanks for coming over and helping me out with Ambrosia. Andrew wasn't here. My father is at some campaign function somewhere. My brother, Malachi, wouldn't even answer his phone, most likely ignoring my calls on purpose. Not that he would have come over anyway, especially if he'd known why I was calling. And he would have made me tell him before he would have agreed to come. I didn't have all that many options left."

"So you thought of me?" Darius said, walking over to the nightstand. "Well, I'm honored to know I'm on your shortlist."

Paris started walking toward the door while holding Ambrosia. "I owe you one."

"You don't owe me. I told you if you ever needed me that all you had to do was call."

"You did. I just didn't expect I'd ever have a reason to take you up on it. I thank you, and Ambrosia *certainly* thanks you."

"Tell you what: Let me have this Snickers bar and we'll call it even," he said pointing at the candy bar on the nightstand.

"Absolutely. Take it. Andrew bought it for me, but I prefer Milky Way bars."

"Are you sure?"

"Yes. Please . . . take it."

He picked it up, dropped it in his shirt pocket, and followed her down the stairs.

"Thanks again," Paris said as she opened the door for him to leave.

Darius stepped outside the door. "Anytime," he said with a bow of his head and a quirk of a smile. "Anytime."

Chapter 7

> Bring forth the blind people that have eyes,
> and the deaf that have ears.
>
> — Isaiah 43:8

Darius came into the bedroom. Tiffany was propped up by two pillows reading the Bible. She looked his way. Darius smiled. "I got you something." He handed her a small brown paper bag.

Tiffany set the Bible down and, taking the bag, peeked inside. "A Snickers bar!" she said, hurriedly taking the candy out. "I love Snickers. Darius, you're so wrong for this. You know I'm trying to cut back on sweets. I want to lose some of this weight."

"I know. But I don't want to deny you something that you love. I keep telling you that you look fine. And I do mean . . . fine. I don't want a bone. I like a little meat on my bones."

"And I love Snickers bars." She tore open

the top part of the wrapper and took a bite, savoring it before taking another one. "It's not good when you eat late, I hope you know that. I'm going to pay for this, I just know I am. But this is *so* good." She looked over at Darius. After she swallowed, she gave him a peck on the lips. He could taste the candy. "Thank you, baby. So you left to go get me this candy bar?"

He tilted his head to the right, then to the left. "Well, not exactly. You know that my phone rang right before I left."

"Yeah. So who was it?"

Darius hesitated for a second. "Nobody you know."

"If it was nobody that I know, then who was it?" Tiffany asked again; her head tilted to one side as she waited.

"Okay. I'm going to be honest with you. I'm going to tell you the truth. Don't get mad now, but it was this beautiful woman with a brand-new Maltese puppy that just happened to have gotten stuck underneath a huge entertainment center in her bedroom. She — the woman, not the puppy — needed someone big and strong with a brain, of course, to help her cute little baby get out of the hole she'd gotten herself into." Darius smiled, then twisted his mouth a few times as he waited for the fallout.

Tiffany stared at him, then took another bite of her candy bar. After a minute of chewing, she smacked her mouth. "Okay, Darius. If you don't want to tell me, then fine. Keep it to yourself, then."

"But I'm telling you the truth."

"It was Big Red, wasn't it?"

"No. I told you who it was. It was a woman with a puppy, a puppy with a cute little purple bow in the top of her head."

Tiffany nodded short, quick nods. "Yep. It was your buddy Big Red. And you went over to his house. Has his wife come back home yet? I know you told me that his wife had left him."

"Nope. She's still at her mother's waiting on Big Red to get himself together."

"What she is waiting on is for him to stop chasing women and to get himself a real job that has benefits. I don't know why you still fool with him."

"Because he's my friend; he needs me. And Big Red loves what he does. He loves to work on cars. He likes working for himself. He can't help it if health insurance is so high he can't afford it. But I'm telling you that I didn't go over to Big Red's tonight."

"Okay, then. What's the puppy's name?"

Darius frowned. "Excuse me?"

"You say you went and rescued a puppy. What's the puppy's name?"

Darius grinned as he rubbed his goatee. "Ambrosia."

"Yep. You went over to Big Red's. And Big Red probably had some ambrosia, most likely from his mama. You made up that cockamamie story about a woman and a puppy so I wouldn't know what you were really up to tonight." Tiffany held out the remaining candy bar to him. "Want a bite?"

Darius laughed and took a bite even though there wasn't much left. "I love you."

"And I love you." She bit a piece of the candy bar again. "And I *love* Snickers bars! Mmmm-mmmm."

CHAPTER 8

Behold, the Lord thy God hath set the land before thee: go up and possess it, as the Lord God of thy fathers hath said unto thee; fear not, neither be discouraged.
— Deuteronomy 1:21

Darius couldn't wait to get home to tell Tiffany the good news. It had finally happened: He'd gotten another job, starting immediately. Things were looking up. He pulled into his driveway and noted a familiar white car parked behind Tiffany's garage door. Tiffany had company. He smiled, parked his car outside of his garage door, quietly went in through the front door, and stood at the bottom of the staircase a few feet away from the den.

He listened in. Just as he thought: Gabrielle Mercedes was there. He heard her and Tiffany talking. They were definitely in what sounded like a deep conversation. He was proud of his wife. She was actually asking Gabrielle questions about what was going on with her. He couldn't hear everything as clearly as he would have liked, but he would get the full 411 when he stealthily grilled Tiffany later. That's what he loved about their marriage: As a couple, they didn't keep things from each other. Well, at least Tiffany didn't keep things from him. He would be the first to acknowledge that God was still working on him and God wasn't through with him yet.

He then heard Tiffany let out a scream. "Oh my goodness! Congratulations, Gabrielle! Oh, my goodness! That's wonderful!" The two women both let out a girlish giggly scream together.

"Daddy," Jade said as she stood at the top of the stairs. "What are you doing?"

Darius looked around for something to use as a cover for his eavesdropping. He looked up at her. "Well, hello there, number one," he said, calling her by the name he sometimes called her, indicating her birth order, while trying not to talk too loudly. "Come and give your daddy a hug."

Jade smiled and trotted down the stairs, hugging her father. He reached inside of his front pants' pocket, pulled out a crumbled-up one dollar bill he'd hurriedly stuffed there, pressed it straight, and handed it to her.

"What's this?" Jade, who had turned nine on April eighth, asked as she held the money in the air.

"It's a dollar."

"I know it's a dollar. But what's it for?"

He smiled, then quietly whispered, "Don't say anything or make a loud sound, but Daddy got a job today so I'm spreading a little wealth around."

Jade's face lit up and she whispered back, "You did? You got a job?"

He whispered back. "Yes. But it's a surprise for Mommy." He pretended to lock his lips. Jade pretended to lock hers as well.

Jade giggled, hugged her father again, then tiptoed back up the stairs. Darius went back over toward the den's opening. He wasn't sure how much he'd missed with the distraction, but they were now talking about things he was sure he didn't care to stand there and listen in on.

"Hello, hello!" he said stepping into the den with a full grin.

Gabrielle had been laughing and her expression dropped completely when she saw him.

"Hi, honey," Tiffany said, standing and greeting him with a quick peck on the lips.

"I didn't hear the garage door let up."

"Oh, that's because I didn't use it."

"Is something wrong with your car? Did you break down or something?" Tiffany asked, worry clearly etched all over her face now.

"Oh, no. Everything is fine. I just parked outside. I needed to run in and get something real quick, and I have to leave and run right back out," he lied. "I decided it didn't make sense to raise the garage door, then turn right back around and raise it in a few minutes later when I leave."

"Oh, okay," Tiffany said with relief.

Gabrielle stood up. "Well, I'm going to get on home."

"Oh, please don't go on my account," Darius said. "I didn't mean to interrupt. I saw your car outside. I heard voices in here and merely wanted to come in and speak."

Gabrielle smiled. "No, I really need to be getting home. Zachary is watching Jasmine for me while I handle a few errands. I don't want to leave them alone for too long."

"I heard you and Tiffany in here all giggly about something. It sounded like some good news," Darius said, trying to be careful that he didn't accidentally say something that was told to him by his wife in confidence.

Tiffany looked at Gabrielle. Darius

couldn't believe it, but his wife was actually waiting on Gabrielle to give her permission to tell him anything.

"Forgive me. I wasn't trying to pry," Darius said. "It's just a good thing when we get some good news around this place. It's like the devil has been messing with so many folks we personally know lately. Anybody who has something to be blessing the Lord for, I want to be a part of it. I know how to get my Holy Ghost shout on." He did a little jig step.

Gabrielle smiled. "I was just telling Tiffany some of my good news. You're right about the devil being busy. But you know our mantra at Followers of Jesus Faith Worship Center."

"The devil may be busy but God is busier!" Tiffany and Gabrielle said in unison. They laughed as they hugged, then high-fived each other.

"True that," Darius said. "So if you share *your* good news, I'll share mine."

Tiffany widened her eyes at Darius. "Honey, you have some good news?"

He primped his mouth a few times, then broke into a full-on grin. "Yes. I got a job!"

Tiffany rushed over to him and hugged him as she jumped up and down. "Oh, baby! That's great. Oh, my goodness! Oh, my goodness! God is so awesome! You got a job? You got a job! Is it the one you've been working so hard to get? Don't keep me in suspense. Tell me everything!"

Darius nodded. "Yes, that's the one. It looks like all of my hard work and networking paid off. God has finally smiled on us. We're about to get up out of this pit we were thrown in and move to a little higher ground."

"Oh, wow! Oh, wow!" Tiffany said. "You got a job and Gabrielle is engaged —" Tiffany quickly clamped her hand over her mouth. She took her hand down slowly. "I'm sorry. I'm sorry." She rush over and touched Gabrielle's hand. "I didn't mean to just blurt that out. It's just . . . God is so good!"

"It's okay," Gabrielle said. "My engagement is not really a secret or anything. It's just with so much going on in my life, I've not been broadcasting it to everybody. But you are so right. God is so good."

"Well, I hope you don't consider me everybody," Darius said, glancing down at the rock on her ring finger. "We're all family here. At least I consider us family. Congratulations, Gabrielle. God truly is . . . good. And His goodness and mercy is blessing us right now."

Gabrielle nodded in a matter of fact way. "God is. And congratulations to you on your new job."

"Thank you, thank you. It's good pay with good benefits. Lord knows, we needed this. And He came through and not a minute too soon. Who said serving the Lord will pay off after a while? Serving the Lord pays off right now, down here on this earth. Because I know it wasn't nobody *but* God who made this way for me and my family."

Darius shook his head, then pinched his nose as though he was trying to keep tears from flowing.

"It's okay, baby," Tiffany said, rubbing his back. "I know. I know. You *know* that *I* know."

Darius held his head up, placing his hand over his lips before shaking himself hard and taking his hand down. "So, Gabrielle. How's the adoption coming along?"

Gabrielle hesitated a few seconds before responding. "Things are moving along." She turned from Darius to Tiffany. "I'm going to get on out of your hair so the two of you can celebrate your good news. But I *so* enjoyed my visit with you, Tiffany. We'll talk again soon, I promise. And if I don't see you before then, I'll see you at Fatima's wedding next Saturday."

"We'll be there with bells on," Darius said.

Gabrielle looked at Darius with a slight smirk. "You're coming?"

"This even *I'll* have to see," Tiffany said with a chuckle.

"Listen, Gabrielle," Darius said. "My wife has grown so much in every area of her life, it seems, since she became part of the dance ministry. The dance ministry is like family around our house. We're going to support Fatima as well as you because you two have been a blessing to every one of us in more ways than you'll ever know. I'm going to be there with my wife. And if you need us — me or Tiffany — we'll be there for you as well."

Gabrielle gave a quick smile as though she wasn't buying any of what Darius was trying to sell. "Thanks, Darius. I appreciate that."

Tiffany eyes were filled with tears. She nodded. "He's right. Darius is right. You and Fatima are like family as are so many at Followers of Jesus Faith Worship Center. You just don't know, you just don't know."

Gabrielle turned to Tiffany. "I know what you mean. Being a part of this ministry feels like home. I had no idea on that January day when I walked up to the front of the church and gave my hand to the pastor and my heart to the Lord, just how much my entire life would change. And to think: It's only been a little over a year. Sure, there are things that have come along in my life, especially lately, that can be dispiriting, disheartening, and discouraging. But I hear God telling me to fear not, neither be discouraged. God has set the Promised Land before each of us. We just have to go up and possess it. God has already given it to us, but we have to go and possess it ourselves."

"You're right, Gabrielle. When we give our lives to the Lord it doesn't mean things will always be easy," Tiffany said. "Far from it. But God places people in our lives who remind us that He's *still* on the throne. He'll show up on our behalf when we may least expect it, when we've given up all hope."

"Yeah," Gabrielle said. "And God keeps reminding me through my trials and tribulations that greater is He that is in me than he that is in the world. No matter what problems come, the peace of God keeps whispering to my spirit, 'I got this.' "

Tiffany did a quick little happy-feet dance. "Girl, don't get me started. I'm about to get my praise on *up in here, up in here*!"

Darius laughed. "You two are something else. I see you don't have to be in church to praise God."

"That's because we *are* the church," Gabrielle said.

"And wherever we are, the church is," Tiffany said, high-fiving Gabrielle again after she said it.

"Pastor Landris teaches us that," Gabrielle said. "So, no matter where we go, the doors of the church are open."

"Well, I'm going to get on out of here before you two get a Holy Ghost party started." Darius smiled, then leaned down and gave Tiffany a quick peck on her lips. "I'll be back shortly and tell you all about my new job."

Darius walked out of the room just as Tiffany and Gabrielle started singing, "Ain't no party like a Holy Ghost party, 'cause a Holy Ghost party don't . . . stop."

He went outside, got in his car, backed out of the driveway, and drove off, singing to himself, "Ain't no party like a Holy Ghost party, 'cause a Holy Ghost party don't stop."

CHAPTER 9

> Meddle not with them; for I will not give you of their land, no, not so much as a footbreadth; because I have given mount Seir unto Esau for a possession.
>
> — Deuteronomy 2:5

Darius sat outside of her driveway, trying to decide whether or not he should go to the door and ring the doorbell. He was thinking that he should have called and asked if it was okay to come over. But when Gabrielle and Tiffany went into all that talk about God, church, and started praising, he just *had* to get out of there. So he'd made up an excuse about not being able to stay, gotten in his car, and driven away with no clear destination in mind.

He'd thought about going over to Big Red's place. Especially since Tiffany had brought his name up four days earlier. He still couldn't believe the one time he'd actually told Tiffany the truth about him going to see another woman, she didn't even believe him. He laughed at the strangeness of it all.

He got out of the car, went up to the door, took a deep breath, exhaled, and rang the doorbell. After a few minutes with no answer, he rang the doorbell again. A few seconds later, the door swung open hard and fast.

"What do you want?"

Darius smiled. "Well, hello to you, too. Are you going to invite me in?"

"Darius, I thought I made it clear on Sunday that I'm not interested in anything with you other than 'hi' and 'bye.' And even that might be stretching things a bit."

"So much hostility. I'm going to have to pray for you." Darius brushed past her and stepped inside. He looked around. It had been five years now since he'd been inside of her home. She'd gotten all new furniture for the living room. It was apparent that Fatima was still doing well financially.

Fatima stepped in front of him to keep him from going any farther. "Darius, why are you here?"

"To be honest," Darius said. "I really don't know. I went home to tell my wife some good news. But when I got there, Gabrielle Mercedes was there."

"Gabrielle was at your house?"

"Yes." Darius could see she wanted to ask him why, but held her tongue.

Fatima closed the front door and turned around to him. "Is everything okay? I mean with Gabrielle and Tiffany." Her tone was softer, not quite as harsh as before.

Darius nodded. "Oh, yeah. Apparently, Gabrielle was there telling my dear wife about her engagement. I assume it's to the good doctor Zachary." Darius smirked. "And I take it from your calm reaction that you already know about it."

"Her business is her business."

"Yeah. You always were good at keeping other folks' business their business. That's what I loved so much about you." He looked into her eyes. "You know I miss you . . . I honestly and truly miss you. I miss *us.*"

"Well, I don't miss you. I'm happy, ecstatically happy. I have someone in my life who loves me. And we're going to be married in nine days."

"And live happily ever after, or so the fairy tale is supposed to go. Reality, on the other hand, doesn't always get that e-mail."

"Now that you've said what you've apparently come here to say, you need to get on home to your wife and children."

"So you're really going to marry that nerd? Really? Although, I will give it to you: You do have him dressing so much better these days. He was pretty pathetic before you came into his life. Not that I was paying that much attention to him. His mismatch of colors and design just used to scream out for it. But everybody is saying how much you've done for him since getting with him. Now if you could just get him to throw away those black square-rimmed glasses, he might *really* be all right."

"To answer your question, I really *am* marrying Trent. And I'm blessed to be doing so. He's an awesome man, but more importantly: He's an awesome man who loves God."

Darius laughed. "Yep. That's what you women claim you're looking for. But you won't be happy. You won't. I know you, Fatima. Or in the more biblical term: I *knew* you." He chuckled. "You need a man with some grit to him, a man with a little edge."

"You mean a man like you?"

"Precisely! A man like me, or even better: me."

"Actually, my taste has improved dramatically. I want the best God has for me. I decided some years ago to no longer settle for less than when God wanted me to have more than enough. And will you just look at what God has done in my life after I changed my mind about what was acceptable and what was not. God blessed me *according to* His riches in glory. And contrary to what many people may think, rich isn't always money."

"Oh, my goodness. Now here *you* go. Why does everybody want to talk about God today? Yeah, I know God woke us up this morning and started us on our way. But, goodness gracious, can we stop being so religious all the time. Give me a break! I certainly didn't come here for this."

Fatima went and opened the door. "Great. Then you can get to stepping. Because I dare say that's *all* you're going to get here: Me talking about the goodness of God. How God kept me even when I was being foolish. Darius, let me give you some advice, and you can take it for whatever it's worth. But the Bible clearly tells us that what we do in the dark *will* come to light. The Bible also says that whatsoever we sow, we're going to reap. All this mess you keep doing . . . it's going to catch up with you someday. Mark my words: I'm telling you this as someone who once loved you. So before you hurt Tiffany and your family any more, get right with God."

Darius threw up his hands in surrender. "Okay. I've had enough preaching for one day. Lord knows I don't care to hear this."

"And the Lord knows how much you need to hear it. All the dirt you've done and are still doing, it's *going* to catch up with you one of these days. And I deeply and sincerely regret the part I played in it. But thank God for deliverance. I've been delivered, do you hear me? I am redeemed. I'm a new creature; old things have passed away. And if I were you, I'd make my way to the altar in a hurry and ask God's forgiveness before it's too late."

"Okay. I'm out." Darius stepped out the door. "Congratulations on your upcoming wedding nuptials. I'll likely be there since I opened my mouth and promised my wife I'd go. But I just wanted to be sure this is what you really want."

"I appreciate that you're *so* concerned about me and what I want. But you don't have to worry about me. In fact, you can delete me from your thoughts entirely."

Darius pretended to hit an imaginary button in the air. "Blip. Delete. Done," Darius said. "Oh, and good *luck* to you." He laughed and walked away. Fatima closed the door.

Darius then began to sing "Superstition" by Stevie Wonder as he walked back and got into his SUV.

Chapter 10

> Furthermore, the Lord spake unto me, saying, I have seen this people, and, behold, it is a stiff-necked people.
>
> — Deuteronomy 9:13

On his way home, Darius received a text from Paris congratulating him on his new job. He smiled as he read the text while driving. Holding the phone against the steering wheel, he texted her back using as much shorthand as possible so as to be safe while driving. Thx. WAYD?

She texted back, repeating the sentiments of his question. What am I doing? Trying 2 decide what I want 2 eat 2nite.

Let hubby decide, he texted.

Hubby working. Won't be home until late.

Darius switched out of text mode to phone and pressed for Paris's number. "Hey," he said as soon as he thought she'd picked up but didn't hear her say anything.

He wasn't sure if he'd hit a dead zone while driving and lost the connection or if something had happened with the call going through. "Hello."

"Hey," Paris said.

Darius held the phone up to his ear with his right hand while steering with his left. "I figured it was stupid for us to keep texting when we could be talking instead."

"I didn't know if it was okay to call, so I opted to text, just in case."

"You're okay. I'm not even at home. In fact, I'm close to your area of town. I had some business I needed to take care of."

"Congratulations on your new job."

"Thank you, thank you. To say that I'm excited would be an understatement. So how did you find out?"

"Daddy told me. He says he wants me and you to work together to get the young folks involved in his reelection bid. I don't know if he or William told you, but that was the stipulation for you getting the job: I had to agree to work with you on this."

Darius laughed. "So Daddy dearest thinks I need a babysitter, huh?"

"No. Daddy would do anything to keep me under his thumb. My working for him gives him a little control over me, or so he thinks. I believe he also set it up this way thinking that you'll be babysitting me. Needless to say: My daddy doesn't have a clue."

"Not if he thinks I can make *you* behave," Darius said.

"That's why Andrew is likely working late tonight. He used to never work late. He was always trying to get home to me. Here lately he's been going on a lot of out-of-town trips without me and taking cases that seem to require more of his time when he *is* here. Frankly, I just think he's trying to get back at me because I refuse to back down on my quest to get Jasmine out of Gabrielle's clutches. I still believe there's something between Andrew and her. I don't know what, but I just have this feeling."

"She's engaged to be married."

"Who's engaged?" Paris said, obviously shocked. "Gabrielle?"

"Yep."

"How do you know that?"

Darius slammed on the brakes, his car stopping mere inches from having almost barreled into the back of a Range Rover that had stopped for the red light Darius hadn't paid attention to. "Whoa!" he said as though he were trying to stop a horse. His heart was now pounding hard.

"What happened? What's wrong?" Paris

asked. "What's going on?"

"This idiot in front of me just stopped, all of a sudden, and made me almost ram into the back of her. I'm sure it *has* to be a woman driving."

"Has to be a woman, huh? It was most likely some man talking on his cell phone and not paying attention, just like you. You know you're not supposed to talk on the phone while you drive, don't you?" Paris said.

Darius laughed. "We don't have a law here in Alabama saying that. But talking and driving is a lot better than when I was trying to text and drive. I'm fine. I'm a man; men can handle stuff like this. It's no different than having someone in the car and talking to them or trying to change the channel on the radio or put in a CD. People make such a big deal about it."

"So you don't have one of those hands-free devices?"

"Nope. I'm holding the phone with my free hand though. I don't need but one hand to drive. That's how real men do it. We drive with one hand. But I bet your husband has one of those hands-free devices, a Bluetooth earpiece, have it come through the radio."

"Yes, in fact he does have an earpiece, as

do I. Okay, real man. But just know that it's dangerous doing that. So I'm going to be a *real* woman and get off the phone so you can concentrate on the road. I don't want to be the cause of you having an accident or something."

"I told you, woman: I *got* this. I got this." He laughed. "I'd like to thank you for all you've done in helping me get this job. What say I stop and pick up dinner for you and drop it by your house?"

"I thought you were struggling financially."

"I am. But I have a credit card. I hope there's enough on there to pick up a bite for you to eat."

"No, thank you. That's not necessary."

"I know it's not necessary. But if it wasn't for you, I wouldn't have this opportunity to make money and hopefully pay off some of these bloodsuckers. You're responsible in more ways than you'll ever know. So tell me what you'd like to eat, and I'll save you the trouble of having to get out and go get it."

"That's okay, Dare. Really. But thank you though."

"Listen, hardheaded woman, let me do this. Okay? All I'm going to do is pick up something and deliver it to your house. That's it. I'm already over this way. If you'll notice, I didn't ask you to meet me anywhere or anything like that. Consider this as part of my job orientation. Your father wants me and you working together. I *know* you don't want to be the cause of me losing my job before I even get started."

"Fine. Just stop wherever it's convenient, call me and let me know what place, and I'll tell you what I want. But I'm going to pay for it, so bring me a receipt."

"All right. Now *that* wasn't so hard, was it? After I drop your food off, I really need to get home to my wife. I'm sure Tiffany is anxious to hear about my new job."

"You haven't told her yet?"

"Oh, I told her I got a job. But she had a visitor when I got home, so I politely excused myself and went for a little drive. You'll never guess who the visitor."

"Dear heart, I don't like guessing games in the least, so just tell me already."

Darius chuckled. "Your friend Gabrielle Mercedes."

"Oooh, do tell."

"I will tell you as soon as I get all of the details." His phone beeped, alerting him that another call was coming through. He pulled the phone away from his ear and glanced at it with a smile. "Speaking of the devil . . . that's my wife calling me now. I'll hit you back when I get to an eating destination to see what you want."

"No. You go on home and take care of your wife. We don't need you messing things up with her at this point. I'll be fine."

"Are you sure? Because it's no trouble —"

"Positive. We'll talk later. Hopefully then, you'll have more to report."

He nodded. "Okay. Bye now." He hurriedly switched over. "Yes, my queen."

"Where are you?" Tiffany asked.

"On my way home."

"So what took you so long to answer your phone?"

"Now you know I'm not supposed to talk and drive or text and drive. Don't you keep telling me that? Isn't that what you keep preaching to me?"

"I tell you that but I know you don't listen. You're driving and talking right now, aren't you?"

"Yes. But that's because I knew if I didn't answer, you'd wonder what was going on."

"Uh-huh. So I'm going to get off the phone before you have an accident or something. How close are you?"

He stopped at a red light. "I should be there in about fifteen minutes."

"Hey," Tiffany said. "Since you're already out, can you stop at the store and pick me up some vanilla wafers and a can of evaporated milk? I think I'd like to make a banana pudding . . . to celebrate your new *job* that I'm still waiting on the details."

"Is that right? Well, if you're making pudding for me, then I'd prefer pineapple pudding much better than banana," Darius said.

Tiffany laughed. "Is that right? Well, in that case, then add a sixteen-ounce can of crushed pineapples to the list."

"How about I just come home and watch the children while *you* run to the grocery store? How about we do that instead?"

"Honey, just stop and do this, okay? You're already out. It makes no sense for you to drive right by the store, then make me have to go."

"Okay, okay. But you know how dangerous it is when you send me to store. I'm the stiff-necked one, remember? I can't turn my head to the right or to the left, I just like to keep it straight. And I always forget something."

"Then work on loosening up your neck. It's just three things: vanilla wafers, a can of PET milk, and a sixteen-ounce can of crushed pineapples, the sweetened kind. And hurry home. You know I want to hear all about your new job. I am *so* proud of you. I hope you know that."

"I'll be home shortly. Just as soon as I find these things on my honey-do list." Darius clicked off the phone and set it on the passenger's seat. "I hate going to the grocery store. I *hate* it!" He turned up the radio and began to sing along with Luther Vandross's "A House Is Not a Home."

Chapter 11

> O the depth of the riches both of the wisdom and knowledge of God! how unsearchable are his judgments, and his ways past finding out!
>
> — Romans 11:33

Darius walked into the kitchen and handed Tiffany the white plastic bag from the store. "Here you go: vanilla wafers, pineapples, and buttermilk."

"What? I said evaporated milk, not buttermilk." Tiffany put her hand in the bag and pulled the box of wafers out. "I can't use buttermilk in a pudding. Now I'm *still* going to have to go out if I want to make this pudding." She pulled out a can and held it up.

Darius started laughing. He pointed his hand and index finger at her like it was a gun. "Got'cha!"

Tiffany grinned. "Boy! You play too much.

I thought you'd actually bought buttermilk." She set the can of evaporated milk down on the counter.

"Tiffany, you know good and well that I know the difference between buttermilk and a can of PET milk. My great-grandmother used to drink buttermilk all the time. She would take cornbread and push it down in a glass of buttermilk."

"I don't want to hear that. Visualizing that turns my stomach every time."

"Well, Great-grandma acted like it was delicious." Darius sat down on a bar stool as Tiffany put the empty plastic bag in the cabinet where she kept them to reuse later.

Tiffany walked over and leaned on the counter across from Darius. "Okay, you've kept me waiting long enough. Tell me about the new job." She smiled. "I'm so excited! I can't believe you left like you did without telling me details. You know I really don't understand you sometimes."

"I left so that you and Gabrielle could finish your talk. I didn't want her to feel uncomfortable or like she wasn't welcome here or able to stay as long as she wanted. She hardly ever comes over here anymore. So I made like I had somewhere to go."

"But she told you we were finished and that she was leaving."

"I know. And how much longer was she here after I left?" Darius raised his eyebrows up and down a few times as he waited on her answer.

Tiffany smiled as she moved her head from side to side like a boxer loosening up before a fight. "Oh, you think you're so smart."

"Exactly, what a thought. So how long was she here?"

She wrinkled her nose, then pulled her right ear. "About thirty more minutes."

"See. I knew she was only leaving because she didn't want to hold you up. The last time Gabrielle was here was last year when she and Fatima came over to help you learn those dance routines. So how did you happen to get her to come by?"

"It's interesting. I called to check on her . . . just to see how she was. She told me she'd been thinking about me and wanted to come by and bring me something."

"Oh, so she brought you something, huh?" Darius leaned in some more.

Tiffany stood up straight. "Yes." She reached into her pocket and pulled out a folded paper. "She wanted to give us this." Tiffany handed him the paper.

Darius took it and opened it. It was a

check made out to Tiffany Connors. "She gave you a check? Gabrielle came over here to give you money?"

Tiffany nodded. "She said God placed it on her heart to sow something into our lives. She knows we've been likely struggling. So she came and brought that to us."

"Is this supposed to be charity or something?" Darius's voice escalated a bit.

"If by charity you mean love, then, yes: It's charity."

"Gabrielle has the kind of money now that she can be passing out five-hundred-dollar checks?" Darius looked at the check again. "Five hundred dollars . . . written to you? Wow. I guess taking in that child is paying off handsomely in more ways than any of us ever suspected. Maybe you and I ought to see about trying to adopt her ourselves. We have room for one more."

"Darius! That's not a very nice thing to say."

"I was only joking. I'm still trying to wrap my brain around Gabrielle writing you a check, let alone one for that amount. I know family members who won't do something that generous."

"I didn't want to take it. Not from her. I know she's had her own financial challenges. You remember last year when something happened with her car?"

"Yeah. The time you and I had to go to her house and picked her up so she could make it to Wednesday-night Bible study. I heard later that her car had been repossessed during that time."

"I don't know about all that. But what I *do* know is that whatever was going on, she was determined to get to church that night. She'd asked Fatima to pick her up, but Fatima's mother died, causing her to leave suddenly. Fatima called and asked me if I could pick her up. I also know Gabrielle lost her job right around that same time. She was cleaning houses trying to make it. Gabrielle has had a hard time for sure."

"But look at her now. Now she's the director over the dance ministry at our church. Doing well enough to be able to take a leave of absence, I assume without pay, *and* take in a little girl who's had serious medical problems. But let's not forget that she's now engaged to marry a doctor. Did she tell you when the big day is?"

Tiffany shook her head. "I don't think they've set a date yet."

"God seems to have turned things around for her to the point where she's now handing out five-hundred-dollar checks? That's all right. And it's not like you and her are best friends, either. Not like Oprah and Gayle by any means."

"I'm not sure Gabrielle is doing all that great. Financially, I mean. But she said God told her to do this, and if I didn't take it, I'd be blocking her blessings."

"Well, it's not like we don't need it. The Lord knows we needed it. I got this job, sure enough. Finally, thank the Lord. But it'll be a few weeks before a check comes rolling in from it. This was definitely God." He handed the check back to Tiffany.

"Only God knew how much we desperately needed this. And only God knew the exact amount we were short of right now." Tiffany began to cry and turned her back to Darius.

Darius stood and walked around to where she was, pulling her close to him. "I know it's been hard. I know it has. But I have this job now, and it pays well, really well."

Tiffany nodded, looked up into Darius's eyes, and smiled. "I'm so proud of you. I am." She stuffed the check back inside her blue jean's pocket and released a deep sigh as though she were pushing out all of the negative feelings taking refuge inside of her. "Now," she said. "Tell me all about this new job." She broke into a grin. "My baby got a job!"

He took a deep breath, then exhaled as he grinned. "You are looking at the new co-chair in charge of getting out the youth vote for Representative Lawrence Simmons's reelection campaign."

Tiffany pulled back. "You got a job doing something in politics? But you don't know anything about politics. In fact, you hardly even vote. So is this just a temporary job or something? The election is in November. It has to be temporary."

He cocked his head to one side. "Wow. Thanks for the vote of confidence. Where's the enthusiasm? Where's the excitement? Where's the thanking God for *this* blessing, even if it *is* temporary?"

Tiffany hugged him. "I'm excited. This is great! But it's already May and the election is the first Tuesday in November. That just sounds like a temporary job to me. But I'm grateful. I am."

"I call this a stepping-stone job. It's all in how you look at a thing." He took her by the hand and led her over to a chair at the glass kitchen table. They sat down. "Aren't you curious to know how much I'll be making for this 'temporary job,' as you call it?"

Tiffany perked up and put a smile on her face. "Yes. How much will you be making?"

"Four thousand dollars a month with a

guaranteed pay of seven months."

Tiffany began to count on her fingers. She did it again, adding one more finger in her count. "So that means you're going to be paid for all of May and all of November, up until December first?"

"Absolutely."

"And you're getting four thousand dollars a month?"

"Twenty-eight thousand dollars, that's three thousand dollars more than what I made at my other job for an entire year, minus the overtime pay, of course."

Tiffany placed her hand over her mouth. "Look at God." She shook her head. "Will you just *look* at God!"

Chapter 12

That I have great heaviness and continual sorrow in my heart.

— Romans 9:2

"Is he in there?" Gabrielle Mercedes asked Mattie Stevens as she pointed toward Lawrence Simmons's closed office door as soon as she entered the office.

"Yes, but —"

Gabrielle walked right past her without even pausing.

Mattie jumped to her feet. "You can't go in there!"

Gabrielle opened the closed office door and closed it behind her. Lawrence was in there alone. "Call your daughter off, Lawrence."

Lawrence was already on his feet. "What is *wrong* with you? You can't just come barging into my office like this. Are you crazy?"

"I want you to call your daughter off!"

"Will you *please* lower your voice," he said. "Come and sit down."

"I didn't come to chitchat or to hear any more excuses. Paris needs to stop this vendetta she's on and leave me and mine alone."

"I'm working on Paris."

"Well, you're not working hard enough. Look at this." Gabrielle pulled a document out of a large envelope and handed it to him."

Lawrence began reading it.

"She's petitioning the courts on having a hearing to take Jasmine away from me. She told me about a month ago that she was planning to do something like this."

Lawrence sat there visibly shaken. He pounded his fist on his desk. "Why won't she just leave it alone?" He looked up at Gabrielle. "I'm doing all I can. I thought I was getting her under control. Paris can be a handful to deal with."

"Well, allow me to tell *you* what I've been dealing with. I have a nine-year-old little girl who has gone through a bone marrow transplant. Before that, she had to deal with the loss of her father. And now she's lost the only mother she's ever known. I know what it's like to lose your mother. I had to grow up without mine."

"I understand."

"No . . . you . . . don't! You *don't* understand. You don't understand that her mother made me promise, right before she died, that I would tell Jasmine she was adopted and who I was to her. But I haven't told her yet. I haven't told her any of it."

"Please, Gabrielle, have a seat and try to calm down."

"I don't want to sit down! I want your daughter to leave me and my daughter alone so I can deal with the things that matter the most right now. I don't need to have to fight Paris as she continually causes trouble . . . trying to take Jasmine from me. It's already a lot to fight without her on top of it." Gabrielle began to cry.

Lawrence pulled out his handkerchief, stood up, and handed it to her. "I'll talk to Paris again. I'll make her understand and back down. I will. I promise. I've already moved on something that should make this all go away. I'm handling Paris."

"If you don't or aren't able to, Lawrence, it's going to get messy. I'm telling you; it's going to get messy. I'm not trying to hurt anyone. I'm trying to handle this the best way that *I* can. But you and I both know that I have more rights to Jasmine than Paris *ever* will. And if the truth has to come out . . . all of it . . .”

Lawrence walked over to her. “I know. You don’t have to remind me. Listen, I’ve just given Paris a job working on my campaign. I’m going to give her so much to do to keep her busy she’ll not have time to do anything else other than work, go home, eat, and sleep. I’ll take care of her. I will.”

Gabrielle dabbed her eyes. “You’d better. Because I love that child, and there’s nothing I won’t do to make sure she’s going to be okay. Nothing. And if Paris really wants to fight, then she’d better come ready. Because I have God and truth on my side, and she won’t stand a chance. And by proxy, neither will you.”

“I said I’ll handle Paris.”

“I pray that you do.” Gabrielle handed him his handkerchief back, turned on her heels, and left.

Chapter 13

> But before faith came, we were kept under the law, shut up unto the faith which should afterwards be revealed.
>
> — Galatians 3:23

"Miss G! You're home!" Jasmine ran into Gabrielle arms just as she cleared the doorway.

"Hi there!" Gabrielle hugged her tightly as she rocked her back and forth.

"Guess what Dr. Z and I did while you were gone?"

Gabrielle looked into her fiancé Zachary Morgan's smiling face, before looking back down at Jasmine. "What did you and Dr. Z do?"

"We played checkers!"

"You did?"

"Yes!" Jasmine giggled. "And guess who won?" She jumped up and down.

"You?"

"One time out of three." Jasmine sternly held up three fingers.

"What? You mean you beat him one time?" Gabrielle smiled at Jasmine, then looked at Zachary and mouthed the word "What?" as she frowned hard at him.

Zachary laughed. "She beat me fair and square. You know I'm not going to throw a game. Not in checkers."

Jasmine looked at Zachary. "Yeah, but you used to let me win when we played Alabama Hit the Hammer when I was in the hospital." She turned and looked back at Gabrielle. "Dr. Z even played the Wii with me."

"You got him to play on the Wii? Wow," Gabrielle said as she and Jasmine headed toward the den.

Dr. Z followed Gabrielle and Jasmine. "I knew you were going to bring that up. You just *have* to tell it all."

"You just don't want me to say anything because I beat you in bowling."

"That's because you're smarter than me."

"That's not why." Jasmine grinned. "It's because I know how to hold the controller correctly, and you don't."

"Yeah . . . well, I'm going to play more with you so you can help me get better."

Jasmine flopped down on the couch. Zachary eased down on one side of Jasmine and Gabrielle sat on the other side. "Okay, you two. It's time we have a serious talk," Jasmine said with a staid look.

Gabrielle laughed. "Is that right?"

Jasmine looked at Gabrielle. "Yes. I'm somewhat troubled. I sense there's something you're supposed to tell me and for some reason you haven't done it."

Gabrielle's stomach quickly turned a flip. She glanced over at Zachary, wondering if he knew what was going on. Had Jasmine somehow overhead something? Zachary gave a quick shrug while shaking his head. "So what do you think I'm supposed to tell you?" Gabrielle asked her.

"If I knew that, then I wouldn't have to ask, now would I?" Jasmine said.

"Are you sure you're only nine?" Zachary said. "You're definitely the smartest nine-year-old I've ever met. I wasn't nearly as smart as you when I was your age, and I became a doctor. Who knows what you're going to be when you grow up."

"I just know there's something you two are keeping from me." She made a funny twist of her mouth and tilted her head first to Zachary, then to Gabrielle. "So spill it," she said to Gabrielle.

Gabrielle's mind was racing a mile a minute, wondering what to tell her.

"Okay," Zachary said. "Why don't you tell us what you *think* we're keeping, and we'll go from there?"

Jasmine sucked in a deep breath and let it out as a loud, frustrated sigh. "Your wedding. When are you two going to get married? It's been long enough. I'm waiting to be a flower girl and nobody's saying anything about a wedding around here. So you must be planning it in secret or something. I see you two whispering about stuff. I want to know. So spill it."

Gabrielle exhaled. "You know what? You're just *too* grown for your age."

"That's because I like to read. My mother said I was reading when I was three. I suppose I'm so smart and so grown because I got a head start in learning." Jasmine suddenly dropped her head and began to look at her hands, folding them into each other now.

Gabrielle reached over, pulled her close, and hugged her tight. "I know, baby. I know."

"I miss her so much," Jasmine said with tears falling.

"I know you do." Gabrielle continued hugging her as she looked at Zachary.

"I've seen her in my dreams," Jasmine said. "It's like she's trying to tell me something, but she can't get the words to be loud enough for me to hear them. There's something my mama wants me to know, but I don't know what it is."

Zachary nodded at Gabrielle. He had to know that she was thinking she needed to tell Jasmine the truth about her being adopted.

"Jasmine, there's something I want to talk to you about. It's a promise I made to your mother before she died."

Jasmine sat up straight and looked into Gabrielle's eyes as she wiped away her tears. "Maybe that's what she's been trying to do but couldn't."

"That's possible," Gabrielle said. "Because she certainly wanted you to know this. She wanted me to help her tell you when she was sick. But she was really sick."

"You mean when she was in the hospital and she died and went to Heaven to be with the Lord?"

"Yes. I told her I would, but things happened so quickly. I knew you were hurting, so I just couldn't do it then."

Jasmine put her arms around Gabrielle's waist and hugged her. "It's okay, Miss G. I know you were hurting just like me. Mom kept telling me how much you loved us."

Gabrielle pressed her right hand to her

chest to hold in a cry that was pressing hard to make its way out. "Yeah."

Jasmine sat up and looked at Gabrielle. "If it's too difficult to tell me now, I understand. I'm a big girl. I know sometimes things are hard to talk about." Jasmine smiled.

"Yes, it's hard. But I think it's time that I do this. For your mother . . . for you . . . and for me."

"Would you like me to leave?" Zachary asked, shaking his head as though he was telling her to say no.

Gabrielle smiled. "No. I'd really like for you to stay."

"Because we're a family. Right?" Jasmine said. "The three of us . . . together."

"That's right," Zachary said, briefly putting his hand on the top of her head.

Gabrielle took Jasmine's left hand. "You know how much your mother and father loved you, don't you?"

"Yes."

"Well, the love they had is even more special than most. You see, some children come into this world to parents who come together to create them. Then there are some who are *so* special that their parents go out and actively look for them to be added to their family."

"Are you talking about adoption?" Jasmine asked.

Gabrielle nodded. "Exactly."

Jasmine pulled away from Gabrielle and scooted closer to Zachary. "Are you trying to say that I was adopted?"

Zachary placed his hand on Jasmine's head again. "You are so special that your parents went looking to find you. That's how badly they wanted you in their lives and family unit."

"No. That can't be possible. I can't be adopted. I look just like my mother. We have the same eyes."

Gabrielle grabbed Jasmine's hand and pulled her close to her, wrapping her arms securely around her. "Oh, baby. Your mother loved you so much! She wanted to tell you this herself because she didn't want you to be hurt or upset."

Jasmine broke away from Gabrielle and stood up. "Okay, so if I was adopted, then where did they get me from?"

"What?"

"Where are my real parents? Did they not want me? Did they throw me away? What?"

Gabrielle stood. "No, honey. That's not it all. Your birth mother wanted you. She loved you, too. She wanted you to have a good life. That's why she gave you up when you were born. She wanted you to have a wonderful family and not have to struggle. She wanted the best for you."

"You don't know that. You don't know what my birth mother was thinking. You're just saying this to make me feel better about my real mother not wanting me and giving me away." Jasmine bolted and ran upstairs.

Gabrielle looked at Zachary. "Oh, Zachary." Gabrielle fell into his arms. "I can't tell her. I can't tell her everything. Not now." Gabrielle pulled away and hurried upstairs. She laid down beside Jasmine, who was crying hard, her body jerking with each sound. "Jasmine, your mother . . . Jessica loved you. Your father . . . loved you. I . . . love you."

"And I love you," Zachary said, coming in and sitting down at the foot of the bed, placing his hand on Jasmine's ankle.

Jasmine didn't sit up or acknowledge either of them. She merely cried until she cried herself to sleep.

Chapter 14

> They profess that they know God; but in works they deny him, being abominable, and disobedient, and unto every good work reprobate.
>
> — Titus 1:16

Pastor George Landris stood before the congregation. "I'd like to direct your attention to the epistle of Paul, the apostle to Titus. Titus, like Timothy, was one of the young men Paul poured himself into so that they in turn would pass on the teachings to others. The letter to Titus dealt with organizing the disorganized work on the island of Crete. You see: Paul wanted to encourage Titus . . . to give him instruction, and to help him rise to the next level in ministry. If you would, and I promise I don't plan to be long today, I'd like for us to focus our attention on Titus 1:16 where it says, 'They profess that they know God; but in works they deny him, being abominable, and disobedient, and unto every good work reprobate.' "

Pastor Landris nodded as he scanned over the overflow of congregants. "Paul, who lets us know in the beginning of Titus that he is a servant of God and an apostle of Jesus Christ, is writing a letter to Titus, whom he calls his own son after the common faith. He's telling Titus that he left him in Crete, which is a large island southeast of Greece in the southern part of the Aegean Sea. Crete is mentioned in the historical analysis in the New Testament three times. The first time is on the Day of Pentecost, where Jews from Crete were in Jerusalem and witnessed those powerful Pentecostal events. The second time is when Paul was being sent to Rome for a trial and his ship passed by Crete. And the third time was after Paul was imprisoned, and he visited Crete, leaving Titus to establish churches there to ordain elders in every city as Paul appointed him to do.

"In Paul's letter to Titus, he gives him the qualifications of elders or bishops, with Titus 1:9 stating, 'Holding fast the faithful word as he hath been taught, that he may be able by sound doctrine both to exhort and to convince the gainsayers.' Gainsayers are folks who contradict, so when you see the word 'convince' in this scripture, it means to convict those folks who contradict. Most of you know those kinds of folks: folks who try to use scripture for their own gain. So in this letter to Titus, Paul was warning against false teachers. In fact, he told Titus when you find these false teachers to 'rebuke them sharply, that they may be sound in the faith.' That's in verse thirteen. Paul goes on to say in verse sixteen that they profess that they know God."

Pastor Landris took a few steps to his right. "If I was to ask right now how many of you know God, I'm sure almost every hand in this building would go up. But, if I were to ask how many of you do your *works* deny that as truth, then we'll be dealing with a whole other matter. Did you know that your mouth can say one thing and that your works . . . your actions can totally deny what your mouth is saying? Well, that's how you can tell false folks. They can talk a good game, but when you look at their actions, when you check out their working record, their works are screaming an entirely different thing. How many of you have heard, 'don't tell me you love me; show me you love me'?" Pastor Landris raised his own hand as he looked out among the congregation.

"Some of you may or may not know this, but my beautiful wife . . . the bride of my affection, Johnnie Mae Landris, was once a big-time author."

There was chattering in the audience as people said things to each other.

"Yes, that's right. Johnnie Mae Taylor is the name you'll find her books listed under. And she was a really good writer, too. Of course, she hasn't written anything new in a long time. She says it's because she's too busy enjoying the best job in town: being my wife, a mother to our two children, and being the rib that was taken from my side as she walks beside me in this ministry." Pastor Landris smiled.

"See . . . some of y'all missed that. I said *beside* me. I know some of you don't like hearing that. I'm talking about those men who run around spouting off 'I'm the head, and my wife had better get behind me.' Well, God created woman using the rib from Adam. I take that to mean, number one, my wife is a part of me. She wasn't taken from my head to go ahead of me. Not to be behind me as she wasn't taken from my back. Not to be stepped on because she wasn't taken from my foot. But to be beside me, as she was taken from my side." Pastor Landris smiled as he shook his head.

"I don't know why I went there. There must be somebody in here who needed to hear that word today. Men, stop treating your wives as though they are second-class citizens. Recognize who she is, and start treating her the way God's Word admonishes a *real* man to treat his bride. Love her, the way Christ loves the church. Okay, let me get back to what I was trying to say." He shook his head again.

"Glory!" Pastor Landris did a little shout and dance. "Somebody better hear what I'm saying. There's a husband in here, you're not doing right by your wife. You're not treating her the way you're supposed to be treating her. You need to get right before you find yourself left. God is speaking to me right now. For some reason, He won't let me move on to what I was trying to say. Okay, I'm going to say it again, Mr. It's-My-Thing-and-I'll-Do-What-I-Want-To-Do. You need to do what God's Word is telling you to do. Obey God. Get right or you're going to get left." Pastor Landris raised his right hand toward the ceiling.

"Okay, okay. I'm through with that. Glory to God. I'm through. But I feel something happening right now. I feel hearts being changed right now. I see some men stepping up into the role God is calling you to. I see some marriages being restored *right now.* I see healing taking place right now."

Pockets of people in the congregation began to stand and clap.

"I feel God moving *right* now. I was trying to tell you what my wife, the author, says about the rule of writing called Show, Don't Tell. But God is doing something right now in this place. He's touching hearts. He's healing broken hearts. Oh, I feel the power of God moving in the place today. The rule of Show, Don't Tell means instead of telling me what happened, show it to me. Let me see it for myself. Hallelujah, I feel the anointing falling all over this place."

Everyone was standing on their feet now, praising God.

"Show, don't tell. Show, don't tell. God is showing us His power right now. I'm up here trying to tell you, but God is showing you. He's showing His love for you, right now. He's touching hearts, right now. He's taking away pain, right now."

Pastor Landris fell to his knees and lifted up holy hands toward Heaven. "Receive! Receive! Receive God's healing, right now. Let God wrap His loving arms around you." Pastor Landris hugged himself. "Let God lift you up from where you are and set your feet on a higher plain. What kind of works are speaking for you? What are your actions telling people? Show, don't tell! Show . . . don't tell!"

Clarence Walker began to play the keyboard and sing, "May the Works I've Done Speak for Me."

The entire congregation was shouting now and in a place of total praise.

CHAPTER 15

> Which in time past was to thee unprofitable, but now profitable to thee and to me.
> — Philemon 11

Darius and Paris sat in William's office waiting for him to come back. It was Monday — their first day of work — and William was doing his version of orientation.

"Did you go to church yesterday?" Paris asked Darius while waiting on William to return.

"Of course."

"Me, too, for what it was worth."

"So it wasn't good?"

Paris shrugged. "It was okay. But once you've had a taste of the real thing prepared and seasoned just right, it's sort of hard to go back to eating cardboard."

Darius laughed. "I got that. There is a difference in something that's good and something that's a 'that'll do.' "

"Absolutely." Paris turned her body more toward him. "So what did Pastor Landris preach about?"

"Oh, it was about people who talk a good game, but their works don't line up with their words. 'Show, don't tell' was his subject. Then he got over into talking about his wife and how much he loved her, how great of an author she used to be."

"His wife is an author?"

"Yeah. I think they say she used to write fiction. But she's not doing that anymore, probably because she couldn't make much money at it. Everybody knows that black folks don't read. And if she's writing for Christians, she can forget them, because they only want to read the Bible and the big-name folks putting out books."

"That's not true. Black folks *do* read."

"Oh, then I stand corrected. Maybe what I should have said is that they don't buy the books. One person will buy the book and pass it around to everybody and their momma." Darius laughed. "You know how we do."

"Yeah. And then when that author is no longer doing it, people wonder what happened to them." Paris raised her hand. "I'm guilty. I've done that. Maybe that's what happened to one of the authors I used to enjoy reading. I never thought about it *or* her, until now."

"You and I know it's all about the Benjamins. If the man ain't making no money off of it, the man don't want to do it." Darius puckered his lips and smacked them. "That's the only reason I'm sitting here in this chair right now."

Paris nodded, then grinned. "Is that right? So you mean to tell me you're not here because you really believe in Lawrence Simmons and you want to be sure he gets reelected?"

"Oh, you're slick. You're trying to set me up." He nodded a few times. "I see who you really are. So, Miss Lady, why are you here? I mean, I can't see you really needing the money. Your Daddy gets paid. Your husband gets paid."

"Don't count out that I don't need the money."

"So you're trying to tell me that you do?" Darius readjusted his body, turning even more to Paris as he leaned in.

"Andrew refuses to help me get Jasmine from Gabrielle. So I have to pay for a lawyer on my own. And I don't know if you know this or not, but lawyers aren't cheap by any means."

"I *heard* that," Darius said. "So you don't

have any rainy-day funds stashed away somewhere that you can tap into? A trust fund maybe?"

"You really *do* watch entirely *too* much television. Because that kind of stuff you see mainly on TV. I buy clothes and shoes with almost every dime I can get my hands on. So, no: I don't have any money squirreled away somewhere that I can tap into. Not the kind of money I'll need in a hurry. Besides, how hard can this job be?"

William closed the door loudly, which had to be on purpose. "Good question. And I'm just the man to answer it for you." He handed Paris, then Darius each a folder. "This is your instruction guide of your duties and what we're expecting from you."

"So Daddy's not coming for this?" Paris asked.

"No. Your Daddy won't be a part of this. I'm his campaign director and right-hand man, as you well know, Paris."

"And don't forget best friend in the whole wide world," Paris said more to be mockingly sarcastic.

William didn't crack a smile. "You two have been hired as co-chairs to work on getting the youth registered, if they're not already registered to vote, and out to the polls on voting day if they are. Our research has shown that young people respond more favorably to young people. We call it the sheep theory."

Darius snickered. "The sheep theory."

"Yes," William said. "Sheep beget sheep. If we want to bring young people over to our side, then who does it better than other young people? Sheep bring in other sheep."

Darius readjusted his body, pressing his pants straight after placing his foot on the floor. "I heard some preacher say once that the reason people are referred to in the Bible as sheep is because sheep are dumb."

William stared at Darius for a few seconds. Darius sat up even taller.

"This job is not a joke. Okay? And we're paying you both very well, so we're expecting you to take this position seriously. You both are receiving the exact same salary."

Paris raised her hand.

"Yes, Paris?" William said.

"How do we know we're getting paid the same salary?"

"Because I just told you that you were."

"Yeah, no offense to you, but just because you say it doesn't mean you're telling the truth or that it's so."

Darius almost laughed out loud but swallowed it before it came out all the way. His patted his chest to ensure it had gone all the way down.

"Paris," William said, "I have no reason to lie."

"You're in politics," Paris said. "Need I say more?"

This time Darius did laugh out. "I'm sorry. But she *does* have a point. You know nobody believes people who are in politics. Y'all always figure out a way to get around the truth. I think it's called creative truth. You know: like creative nonfiction."

"Okay, fine, then," William said. "Darius, tell Paris how much you're being paid."

"You want me to tell *her*?"

"Yes."

Darius placed his hand up to his mouth. Other than his wife, he'd never really told anyone how much he made. And even the other day when he told Tiffany what his salary was going to be, he hadn't told her the whole truth.

"Darius, please tell Paris how much we promised you," William said, taking his time to emphasize each word spoken.

"Five thousand dollars for seven months, which includes paying for the whole month of May and the whole month of November regardless of November's outcome," Darius said.

Paris nodded. "Okay."

"So you're satisfied?" William asked, his face set on Paris.

"I'm good. I just figure if we're doing the same job, we should be getting the same pay. I know you and Daddy think I'm useless . . . that I'm not worth much —"

"That's not true, Paris. In fact, if you must know: It was your father who suggested we hire you for this position." William smiled. "So are there any more questions regarding the money aspect of this job?"

"Nope," Paris said. "I'm good."

"I'm good," Darius said. "Unless you want to up the amount."

William rolled his eyes at Darius. "All right, then, we'll move on. As I was saying, you're both receiving the same salary, so we expect to get the same effort. You *will* be working long and hard hours. The monies we're paying you are from hardworking donors who expect us to be good stewards. Because you're dealing with getting to the young folk, you're going to have to go where they are. That means high schools —"

"High schools?" Paris said, pulling her body back in recoil. "People in high schools are too young to vote."

William nodded. "High schools have high school seniors, many of whom are already eighteen, and others who will turn eighteen before the November election. We'd like to get them before the other candidate can get to them. Let's get them registered and let them know that we respect them enough that we've taken time and effort to court their vote. People love to feel wanted."

"Okay, so high schools," Darius said. "Where else?"

"High schools, colleges, universities, churches, and nightclubs."

"Nightclubs?" Paris said. "You want us to go to nightclubs?"

"I want you to go wherever young people congregate," William said. "That includes the park and various church functions. Barack Obama got the young people out and you see how that worked out for him."

"Do you have a Facebook and a Twitter account already for the campaign?" Darius asked.

"A face what and a twit who?" William asked.

Darius leaned in. "Social media. It's the growing thing these days. We can send out tweets and start a Facebook fan page. That's where a lot of young people hang out."

"Well, you two know more about all of that stuff than I do. Get together and work it out. That's what we're paying you for," William said. "And if either of you have jealous spouses, then you need to bring them on board about what's expected of you. Because neither I nor Lawrence have the time to babysit or intervene with marriage counseling. And if you have other projects that are in need of you taking any time off, then you may as well put it on hold until after this election is over. I'm telling you: You're about to enter the *crazy* work zone."

"So you're saying we won't be getting any days or time off?" Paris asked. "We're working seven days a week?"

William sat down for the first time since he'd entered the room. "Pretty much that's what I'm saying. But look at it this way: You're being paid thirty-five thousand dollars for seven months work. In fact, not even a full seven months, since you missed working at the beginning of this month and there won't be anything much to do after the first part of November and the election has been decided. Most folks don't make that much in a year. You can rest and take care of personal business after you're done. But this election is going to be a hard-fought one. Frank Johnson's folks aren't going to be taking off and letting up. Therefore, we need all hands on deck, every hand to the plow. So if either of you have changed your minds, then speak now." William became quiet and looked first at Paris, then Darius. "Or forever hold your peace."

"Or at least hold it for the next six months," Darius said, looking over at Paris.

"Now . . . does anyone have any more questions?"

"Yes," Darius said. "What about an expense account?"

"That packet I just gave you has instructions and forms that you'll need to fill out and turn in to Mattie Stevens, Lawrence's administrative assistant. She'll process them and reimburse you for any legitimate monies spent on the campaign."

Darius began to shake his head. "Oh, no. That won't work for me. That's too old school. I need operating funds upfront. I can't be using my own money and waiting on a reimbursement. You need to get us a credit slash debit card with access to instant money. If you're looking for us to be doing all this driving around town, using up gas as high as gas is, we need money upfront for that. Well, let me just speak for myself: *I* need money upfront."

"You and Paris will likely be going to many of these places together," William said.

"And — ?"

"And that will cut down on the gas expense."

"You still have to put gas in the car," Darius said. "Trust me: Prayer does *not* fill up your tank. I know because I've tried it. Getting into clubs costs money, especially if you're a guy. Trust me: I know that, too. And going to churches" — Darius shook his head — "those preachers be looking for you to put something in the collection plate and they hate money that makes noise. They like the quiet kind. I know because I've gone to some churches that actually have a credit card and an ATM machine in the place. I kid you not. So you need to talk to whomever and get us both a card with a balance of cash on it. Then we can fill out those forms, turn them in, and when the money comes back, whoever needs it, can be reimbursed."

Paris laughed.

William smacked his lips a few times. "Fine. I'll get you both credit cards."

"Now we're talking." Darius sat back against his chair as he smirked. "And while we're asking, what are the chances of maybe getting a company car. I mean, I don't want to put all those miles and wear and tear on my vehicle. If my vehicle breaks down, I'm the one having to take it to Big Red to get it fixed. Big Red is reasonable, but he still charges for his work."

"You're really pushing it," William said, staring hard at Darius.

"Well, you know what the Bible says. 'You have not because you ask not.' And don't you dare ask me where that is in the Bible because I am *no* Bible scholar."

"I'll check on these items. Then I'll show you two the office you'll be working out of," William said. "And before either of you ask: No, you will *not* be getting separate offices. Period. End of discussion."

"I'm good," Darius said. "The way it sounds, we're not going to be in the office that much anyway." Darius rubbed his hands together and readjusted his body.

William left.

Paris laughed. "You are crazy!"

"Well, get ready. Because you and I, Paris, are going to have a great time." Darius stood up and stretched. "Let me ask you something? Are they actually paying you the same as me?"

Paris cocked her head to the side and twisted her mouth.

"Girl, I'm just playing with you." He laughed. "But for real, are they? I mean, I checked MALE on my form. They must not have gotten the memo. Women are *supposed* to make seventy-seven . . . seventy-eight cents of every dollar a man makes. We have families to provide for."

"It's 2010. President Obama signed the Lilly Ledbetter something or other act. All I know is it's supposed to put employers in check: equal pay for equal work. Y'all better *recognize.*" Paris primped her mouth and wiggled her neck as she snapped her fingers twice.

"Look at you . . . trying to be all southern and hip. 'Y'all better *recognize.*' " Darius mocked Paris, who he knew was mostly messing with him. "Girl, I'm going to enjoy working with you. I can see that already. Yes, yes. And they gonna pay me handsomely for doing this? Oh, yes! There *is* a God in Heaven."

CHAPTER 16

> For all that is in the world, the lust of the flesh, and the lust of the eyes, and the pride of life, is not of the Father, but is of the world.
>
> — 1 John 2:16

"Okay, so what are we going to do first?" Darius asked Paris as they stepped in a small office that at least had a door to close to keep unwanted folks out.

"Well, let's see," Darius said, looking around the office as Paris went and sat in a black leather chair at one of the two desks. "We have our own desks. We each have a computer. There's a printer in here."

"Yeah, I like that. I hate sharing." Paris swiveled the chair a few times, adjusting it upward to fit her height better. "I hope you know what you're doing, because I'm going to be honest: Except for my people skills, I don't have any idea *how* we're going to do this."

"Sure you do. Let's look at it like an elaborate party you want to put on." Darius sat in the chair on the other side of Paris's desk and leaned forward. "What would we be doing if this was a party we wanted to be successful?"

Paris leaned back in her chair and looked toward the ceiling. "We need to make a list of everybody we'd like to invite to attend. Then figure out ways to get the word out."

"There you go. See, we're already on our way. You need to get a pen and paper and write all of this stuff down." Darius took his hand and shooed it at her as to tell her to get going.

Paris sat up straight, then leaned in toward him, her body now resting on the desk on her folded arms. "*You* write it down. What do I look like . . . your secretary?"

"I tell you what: Turn on the computer and we can put our plans there."

Paris sat back straight, her arms still folded. "How about *you* go over to *your* little desk, you turn on *your* computer, I'll come over there, and *you* can put our plans there?"

"You do know we're not going to get anything done if we don't figure out how to work together. You do know that, don't you?

And if we don't get anything done, then we're going to get fired. Do you know what fired means?"

"My daddy's not going to fire me."

"You keep sitting there and thinking that if you want to."

Paris stood up and cupped her hands around her neck. "You do know the only reason either of us got this job is to keep us busy and out of the way."

Darius stood. "First off, you're going to have to stop wearing stuff that makes you look so doggone good. It's hard enough working with you and trying to concentrate while keeping from falling for all that beauty and charm you exude."

"Okay, you're trying to be funny now."

Darius shook his head. "Nope. I'm just a good Christian man who's trying to keep focused on the job at hand. And I'm telling you that you can help me out tremendously if you'd maybe tone down the beauty and the charming way you talk, and dress down a bit. You're all *gussied* up. Have men lusting all after you."

"Well, you know what the Bible says about that, don't you?"

"Oh, so you're breaking out the Bible on me now, huh?" Darius puckered his lips. "All right, hit me, Paris. What does the Bible say about having men lusting after you and what we should do about it?"

"It says if your right eye offends you to pluck it out." Paris moved her hand in a plucking manner. "Blip. Just like *that*!"

"Oooh, girl. Before I do something like that, I'll just turn and look away."

Paris sat back down and turned on her computer. "Same difference; it works for me. Because I *will* be dressing up and I *will* be both looking *and* smelling good. So you'd best learn to deal with it. Or else this is going to be a long six months."

Darius held his hands up in surrender and went and sat down at his own desk. He turned on his computer.

Paris opened her purse and pulled out her cell phone. She pressed a number, then swiveled her chair slightly away from Darius. "Hi, honey. I'm calling you from my new job. I told you I was going to do it." Paris listened, occasionally turning as if to see whether or not Darius was trying to actively listen in.

Darius had become quite artful at pretending that he wasn't paying attention when he was. He began typing on the computer, frowning and such to give the air that he was in deep thought. He could hear that things weren't going well with Paris and her husband, just as she'd said. She was telling Andrew that she wasn't going to back down from her idea of getting Jasmine, she didn't care *what* he said. Her husband must have said something about her and her pride, because Paris started giving him the rundown about pride.

"While you're criticizing me, do you want to know what your downfall is going to end up being? Well, I'm going to tell you anyway. You're going to realize what you had and see that it was your stubbornness to stick to your stupid principles, regardless of how it affected me, is what is going to be the cause of you losing the best thing that you ever had." Paris was quiet for a minute. She suddenly made a growling sound. "Argh! Okay, Andrew. All right. Okay. Good-bye!" She clicked off her phone and almost tossed it onto her desk.

Not a true typist, but one who had learned to master the index finger on both of his hands, Darius was pecking away on the computer. He refused to acknowledge Paris's outburst, pretending he neither saw nor heard a thing.

Yes. He was going to enjoy this job immensely!

CHAPTER 17

The elder unto the elect lady and her children, whom I love in the truth; and not I only, but also all they that have known the truth.

— 2 John 1:1

It was ten days after Gabrielle told Jasmine she'd originally been adopted. Zachary and Gabrielle sat at the kitchen table. Jasmine was with Tiffany Connors and her nine-year-old daughter, Jade. Tiffany had called to ask if it would be okay for Jasmine to come over. Jasmine was so excited about that prospect, especially since she and Jade had become acquainted at church and were developing quite a little friendship. In fact, the timing of Tiffany's call was interestingly suspect, as though the nine-year-olds had plotted the whole thing themselves.

Other than school, Gabrielle hadn't allowed Jasmine to go too many places without her. She wanted to be certain that wherever Jasmine was, she'd be in good hands. Tiffany assured Gabrielle she would be all right with her (after all, she did have three children of her own and they appeared so far to have survived just fine). And it would be good for Jasmine to get out and be with other children her own age outside of school and church.

"We need to talk," Zachary said to Gabrielle as they sat there. "I know these past days have been hard on both you and Jasmine."

Gabrielle merely nodded as she stared out onto the back deck.

"Gabrielle? Talk to me." Zachary began to look where Gabrielle's eyes seemed fixed.

Gabrielle smiled. "Do you see that bird?"

Zachary moved around, trying to see what bird she was talking about.

Gabrielle stood and walked over to the door. "Come here and look. The red one. See? She's right there." Gabrielle pointed toward the top banister of her deck.

Zachary came and stood next to her. "Yes, I see her now."

"I like birds. I especially like redbirds. I think they're supposed to have a special meaning. When you see one, I mean. I can't remember what it means, but I think it's supposed to mean something special."

Zachary stepped behind Gabrielle and placed his hands on the sides of her arms, rubbing them up and down as though he was warming her. "Oh, Gabrielle. It's going to be all right."

She nodded. "I know it is. I just don't know if I'm handling things the right way." She broke from his slight embrace and went and sat back down.

Zachary followed her, taking her hand after he sat down. "You're doing fine. So what time is Jasmine coming back home?"

"Tiffany said she'd call right before they were leaving. Jasmine didn't have any homework today. You know how it is when it's close to the time for school to let out for the summer."

"Yes, I know. Gabrielle, please talk to me."

"I am talking." Gabrielle looked at him and forced a gentle smile.

"No, you're avoiding. You're trivializing. You want to talk about redbirds and whether or not what you're doing is the right thing. Tell me what's going through your mind right now. Tell me what's bothering you . . . tell me what you're *really* thinking."

Gabrielle began twisting her three-carat, princess-cut, diamond engagement ring around her finger. "Why didn't I tell her all of it? That night, when I was telling Jasmine that she was adopted. Why didn't I just go on and tell her who I am to her? I should have just laid it all out on the table. That's what Jessica wanted to do: She wanted to tell her everything at one time."

Zachary grabbed her hand and gently squeezed it. "Because you didn't feel it was the right time. You'll have plenty of time to tell her."

Gabrielle frowned. "When? Exactly when *is* the right time? How do I bring it up now? I should have told her while we were already on the subject."

Zachary stood, pulling Gabrielle up with him as he arose. "Don't be so hard on yourself. You and Jasmine have a bond. You'll know the right time to tell her. And when that time comes, you will."

Gabrielle shrugged her shoulders. "I'm a coward. That's what I am: a coward. I didn't tell her because I didn't want her to hate me."

Zachary moved Gabrielle back a little so he could better look into her eyes. "No . . . you're not a coward. You're a mother who loves her child dearly. You didn't want to overwhelm her with too much information to have to process all at once. You said she was okay the following morning when she woke up, right?"

"Yeah. It was almost like we never had a conversation about her being adopted. Do you think she's in shock or something? Maybe I should have spoken with someone about how to properly do this instead of just telling her the way that I did."

"She's okay, Gabrielle. She knows she's loved."

"Would you like something to eat?" Gabrielle broke away from him and walked over to the cabinet. "I cooked a really nice dinner. If you'd like to eat now, I can fix you a plate. Or you can fix it. Whichever . . ."

"I'm fine." He walked over and hugged her again. "But you know what I'd *really* like?"

Gabrielle sheepishly looked up at him. "What?"

"I'd like to do what Jasmine said and talk about our wedding. Let's pick a date. Come on."

Gabrielle quickly pulled away again, opening the cabinet and taking down a white plate. "There's too much going on." She set the plate on the counter. "I have Paris to deal with . . . Jasmine learning all these things that she never even had a clue about. There's this long drawn-out process I'm being forced to go through to officially adopt

Jasmine. We can talk about a wedding after everything is settled."

"And when do you think *that* might be?"

Gabrielle went and sat back down in the chair at the table. She covered her face with both hands, rubbed her face, then took her hands down. "I don't know."

"Well, have you heard any more from Paris and her lawyer or the court?"

Gabrielle shook her head. "Not in the last few weeks. But that doesn't mean anything."

"So what's your lawyer saying?"

"I'm still using the lawyer Jessica had . . . Robert Shaw. For now, he believes things will progress as they should, barring any more interferences from Paris and her lawyer." Gabrielle leaned her head back and looked up at the ceiling. "Why won't she just go away and leave us alone? This has nothing to do with her." Gabrielle straightened her head and looked at Zachary as though he was the enemy. *"Nothing."*

"Didn't you tell me the last time you talked to her father he said he would handle his daughter?"

"Yes."

"Then maybe he was successful. Face it: He has just as much, if not more, to lose as you if this comes out. He's the one up for reelection," Zachary said.

"Maybe. I pray he succeeded in convincing Paris to drop this silliness."

Zachary took Gabrielle's hand again and began stroking each finger individually with his other hand. He touched her engagement ring and lingered there. "Well, I don't want to predicate our wedding or our happiness on what other people are doing or not doing. I want to marry you, Gabrielle Mercedes. Plain and simple. And honestly, I really don't want to wait too long."

"If we plan a date, then that's merely another battle for us to have to fight," Gabrielle said. "Your mother is not going to be happy about us getting married and you know that. I know she's your mother, but I just feel like she's not going to let us ride off into the sunset and live happily ever after if she has anything to say about it. She's already fired the first shot over the bough."

"My mother knows we're engaged."

"And she knows that engaged doesn't mean married yet and that there's time for her to talk you out of it."

"It's not going to happen," Zachary said. "She can talk until she's blue in the face; it's not going to change how I feel about you. But my mother really does like you."

"No, she doesn't."

"Yes, she does. She's just being an overprotective mother who thinks she knows what's best for me. My daddy is crazy about you. And my aunt Esther acts like you're the child she never had. In fact, I'll let you in on a secret." He leaned in close. "Aunt Esther is the one pushing so hard on us setting a date. She keeps saying she doesn't know how much longer she has left on this earth. And she doesn't want us to wait too long and she ends up missing the wedding because she never knows when she'll be called to glory. She says she doesn't want to have to watch our wedding from Heaven —"

Gabrielle laughed. "She isn't saying all that. You're just making this up."

"I promise you that's what she said. Call her up and ask her. I told her that I would marry you today if you'd do it, but that you're the one dragging your feet. I'm trying to protect you from the wrath of Aunt Esther. She keeps threatening to come down here and straighten you out."

Gabrielle grabbed Zachary by his forearm. "Oh, Zachary, I would love that! I would love for Miss Crowe to come and visit."

Zachary shook his head. "I think you're missing the point here. She wants to come to a wedding. Jasmine wants us to get married. *I* want us to get married. People at church want us to get married. Even my sister Queen is asking when, so she and the baby can come. She even thinks her husband will come with her according to when the wedding is, as long as he can get off work."

"I want to see little Warren. Pictures don't do him justice with his little cute self. I know he's just as cute as he wants to be. He looks so much like his mother, it's amazing."

"Okay, then let's plan our wedding." Zachary pulled out his cell phone and went to the calendar. "Saturday, May twenty-ninth would be perfect! We can do like Fatima and Trent just did and marry within a day of your birthday on May thirtieth."

"Wasn't their ceremony beautiful!" Gabrielle released a satisfied sigh as she looked dreamy-eyed while talking about Fatima and Trent's Saturday nuptials.

"It was really nice."

"Tiffany was there all by herself with the children. She said Darius had planned on going, but he started a new job and had to work or something."

"Indeed, it was a beautiful ceremony. They're on their honeymoon now in Jamaica. It's our turn to do this. Come on. Let's go for it."

"Oh, I get it. You're just trying to get to the honeymoon." She laughed.

He laughed as well. "Now I'm not going to lie to you: I can't *wait* for that part. But honestly, the part I'm *really* trying to get to is the 'you may kiss your bride' part." Zachary smiled. "I want to kiss my bride."

"But May twenty-ninth . . . a day before my birthday?" She shook her head. "I don't know about that. I don't know that I'd want our wedding date to be that close to my birthday."

"I promise you we'll still celebrate both . . . royally. I won't shortchange you. You can believe *that.*" He took her by the hand. "So what do you say? May twenty-ninth?" He made his eyebrows rise and fall several times as he plastered a smile on his face.

Gabrielle shook her head. "A little less than two weeks is not enough time to plan a wedding. It's not enough time for folks to make plans to be here, not that we'd invite that many people. But your family is mostly in Chicago, with Queen in Florida." Gabrielle bit down on her bottom lip. "It's funny. When I was a teen growing up living with my aunt and thinking about my wedding day someday, I always said I wanted a big Cinderella-type wedding."

"Well, I'm no prince, but we can still put

together a beautiful wedding. And as for my family, they can all fly in."

"The tickets will be higher because they'll be last-minute purchases."

"My family should have *some* money, and if not, there's always a credit card."

Gabrielle laughed. "You're determined for us to do this, aren't you?"

"When I asked you to marry me, I thought when you said yes it was because you actually planned on marrying me."

Gabrielle let out a short laugh. "I did. I do. I will." She sighed. "I just don't want to plan this with all of these things still in limbo. If I knew for sure that Paris was dropping this notion of trying to either take Jasmine or just make sure I don't get her, we could plan a wedding. But I don't want to have our special time ruined by things happening outside of us. I need to stay focused when it comes to Jasmine. I'm not saying I'm choosing Jasmine over you, but for now, I need to put Jasmine's welfare first."

"You know I'm going to wear you down, don't you? You're going to marry me if I have to pull a troglodyte move on you."

Gabrielle let out another short laugh. " 'A troglodyte move?' "

"Yeah. You know a caveman move: Grab

you by the hair and drag you where I want you to go." He then lowered his bass voice to sound primitive. *"Come here!"*

Gabrielle grinned. "You wouldn't." She tilted her head ever so slightly as she chuckled.

He shook his head. "Nah. I wouldn't grab you by the hair." He lifted a spiral curl of her hair, then let it drop back to her shoulder. He smiled. "But I *would* throw you over my shoulder and carry you to the altar. Don't make me prove it, because I *will* now."

She lovingly placed her hand on his face. He closed his eyes as he experienced the warmth of her touch. "I love you. I really do." He opened his eyes as she continued speaking. "We're going to get married. Just not right now. When we do, I want it to be all about you and me standing before God. I don't want to feel you're doing this because of what I'm going through and your need to protect me."

"But I'm not trying to just protect you. I love you. I want to be there beside you: for better or worse. I don't care about right timing. I want to spend the rest of my life with you as your husband, and I want to get started now." He looked at his watch. "In fact, we could call Pastor Landris and see what's on his schedule for tonight."

"Sorry, but we couldn't do it tonight even if we wanted to."

"And why not?"

"We need a marriage license. Nobody will marry us without a license."

"You know, by plane, Las Vegas isn't that far away . . ."

Gabrielle shook her head. "You really know how to court a woman, don't you? We're going to be okay. I know we are. For now, we'll just wait."

Zachary took her by her hands. "Let's pray."

Gabrielle gave two quick nods. Zachary saw her eyes fill up with tears, then one spilled over and made its way slowly down her cheek. He took his thumb and gently wiped it way. She closed her eyes, and he began to pray.

Chapter 18

As sorrowful, yet always rejoicing; as poor, yet making many rich; as having nothing, and yet possessing all things.

— 2 Corinthians 6:10

Gabrielle sat in Robert Shaw's office. He was the lawyer Jessica Noble had retained to handle her affairs before she died. He was the one who had filed the power of attorney paperwork, enabling Gabrielle to act on Jessica's behalf in all matters. He was the attorney working to ensure a smooth adoption for Jasmine over to Gabrielle, the person his client had desired to have custody of her child in the event of her death.

Robert had all but promised in the beginning that this would be smooth and pretty simple. Jessica had a will. She'd specified her desire for Gabrielle to take Jasmine upon her death. She'd left a nice amount of money in a trust fund and her house to Jasmine with the trust that Gabrielle would handle and manage things as needed with honesty and integrity. Everything was in order. Everything except for Gabrielle having to fight with Paris Simmons-Holyfield about Jasmine's custody.

"Who could have anticipated any opposition or problems?" the short, balding Robert Shaw said to Gabrielle as she sat in his office across from him. "This absolutely baffles the mind." He rubbed his hairless part of his head. "This woman is not going to quit *or* let this go."

Gabrielle shook her head. "Jasmine doesn't need this in her life. She doesn't need this right now. She hasn't gotten over losing her mother yet. She doesn't even know Paris."

"Well, Paris Simmons-Holyfield is not backing down. I petitioned the court to dismiss her objections *and* her petition for custody of the child," Robert said. "At this time, anyway, it doesn't look like the court is inclined to dismiss it, not saying that they won't later. And Mrs. Simmons-Holyfield doesn't appear to be poised to let it go. So we're sort of stuck at an impasse."

"Well, I've already told you I'm going to fight Paris on this. She's not going to take Jasmine from the only safe home she has right now, I don't care how much Paris claims she can give her a better home than I can." Gabrielle rubbed her forehead. "This is crazy!"

"Barring her dropping this, we're headed for a court battle to fight it out there. But I have someone coming by to help with this case. He's a really good lawyer. He's not with our firm, but we have an association with them. He's coming to meet with you today."

"Today?" Gabrielle said.

There was a knock on the door. Robert smiled. "Right on time. That's probably him." Robert went to the door and opened it. "Oh, I'm sorry. I thought you were —"

"Neal Michaels? He had an emergency. They sent me to take his place."

"Come on in," Robert Shaw said. "It's good to see you again."

Gabrielle turned as the man stepped inside.

"Gabrielle?" he said.

"Andrew?"

Gabrielle stood and they hugged.

"So I take it you two know each other," Robert Shaw said.

"Yes, we do." Gabrielle took a step back and looked at him. "What are you doing here?"

"Our firm was asked to help out with a case Attorney Shaw is working on. I wasn't told the client's name, only general information concerning the nature of the case," Andrew said directly to Gabrielle.

"Please, Andrew, have a seat," Robert said.

Both Gabrielle and Andrew sat across from Robert.

"Well, I suppose we can skip the introductions," Robert said. "But before we proceed, I need to ask you, Gabrielle, whether you have any objections to Andrew here taking part in your case."

Gabrielle swallowed hard. "No offense to Andrew, who I'm sure is an *awesome* and *competent* lawyer, but the person causing all the havoc in my life right now happens to be his wife."

Robert frowned as he looked down at the open folder before him. "Paris Simmons-Holyfield . . . Andrew Holyfield." Robert looked up. "Mrs. Simmons-Holyfield is your wife?" Robert looked at Gabrielle. "I am *so* sorry. I didn't even immediately make the connection. In fact, I didn't know they were sending Andrew. I only relayed general information about what I needed. They told me they were sending Neal Michaels."

"As I said, Neal had an emergency so they asked me to come in his place." Andrew turned to Gabrielle. "But if I can help you with this, I really want to do it."

Gabrielle slowly shook her head. "That won't work. Aren't you standing with Paris on this?"

"Actually, I'm completely opposed to what she's doing." Andrew looked at Robert. "Would you mind giving me and Gabrielle some time alone to talk?"

Robert looked at Gabrielle, who nodded her okay. He stood. "I'll be right outside. If not, just ask one of the secretaries to find me." He stepped out.

Andrew stared at Gabrielle without saying anything for an entire minute after Robert closed the door. "It's truly good to see you again."

Gabrielle smiled. "You, too. The last time was sort of awkward."

"To say the least. And believe me, when I got home, it didn't get any better for me."

Gabrielle chuckled. "I take it Paris gave you the what for and 'how come'?"

"Yes, except more like the 'when did you.' She picked up on you calling me Drew and wanted to know what was going on between us. She thinks you and I have some secret we're hiding."

"Well, she's right," Gabrielle said. "We do."

"Yeah," Andrew said. "Now here we are again." There was a moment of silence. "Listen, Gabrielle. I'd really like to help with your case. I came thinking I was working on something that had to do with garnering child custody. They didn't tell me much else, so I certainly was surprised, pleasantly though, when I saw you sitting here."

Gabrielle shook her head slowly. "I don't know about this, Andrew. You're sleeping with the enemy. And Paris really is portraying herself as my enemy, that's a fact."

"And you don't think you can trust me," Andrew said in a matter-of-fact way.

"I don't. I'm being honest with you."

"But you know me, Gabrielle."

Gabrielle smiled. "I *knew* you. And if you asked me to be honest on this, I would say that I know you wouldn't deliberately *try* to hurt me, not deliberately. But you're married to Paris. I would think both of you are together in trying to take Jasmine from me."

"Well, you'd be wrong. I completely disagree with what my wife is doing. And I've told her as much."

"And yet, she's moving forward, full steam ahead."

"You know Paris."

"Yes. Unfortunately, I do." Gabrielle stood

up and walked toward a glass case with awards and knickknacks inside of it. Her back was now turned to Andrew.

"I'd like to stop her," Andrew said. "This just might be the answer to a prayer."

Gabrielle turned around. "You would actually team up with me against your own wife? Even if anyone allowed it, it just doesn't seem right."

"Paris shouldn't be doing this. I realize she doesn't care much for you. I just didn't know how much she didn't care. Part of this may even be my fault."

"How so?"

"Paris wants to get back at you because she thinks you and I are keeping something from her."

Gabrielle came back over and sat down next to Andrew. "Then why don't you tell her the truth?"

"Because if I tell her that I was the one who picked you up after she put you out that day and took you home with me, she'll never forgive me for having kept that information from her all this time."

"So you're being a coward and making me and Jasmine pay."

Andrew shook his head as he frowned. "That's not it. Paris really wants a child."

"Then tell her to have her own and leave

mine alone."

Andrew tilted his head. "What do you mean yours?"

Gabrielle threw her hands up in frustration. "Listen, Andrew. I appreciate you for coming. I'm sorry it ended up being a waste of your time. I'm going to fight Paris, you can believe that. But I'll be doing it without your help."

"I'm good at what I do, Gabrielle. I can help you win this. I can." His dimples were really doing a number on her. She always thought he had the cutest dimples.

"Why don't you just give Paris her own baby and maybe she'll go away and leave us alone," Gabrielle said.

Andrew covered his face with his hand. He took his hand down and looked at Gabrielle. "We *have* been trying, for almost two years now. That's why she's acting so crazy. She's having a hard time dealing with not being able to conceive."

"So for sport, and to take her mind off her troubles, she comes after the only child connected to me. All the other children in the world praying for a home, and she decides to go after one who is already spoken for. And for what reason? Because she wants to hurt me? She wants to get back at me? Because she thinks I was trying to take her boyfriend some ten years ago?" Gabrielle began to laugh. "It's crazy. And the funny thing about all of this is: She was the one who went after her boyfriend's best friend — that would be you. And she ended up marrying you. If she only knew the whole truth about everything."

"Then maybe you should tell her. Maybe that will make her back off."

"Andrew, I'm trying to make sure that little girl doesn't have to deal with any more drama in her life than she's forced to. Paris is a loose cannon right now. Telling her the truth won't shut her down. She'll either not believe it or try and use it against me." Gabrielle touched Andrew's hand. "You're a good man, Andrew. But if your wife wants a fight, then I'm going to give her one. But she won't be taking Jasmine from me. That's one thing I can promise. As God is my witness and as God is on my side, Paris will not take Jasmine from me." Gabrielle primped her mouth.

Andrew took out a business card and held it out to Gabrielle. "I want to stop Paris on this as well. Together, I believe we can do it and with minimal damage. Think about it. Pray about it. And if God leads you to, then give me a call. Okay?"

Gabrielle took his card. "I'll pray about it

and we'll see what God says."

Andrew stood to his feet. "I hope to hear from you soon." There was a quiet rap on the door. Andrew went and opened it. "We were just finishing up," Andrew said to Robert. "I'll call you later."

Robert nodded as Andrew brushed past him. He came and sat down at his desk. "I apologize for any discomfort that may have caused. But what are the chances of something like that happening?"

Gabrielle nodded. "It's okay. He once was a good friend to me."

"So, how would you like to proceed? I can ask that they send another lawyer —"

"Let me get back with you on that. I want to think about it." Gabrielle put Andrew's card in her wallet in her purse. She stood up; he stood. She started for the door, then turned around. "It looks like I have something else to add to my prayer list."

Robert walked to the door with her. "If I may, let me say this. I've worked with Andrew before a few times. He's a good man and a *really* good lawyer. He doesn't do things for the money. If there's anything he can do to help with this —"

"I know." Gabrielle smiled. "I'll be in touch."

Robert opened the door and Gabrielle left.

Chapter 19

> In whom also we have obtained an inheritance, being predestinated according to the purpose of him who worketh all things after the counsel of his own will.
>
> — Ephesians 1:11

Zachary called Gabrielle to see how her visit to the lawyer had gone. She'd gotten home mere minutes before Jasmine got in from school and didn't want to tell him anything over the phone for fear Jasmine might overhear her.

Zachary came over around six o'clock that evening.

Jasmine greeted him at the door. "Dr. Z, would you like to play Jenga?"

"Sure, Miss Jazz," Zachary said to Jasmine before looking over at Gabrielle. "You set up the blocks, and I'll be with you as soon as I speak to Miss G." He and Gabrielle stepped privately into the kitchen.

He lowered his voice. "Okay, you know I want to know how things went with the lawyer."

"Something happened while I was at Mr. Shaw's office that I'm praying about. Andrew Holyfield showed up."

"Andrew Holyfield? You're talking about Paris's husband?"

"Yes . . . him."

"What was he doing there?" Zachary shook his head deliberately. "And don't dare tell me he was trying to strong-arm you and your attorney. I knew I should have rescheduled my appointment and gone with you. I had a feeling in my gut today —"

"No, it was fine. Andrew's not like Paris at all." Gabrielle sat down at the kitchen table. "It was actually kind of funny."

"He's a lawyer. I don't see how there can be anything funny about the lawyer slash husband of the woman who's causing you so much trouble showing up at a meeting you had scheduled with your lawyer. Maybe you should consider finding another lawyer entirely. It looks to me like they may be in cahoots or something."

"Mr. Shaw didn't know Andrew was coming to see me. Not exactly."

"I'm ready, Dr. Z!" Jasmine yelled from the den.

Zachary yelled back. "I'll be there in a minute." He returned his attention back to Gabrielle. "How do you know that? Because he told you that. You apparently don't know how some of these all-boys networks operate. They can be quite deceptive."

"Mr. Shaw wants me to win this but he doesn't feel he's the best person to represent me since it has become a little more complicated. So he called to another firm and asked them to send over someone to assist us. The person who was supposed to come was unable to, so they ended up sending Andrew by sheer coincidence."

"And you seriously believe that when Andrew heard about it, he didn't know it was you?"

"If what he said is true, then I'm pretty sure he didn't know until he stepped into Robert Shaw's office and saw me sitting there."

Zachary nodded. "Okay. If you say so."

Jasmine yelled again in a singsong voice, "Dr. Z, I'm going to start without you!"

Zachary yelled back. "And you'll be cheating if you do!"

"You go on and play with Jasmine. We can talk about this later."

Zachary and Gabrielle went back in and played with Jasmine. After they'd eaten supper and Jasmine was in bed, Gabrielle told Zachary what Andrew had proposed.

"So he says he wants to help you?" Zachary said.

"Yes."

"And you believe him?"

"I do."

"Then what are you going to do?" Zachary asked.

Gabrielle sat back against the couch. "I don't know. Mr. Shaw trusts him. I trust him. I believe he really isn't going along with Paris on this. And I believe he's thinking that if Paris learns he's going to be representing me, it will make her back down and not take this to a court hearing."

Zachary put his hand slightly over his mouth. "That's a thought." He took his hand down. "But if he's your lawyer, you'd have to tell him things that he *could* possibly use against you."

Gabrielle shook her head. "Andrew would never do that."

"The Andrew you may have *known* would never do that. How well can you say that you know him now?" Zachary squared his body with Gabrielle. He took her hand and locked his fingers with hers. "People change. He's married to Paris now, the evil queen."

"I wouldn't go as far as to call Paris the

evil queen," Gabrielle said.

"She invited you into her home. She then kicked you out without notice for reasons you can't even tell me, I might add. Years later, she sees you, learns you're about to adopt a nine-year-old child who has been orphaned by the death of both parents, at least that's all she knows from the outside, and what does she spend her waking moments doing? Thinking of ways to keep you from getting that child. And for what reason? What reason does she have in doing this, other than feeling like she may be able to hurt you? She doesn't care how any of this might affect poor little Jasmine. She doesn't care that this is what Jasmine's mother wanted. She just wants to put a dagger in your heart. *That* sounds like evil to me."

"I can't answer what's motivating Paris to do what she's doing. Maybe she honestly believes she's doing an honorable thing. It appears she really thinks I'm an awful person. So in her mind, she believes she's actually rescuing Jasmine from the likes of me."

"Why don't you try and talk to Paris?"

"That's what Andrew said, to which I say: Why don't I just talk to this wall here instead? It would yield the exact same results."

Zachary laughed. "You may be right. But if you were to tell Paris the truth —"

Gabrielle shook her head. "No. I wouldn't do that. Not Paris. Never."

Zachary rubbed her hand he still held with his other hand. "I don't mean all of it. Just the truth that Jasmine is your daughter you gave up for adoption."

Gabrielle quietly pulled her hand out of Zachary's. "I shouldn't have to tell her that for her to leave me alone. None of this is her business."

Zachary captured Gabrielle's hand back. "If it will make her abandon this ridiculous endeavor, wouldn't it be worth it? Huh? Wouldn't it?"

"I don't know. It might make her start thinking. What if she puts one and one together and realizes who Jasmine's father is? That would be nothing but more ammunition for her to use against me and, sad to say, even against her own father."

"You think she would use something like that against —"

"Shhh. Not so loud." Gabrielle looked in the direction of upstairs.

"She's asleep. She can't hear us."

"You never know. I don't want to take any

chances and end up making a misstep in all of this."

Zachary nodded. "Okay. But if you were to talk to Paris and let her know she doesn't have a legal leg to stand on, maybe she'll back down and let this go. So what do you think you want to do? About Andrew representing you?"

Gabrielle shrugged. "I don't know. Mr. Shaw thinks we should let Andrew in on the case. You think I should tell Paris the truth. I don't know the right thing to do."

"Well, in that case, there's only one person for us to go and talk to."

"You're right," Gabrielle said. "So do you want to do the honors and call or would you rather I?"

Zachary smiled. "It doesn't matter. You can do it." Zachary stood up.

Gabrielle stood up next to him. Zachary took her hand and kissed it. "If anyone can set you in the right direction, He most definitely can." Zachary released her hand.

Both Zachary and Gabrielle kneeled down in front of the couch. She took Zachary's hand and held it as she bowed her head and began to pray. "Heavenly Father, I come to You today, thanking You for who You are. Lord, I need Your help; I need Your divine counsel. I'm in need of Your direction. I want to do the right thing. Lord, please . . ." Gabrielle began to cry.

Zachary placed his arm around her. "Guide us, O thou great Jehovah. Bless Gabrielle. We know that the battle is not ours, it's Yours. Thank You for Your love. Thank You for Your peace. Thank You for Your grace. In all of our ways, we will acknowledge You, and we know You *will* direct our path. We thank You in advance, and as always, we give You all the praise and all the glory, in Jesus's name. Amen."

Zachary helped Gabrielle up and back on the couch. She was still crying. "Thank you," she said in between her sobs.

He hugged her. "I told you, Gabrielle: We're in this together. I'm here and I'm not going anywhere. Do you hear me?"

She nodded. "Zachary?"

"Yes."

"I'm going to work with Andrew on this."

Zachary placed his hand under Gabrielle's chin and lifted it up. "Are you sure? Are you *sure*?"

She nodded. "Yes. I'm sure."

Chapter 20

Wives, submit yourselves unto your own husbands, as it is fit in the Lord.

— Colossians 3:18

Paris greeted Andrew at the door. "Ask me how my day went," she said.

Andrew looked at her. "Oh, so you're talking to me now." He walked over and set his briefcase down at the bottom of the staircase.

"Andrew, please don't. I'm really trying here."

Andrew stood like a statue and looked at her.

"So, you're not going to kiss me?"

"Paris, you and I need to talk."

Paris grabbed him by the hand and led him into the den. She sat down, pulling him down with her. "You're right. You're my husband and I need to give you the respect of hearing what you have to say."

"I want you to drop this thing you're pursuing with Gabrielle. I want us to concentrate more on us and *our* family." He frowned. "Do you understand?"

"I hear you. And I know what you're trying to say. But, Andrew, I'm telling you: I don't want that little girl having to grow up with Gabrielle for a mother."

"Why not? Why do you keep pushing this? It's none of your business. In fact, when we were all trying to help that little girl by seeing if we might be a match as a bone marrow donor, you were the only one who wanted no part of it."

Paris smiled as she turned her body more toward Andrew and leaned in. "That's true. But things have changed. Things are different now. You always tell me I need to learn how to care about someone other than myself. Well, Andrew Holyfield, I'm doing just that. We'd like a family of our own. For whatever reason, you and I haven't been able to start one. This little girl needs a family and a good home. Now, I might not have stepped up when Jasmine needed me before, but Imani did. It was Imani's bone marrow that saved that little girl's life. What good is saving a life if we're not willing to do whatever we can to ensure the *quality* of that life?"

"Gabrielle is a good person."

"And you know that *how*? Have you ever lived in the same place with her?"

Andrew dropped his head down. "I need you to let go of this vendetta you have against Gabrielle. If you don't, you're going to force me to do something you're not going to like. I'm telling you, Paris. Don't make me have to go against you."

Paris grinned. "You're not going to do anything to hurt me *or* make me look bad. You love me too much, Andrew. I know you say you're not going to help me get Jasmine, but you'll come around and see things my way. I believe that. I'm praying for that."

"Why are you so bent on doing this? You see it's not something I'm going to support you on. You can't go to court to take a child away from someone who you claim is unfit because she's a single mother, and then you go in there doing this as a single person."

"What are you saying? You'll divorce me if I continue this?" Paris stood up and placed her hand on her hip. "Is that what you're saying, Andrew? That you would actually *leave* me over somebody like *her*?"

Andrew stood and gathered her up by the shoulders. "No, that's not what I'm saying at all. What I *am* saying is that I'm not with you on this. And if you force me to choose between what I believe to be right, and you, then I'll choose Gabrielle Mercedes's side."

"Because you and Gabrielle were once lovers." Paris had a defiant look in her eyes.

"I told you that Gabrielle and I were never lovers. I don't know how many times I have to tell you that."

"Then why are you taking her side over mine?"

"I'm not taking her side over yours. I'm taking the right side over wrong. You're wrong in what you're doing, Paris. I realize I've allowed you to do things like this in the past. If you wanted something, I went along with you. But I'm not doing it on this. You're playing with people's lives. That little girl is not a collectible doll or a Maltese puppy, for that matter, that you can get when you want, then throw to the side when you get bored or decide you're tired of it."

Paris abruptly pulled away from him and flopped back down on the couch. She folded her arms hard against her chest. "I didn't get rid of Ambrosia. I'm working now, and I can't take care of her like she needs. I sent her over to my folks' house until I can manage things better around here."

Andrew slowly eased down next to Paris. He tried to take her hand. She snatched it out of his. He tried again, and again, she snatched her hand from him.

"Look at me," he said.

Paris continued to look away.

"Paris, please look at me."

Paris turned toward him.

"I'm proud of you for deciding what you want. You wanted this job and now you're doing it. But be honest, though. You wanted that Maltese and after about a month, you lost interest and moved on to something else. I'm not saying anything is wrong with that."

"Ambrosia needed more attention, and with me working the way I'm doing, I can't give her the attention in the way she needs. Imani loves having her over there. She has more time to take care of and play with her. So everything is working out."

"Okay, tell me this. Let's say Gabrielle decided to just let you have Jasmine. Right now, she agrees we'd be the better parents for her. What would you do then?"

"Why would she just up and agree right now?" Paris tilted her head. "If I didn't know better, I'd wonder if *you* were Jasmine's father."

"What do you mean if you didn't know better?"

Paris grinned. "Nothing. I was just saying

that the way you're championing on her and Gabrielle's behalf, it's almost as though you have a vested interested in this."

"I do." He touched Paris's cheek. "I want you to drop this and concentrate on *us*. Let's keep the focus on *our* family."

"I *am* concentrating on us. And believe me: I'm focused on *our* family. I just believe you'd be an amazing father. And whether you want to admit it or not, I'd be a pretty good mother. Jasmine is a beautiful little girl with a bright future ahead of her. I want her to have the best, and I think you and I are in the best position to give her just that."

Andrew smiled. "You're right. You're going to be a great mother. So we'll keep trying to have our own little bundle of joy and leave Gabrielle alone." He shrunk down to look into her eyes. "Okay?" He took her by her shoulders with her arms still folded.

Paris looked sheepishly into his eyes and smiled. "Whatever you say." She unfolded her arms. "You're the man of this house. You're my husband."

Andrew squinted one eye and leaned his head to one side. "Okay. So does this mean this is settled?"

"You're my husband. You say it's settled, then it's settled."

Andrew nodded slowly as though he was

skeptical. He grabbed her hand. "Okay, so tell me about your day."

She grinned. "I told you I am co-chair with this guy named Darius Connors. We've put together this amazing plan to reach the young voters. I am *too* excited."

"Sounds like you and this Darius Connors guy make a good team."

"That what he says. So far, he's okay. It's only been a few weeks. But we're definitely going to be working some long, hard hours. We'll likely be out late a lot of nights."

"Should I be jealous?"

"Of what? We're working . . . hard. And Darius is married with three children. William wants us working nightclubs and going to college campuses and various college and church functions."

"As long as you're happy doing this for however long you decide to do it."

Paris pulled back from Andrew. "What are you implying now? You don't think I'm going to stick with this?"

Andrew laughed and threw his hands up in the air. "I am *not* going there. This is between you and whoever hired you. I'm just going to be your loving, supportive husband."

"Yeah. My loving, supportive husband who supports me in everything except when it comes to helping me rescue a sweet little girl from the clutches of that wretched woman and into our loving home."

"Paris —"

Paris threw up her hands in surrender. "I'm done. I'm done. I've said all I have to say to you on the matter. But at least you know where I stand."

Andrew pulled her close and gave her a quick peck on the lips. "I love you."

She smiled and rocked her head from side to side. She widened her eyes. "I love you, too."

Chapter 21

> Husbands, love your wives, and be not bitter against them.
>
> — Colossians 3:19

"How do you know? Have you ever lived in the same place with her?" After Andrew went upstairs to change out of his suit, he replayed the question again in his mind his wife had just asked him earlier about Gabrielle. He *could* tell her the truth: Yes, he *had* lived in the same place with her once. He knew what kind of person Gabrielle was. And after speaking with her in Robert Shaw's office today, he saw that she was the same caring person he'd known before. Paris had been wrong in how she'd treated Gabrielle. And she was wrong in what she was trying to do now.

He did love Paris. And as great of a father as he believed he would be, he also believed she would be a good mother. She'd been great with Ambrosia for those three weeks she'd had her. In fact, he was feeling a bit jealous in the beginning with how much love and attention she was lavishing on the puppy. She bought the puppy a beautiful sparkling collar that, at first glance, looked like diamonds. She assured Andrew she wouldn't be crazy enough to spend that much money on a diamond collar for a dog. The collar was purely cubic zirconia made to appear to be diamonds.

Paris dressed the puppy up in little foo-foo outfits. She carried her around like she was a baby. Paris puppy-proofed the areas where the puppy might be. She even started cooking for the two of them just so they could be at home with the puppy.

Then Paris's father offered her a job working on his campaign. Andrew didn't even know Paris was interested in working outside the home. In the past, she'd told him that wasn't something she cared to do. And he wasn't the type who felt he should tell his wife what she should do, not when it came to things like that. So if she wanted to stay home, it was fine with him. If she wanted to work outside the home, that was also fine with him. They were a team.

He wasn't so sure about the guy she was working with, though. Andrew could see how her eyes seemed to light up now. She even appeared more receptive when he asked her to drop her campaign of going after Gabrielle to take Jasmine away from her. That was just senseless to him. If at some point the two of them were to learn that they needed to adopt a child, then there were lots of children who needed parents and a loving home. They didn't need to go after the same child Gabrielle already had.

The next day, his phone rang at his office. It was attorney Robert Shaw.

"Andrew," Robert said. "Gabrielle Mercedes called. If you're still willing and haven't changed your mind, she's agreed to allow you to work on her case."

Andrew scratched his head. "I'm willing. But let's just pray that it's over and it won't come to going to court as a challenge."

"Do you know something I don't know?"

"As much as my firm would love to have the money from this, I'm praying I may have negotiated an out-of-court settlement without any shots fired."

"That would be good news indeed, if that turns out to be the case," Robert said.

"Time will *definitely* tell." Andrew hung up after saying good-bye. His cell phone began to ring. He pulled his phone out and looked. It wasn't a familiar number. "Hello," he said.

"Hello, Andrew. This is Darius Connors. I work with your wife."

"Yes. My wife told me about you. Is everything all right?"

"I hope so. I was calling because Paris was supposed to be here this morning no later than nine o'clock for an appointment we have scheduled, and she's not here yet."

Andrew glanced at his watch; it was 9:37 A.M. "I suppose you've already tried calling her at home and on her cell."

"Yes. I've tried both." He paused a second. "Hold on. This may be her calling me back now." He placed Andrew on hold. A minute later he switched back to Andrew. "I'm back. That was her."

"So everything's all right, then?"

"Yeah." Darius chuckled. "She said she overslept."

Andrew nodded. "That's what I was thinking. My wife's not actually a morning person."

"I heard that. My wife doesn't have that problem. With three children, you become a morning person, a noonday person, *and* a midnight person."

"Paris tells me you two are about to be stretched for the next few months."

"Yeah. I told my wife last night that the way things have been set up for the next several months, we'll be lucky if we happen to pass each other during the night. It's going to get crazy. But I'm just thankful to have a job. It's tough out there."

"I hear you," Andrew said.

"I don't know if wives always get what it's like to be a black man trying to make it out here in the world. It's not like slavery, when every black man was guaranteed a job." He chuckled. "It was long hours without pay, but we had work. Women seem able to get a job easier these days than a man can. I'm not mad at them though. And other than being a typical wife who becomes more alert when her husband works around or with other women, my wife is pretty okay. I've told her all about Paris. Your wife is smart. She has a good head on her shoulders."

"Yeah, she's pretty smart," Andrew said.

"Well, I'm sorry I bothered you. It was nice meeting you over the phone. Maybe the four of us can get together and have dinner or something," Darius said.

"That would be nice."

"Well, I'm not going to hold you. I suppose I'll go warm up the car so I'll be ready to hit the road when Paris does get here." Darius laughed. "That was a joke, you know. I don't really have to warm up the car."

"I figured as much." Andrew said bye and hung up the cell phone. His cell phone rang almost immediately. He looked, then hurriedly answered it. "Paris."

"Hi, honey. I was calling to let you know that I was okay. Darius told me he had you on the other line."

"I'm just glad nothing happened and that you're okay."

"Yes, I'm okay. I just have to get used to this pesky alarm going off. I guess I hit the snooze button one too many times and ended up turning it off completely. I'm sorry that Darius had to call and worry you."

"He seems to be a pretty nice guy."

"He is. Well, I'm leaving the house now. I'll talk to you later."

Andrew hung up and stared at his phone. *Maybe this job is going to be good for Paris after all,* he thought. If nothing else, he hoped it would keep her too busy to even think about Gabrielle and Jasmine, let alone go after them. It might also show her that things don't always go as smoothly as we hope, no matter how much we believe that they will.

CHAPTER 22

Children, obey your parents in all things: for this is well pleasing unto the Lord.
— Colossians 3:20

Darius opened the door to their office as he and Paris laughed about a man they'd passed coming in the building. Paris instantly cut off her laugh as soon as she saw her father sitting there.

"Hi, Daddy. What are you doing in here?"

"Waiting on you, Daughter."

"Mr. Simmons," Darius said, acknowledging him with a quick nod.

Lawrence returned the nod. "Darius, if you don't mind, I'd like to speak to my daughter . . . in private."

"No problem. I need to go check with the graphics folks on our flyers." Darius grabbed a folder off his desk, then left, quietly closing the door behind him.

Paris bent down and gave her father a

quick peck on the cheek. "Are you checking up on me, Daddy?"

"Not exactly." He pointed to the empty chair next to him for her to sit down. Instead she walked around to her desk and sat in her own chair. "I got a call from Blake today."

Paris sighed. "Your attorney."

"*Our* attorney, it appears. He tells me that you're still pursuing trying to take that girl from Gabrielle."

"I told you, Daddy. If you're not going to do anything about it, then I will. If I don't, who else is there left to do it?"

"It's not your place, Paris. I've told you I want you to leave it alone."

"You thought the Maltese puppy would work, and it didn't. So I guess you thought giving me a job to keep me busy slaving away on your campaign would do it. Well, I'm not going to let it go. I can't tell Andrew the whole truth about why I'm pursuing this because I really don't want to mess things up for you. But I can tell you. You know *exactly* why I'm doing this. I would think you, of all people, would support me. But I guess winning reelection is more important to you than winning back your own child."

"Which child are we talking about? You?"

Paris leaned forward. "No, Daddy. I'm

talking about Jasmine."

"I told you: I never slept with Jessica Noble. And as your father, I've asked you as nicely, and as forcibly as I know how, to drop this ridiculous notion. You're opening doors that none of us need open right now, Paris Elizabeth. How many times have I told *all* of you: A story doesn't have to be true for it to bring a person down? If something like this should get out, it doesn't matter whether it's true or not; I'll be slammed with it. Is that what you want, Paris?" He leaned in. "Is that what you're trying to accomplish by doing this?"

"I want that little girl out of the clutches of Gabrielle Mercedes. I want her raised in a family with true family values. If you and Mom can't take her in, then Andrew and I will. I wish you would support me on it. But I see that when it comes to choosing, you choose your career over your flesh and blood every time."

"I'm going to tell you this one last time: Drop it, Paris. You need to put your energy on your own marriage."

Paris frowned. "What's that supposed to mean?"

"It means you're going to mess around and drive Andrew away if you're not careful. Whenever a person puts too much attention into the wrong things, they generally make mistakes they later regret." Lawrence stood up. "I love you. And I want you to be happy. Take care of your husband. Work on having your own baby. Listen to your father for a change, why don't you. And drop this notion of going after Gabrielle and that child."

Paris stood up and straightened her yellow suit jacket by tugging it down. "Okay, Daddy. I'll drop it. I'll work on making my husband happy. I'll keep working on having a baby of my own. And I'll work hard to get you reelected. Happy now?"

Lawrence nodded once, then opened his arms wide. Paris walked around her desk and stepped into his awaiting arms. He hugged her. "I love you, baby."

"Love you, too, Daddy. Love you, too."

Chapter 23

Fathers, provoke not your children to anger, lest they be discouraged.

— Colossians 3:21

Having walked her father to the door, Paris stood with her back against it. Tears rolled down her face. She wiped hard, then walked over and picked up her purse, took out her cell phone, located the number she was looking for in her phone's address book, and called. "Blake Daniels, please. This is Paris Simmons-Holyfield calling." She waited for him to pick up.

"Blake Daniels."

"Hi, Mr. Daniels, this is Paris Simmons-Holyfield. I'm calling to let you know that I will no longer be requiring your services."

"Oh, okay, Paris. You know I think that's best. This was going to be a pretty messy case and possibly long, not counting an uphill and hard fight."

"Yeah, I know. You told me."

"And you know I was also concerned that your husband is a lawyer and he wasn't doing anything to indicate his approval toward your efforts," Blake said. "That's troubling not only to me, but the court, when you're taking on something of this magnitude."

"Yes, yes. You're right. And my husband and I definitely weren't on the same page when it came down to this. Well, I just wanted to call and let you know that I'd no longer be using you or your firm in this matter. I thank you for your wise counsel and for having originally filed the papers as you did on my behalf."

"So I can withdraw your petition?"

"Yes, you can."

"Okay, Paris. I'll take care of this right away. And if I can assist you in the future on anything else, please know that I'm here."

"I'm certain I won't be calling you for anything else. Thank you, Blake. Goodbye." Paris clicked off the phone and stared at it.

Darius opened the door slightly and stuck his head in. "Is the coast clear?"

"My father's gone, if that's what you're asking."

Darius fully opened the door and walked

in. "What's the matter with you? You look like someone stole your rainbow-colored lollipop or something."

Paris sat down, gently placing her cell phone on her desk. Darius sat in the chair across from her. She looked at him with a stern face. "I need a lawyer."

"That shouldn't be a problem for you. Didn't you tell me that your husband is one? I'm sure he knows plenty of them."

"He is and he does. But I need a lawyer that doesn't know Andrew or my father, for that matter." Paris stared out into nothingness. "I need my own lawyer, one who will be working for me and my interest."

"I'm sure you can find one in the phone book. Let your fingers do the walking. Do we even have a physical phone book in this place? Do they still even put out physical phone books? Everything is online now." He sat back against the chair and steepled his fingers.

"I don't want to find one in the phone book. I need a personal recommendation. I need a good lawyer, and one who's astute in family matters."

Darius leaned in. "Are you thinking about getting a divorce or something?"

"No. I need someone to help me get Jasmine from Gabrielle."

"I thought you had someone for that already. That lawyer you said you went to see this morning, which was *actually* the reason you were late getting here. I wish you'd told me what you were doing and I wouldn't have called your husband."

"Yeah, I had one. His name was Blake Daniels. But it turns out he's more my father's lawyer than mine even though I was paying him an outrageous amount of money for his services." She looked hard at Darius. "He must have called and told my father I was there today about Gabrielle."

"That's why your father was here?"

"Yep. He was here strong-arming me about dropping this . . . *again.*"

"You know I'll help you in any way that I can. But please don't cause me to lose this job. You and I both know that the only reason I got this is because of you."

"You know: You're just like all the rest of them. All you care about is yourself and what happens to you." Paris stood up and looked hard down at him.

Darius stood and walked around her desk to her. "That's not true. But if we're going to do anything, let's be smart about it. If you lose this job, how are you going to pay a lawyer? If I lose this job, how am I going to be able to continue helping you?"

Paris laughed, mostly to get under his skin. "How have you helped lately?"

"Okay, how about this." Darius closed the distance between them by stepping even closer to her. "My oldest daughter, Jade, is friends with Jasmine. Last night, I happened to overhear Jade talking to my wife, Tiffany. And Jade was telling her about Jasmine being upset about being adopted."

"So, she's upset because she's about to be adopted. Big deal. What child wouldn't be?"

Darius smiled. "You're missing it."

Paris leaned, almost sitting on the edge of the desk. "Missing what?"

"Jade didn't say that Jasmine was upset about the fact that she was *going* to be adopted. She's upset because she found out that she *was* adopted."

Paris frowned. "That makes no sense."

"When I talked to Tiffany about it, she told me that when Jasmine came over to our house for a visit, she'd just learned about a couple of weeks earlier that her parents actually adopted her. Apparently Jasmine was having a difficult time with that new revelation."

"Did Jasmine tell your wife any of this?"

"No, Jasmine only talked about it with my daughter. They're the same age. I'm sure you know how that is, especially with girls."

"But that doesn't make any sense." Paris was clearly puzzled now. "Maybe your daughter got it wrong. Maybe she misunderstood. You should talk to her and find out for yourself exactly what was said."

"That's not a good idea. I don't want to push my daughter in the wrong direction. If I get in it, she'll become suspicious and maybe even shut down in telling her mother anything else. As I said: I overheard them."

Paris stood up from sitting on the desk, then sat down in her chair. "Yeah, you're right. That's how I used to be. If I told my mother something and she told my dad and he questioned me, it made me not want to tell her anything else for fear that she'd break the confidentiality and tell him again. My baby sister is that way now with our folks." Paris picked up a pen off her desk and stuck the top of it in her mouth. She took the pen out and looked up at Darius. "But if what you're saying is true, then that could only mean that Jessica Noble *wasn't* her birth mother."

Darius went and sat back in the seat across from Paris. "Another scenario could also be that Jessica's husband wasn't the child's father and *he* adopted her."

Paris nodded. "That's possible. That's why I suppose it would be good if we could find out the exact words Jasmine said to your daughter."

Darius pulled out his cell phone. "I'll just call Tiffany and ask her." He held the phone, his eyes shifting a few times as he waited. "Tiff, can you talk a minute?" He paused. "I just have something that I need to ask you real quick. You remember when Jasmine told Jade that she was adopted. Did Jade say her parents adopted her or just her father?" He was quiet a moment. "No real reason. I was thinking about it but I couldn't remember if she said it was her parents that adopted her or just her father. You know, like maybe after having her daughter, her mother had gotten the man she married to legally adopt her." He nodded. "Okay. Thanks. I'll see you when I get home. No, I should be home at a decent time today. Tomorrow, who can say?" He clicked off his phone and put it back up.

"Well? What did she say?"

"It was her parents that adopted her. Neither of them were her birth parents."

Paris nodded as she again stared into nothingness. "Okay, then. Now I'm *totally* confused."

"Just another piece to the ever moving puzzle."

"Yeah. As they say: The plot thickens. But

I'm not shy about stirring things up. I'm going to get to the bottom of this if it's the last thing I do." She smiled and looked at Darius. "I need a lawyer. Now."

Darius leaned back against his chair, his hands cupping his neck. "Then *we* shall find you one."

CHAPTER 24

> Let no man despise thy youth; but be thou an example of the believers, in word, in conversation, in charity, in spirit, in faith, in purity.
>
> — 1 Timothy 4:12

"They're going to work us to death," Paris said to Darius as they walked back to the car provided to them by the campaign but driven solely by Darius. A little white midsize car Darius wasn't crazy about, but at least they had a car that wasn't his to experience all this wear and tear.

He opened the door for Paris. "You have to admit: This *is* fun though."

"Oh, you just like being around all these cute young women, many of whom are half dressed and putting everything they have on full display," Paris said.

"You're starting to sound like my wife now." Darius closed the door and walked around to the other side and got in.

Paris put on her seat belt. "You'd better be glad that I'm *not* your wife because I would have clocked you big-time today."

"Yeah, like your eyes weren't roving. I saw you looking at that collection of guys with the muscle shirts on. My friend Big Red says you women look just as much and as hard as we men. Y'all are just slick with yours."

"Well, I got them signed up to vote, didn't I? And they said they'd vote for my father."

"What a guy *says* and what he *does* is entirely *two* different things." Darius started the car and angled his body slightly as he backed out, placing his arm around Paris's head as it rested on her headrest.

Paris looked straight into his face. "I know that. I majored in Men One-oh-one."

Darius turned his body back forward, but allowed his arm to remain on Paris's headrest. "I believe that."

"Don't you think you need to drive with both hands on the wheel?"

"Why? I can drive with my left hand just fine. Is my arm bothering you?"

"Yes, as a matter of fact, it is."

Darius laughed, then took his arm down. "You are so high maintenance. It's amazing that your husband hasn't left you yet."

"I could say the same thing about you. I don't know why your wife puts up with somebody like you. It's obvious you *love* to chase skirts."

Darius laughed. "There are worse things she could be worried about. But my wife knows she's not going anywhere. That woman loves her some Dare."

"Oh, okay." Paris nodded a few times as she smiled. "I see you have her good and fooled."

"No more than you have Andrew."

"You don't know anything about me and Andrew."

Darius alternated his attention between the road and Paris. "I know that he's crazy to let you go out of the house looking like you do. All sexy and all. Now if you were *my* wife, I'd make you cover up all of that. You wouldn't be advertising how fine you are to other men. Nope. Not if you were mine."

Paris laughed. "From that picture you showed me, your wife is really cute."

"Yeah, but if you noticed, I make her cover up her goods. I don't believe in sharing, not even a good look. What my wife has is for me and my eyes only. You're hanging out here . . . around all this high testosterone. Your husband better be glad I'm hanging with you so I can keep you out of trouble."

"I'll have to tell him that."

He looked at her as he pulled up alongside her car in the parking lot. "Okay, so we're supposed to hit the club tonight. What time would you like for me to come and pick you up from your house?"

"You're going to come pick me up from my house?"

He chuckled slightly. "Of course. It makes no sense for us to meet up down here when I can just as easily swing by and pick you up. Besides, I'm a gentleman and a godly man. What kind of man wouldn't want to be sure you're safe the whole time you're in his possession?"

"I'll not be in your possession."

"You and I are showing up at the nightclub together. You'd better believe I'm going to keep an eye and a rein on you. Your father and husband are not going to be looking for me if something were to end up happening to you."

Paris opened her car door and set one foot down on the parking lot to get out. "In that case then, I'll see you at my house around eight." She got out of the car fully.

"The party doesn't start jumping until ten," Darius said, scrunching down low so he could see her.

She stooped down a little. "Yeah. But we're not there to party. We're there to work. We still need to set things up for the work aspect of this outing. Remember?"

He smiled and gave her a salute. "Right. Then I'll see you at eight."

Paris wiggled as she pulled down and brushed smooth her clinging canary yellow dress. He honked his horn as he slowly drove away, ensuring that she'd gotten safely into her black Lexus ES 350.

Chapter 25

Drink no longer water, but use a little wine for thy stomach's sake and thine often infirmities.

— 1 Timothy 5:23

Darius gave Tiffany a drive-by kiss as he was on his way out the door.

"Behave yourself now," she said as he briskly walked away. "Don't have *too* much fun while you're working."

He turned around. "It's only work. I'll be home really late, so don't bother trying to wait up."

Tiffany nodded, then blew him a kiss as he went out the front door to the car.

He pulled up at Paris's place with five minutes to spare, surprised when she came out before he even turned the car off. He jumped out of the car and hurried to open the passenger's side door for her. "Will you look at you?"

She tossed her head from one side to the other a few times and got in, placing her Gucci briefcase on the floor in front of her Prada shoes.

He went around the back of the car and got back in, then turned to her. "I first need to call the fire department. Because, woman, you are *smoking*!"

Paris playfully hit at him. "Boy, I thought at first you were serious."

He shook his hand as though he'd been burned by fire. "I *am* serious. You are wearing the *heck* out of that little red dress and those red stilettos. Fi-yah!" He backed out and began driving down the road.

"I called the manager of the club to be sure they have a place already set up for us to work from." Paris pulled down the sun visor. The light above it automatically came on. She freshened up her lipstick.

"That's good." He glanced over at her. "Really good." He grinned.

She cut her eyes over at him. "What are you grinning like a Cheshire cat about?" She took out a tissue and dabbed the corners of her mouth.

"Oh, just enjoying the scenery, that's all." He looked at her and smiled some more.

She put the sun visor back in place, effectively turning off the light. "Well, what you need to do is keep your eyes on the road."

They arrived at the nightclub and there was a line outside the door two people deep and already the entire block long.

"I thought you said the party didn't get started until ten?" Paris said.

Darius jumped out and hurried to open her door. He took her by the hand to help her up. "It doesn't. But now you know why this spot is called The Fire Place."

They walked toward the front, passing a few folks who made it known that they didn't appreciate the appearance that they were trying to jump in the line.

The door wasn't opened yet. Paris called the manager and, four minutes later, a big burly man came and let them in.

They set up items on a table inside the dance hall close to where people entered and exited. When the doors opened, they signed up lots of unregistered voters as well as talked with folks about their candidate, Lawrence Simmons, highlighting his past accomplishments, not pointing out that he was now a Republican. When asked about his switch in parties by the more informed voters, Paris was deft in letting the person know it was strictly for tactical reasons.

It was close to one in the morning. Most

of the people were on the dance floor. Darius smiled at Paris sitting at the table and grooving to the beat.

He stood up. "Let's dance."

She shook her head. "I'm not that great of a dancer."

"So. This isn't a dance competition." He held out his hand to her. "Come on."

She shook her head again. "We're supposed to be working. Remember?"

"We *have* been working. Hard, too. No less than twenty guys have asked you to dance and you turned them down but managed to still turn most of them into registered voters who promised to cast their vote for your father."

"Some of them were lying, asking me for my phone number so they can talk to me more about politics later."

"Oh, I heard them," Darius said, his hand down by his side now.

She smiled. "Don't be acting like I'm the only one who was getting hit on. I saw those scores of women giving you their phone numbers. You'd just better remember to empty your pocket before you go home and your wife finds them."

He chuckled, then held his hand out to her again. "Let's dance. Come on. We're pretty much done for the night."

Paris looked over at her Gucci briefcase.

"Just hide it under the table. The tablecloth will keep people from seeing and trying to steal it. Come on."

She put her briefcase under the table and took his hand.

They danced to five songs in a row before going back to their table. Paris sat while Darius remained standing.

"Would you like something to drink?" he asked.

"Yes. A peach Fuzzy Navel."

"Coming right up." He left and returned shortly. "At your service. One peach Fuzzy Navel." He set it down in front of her and sat down with a glass of rum and Coke.

She nodded her approval. "This is good."

"So are you," Darius said. "I mean, you're a good dancer, in spite of your insistence otherwise."

"I suppose I have some moves still left from my young days. My brother, Malachi, and I used to love to 'cut the rug,' as my grandfather used to say. Andrew was never a big party guy though. So we don't go out to places like this. If we dance, it's generally at one of my father's campaign functions, the one with all the old folks in attendance. Have you ever seen a room full old folks doing the Electric Slide?"

Darius smiled. "Looks like this job might be just what the doctor ordered." He turned up his glass, finishing it quite quickly. He watched Paris slowly drink hers from a straw. He began to snicker.

"What's so funny?"

"The way you're drinking that Fuzzy Navel. All cute and dainty. If you're going to drink it, then you ought to drink it."

She held the glass up in the air, grinned, then turned it up, taking several nonstop swallows. When she was finished, she set the glass down hard on the table.

"Oh, I see you can drink like a big girl." Darius moved in closer. "Would you like another one?"

"Are you planning on having another drink?"

"I was thinking about it."

She shook her head. "Then I suppose not. One of us needs to be sober enough to be the designated driver."

"I can drink more than one of these watered-down babies and drive just fine."

"Not with me in the car you can't. If you're drinking, then I'm driving."

He twisted his mouth. "Then I guess that's it for me."

"Seriously?"

"Seriously. I'm supposed to be taking care

of you. That means making sure I return you to your home in the same condition that I picked you up. That's how I was taught to treat the women in my life."

Paris sat back against her chair. "I'm not one of the women in your life. We merely work together. That's it."

"Still, you're a woman. And whether you want to admit it or not, you're in my life. Your father has threatened me one time already; I dare not push it by putting his precious daughter in danger. So I'm out. But if you want another drink, there's nothing stopping you now."

"You're just trying to get me tipsy or something."

"Nope. I just want you to enjoy yourself. If we have to be here working, then we might as well take advantage and make the best of it."

A guy walked up to the table. "I hear you're here about voting. I'd like to hear more." His words slurred slightly from too much alcohol consumption. He was looking totally at Paris as he played with his finely trimmed goatee.

Darius stepped up to him. "What can we help you with, my man?"

The guy turned his attention briefly to Darius. "I'm good. I'm talking to this beautiful lady here, this Venus of beauty. I'm sure she can help me just fine." He turned his attention back to Paris. "So what do you say, pretty lady? Why don't you and I go somewhere a little quieter, like say my crib, where you can tell me all about this voting stuff and why it's in my interest to even vote?" He stumbled backward a few steps, then stepped forward to gain back his lost ground.

Darius picked up a brochure off the table. "Why don't you take this and read through it when you get back to your *crib.* It tells all the different ways you can register —"

The guy grinned at Paris. "I'm already registered. I just want to know more about this dude that you think I should vote for. And if he has somebody like you advo— advo— advocating for him, he has to be all right."

Darius pressed the brochure into the guy's chest. "That's the beauty of this glossy. It gives you all the information you'd ever want to know about Lawrence Simmons."

The guy refused to take possession of the glossy. "Come on. Let's dance." He held his hand out to Paris. "Come on, sweet thang."

Darius put the brochure down and stepped over to the guy's awaiting hand. "Listen —"

"I got this," Paris said, standing up. "Look. I'm working. This is my job. This is what I do to make a living. Now . . . I don't come on *your* job asking you to come home with me and show me how to make hamburgers, now do I? So show me the same respect and courtesy. If you want to know more about why you should vote for someone like Lawrence Simmons, then I'll be glad to answer your question. Otherwise —"

"What I'm *interested* in is getting your name and phone number. You're a hot little number. I bet you and I can make beautiful sparks together." He stumbled closer to Paris.

"Well, I *happen* to be married, and I'm not interested in anything other than getting the word out about voting," Paris said. "That's it. Understand?"

"Oh, so you can dance with this dude here" — he pointed his head at Darius — "but you're too good to dance with somebody like me? Is that it?"

"It *is* okay to dance with your own wife, right?" Darius said to him.

The guy took a few stumbling steps back. "Oh, oh, this *here* your wife? Man, I didn't know. My bad. No harm, no foul."

"Well, I think you owe her an apology," Darius said, his face stern, his eyes bearing down hard on him.

The guy looked at Paris and bowed slightly with his head, stumbling as he tried to remain steady. "My *sincere* apologies to you, Miss Married Lady." His words continued to come out slurred.

"No problem," Paris said.

The guy left.

After he was safely out of range, Paris laughed. "You are *so* crazy."

"Well, it got him to leave, didn't it?"

"Yeah, it did."

A cocktail waitress came over and set a glass down in front of Paris. "Our finest and most expensive red wine, compliments of that gentleman over there." She pointed at a nicely dressed man in an Armani suit who nodded at Paris.

"I don't care for it," Paris said to the waitress. "Please return it to him for me."

Darius picked up the glass of wine, held it up like a toast to the man who'd sent it, and turned the glass up. "Thank him for us, will you?" Darius said to the waitress. He then turned to Paris. "They say a little wine is good for the stomach." He winked. "So, are you ready to go?"

Paris nodded, gathered up her things, and they left.

CHAPTER 26

Some men's sins are open beforehand, going before to judgment; and some men they follow after.

— 1 Timothy 5:24

"We've covered a lot of ground over these past seven weeks," Darius said to Paris while in their office. "It's too bad after all we've done to date, we *still* have to work on the Fourth of July. I was thinking we'd at least be off for *that day.*"

"Well, I missed being able to celebrate *my* birthday."

"I did my part to help make up for it. I bought you a cupcake." Darius smiled. "A red velvet one with cream cheese icing."

"Yes, you did. But I wanted to do something special, not attend some fund-raising event where we were begging for donations. I guess I'll make up for it when this is all over, just like I'll make up for the Fourth.

William says holidays like the Fourth are good times to catch people out and about. William seems impressed with us so far. I don't think he thought what we were doing would end up being this productive," Paris said. "I saw him earlier; he said we're exceeding expectations."

"I told you you're a natural at this. We make a good team."

Paris nodded. "We do. Oh, and I appreciate that lead you gave me on that lawyer. She's good . . . *really* good."

"You can thank my wife. She's the one who gave me her name. I asked if she knew of any good family lawyers, and she came back with her."

"Well, she's good. I absolutely like her."

"So I suppose that means you're not giving up on getting Jasmine?"

"Nope. I'm not stopping until I've gotten that child from Gabrielle's greedy little grips. My lawyer has learned that there's a sum of money on the line and will ultimately be under the authority of the person who ends up with Jasmine. I guess now we've figured out Gabrielle's motivation for wanting to keep little Jasmine so bad that she'd fight me to hold on to her."

"Was your lawyer able to find out whether Jasmine was really adopted?"

"I thought I told you that last week." Paris shrugged. "It's been so busy, maybe I didn't. But, yeah, Jasmine was originally adopted. Who her birth parents are is another matter, and not so easy to find out."

"Then my daughter Jade was right."

"Yep. She was telling the truth."

"So that blows a hole in your theory about your father and Jessica having had an affair and Jasmine being your father's child."

Paris shook her head and placed her finger up to her lips to tell him to be quiet. "Yes, I guess so." She placed her finger up to her lips again and pointed toward the closed door. "You want to go get something for lunch?"

"Yeah. I was just about to ask," Darius said, trying to keep from laughing.

Paris got her purse. They left the office and went to the car. After they were inside and the doors closed, Darius started laughing. "What was *that* all about?"

"I don't know exactly why, but I don't trust saying too much, especially lately, and particularly about personal private things, in our office," Paris said.

"You think maybe our office is bugged or something?"

"I wouldn't put it past my father *or* William. In any case, I'd rather be safe than sorry. For now, my father believes I've dropped this whole notion about getting Jasmine from Gabrielle. I'd like him to keep thinking that way."

Darius drove away. "What do you feel like eating today?"

"Barbecue."

"Ooh, good choice. I was just thinking about that myself." He looked from her, back to the highway. "I'm telling you: You and I were made for each other. We go together like ham and cheese. Like peanut butter and jelly. Like eggs and grits."

Paris shook her head. "You are *so* crazy."

"You're in good company: My wife says the same thing."

"How is your wife these days?"

"Loving the fact that I'm bringing in a nice, fat paycheck bi-weekly. There's nothing that makes a marriage work better than having enough money to keep down frivolous arguments." He glanced at Paris. "We still need to get our spouses together one of these days. Tiffany *really* wants to meet you."

"Then have her stop by our office one day, whenever we're there."

"Truthfully, I'm not that crazy about the two of you meeting."

Paris frowned. "Why not?"

He smiled, looked at Paris, then back to the road, where he was now turning into the barbecue place. "Some things I just like keeping exclusively to myself. So what's your husband saying about you working the way we've been doing, out all hours of the night with a hunk of a man like me?" He laughed.

"He's not crazy about the nights we're out late or the various nightly events we attend. But he's the type of man who wants me to be happy. And he can see that I look like I'm happy."

Darius parked the car. "You two still trying to create a mini you or mini him?"

"Look at you: all up *in* my Kool-Aid." She quickly opened her car door.

"That's what friends do. At least I *hope* you consider me a friend." He opened his door and stepped out, meeting up with her. They walked toward the restaurant.

"I do consider you a friend. All joking aside, I really do. You're the only person, other than my new lawyer, that I can confide in about Gabrielle."

"So you haven't told your husband that you're still pursuing this?" Darius opened the door to the restaurant and held it open for Paris.

"Nope. He's made it clear that he's not

going to support me on this. So why bother talking to him when he's becoming more and more like the enemy."

"Two?" the hostess asked when they walked up.

"Yes, please," Darius said.

"Oh, and can you put us in a place where we can talk more privately?" Paris asked.

"Of course." She led them to a booth away from where most people were seated. "Is this okay?"

"Perfect," Paris said as she beamed.

Paris and Darius sat down.

Darius leaned in. "So what do you think Andrew is going to do when he learns you *haven't* dropped this?"

Paris picked up the menu and looked down at it. "I don't know. I hope he'll come around and see things my way."

"But if you've learned that Jasmine was adopted, then it sounds like she's really not your father's child, just like he said she wasn't. And if that's the case, then there's no real reason for you to care anymore."

"I thought about that . . . that Jasmine's not my father's daughter the way I was thinking. But the truth is: My father still has never denied this is his child. My father denied that he ever slept with Jessica Noble. Think about it: My father is a true politician from his heart. And *true* politicians are skilled at word manipulation."

Darius laughed. "You're so cute. The way you come up with those sweet little phrases like 'word manipulation.' Okay, so that means you still think he's lying."

"No. He would say he didn't actually lie. He told the truth. He *didn't* have an affair or sleep with Jessica Noble. But now that I've learned Jessica Noble is not Jasmine's birth mother, I just need to dig a little deeper and see if we can't find out who is. That just might be the person my father *did* sleep with to produce Jasmine. See? Simple enough."

"You know you have some kind of an imagination on you."

"Not really, but picture this. What if Jessica Noble knew the person my father slept with and agreed to adopt Jasmine to throw my father off the trail? My father may honestly not know that Jasmine is his child. Then again, maybe he does and everybody involved was in on this deception from the start." She shrugged.

"See what I mean," Darius said. "The little wheels inside your head just be turning. Remind me not to ever lie to you. You'd bust me for sure."

Paris sneered. "And don't you forget it."

"But it's also possible," Darius said, "that Jasmine is not your father's child and everything was just a coincidence. The fact that he got involved with trying to help find her a bone marrow donor, the fact that one of his children turned out to be a perfect match . . ." Darius shook his head. "I'm not helping his case any, am I?"

Paris shook her head. "Not at all."

The waitress came over, took their orders, and left.

"So tell me," Paris said. "How many affairs have *you* had?"

Darius leaned in on his elbows. "You mean counting you?"

Paris laughed. "I've never had an affair with you."

"But you will."

Paris chuckled again. "No, I won't."

"Care to put some money where your mouth is?" Darius leaned back and leered.

"Nope."

"Because you know you'd lose," Darius said with a smirk.

"Nope. Because I don't take money out of the mouths of babes. And if I bet you, which I don't bet, but if I were to bet you, you would lose. Of course, I could use a new pair of shoes. I saw this pair of Christian Louboutins I'd *love* to have, and they would look *so* good on my feet. They're gold glittered, which looks good with those red bottoms, and about five inches high. But they cost too much for me to feel right paying with my or my husband's money. But I wouldn't have a problem winning the money from you and using it to buy them. So don't you *dare* tempt me."

"You're that confident, huh?"

"I know me," Paris said.

"Are you saying I'm not your type?" He leaned in even closer, licking his lips.

"You're my type. You're not bad on the eyes . . . have a little charm on you."

He sat back against his seat. "Why thank you, ma'am, and right back at'cha."

"And you *can* be funny at times."

"I've been told that." He rubbed his chin. "You women seem to like a man with a sense of humor."

Paris chortled. "Okay now. Don't push it."

"So why do you feel you and I would never have an affair?"

"Because I'm not like those other weak women you've likely tricked into sleeping with you."

Darius sucked his teeth. "I wouldn't call any of them weak now. And I don't have to trick *any* woman into being with me. It's something they wanted to do."

"Aha! I knew it! You just confessed." She grimaced as she shook her head. "You're such a jerk. Cheating on your wife. Well, you'll never cheat on her with me."

He simpered. "We'll see. A lot can happen in five months working closely together."

"Yeah, we'll see all right. So far you've tried getting me drunk and that hasn't worked."

"I've never tried to get you drunk. I don't have to get a woman drunk for her to want me. And I'm offended you'd even think that about me. She may get drunk just to let her true feelings run free. But I don't need a woman impaired to want to be with me."

Paris laughed. "Yeah, you're offended, all right."

The waitress came over with their orders.

Darius looked at Paris after the food was on the table. "These ribs look *good.*"

"Yes, they do."

"It's your turn to say grace," Darius said.

"But I did it the last time."

"And you do it oh so well, too." Darius bowed his head.

Paris made a loud, deliberate sigh, and then said grace.

Chapter 27

> Likewise also the good works of some are manifest beforehand; and they that are otherwise cannot be hid.
>
> — 1 Timothy 5:25

Gabrielle, Fatima, and Tiffany pulled up at the restaurant at the same time.

"I'm so glad you suggested doing this," Fatima said to Tiffany as they hugged. "I haven't been to this place in years. And I definitely needed a girls' night out." Fatima looked at Gabrielle before they hugged. "You look like you needed a night out with the girls, too."

"It's always good seeing the two of you," Gabrielle said. "I've never been to this restaurant before."

"My husband was telling me about it the other day," Tiffany said. "He says the food here is outstanding. I told him I was going to check it out."

"So he's never brought you here before?" Fatima asked with a frown.

Tiffany smiled. "No. But he's been working so hard these past few months; we barely ever see each other lately."

"I'm sure you're glad he got another job," Fatima said.

Tiffany nodded with a smile. "Yes, thank the Lord. It was getting so hard with just me working. Bills get behind . . . folks calling the house looking for their money."

"But at least he was getting unemployment, wasn't he?" Fatima asked.

"Oh, yeah. But that's only enough to keep you thinking you might be able to stay afloat until another boat comes along." Tiffany smiled.

"I'm surprised he was able to find something in this economy," Fatima said. "My husband says —"

"Oooh, listen at you," Tiffany said in a singsong way. " 'My husband.' Trent is *such* a nice guy. God really blessed the two of you to find each other."

Fatima blushed. "Yes, God did. And I couldn't have asked for a better man."

"I know how you feel," Tiffany said. "That's how I feel about Darius. Don't get me wrong, now. He has his faults. But we're still together after all these years. All in all, he's a pretty good man. Like when he found out we were talking about meeting up. He shocked me by volunteering to keep the children tonight. He *never* volunteers. Never. Yes, Fatima, you'll have your ups and downs. But with lots of prayer and lots of love, you can make it. Darius and I are a living testament of that."

Fatima turned her attention to Gabrielle. "So why are you so quiet tonight?"

"Because she's going to be the next one inducted into our marriage club," Tiffany said.

Fatima scrunched down and tilted her head slightly. "Gabrielle, are you all right?"

Gabrielle smiled. "Oh, yeah . . . yeah. I'm fine. I'm sorry. I was just sitting back listening to you two. I'm excited that things are going so well for both of you. That's a blessing for sure."

Fatima reached over and touched Gabrielle's hand. "I'm the one who's sorry. We're over here being all cheery . . . going on and on, all happy-go-lucky about how great things are going in our world, while you have stuff going on in yours."

Gabrielle shook her head and stretched her neck, causing her head to rise higher. "No. No. Please don't feel bad about the good reports you have in your life. It's good for me to hear great things like this. It gives me hope."

The waiter came over to their table. "Are you ladies ready to order?" he asked.

"We've been sitting here running our mouths," Tiffany said. "We haven't even had a chance to look at the menu."

"You work here," Fatima said to him. "What would you suggest?"

"The platter meals are our best bang for the buck. The platters come with our famous coleslaw, the best French fries around, and light bread toasted on a grill. We have one with chicken, one with ribs, and our combo that gives you a little taste of both. If you happen to be a vegetarian —"

"Oh, no. No vegetarians here," Fatima said. They all laughed.

"I'd like the rib platter," Gabrielle said.

"Chicken platter for me," Tiffany said, holding her hand up and waving her fingers.

Fatima closed her menu and handed it to him. "Both of those sound good. I think I'll stick with what I've done the last time I was here and go with the combo platter."

"And to drink?" the waiter asked.

Tiffany lifted her hand. "Sweet tea for me. Love my sweet tea."

"We have raspberry tea," the waiter said.

"Raspberry?" Tiffany said with excitement. "Oooh, that sounds good. I want to try the raspberry tea."

"Raspberry sweet tea sounds good to me as well," Gabrielle said.

Fatima laughed. "Cola for me, please." She looked at Gabrielle, then to Tiffany. "I always have to be the odd woman out, huh?"

"You just know what you like." Tiffany handed her menu to the waiter.

"There's not a thing wrong with going in a different direction from the crowd," Gabrielle said, handing her menu to the waiter.

"I'll be back shortly with your drinks," the waiter said. He came back within minutes and set down their drinks in boot-shaped glasses. "Your food will be out soon."

"Thank you," they said, to which he bowed slightly from the waist and left.

"Okay, so what were we talking about before we were interrupted?" Tiffany said. "Oh, yeah. Gabrielle and what's going on."

"Have things settled down any better yet?" Fatima asked. "I mean from the last time we talked?"

"It seems like it has. I have a new lawyer, sort of, working on it. I'm hoping things wrap up soon and that there are no more complications. But there's still a lot of time between now and when things become final. I just continue to pray without ceasing, standing on God's promise that all is well. And Zachary has been *so* wonderful. He's been right there by my side."

"You always have such a positive outlook on things," Fatima said. "Ever since I've known you, you've seemed so strong in your faith in God. I was saved long before you were, but your faith always seems to surpass mine."

"It's not a competition. I merely take God at His Word," Gabrielle said. "And Pastor Landris said the only way you can know the promises of God is to read the Bible and find out what's in there for yourself. I've read it. I know some of the promises that speak to my life and situation. I know that I'm more than a conqueror. I know that the prayers of the righteous availeth much. I know that I'm made righteous not by my works but by what Jesus did on the cross and Him declaring me the righteousness of God."

"Preach!" Fatima said, throwing one hand up in the air. "See there? Now *that's* what I'm talking about!"

"I know Pastor Landris and Johnnie Mae have been a blessing to me," Tiffany said. "I've learned so much from both of them. Then seeing someone like you, Gabrielle, come in and do what you've done in the short time that you have. It encourages me as to what I can do."

"The Bible says we can do all things through Christ Jesus, who strengthens us. I just take God at His Word. The Bible says I can, so I say I can." Gabrielle picked up her glass of tea and took a sip. "This raspberry tea is delicious."

Tiffany picked up her glass and took a swallow. She nodded. "It is."

"Not that I want to divulge anything I'm not supposed to," Fatima said. "But how are things going with Jasmine? Is she continuing to adjust okay?"

Gabrielle nodded. "She is. Both of you know that I told Jasmine she was originally adopted."

"Yeah. I didn't want to say anything I wasn't supposed to, just in case," Fatima said.

"It's okay. Tiffany knows." Gabrielle rubbed her hands together as though she was warming them.

"I didn't mean anything by that," Fatima said to Tiffany. "I just don't want to say the wrong thing. That's how gossip grows wings and takes off flying."

"I understand," Tiffany said. "I wasn't offended. Actually, I was thinking the same way. I didn't know whether you knew. Jasmine told Jade and Jade told me. I called Gabrielle to let her know what was going on, and she told me everything."

"Well, after the initial shock wore off, Jasmine seems to be taking it fine now. I've tried talking to her about it to see where her thoughts are. But she's nine. And I'm not sure if it really matters to her as much as we think. She knows she was loved by her parents, the Nobles. And I believe that's what's most important to children."

Tiffany frowned. "It does matter though. Because she still talks about it a lot with my daughter."

"I'm just glad she has someone she feels comfortable enough to open up to and to express her thoughts and feelings," Gabrielle said. "I just wish she would talk to me like she seems to talk to Jade about it."

"Maybe you should take her to see a professional counselor," Fatima said. "There's a woman at our church who does that. I don't know if you know her. Her name is Sapphire."

Gabrielle nodded. "Yes, I know Sapphire. She and I have already talked. Johnnie Mae introduced me to her when I first became involved in all of this. I talked to her about Jasmine. She asked me a few questions after I told her that I'd told Jasmine. She said I shouldn't worry because Jasmine appears to be handling it fine."

"Well, I know she seems fine whenever I see her," Tiffany said. "Not that I'm any kind of an expert or anything. Oh, and Jade's been on her head for Jasmine to come over. You know how bored children get after about two weeks of summer vacation."

"I was thinking about having Jade come to my house for a sleepover or maybe a slumber party," Gabrielle said to Tiffany. "I don't know if there's a difference in the two, but it's something Jasmine said she'd like to do."

"That would be great! Like I said, school's out, and Jade is *past* bored. The younger ones do okay; they're content at daycare and sitting in front of the TV when they're home and playing video games. Not Jade. So whenever you want to do that, let me know."

Gabrielle nodded. "Wonderful. Then we'll do it."

"I want to come to a slumber party," Fatima said. "Hey! We should have one for the three of us. That would be so much fun."

"What?" Tiffany said with shock in her voice. "Are you trying to figure out how to get away from your husband this soon after the wedding? Is the honeymoon over already?"

Fatima laughed. "No. But I was just remembering back when I was growing up and how my friends would have slumber parties. I was thinking that might be fun for us now. Just because we're grown doesn't mean we can't still have fun, right?"

Gabrielle buttoned her lips tightly, then relaxed them as she looked down at her hand. She looked up. "I've never been to nor had a slumber party before."

"What? You've never been to a slumber party before?" Tiffany said.

Gabrielle shook her head slowly. "Nope."

"Your folks must have been overprotective or something," Tiffany said.

Gabrielle shrugged nonchalantly. "Actually, my mother died when I was close to four. I was raised by my aunt and her husband." Gabrielle stopped referring to him as her uncle years ago after what he'd tried to do to her when she was in her teens.

Tiffany reached over and touched Gabrielle's wrist. "I'm sorry. I didn't know. If you don't mind me asking, what happened with your mother? Was it cancer?"

Gabrielle tried to smile so her words wouldn't seem so heavy when she spoke them. "No. Domestic violence. My father killed my mother. He's still in prison, although he's up for possible parole at the end of this year, in fact."

Tiffany jumped to her feet and went and threw her arms around Gabrielle's neck. "Oh, Gabrielle. I'm so sorry. I shouldn't have pried. I had no idea."

"It's okay." Gabrielle patted Tiffany's arm, which was still around her neck. "It's a part of my life, and I've learned to keep going in spite of what may have happened in my past."

Tiffany sat back down. "Well, I agree with Fatima. I think we should plan a slumber party for the three of us. We could have it the same night you have Jade and maybe a few other girls over for Jasmine. There's Johnnie Mae's little girl, Princess Rose, and Sasha's little girl, Aaliyah. They're all close to the same age. I think Princess Rose is around eleven now. Having a slumber party for them and for us would be so much fun! I'll help you plan it, Gabrielle."

Gabrielle nodded. "It really *does* sound like fun."

"Then is it a go?" Tiffany asked. "A slumber party for the girls and a slumber party for the three of us?"

Gabrielle smiled. "Yeah." Gabrielle clapped her hand one time. "Let's do it."

Fatima began to look toward the direction of where the waiter had disappeared to. "I wonder where on earth is our food? What could be taking so long?"

As though he'd heard her, the waiter stepped into view with a large tray. "I apologize, ladies, for the delay."

"I was starting to wonder if the chef had to go out and catch the pig and the chicken himself before he could cook them," Fatima said with a chuckle.

The waiter gave a short laugh as he set the food down in the appropriate places. After ensuring they had everything they needed, he left.

"This looks and smells *so* good," Gabrielle said. "Let's pray."

"If you don't mind, I'd like to do it," Tiffany said. They held hands and Tiffany prayed.

After the prayer, Fatima passed around a small bottle of hand sanitizer. They all squirted some in their hands and rubbed their hands together.

"Okay, women of God, let's dig in!" Fatima said. "And let's not be cute. Tonight, we're using our hands."

Chapter 28

> Therefore thou art inexcusable, O man, whatsoever thou art that judgest: for wherein thou judgest another, thou condemnest thyself; for thou that judgest doeth the same things.
>
> — Romans 2:1

"Would you like to go out to dinner?" Andrew asked Paris Thursday evening when she came in. It was the first evening she'd been home when he got there in a long time.

She shook her head. "No. I'm tired. This work thing is no joke."

"I told you so. You were always questioning why I didn't want to go out after I came home from work. Now you see why."

"Yeah." Paris smiled and tilted her head slightly. "Now I see why."

Andrew grabbed her around her waist and rocked her in his arms. "So what would you like to do for dinner? Call for delivery or fix something ourselves?"

Paris pulled out of his embrace. "I'm really tired, Andrew. Why don't you get us something? I don't care what. I'm going to my room to relax."

"Okay, then. We can just have a nice romantic evening here together, if that's what you'd prefer to do. Although I still owe you a birthday dinner since you were working the night of your birthday. And we missed celebrating the Fourth together."

"I really don't feel like doing anything much. We were out until after one this morning. Then we had to be at this rally they were having downtown for almost six hours that started at nine this morning. I am *so* beat, Andrew, you just don't know. And tomorrow, it's another late-night function. I'm about ready to crash and burn."

"By 'we' you mean you and Darius?"

"Yeah."

"So you have the time and energy for that, but when it comes to me, you don't feel like being bothered?"

Paris walked over to him and placed her hand on his chest. "I told you from the beginning: Darius and I only have a working relationship. That's it. That's all it ever will be. Just like the women on your job, including your secretary and paralegal assistant. Darius and I are together because we have to be . . . it's our job."

"I haven't accused you of anything more than that. I'm just pointing out that you can do all of these things, but when it comes to you and me, you never feel like doing anything much anymore."

"It's July eighth. It's only been two months. You act like it's been years. Maybe had you supported me more when I was trying to do something that meant something to me, things would be different between us."

"You mean if I had gone along with your plan to try and take Jasmine from Gabrielle," Andrew said. "I told you: I'd rather spend my time and energy on making our own little family and leave Gabrielle and whatever she's doing alone."

Paris stepped back. "Look, Andrew, I don't care to talk about Gabrielle. I still say there's *something* between the two of you that you haven't told me, I don't care how much you say differently. But if you want to keep your little secrets, then just know that two can play that game."

Andrew stepped in front of her and looked into her eyes. "What do you mean by that remark?"

"I mean: If you want to keep things from

me, it's fine. Just don't be mad when you feel like it's coming back on you."

"So you have some secrets you're not telling me?" He crunched down and gazed into her eyes.

Her face was stern, not a smile to be found. "Nope. I'm just saying that if later on it feels like I've kept anything from you, then don't judge me since you're doing the exact same thing with me. That's all I'm saying."

"All right, Paris. You have *your* job to do and *I* have mine."

"See what I mean?" Paris said, pointing a finger at him. "It's little things like that. 'You have your job to do and I have mine.' We're both bringing money into this household now." She shrugged. "Enough said on the subject. But whenever you want to come clean about your secrets" — she started walking away — "then I'll be happy to come clean with mine. It's as simple as that."

She strutted up the stairs, turning once to look back at him still standing there with a grimace on his face.

CHAPTER 29

> Therefore remove sorrow from thy heart, and put away evil from thy flesh: for childhood and youth are vanity.
>
> — Ecclesiastes 11:10

The slumber party was on and getting ready to be popping. Despite the disappointing news Gabrielle had received hours earlier from Robert Shaw about her court case, Gabrielle found herself more excited about the party than even Jasmine, who was literally skipping and dancing around the house, counting down the minutes until six o'clock.

Gabrielle and Tiffany had worked hard putting together a princess-themed party complete with crowns and royalty party favors. All of the girls invited (Jade, Princess Rose, and Aaliyah) were now in the middle of the den Gabrielle had transformed to look like a castle, along with Jasmine, in a group hug, jumping up and down, and screaming as only young girls can do.

Gabrielle couldn't stop smiling. Fatima and Tiffany were also there for their slumber party time together.

"I'm *so* glad you decided to do this," Tiffany said while they were in the kitchen making hot dogs. "This is *just* what I needed. I am so stoked!"

"What did you do with your other children for tonight?" Gabrielle asked.

Tiffany speared a hot dog and placed it inside of a bun. "Brace yourself. Wait for it . . . *wait* for it . . . Darius has them." She beamed.

"He's their father; he *should* have them," Fatima said with a little more edge than was probably necessary or expected.

Tiffany frowned. "I know he *should.* But he's been working so much lately. I was surprised when I told him we all were doing this and he said he'd make sure he was off work to keep Dana and Junior so that I could come. This new job has changed him so much. I just hope he survives at home with those two all by himself. Junior, especially, can be a handful."

"I'm sure he'll be fine," Gabrielle said. "Zachary keeps Jasmine for me when I have things I need to do, and he manages just fine."

Tiffany picked up the plate of finished hot dogs, two for each girl. "Well, Darius is *no* Zachary."

"I know that's right," Fatima said, again with smugness to her tone.

Tiffany laughed. "Wow, Fatima. Go easy on my husband, why don't you?"

"Sorry. I shouldn't have said that. It's just Zachary is such a good man." Fatima picked up the tray with the condiments for the hot dogs. "I'll carry this in," she said to Gabrielle, who had the bowls of chips and dip and was reaching for the tray before she scooped it up.

They took the things in to the girls, who now had on their matching pink and purple princess pajamas Gabrielle had bought for them. Pillows and lounging things were positioned in the room already.

"Did you also make us strawberry milkshakes?" Jasmine asked.

"Yes," Gabrielle said. "We have strawberry milkshakes in the kitchen, with *real* strawberries in them. They're coming in a second."

Jasmine got up off the floor. "I'll go get them."

"We can *all* go," Jade said, standing to her feet as well.

"We're going to bring them to you,"

Tiffany said. "You princesses stand down, why don't you. Y'all say your grace and get started eating. Milkshakes are on the way."

"We just don't want y'all thinking we're too much trouble," Jade said. "We'd like to do this again. We're having so much fun!"

"Don't worry," Gabrielle said. "We'll definitely do this again."

"Yay!" all four girls said in unison as they jumped up and down.

"I'm having so much fun!" Princess Rose said. "Maybe I'll ask my mother to have one next."

"That would be so *awesome,*" Jade said. "We could have a slumber party every week for the next three weeks if all of us get our folks to have one." Jade turned to her mother. "Mommy, can we? Please?" She put her prayer hands together. "Please, please, please."

"Whoa," Gabrielle said. "Now don't go getting me in trouble with all your folks. I don't want anyone mad at me for starting something here."

"My mom would probably be the only one who doesn't want to do something like this," Aaliyah said. "But my dad and Mama Melissa would. I'll ask my daddy."

"You have two mothers?" Jasmine said to Aaliyah.

Aaliyah paused for a second. "I guess you can say that. My mother is Sasha. But my daddy married someone else and she's like a mother to me. I stay with them a lot, *a whole lot* — my daddy, Mama Melissa, and my little brother, Marc-Marc. They're about to have another baby soon. Daddy says it's a little girl. I saw a picture of her inside Mama Melissa's stomach. I don't know how they can tell she's a girl, but that's what they say. So I'm going to have a baby sister soon."

"I have two mothers. My other mother died. Now I have Miss G," Jasmine said. "She's like my mother now."

"I thought you said you have three mothers?" Jade said. "You remember you told me that you have three mothers."

Obviously uncomfortable, Tiffany twisted her mouth a few times, then left and went to the kitchen.

"Three?" Aaliyah said, shaking her head slowly. "That's a lot of mamas."

"How do you have three mothers?" Princess Rose asked. "I guess you could actually say that I have two daddies or I would have. My real daddy died when I was too young to remember. Now Daddy Landris is my father. He's a great father, too. Mama says we're both blessed to have him in our lives.

And I agree."

Gabrielle thought about shutting down the conversation, but decided it was better to let them talk unhindered. That's what she was told was part of the slumber party experience: being able to talk about secret things and things that were on your mind. And Jasmine wasn't saying any of these things to her, so this just might be her only opportunity to hear what Jasmine was *really* thinking and feeling. Although she was pretty certain what Jasmine meant about her having three mothers, she was curious to hear why Jasmine had told Jade that. *What was going through Jasmine's mind at this point?*

"Here you go," Tiffany said, bringing in a tray of capped, tall plastic princess cups. "Strawberry milkshakes for everyone!"

The girls started jumping up and down again. "Yay!" They took the milkshakes off the tray and went to the princess tent Gabrielle had made using pastel-colored chiffon strung from the ceiling in the corner of the den.

And just like that, the conversation was over.

Chapter 30

> Let thy garments be always white; and let thy head lack no ointment.
>
> — Ecclesiastes 9:8

Gabrielle, Fatima, and Tiffany went up to Gabrielle's bedroom after playing a couple of games with the girls and dancing to a few songs. The women changed into the white satin pajamas Gabrielle had bought them for the slumber party.

Fatima did a little dance. "Look at us: we look like triplets with our identical white pajamas. Thanks, Gabrielle. These are *too* cute."

"You're very welcome," Gabrielle said.

"That was such fun!" Fatima said. "I still got it. Thirty-seven years young and *I* still got it. Did you see me doing the Twist down there?" She started doing the dance called the Twist.

"What decades did you get those dances

from?" Gabrielle said.

"Those are classics," Fatima said as she went and got her bag with her rollers in them, a pale pink comb, and a jar of hair grease. "Don't act like you don't know."

"You had my daughter cracking up." Tiffany began to move like a movie scene being advanced one frame at a time with one-second pauses. "What was *that* supposed to be? I thought I was watching a rerun of *Soul Train.*"

"It was the Robot," Fatima said. "And I was doing it way better than whatever that is you just called yourself doing." Fatima opened the jar of hair grease, took her comb and, parting her hair, greased her scalp.

Gabrielle laughed. "Both of y'all were funny, if you ask me. Where did you two learn to do the Bump?"

"Girl, that was the *dance* back in the day. At least, that's what my mother used to tell us when she was showing us how they did it when she was growing up. These children don't have anything on us." Fatima stopped and stood up. "I started to break out with the Funky Chicken on them." Fatima tucked her fists under her underarms and began flapping them like they were chicken wings while wobbling her legs.

"That's called the Funky Chicken?" Tiffany said. "If you hadn't told me, I would have guessed you were trying to do the Stanky Legs or the Butterfly or something, only badly. If you had done that, those girls *really* would have laughed us from down there even faster than they ended up doing."

"Gabrielle let Jasmine turn on the Wii and put in that Just Dance game," Fatima said, sitting back down and continuing to roll her hair. "They have all kinds of songs on that thing. 'U Can't Touch This' by MC Hammer, 'Pump Up the Jam' by Technotronic, 'Le Freak' by Chic." She stopped rolling her hair. "I didn't get that song called 'Dare.' But Tiffany seemed to like it."

"That's because it was slow enough not to wear me out and I could get the steps easier," Tiffany said.

Fatima finished with her last roller, put the grease and her comb back in her bag, and zipped it closed. "What was the name of that song the girls kept playing over and over again?" She crossed her eyes to show how crazy that had made her.

" 'I Like to Move It,' " Tiffany said, singing the title of the song.

"I'm not familiar with that one, but they sure knew it," Fatima said.

"If you had children, you'd know it. It was

in a movie called *Madagascar* and later in one called *Happy Feet.*" Tiffany began to sing the hook of the song again. "I've seen both of those movies so many times I know most of the characters' parts by heart." She grabbed a can of hair sheen and sprayed her hair, then began wrapping it as she continued talking — brushing it to make it lay down as she wrapped. "I don't know what it is about children, but when they find a movie they like, they want to watch it every single day." Tiffany pinned her hair in place with large bobby pins.

"That was how one of my cousins was," Gabrielle said. "We had VHS back in the day. And my cousin Luke taped *Ghostbusters.* He would watch that movie over and over again; it absolutely drove us crazy. And we didn't have but one good television, so if we wanted to watch television, we had to watch that or go somewhere and play. I hated it. 'Don't cross the streams.' That's all he ran around saying from that movie."

Fatima placed a baby blue satin bonnet over her rolled hair.

They all sat on the floor on the pallet Gabrielle put down for them.

"You're not going to do anything with your hair?" Tiffany asked Gabrielle.

"Yeah. Of course."

"Oh, I want to see this," Fatima said. "I've always wondered how you manage to keep your rods curly and not all flattened, squashed, and muffled up."

Gabrielle laughed, then got up and went to her bathroom. She came back out with four large bobby pins and a black satin bonnet.

"Okay, so you wear a satin bonnet just like me," Fatima said.

Gabrielle grabbed a handful of the Shirley Temple–like curls in the back that rested on her shoulders and lifted them to the top of her head. She placed bobby pins in several places to hold the hair up.

"Cute," Tiffany said. "You know you really *could* wear your hair like that. That's a style. It's real dressy looking."

"I was just about to say that it would look good with an evening gown or a nice little cocktail dress," Fatima said. "I like your hair that way, too. You should do that sometimes even if it's not to a fancy event."

Gabrielle laughed. "Y'all are funny." Gabrielle put the black satin bonnet on her head. "Voila!" She held her hands out, crossed her legs at the ankle, and sat down on the pallet with them.

Fatima clapped. "So that's how you do it. I always wondered. Now I know. And that's why your rods don't get smashed and come out so fresh looking."

"Yep. I think pulling my hair up like that, when I lay down, protects the curls because they're up and out of the way. Otherwise, they *would* be flat," Gabrielle said.

"I thought you just slept with your head hanging off the bed or maybe slept on your arm and didn't move," Fatima said. "That's why I wouldn't ever get rods. I like a good night's sleep too much to be worried about my hair. Not that these rollers are all that comfortable. I'm seriously thinking about letting my hair go natural. That's the growing craze now. I could sport an Afro like my late mother did back in her day when she was growing up." Fatima turned to Tiffany. "So, Tiffany, you don't put anything on your head after you wrap it?"

Tiffany got up and reached into her bag, pulling out a black hair wrap meshed scarf with Velcro, and placed it around her hair. She sat back down.

"Do you think we should check on the girls?" Gabrielle asked. "They're awfully quiet down there. I know they're not asleep."

"Oh, they're fine," Tiffany said. "If they weren't, they'd be calling for sure."

"Oh, wait. I have something special for us

to drink. I'll be right back." Gabrielle got up and quietly went downstairs. She came back with three wine glasses and a bottle.

Fatima started laughing. "Grape juice? You have wine glasses with a bottle of grape juice."

"It's the real grape kind," Gabrielle said, handing them each a glass. "But it's like red wine."

"So what were the girls doing?" Tiffany said. "Because I know you sneaked and checked on them."

Gabrielle smiled. "They're down there whispering. I suppose they'll get sleepy and go to sleep at some point."

"Not after eating that cotton candy you made and gave them. Sugar, children, and bedtime don't go together," Tiffany said. "Now that Jade knows Jasmine has a little cotton candy machine, she's going to be asking for one."

"Well, as long as they had fun," Gabrielle said. "That's what counts. And they definitely *did* have that." She poured grape juice in each glass, then put the cap back on and set the bottle down next to her.

Fatima raised her glass. "To sistership," Fatima said.

Gabrielle and Tiffany raised their glasses. "To sistership!"

They drank their grape juice. Gabrielle set her glass down. "Let's pray."

"Wow, I was just thinking the exact same thing," Tiffany said.

"I'd like to do it," Fatima said.

Setting their glasses down, they joined hands, and Fatima led them into prayer.

CHAPTER 31

As thou knowest not what is the way of the spirit, nor how the bones do grow in the womb of her that is with child: even so thou knowest not the works of God who maketh all.

— Ecclesiastes 11:5

"All right, my spiritual sisters," Tiffany said. "Let's be like girls at a *real* slumber party. I want Gabrielle to get the full slumber party effect."

"So far, I've had a really great time," Gabrielle said. "Seeing the girls and how they were acting has been a blessing. Jasmine's been grinning so big. It blessed my heart to see her so happy. She told me she'd never had a slumber party before."

"Well, part of the ritual of slumber parties is to sit in the dark, tell secrets, and talk about stuff you might not normally talk about in another setting," Tiffany said. "If we were young girls, our conversation would likely be about boys. But since we're all grown . . ." Tiffany hunched her shoulders.

"We're talking. And the lights are off, except for that small one I left on," Gabrielle said.

"Well, I have something I want to talk about," Fatima said. "I think Trent wants us to have a baby."

Tiffany spoke up first. "That's great!"

"Oh, it is." Fatima was trying to sound enthused; she wasn't pulling it off very well.

"But?" Gabrielle said. "I hear a but in there somewhere."

"It's not so much as a but . . . but —"

Gabrielle and Tiffany laughed. "I knew it," Gabrielle said.

"Don't laugh, you two. I'm thirty-seven years old. I think I may have waited too long. What if my eggs are too old? What if I don't have many eggs left to work with?"

"Woman, please," Tiffany said. "You're at just the right age. But you need to go on and do it. You can't be dillydallying around about it. And after the baby gets here, if you need a babysitter, I'm sure Gabrielle will be more than happy to step up."

Gabrielle laughed. "Oh, so you're volunteering me, huh? I thought you were about to tell her you'd be there for her."

Fatima let out a loud sigh. "But I'm not sure that I want children. Is that selfish?"

"If you don't want any, I suppose it's better to admit it than to bring a child into this world that you don't want," Tiffany said. "There's nothing worse than people having children and mistreating them because they don't want to be parents."

"It's not that I don't like children, because I do," Fatima said. "I'm just scared. What if I really suck at being a mother? What if the baby cries and I don't know what to do to make him or her stop? I don't have my mother to turn to anymore for advice. What if I mess up? What if my baby doesn't like me?"

It was Gabrielle's turn to laugh. "Your baby will like you. I'm sure about that. You're going to be a great mother. You'll know what to do when the time comes. You'll hold her in your arms and you'll feel such love for that child that you'll know in your heart the right thing to do."

"How do you know? You've never had a baby before," Fatima said to Gabrielle.

Gabrielle became quiet.

"Hey, I'm sorry. I didn't mean anything by that," Fatima said. "I'm sorry if I offended you."

Gabrielle looked at Fatima. "It's okay."

"Well, I'm sure you and Zachary will have lots of children after you get married," Fatima said.

"It's okay, Fatima."

"Darius says he doesn't want any more children," Tiffany said. "I actually wanted one more. I would have loved to have another boy, although another girl would have been just as great. But he said three children were enough for him, so we decided to have my tubes tied."

"Why didn't you make him get a vasectomy?" Fatima said. "He was the one who didn't want any more children. I wouldn't have closed my options. You never know; you might end up getting married again someday and wished you hadn't done it."

"Why on earth would I ever marry again?" Tiffany said with a puzzled look. "Darius and I are planning to grow old together."

"Look at me: I'm just putting my foot all in my mouth tonight," Fatima said. She turned to Gabrielle. "Are you sure that was only grape juice we had?" She laughed, then turned back to Tiffany. "Not saying it will be the case, but I was thinking about if something were to happen to your husband you might marry again and regret having done that."

"Well, I don't envision myself ever remarrying. As I said: Darius and I plan to grow old together."

"That's good," Fatima said. "If you're happy and everything is going well, then, hey, don't mind me. I was just trying to decide what I'm going to do." Fatima turned to Gabrielle. "What do you think, Gabrielle? If you were me, would you have a baby?"

Gabrielle suddenly started to cry.

"What's wrong? What's the matter?" Fatima leaned over and hugged Gabrielle. "Are you thinking about what's going on with you right now? Is it something to do with Jasmine that you haven't told us?"

Gabrielle nodded. She was really losing it. She pulled away from Fatima's embrace. "Yes. It's hearing from my lawyer today about the adoption and all of the problems we're still encountering. It's Jasmine talking about having three mothers."

"It's Jasmine wondering about her birth parents," Tiffany said, now rubbing Gabrielle's back. "That's it, too, huh? She wants to know who her birth mother is and you're worried that her birth mother might somehow possibly come back into her life and try to take her from you?" Tiffany got up and got the box of tissues off Gabrielle's dresser. She yanked out a few pieces and handed some to Gabrielle as she sat back down and set the box next to Gabrielle.

"Hey," Fatima said, grabbing Gabrielle's free hand. "You're not supposed to be sad at a slumber party." Fatima bent her head down to be able to look directly into Gabrielle's eyes. She smiled. "Okay, enough talk about babies and children. Let's talk about something else, something fun and exciting. Let's talk about —"

"No," Gabrielle said, holding her head back as she dabbed her eyes. "I want to talk about this." She took a deep breath and exhaled. "I *need* to talk about it."

"Okay, then," Fatima said. "We can talk about it if you want to."

Gabrielle was down to only sniffles now. "If I tell you both something, will you promise not to tell anyone? I'm talking, not even tell your husbands."

"Sure. If that's what you want," Fatima said.

"Of course," Tiffany said. "That's what sisterfriends are for."

"It's about Jasmine."

"Okay," Fatima said. "Take your time; we're not going anywhere. We have all night."

Gabrielle nodded. She wiped her eyes. "It's about Jasmine's birth mother."

"Are you saying that you know who her birth mother is?" Tiffany asked. "Have you spoken with her?"

Gabrielle nodded again. "Yes." She rubbed her neck. Should she tell them? Other than her, the only people who presently knew the truth about Jasmine's birth mother were Zachary, Johnnie Mae, Pastor Landris, Lawrence Simmons, and his right-hand man, William. She hadn't even told her lawyer, Robert Shaw. She'd had no reason to disclose it to him yet. And as far as she knew, only Zachary, Lawrence, and William knew the entire truth: that Lawrence Simmons was Jasmine's birth father. She saw no reason to disclose that information to anyone else, not at this point anyway.

If she told Fatima and Tiffany the truth about her true relationship to Jasmine, could she really trust them to keep it? But after what Robert Shaw just told her earlier today on the phone, the truth was most likely going to have to come out. Her back was being forced against the wall by Paris. She would have no choice *but* to come out swinging with everything in her arsenal. Paris had hired a new lawyer. The lawyer had contacted Robert and informed him that her client was proceeding with her petition and custody objection and fight even more vigorously than before. It was pure nonsense for Paris to continue, Gabrielle's word not Paris's lawyer's or Robert's. Robert, in fact, was taking this newest threat *very* seriously. For the first time, he really sounded worried.

Gabrielle took a deep breath and slowly released it. She looked at Fatima, then Tiffany. "I'm Jasmine's birth mother. Jasmine is my daughter I gave up for adoption nine years ago."

There was dead silence.

Chapter 32

> He is proud, knowing nothing, but doting about questions and strifes of words, whereof cometh envy, strife, railings, evil surmisings.
>
> — 1 Timothy 6:4

Andrew Holyfield was sitting in the conference room at his firm. He turned to Gabrielle, who was sitting in the chair right next to him. "Are you sure you're okay with this? Are you sure?"

Gabrielle nodded. "I prayed and God gave me such a peace in my spirit about it. I'm sure."

"As long as you're sure now," Andrew said. "Because if you can't trust me, then you can't feel comfortable that I'm truly working on your behalf."

Gabrielle chuckled. "And, of course, it doesn't help that you're the husband of the one bringing all of this misery and trouble to my doorstep."

"When my superior heard that, he ordered me to turn this case over to someone else. He feels this is a *total* conflict of interest," Andrew said as he adjusted his notepad slightly. "I assured him everything was and would be aboveboard. I was really hoping it wouldn't come to a lawyer having to be involved. I tried my hardest to convince Paris not to pursue this. She assured me she wasn't. I guess her actions tell me otherwise and just another level of truth about my wife."

"So have you told her about us?"

Andrew smiled. "What's to tell?"

"I'm sure she questioned you about whether you knew me or not, possibly slept with me at some point in your life. I know Paris. If nothing else, she's consistent."

"She did ask me if I knew you, but I didn't tell her anything," Andrew said.

Gabrielle shook her head. "I wish you would tell her. I don't believe in lying. That's why I told Zachary everything."

"I don't consider what I'm doing as lying exactly. I just didn't voluntarily disclose everything, like she has no idea that I offered to represent you in this case."

Gabrielle shook her head again. "I don't like it. I'd rather you tell her everything.

Something like this can come back and bite all of us. I don't want to win this thing for it to later come back on appeal or something and be overturned or haunt me due to legal technicalities."

He touched her hand. "Withholding information is not the same as lying."

"It is in my book. I'd prefer you tell Paris everything," Gabrielle said. "Tell her about our past. Tell her that you're representing me. Tell her."

"It's too late to tell her now. If I know my wife, and trust me: I know my wife; she'll be worse than she is right now just *because* she wants to hurt you."

"So what do you think is motivating her to pursue this now?" Gabrielle said with a sneer. "It's because she just wants to hurt me."

"Well, my first and only priority at this point is to make sure that your adoption of Jasmine goes through as her mother wished." Andrew sat up straight in his seat. "But I need you to help me do that. So I need you to tell me everything you can. If I ask you a question, I need an honest answer. You're completely covered by attorney-client privilege. If I don't ask you something but you believe it's relevant for me to know it, then I need you to tell me."

Gabrielle chuckled. "As opposed to what you say you're doing with your wife?"

"Can we please just stay focused on your case?"

"I'm just pointing out that you aren't exactly practicing what you preach. Personally, I think it's a mistake for you not to tell Paris. If she knew you were my lawyer, I dare say she likely might drop this whole pursuit. I know if you were my husband and you were siding with *my* enemy —"

"You're not the enemy."

Gabrielle wrinkled her nose. "In Paris's eyes, believe me: I'm the enemy. If she didn't believe you and I had something going on before, I assure you she will be convinced that we definitely are now, if this thing goes to court and she learns you're the attorney representing my interest."

"I still wish I knew why she is so bent on taking this child from you," Andrew said. "It baffles me. We've been trying to have a child of our own. I even consented to adopting a child if it comes to that, but not the one you have in your custody." He shook his head.

"But Paris wants this one, the one that's in my heart . . . the one in my home. Well, if she wants a fight, then that's what she's going to get. Because she's not taking my child from me. She's not taking my little girl from me."

"The lawyer Paris has retained is a good one. I'm going to be honest with you, Gabrielle: There *is* a possibility we might lose this." Andrew leaned in. "Your past profession will likely come into play."

"That's in my past. I'm saved now. I'm a new creature in Christ. That old woman, along with her past, is gone. She died taking my past with her."

"That plays well in church. But if this stays on track, we're going into a court of law. If Paris is contending that you'd be an unfit mother —"

"But I'm *not* unfit."

"But Paris is going to say that you are. She's going to advocate that you're not the best parent for this child. Her intention is to prove she would be a better parent."

"Actually, she's saying the *two* of you would be better for Jasmine — the married couple with a stable home — than me: the unmarried ex-stripper." Gabrielle stood up and slowly walked around. "I hate this! I wish God would just make it all go away." She stopped and looked at Andrew.

Andrew was already looking her way. "Maybe I could get Paris to sit down and talk with you, woman to woman. If I could get you two in a room together like this, maybe the two of you can come to a civil resolution."

Gabrielle laughed as she sat back down, writhing her hands now. "Paris Simmons? We're talking about Paris Simmons-Holyfield."

He chuckled. "That's praying for miracles, but it's worth a try. You never know. God has been known to move in mysterious ways. His wonders to perform."

"Why don't you just tell her everything, Andrew? Tell her we knew each other back during the time she put me out of her apartment all those years ago. Tell her I stayed at your place with you and your mother for ten days, almost two whole weeks. Tell her you've agreed to represent me against her. Tell her."

"And then you can prepare for the fight of your life. Because then this will become about even more than her trying to take this child from you. Then it becomes a personal vendetta to make both me and you pay." Andrew nodded. "Had I told her in the beginning when she asked if we knew each other, I can't sit here and assure you that we wouldn't be in this exact same place right now."

"You mean you representing me against

your wife?"

"Absolutely. When Paris gets a thing in her head, the truth doesn't deter her. It may slow her down, but it doesn't stop her. I know; I've seen her. She doesn't care what anybody says. It could be her father, her mother, me . . . she's going to do what she wants to do, regardless. So you and I just need to figure out how to put this to bed once and for all. We need to drive a stake in it. And I need you to help me do that."

"So you want me to tell you everything?" Gabrielle leaned in closer. "Everything?"

"Please."

"Okay." She sat up straight in her chair. "For starters, Jasmine . . ."

"Yes."

"Jasmine is my child. She's my daughter."

He tilted his head slightly and sighed. "I know this already. As far as you're concerned she's your child . . . your daughter. I get that. But legally, that's not so."

Gabrielle stood up and wrung her hands as she paced a little. "You're right. Legally, it's not so. Legally, she's not mine. Not anymore anyway. I signed that right away a little over nine years ago."

"Excuse me? You want to run that by me again?"

Gabrielle sat down and looked squarely in

Andrew's eyes. "I'm Jasmine's birth mother. I gave birth to her and I gave her up for adoption. Jasmine is my biological child."

"Gabrielle, don't play with me now. We don't have time to play games."

Gabrielle sat up straight. "I'm not playing with you, Andrew. When you found me walking down the street, picked me up that day, and took me home with you, I was pregnant with Jasmine. Jasmine is my daughter. And whatever I have to do, I'm not going to lose her again. I'm not. I'm not giving her up again. I won't."

Andrew fell back hard against his chair. "Wow! Wow! Well, I'll be John Brown. Who knew?"

Gabrielle laughed. "You'll be John Brown?" She laughed again. "I haven't heard anyone say that in like . . . *forever.* Wonder who came up with that and why?"

He shook his head. "Give me a minute here. I'm trying to soak all of this in. Jasmine is your daughter. You were pregnant with her and I didn't even know it."

"Nor did your mother. That's why I left like I did. I knew your mother would figure it out soon enough. Morning sickness and a growing belly will give it away every time. I didn't know what to do. So I went to a place for unwed mothers-to-be, had her, then gave her up for adoption."

"So how . . . If . . ." He shook his head. "I don't get it," Andrew said, clearly having a hard time grasping all of this.

"Jasmine needed a bone marrow transplant. Jessica Noble, Jasmine's adoptive mother, was desperate to save Jasmine's life. So she did what any caring, loving mother would do. She put away pride and man-made technicalities, and she found a way to save her daughter. Now, it's my turn to do the same."

"Does she know? Jasmine, I mean . . . does Jasmine know who you are to her?"

Gabrielle shook her head. "No. She knows she was adopted. I just recently revealed that to her about two months ago. It was something Jessica asked me to do before she died, so I told her. She seems to be coping okay with that knowledge. I've been told by a professional that when she's older she may have some setbacks in dealing with it. But to answer your question: No, I haven't told her that I'm her birth mother. I should have, but I couldn't bring myself to do it. What if she hates me for giving her up? There's too much going on right now for me to let her know all of this in one whack. I do plan on telling her; just not at this point. I want to get this adoption finalized first, and when the time is right, I will."

Andrew shook his head. "Well, this is a bombshell for sure. Something like this will most definitely give you a leg up in court. But I think we should tell Paris and see if this information will avert battling it out in court all together."

"No. I don't want to tell Paris this."

"But if she knows, I truly believe she'll back off."

"Okay, let's think about this. What if we do tell her? She already thinks you're keeping something from her about us. What if she learns we in fact did know each other back then? Knowing Paris, she'll start accusing us of having slept together. Before you know it, she'll be declaring that this child is possibly yours." Gabrielle shook her head. "I don't need that drama. Not at this point in the game."

"But since you and I both know that's not the case . . ." He paused, then looked at her. "Jasmine isn't mine, is she?"

Gabrielle laughed out loud. "Boy, stop playing. You know me and you never were together in that way."

He smiled. "I don't know. You might have drugged me or something, then took advantage of me."

Gabrielle smiled. "You always did know

how to make me laugh."

Andrew nodded. "But on a serious note. You *do* know who the father is, don't you?"

"Yes."

"Well?"

"The father is irrelevant at this point. He's not trying to get Jasmine. I'm not looking for child support. He didn't care back when I was pregnant with her, and I can assure you with pretty much certainty that he doesn't care now. I'm the one trying to get custody of Jasmine. That's all you need to know. Let's just keep the focus on me."

"You know Paris is going to want to know. If for no other reason than to see whether you actually *did* sleep with her boyfriend Cedric at the time, just like she accused you of doing."

Gabrielle thought about it. She didn't know what all Paris knew. She could see Paris thinking like that. But what if Paris put things together and figured out that Jasmine was her father's child. Gabrielle didn't want to go that route or take that chance.

"If there's any way you can argue my rights without Paris finding out that Jasmine is my biological child, I would appreciate it."

"I'll see what I can do. Although as I said: Paris's lawyer is good, really good."

"Yeah. But I'm counting on *my* lawyer being even better."

"For you, I'll be at my best."

"That's all I'm asking for."

"But if this information has to come out —"

"Then it will just have to come out, and I'll deal with the fallout. We'll deal with things as they come."

Andrew nodded, then stood to his feet. Gabrielle stood up as well.

"I'll be in touch," he said as he shook his head, then, as an almost whisper under his breath, said, "I'll be John Brown."

CHAPTER 33

> But they that will be rich fall into temptation and a snare, and into many foolish and hurtful lusts, which drown men in destruction and perdition.
>
> — 1 Timothy 6:9

Paris was fit to be tied. She paced back and forth like a caged lioness. "He's representing her!" Paris said as she wrung her hands. "Her!"

"I know, and that stinks to high heaven," Darius said. "But you have to stay focused. We have this event tonight in that ballroom. We've worked hard all day getting things ready. I need you focused, Paris."

"I don't care about that! I don't even want to go to this stupid function tonight, not now." She stopped pacing and stepped right up in Darius's face. "I find out he's representing *her* against me. And on the same day, I also learn that Gabrielle is actually

Jasmine's birth mother! Really, Darius? Really? I mean: It doesn't get any worse than this! And all you can think about is some silly event with a bunch of losers who likely can't wait to get wasted? Well, I'm not going."

"Yes, you are."

She clenched her teeth as she spoke. "No . . . I'm . . . not!"

He grabbed her up by both shoulders. "Yes . . . you . . . are. Your father will be speaking there, and he and William need to see what a great job we've done. This is like the playoffs at this point. We have to bring our A game. We can't quit now."

She jerked away from him. "You might not be able to quit now, but I can. I don't care anything about this election. Either my father is going to do what he needs to do to win or not. Most of these folks we've already signed up and gotten to say they'll vote for him in November aren't going to even bother to show up at the polls. *You* know it, and *I* know it."

"Paris, pull yourself together. We've come this far; we're going to finish this. So let's just put this in a mental compartment for now, go do this event tonight, and tomorrow, you can put your gloves on and fight another round."

"Why is God doing this to me? Why does He always seem to let Gabrielle win? I don't get it. I've always been a better person than her. I know God knows that. I let her stay at my apartment when she had nowhere else to go, and what does she do? She steals my boyfriend. I run into her while seeing about a friend's sick child and what does she do? She steals my husband and makes him her lawyer against me." Paris started crying. "My own husband who wouldn't represent me and my interest made a conscious decision to be *her* lawyer against *me. Her* lawyer! How do you explain that? And when it looks like I might have a chance to win, then what happens? I learn that the anointed Gabrielle Booker . . . yes, I said Booker because that's her real name with her phony conniving self!"

"But she changed it to Mercedes," Darius said, adding fuel to a fire he clearly saw burning hot out of control.

"I don't care what she changed it to! She's still a Booker as far as I'm concerned. According to you, she was going by . . . What was her stripper name again?"

"She was an exotic dancer. They didn't call them strippers; it was exotic dancers. And her moniker was Goodness and Mercy." Darius put his arm around her shoulder and pulled her close to him.

"Goodness and Mercy. What a stupid name to call yourself. I'm surprised she didn't change her last name to Goodness. Gabrielle Goodness. She may as well have; it looks like God treats her like she's goodness or something. The wicked . . . the evildoers always seem to win."

"You're just upset."

Paris pulled away from his embrace. "You're right! I *am* upset! I'm over here looking like a complete fool while she gets to waltz away completely unscathed."

"You don't look like a fool; Andrew does. Because he can't see the great woman he has right in front of him. But you can't blame him."

"Why not? He's a grown man with a mind of his own. Gabrielle didn't force him at gunpoint to represent her. That was something he chose to do. And he did it to let me know that he's the boss in our family. He did it to put me in my place." Paris made a snorting sound when she breathed in too quickly. "Well, I'll show him. You're right. I *am* going to this function tonight. And I'm going to show my father what a great job you and I have been doing. And you know what else?"

Darius smiled, then cut it off to look dead

serious before she caught him grinning and appearing otherwise. "No. What?"

"I'm going to have a good time. And don't you *dare* try and stop me. I'm not going to worry about Andrew or any of this. I'm done thinking about other people before I think about myself. I'm done putting other folks ahead of me. Done, do you hear me? D-O-N-E, done!"

"I hear you. So what time do you want me to pick you up tonight?"

"It starts at seven. Everything is set up and ready. Five thirty will give us plenty of time to do one final walk-through. But I can drive myself. I don't need you to pick me up. It's not like when we go to a night-club or way off somewhere."

"I'll be at your house at five thirty."

"You just don't trust me to show up?"

"Nope. So be ready when I get there. And please, if your husband gets home before you leave, don't say anything to him about any of this. Please. Just wait until this event is over tonight, and then you can go at it with him all you want. Okay? For me? Promise?"

She pouted her lips. "Okay."

Darius picked her up as promised. After her father and William left the event a little after nine o'clock, complimenting them both on how well everything had turned out, Paris was true to her word. She let her hair down and drank and drank, and Darius didn't dare stop her.

Everyone was to be out of there by ten o'clock.

Darius called home a little after ten. "Hey, babe. I wanted to call and let you know that I won't be coming home tonight. This event has us on the other side of where I thought we were going to be, and dare I say that this is turning into a longer night than originally planned. The campaign is putting us up in a hotel for the night. And because I'll be working so late, I'll likely not see you in the morning before you leave for work."

"Oh, okay. You'll have to tell me all about it when you get home."

"What's to tell? It's work. Work is always work."

"I still don't get why you don't want me to tell anybody what you're doing and who you're working for. They would be *so* impressed. At least, I think so," Tiffany said.

"Nobody cares what I'm doing *or* who I'm doing it for. Most folks hate politicians. Trust me, your friends don't care nor do they need to know who my employer is. And if they're not in his district to vote for him, what's the point? All it will look like is that you're bragging for bragging sake."

"I only wanted to tell Gabrielle and Fatima and maybe a few other friends. None of the ones I want to tell are like my other friends you're thinking about. But I suppose you have a point." She sounded disappointed.

"Well," Darius said. "I have to go. As they say: A man's work is never done. But you can believe I'm getting paid. And when I get paid, that means *we* get paid."

"And as you say: That's all that counts these days," Tiffany said. "I'll see you later. Be good now."

"Always," Darius said. He clicked off the phone and walked back into the ballroom, locking his eyes on Paris, who was gulping down another drink. "Always, my dear wife." He strolled toward Paris with a grin.

"You're back," Paris said with a smile and clearly having had one too many to drink.

"Yes. I just called my wife and told her I wouldn't be home tonight."

"Why not? Where are you going?"

"Taking you somewhere to sleep this off," Darius said.

Her words were slurred. "I'm great. I'm having the time of my life."

Darius helped her to her feet. "You might

be great right now. But if you go home like this, who knows what you'll say to your husband. I have too much invested to let you ruin things when we're so close to the finish line."

"You mean Mr. Traitor? My hus . . . hus . . . husband the traitor."

"Yeah, that's exactly what I mean." Darius walked her toward the doorway and out into the hallway. "Come on."

They walked to the hotel lobby adjoined to the ballroom areas.

"My name is Darius Connors. I'm with the Lawrence Simmons reelection campaign. I'd like a room, please. I believe they have one already booked."

"Yep," Paris said. "Because I *booked* it, and we *used* it when we were here earlier today setting things *up.*"

The person at the counter looked at Paris, then to her computer. "Actually, we thought you were finished with it."

"Well, it looks like we're not," Paris said. "Choirboy here thinks he's my babysitter."

The woman behind the counter smiled. "No problem. I'll get your key. Will that be one key or two?"

"Two," Darius said.

"Whatever," Paris said with the wave of her hand. "He's not my daddy and he's *definitely* not my traitor of a husband."

"But I *am* responsible for you," Darius said. "And you're in no condition to go home right now." He looked at the clerk. "I think it may have been something she ate."

"Of course." She handed him a small holder with two plastic keycards inside. "Checkout time is at eleven."

Darius nodded, then doll-walked Paris over to the elevator.

Chapter 34

Surely as a wife treacherously departeth from her husband, so have ye dealt treacherously with me, O house of Israel, saith the Lord.

— Jeremiah 3:20

"Wake up, sleepy head," Darius said as he stood over her. Paris grabbed up the covers and pulled them completely over her head.

"Come on now; you need to get up." He sat down on the bed next to her and pulled the covers off her head.

She made her way to a sitting position, refusing to open her eyes. "My aching head," she said, pressing the palms of her hands tightly against both sides of her face.

"I told you you were going to feel this way when you got up, but you didn't want to listen," Darius said.

She kept her eyes shut, turning her head in the direction of where the voice was coming from. "What are you doing here? Did I oversleep or something? Where's Andrew? Did he let you in?" She slowly opened her eyes, then nippily looked around. "Where am I?"

He chuckled. "You're still in the hotel room. It's almost eleven o'clock and we have to vacate the premises. So up and at 'em. Come on, sleeping head. Let's get moving."

She grabbed the white duvet and pulled it up to her chin. "How did I get here?"

"You stumbled most of the way. But some of it, I suppose we can say you walked."

"Oh. Last night. I was drinking. Heavily. That's right."

"And I told you it was a bad idea that you would *most assuredly* regret in the morning." Darius smirked. "Good thing you and I are such a great team."

"You brought me here."

"Yep."

"And you left me here to sleep it off, and now you've come back to get me."

Darius laughed. "Not quite. So I guess you don't remember?"

"It's a bit hazy, but it's starting to come back. I was upset with Andrew."

"*That's* an understatement. You called him after you came in here —"

"I called him? And you *let* me?"

"Like I could have stopped you from doing whatever you pleased. At least, that's what you told me last night when I was trying to get you to stop a lot of things." Darius got up and went to the closet. He took the hotel-provided white robe off the hanger and laid it on the bed. "Your clothes are over there on the chair. Not that I would see anything *now* that I haven't already seen, compliments of last night."

"You didn't? Please tell me that you didn't . . . we didn't."

"Let's just say that if you had bet me like I proposed, I'd be oh so much richer this morning than when I started last night."

"Tell me you did *not* take advantage of me while I was drunk. Please tell me you didn't." She cringed.

"Paris, don't even try it. I brought you up to this room with good and honorable intentions. You, on the other hand, were like an animal in heat. I'm *only* human." Darius pulled a folded piece of paper out of his pocket and handed it to her.

She looked at it without opening it. "What's this?"

"Something you insisted on writing and giving to me. To sum it up: It says you were of a sound mind and doing what you were doing of your own free will."

"I was drunk. And you knew that I was drunk." She grabbed her head.

"Shhh. Not so loud. When I said pretty much those same words to you, you tried to fight me — literally. That's when you got the notepad they put in these rooms, wrote that note there — see, it has the hotel's logo up top — and you signed it. You said you were 'legally protecting and exonerating' me. Then you proceeded to tell me how long you've wanted me and how incredibly fine and hot you find me and my body."

"You're making that up."

"Okay. The part about me being hot, I did make up. But all the other stuff is true."

She scooted to the edge of the bed, holding the duvet up to her neck, and placed her feet on the floor. She reached over and retrieved the robe. "Turn around please."

Darius giggled. "No problem." He turned his back to her.

She put on the robe, got up, and walked briskly to the chair that held her clothes. "Okay, so I got drunk. You brought me up here. But instead of doing the honorable and decent thing and leaving me, you stayed the night with me?"

"You got drunk. I made sure you were okay. I didn't dare want to leave you alone because if something were to have happened to you, like say you had died or something, then who do you think is the person they'd come looking for?"

"But you didn't have to *sleep* with me."

"You're right. I didn't. And if I was prayed up a bit more and you weren't so doggone fine and irresistible, I might have been able to turn you down. But . . . I'm only human. Believe me though: My original intentions were *purely* honorable."

She stopped next to him. "You say I called Andrew?"

"Yep. And you let him have it. Pow! Right between the kisser. I mean you gave him the what for. You read that man like a page-turner book a friend had loaned you and wanted back now before you were finished."

"Did I tell him what all I knew?"

"No. Fortunately for you, I was here. I took the phone from you. The way you were going off on him, I just knew you were also about to tell him I was here with you."

"Then he's undoubtedly worried about me?" Paris looked around the room.

"What are you looking for?"

"My cell phone."

Darius went and got it off the nightstand and handed it to her. "You can calm down. I fixed it with Andrew for you."

"How? What did you do?"

"I texted him and told him, well, actually he thought it was you texting him, but you told him that you'd had too much to drink and you'd checked into a hotel."

Paris shook her head. "That wouldn't work for Andrew. He would have come looking for me. I know him. He would have come and gotten me."

"I handled that as well. I texted him that Doris was here with you . . . that you were fine, but that you were going to turn off your phone and get some much-needed rest and for him not to bother calling or texting you back."

Paris hurriedly powered up her phone. After it was functional, she read the unread text message and listened to a voice mail message Andrew also left.

"Is everything okay?" Darius asked.

"Yeah. Andrew said he was glad 'Doris' was here with me, and for me to call him as soon as I got his message."

"See, everything worked out, then."

"It looks that way. But I do have one question," Paris said.

"Give it to me."

"*Who* is Doris?"

He laughed. "Beats me. But I supposed you'd better have an answer for Andrew when you talk to him and he asks."

Paris went to the bathroom, got dressed, and Darius drove her home.

Chapter 35

Dare any of you, having a matter against another, go to law before the unjust, and not before the saints?

— 1 Corinthians 6:1

Andrew called Gabrielle. "I need to see you."

"Today?" Gabrielle said.

"If possible. I'm not sure what's going on, but something seems to be."

"Sure. I'll see if I can get someone to keep Jasmine, and I'll be there sometime today."

"If I'm busy, please wait. Just tell my secretary that I'm expecting you so she'll be sure to announce when you've arrived."

"Okay. You have me worried now."

He didn't say anything else to calm her worries. She knew whatever it was, it was either important or serious.

Gabrielle called a few people to see if one of them could keep Jasmine. The list of people she trusted enough to leave Jasmine with was short. She was just about to call Zachary as a last resort when Tiffany called her.

"Hi, Gabrielle. I know this is short notice, but I was wondering if it would be okay for Jasmine to come over to play with Jade today."

"You're off work today?"

"Yes. Darius worked late last night and Junior woke up this morning with a fever. I was trying to wait on Darius to arrive so he could take him to the doctor. I tried calling him, but his phone was off. At first I called in and told them I would be a little late, thinking Darius would be home soon. But after nine o'clock, I called and told them I needed to take the whole day off and I took Junior to the doctor myself."

"Is Junior all right?" Gabrielle asked.

"It was an ear infection. The doctor gave him some medicine. His temperature is back to normal now, so he's fine. But I was home and Jade asked if Jasmine could come over. I told her I'd call you and ask."

"You know . . . this is nobody *but* God," Gabrielle said. "Would you believe I need to go see my lawyer, and I was trying to find someone to watch Jasmine until I got back?"

"Wow, God is awesome, isn't He?"

"You haven't said *nothing* but a word. 'Awesome' doesn't even come *close* to describing our God."

"I know that's right. Well, you just bring Jasmine right on over. I'm here for as long as you need me to keep her."

"Thank you, thank you, thank you. I owe you."

"No, you don't. That's what friends are for," Tiffany said. "Besides, you're doing me a favor by letting Jasmine come. Jade's been moping around for the past few days, talking about how she doesn't have anyone to play with. A street of houses with girls all around her age, and she doesn't get along with any of them the way she does with Jasmine."

"Well, we'll be there shortly."

Gabrielle called Jasmine downstairs and told her she was going over to visit with Jade. Jasmine began jumping up and down with joy. She wanted to change clothes though before they went. Gabrielle shook her head as she smiled, telling her to hurry up because she had somewhere she had to be before it got too late.

Now, if only Andrew would have some positive news for her for a change. "Please, God. I know You're able. Let Andrew have some good news. Please."

The doorbell rang. Gabrielle wondered who that could be. It couldn't be Tiffany, even though it would be just the sort of thing Tiffany would do to help her out. But there hadn't been enough time for her to have gotten there that quickly.

Gabrielle looked out to see who it was. With her back turned, all Gabrielle could tell was that it was a woman with a lot of height on her.

Gabrielle opened the door. "Yes?"

The woman turned around.

"Paris? What are you doing here?"

Paris took her shades off. "We need to talk."

"How did you find out where I live?"

"May I come in?" Paris said, ignoring Gabrielle's questions.

"Well, actually, I was on my way out."

Paris stepped inside anyway. "This shouldn't take long."

"All right," Gabrielle said, closing the door. "Let's go into the den. This way." She led her to the den.

Paris sat down in a wingback chair without being asked and crossed her legs. Gabrielle sat on the sofa.

"I'll get right to the point," Paris said.

"What's the deal with you and my husband?"

"Who? Andrew?"

"Don't try to play dumb with me. That's the only husband I have. I know everything. So let's put the whole shebang on the table so we can resolve this between us, once and for all."

Gabrielle scooted back a little. "Fine. But don't you think you should be talking to your husband about this, instead of here harassing me?"

"Who's harassing you? I came here so you and I can solve our issues, woman to woman . . . Christian to Christian. The Bible tells us that if we have a matter against one another, we should work it out amongst ourselves."

"And yet, the first thing *you* did was take our matter to the court system," Gabrielle said.

"That's because that's where *that* should have gone. It was a legal matter. You wanted to adopt a child and I didn't believe that was in the child's best interest," Paris said.

"But why? What have I ever done that would cause you to believe I'd do anything to harm a child?"

Paris chuckled. "You took my boyfriend from me. After I opened up my home to you, you stabbed me in my back, and you slept with my boyfriend."

"I did not," Gabrielle said. "I never slept with Cedric. I'm telling you the truth. I never slept with him. How many times do I have to say that before you believe me? But you, on the other hand, betrayed Cedric and got with his best friend."

"Oh, okay. So you want to go there, huh? Well, tell me, Miss Gabrielle. How would you happen to know that? If you and Andrew never met, then how would you happen to know that Cedric and Andrew were even friends, let alone best friends?"

"Fine," Gabrielle said, scooting closer to the edge of the sofa. "I told Andrew he should tell you everything."

Paris stood up and walked over to Gabrielle, towering over her. Gabrielle immediately stood to her feet.

"I'm not going to fight you," Paris said. "I have more class than to get down in the gutter to your level. So do you want to inform me when you've had the opportunity to tell *my* husband anything he should be doing with *his* wife?"

"Sit down," Gabrielle said in a soft voice.

"You don't tell me what to do."

"Please," Gabrielle said nicely. "Will you have a seat?"

"You didn't offer me a seat when I came in here." Paris sat down in the wingback chair and crossed her legs again. "In fact, you didn't even have enough manners to ask me to come in when I rang your doorbell. That's why I didn't think you needed to get that child."

"Can we just please stay on one subject at a time?" Gabrielle said as she eased back down on the sofa.

Paris began to swing her top crossed leg. "So when did you and my husband have an occasion to speak about what *he* should be telling *me*?"

"I asked Andrew to tell you that we did, in fact, know each other."

"Well, I already know that now. Why he couldn't tell me the truth in the beginning when I first asked him, I'll never know. But that's beside the point. What I want to know is why you felt the need to go out and hire *my* husband to work against me?"

"I didn't seek your husband out."

Paris stopped swinging her leg and uncrossed them. She leaned forward. "So you really want me to believe that he came looking for *you* to represent *you* against my challenge of you getting to adopt Jasmine."

"If you don't mind, will you please keep your voice down," Gabrielle said as she looked toward the door opening of the den. "Jasmine's here. I don't want her to overhear us."

"If you don't want me to talk loud, then I would suggest you answer my questions so you don't get me upset. You probably recall: I tend to get loud when I'm upset."

"My original attorney, Robert Shaw, put in a request for a lawyer versed in the problems your challenge was posing."

"And he just *happened* to contact the firm where my husband works. And they just *happened* to send out the husband of the woman who was doing the challenging? How convenient. Forget about the ethics and conflicts of interest screaming all over the place." Paris sat back hard against the chair and crossed her arms.

"Would you mind if we pray before we proceed? I just feel you and I should pray together."

"You can pray all you want. I didn't come here to have church with you. I came here for answers. I came here to get to the other side of the lies I've been fed."

"I've not fed you any lies, Paris."

Paris unfolded her arms. "You're a Christian, right?"

"Yes."

"And Christians aren't supposed to lie, right?"

"Correct."

"Okay, Gabrielle. Let's see how much of the Christian talk you actually walk. Did you know Andrew prior to us meeting in the hospital cafeteria that day? Yes or no."

"Yes."

"Did you meet him prior to me kicking you out of my apartment back when you and I lived together? Yes or no."

"Yes."

Paris tightened her mouth as though she'd just eaten something sour. "Did you sleep with Andrew while you were living in my apartment?"

"No."

"When I put you out, did you see him at all after that?"

"Yes."

Paris stared hard at Gabrielle. "When?"

"When he picked me up . . . as I was walking down the street from your apartment with nowhere to go."

"Andrew picked you up? *My* Andrew?"

"He wasn't *your* Andrew at the time. You were with Cedric, remember?" Gabrielle's house phone started ringing. "I need to get that. It's probably the person where I was headed, before you barged in, calling to see where I am."

Paris shrugged. "Let your answering machine or voice mail get it. We're busy, and it would be rude for you to just up and answer the phone when you're entertaining company."

"Not if it's important. And not if my 'company' was an understanding person."

"But it's *not* likely that important. And I'm *not* the understanding type. So let's carry on. This shouldn't be too much longer, especially if you keep answering my questions the way you've been doing." Paris flashed Gabrielle a short, snarky smile. "When Andrew picked you up that day, where did you get him to take you?"

"I didn't get him to *take* me anywhere," Gabrielle said.

"Excuse me? So what did you do? Live in his beat-up old car?"

"He took me home with him."

Paris stood up and held her hand up like a person directing traffic. "Hold up. Did I just hear you correctly? Did you just say that *Andrew* took you home with him?"

Gabrielle stood up, too. "Yes."

Paris scratched the top of her head. "So you were living with my husband?"

"Again, he wasn't your husband at the time. In fact, he wasn't even your boyfriend at the time. The way I understand it to have happened, that came later . . . much later, after you dumped Cedric for him."

Paris frowned. "Did Andrew tell you that?"

"Look, Paris. I don't want to rehash every bit of the past that doesn't amount to a hill of beans." Gabrielle put her hand on her hip. "What's important is: I met him. I knew him back when I lived with you. And he and I never . . . *ever* slept together."

Paris nodded. "So you didn't sleep with my boyfriend Cedric, according to your truth. And you didn't sleep with Andrew, my soon-to-be boyfriend who eventually became my husband?"

"Right. So if your question is why Andrew has stepped up to help me against what you were doing, the answer is: He's a really good man with a really good heart who believes in *really* doing the right thing. He knows it's wrong for you to try and take Jasmine from me."

Paris nodded again as she smirked. "Okay. I have just one more question and I promise then that I'm done."

"All right."

"The baby you were pregnant with . . . the one you gave up for adoption . . . the baby that would be named Jasmine Noble, whose baby was it? Who is her father?"

Gabrielle's legs became wobbly, and she quickly sat down on the sofa to keep from falling to the floor. "Who told you that?"

"Do you dare deny it's the truth?"

Gabrielle shook her head in sheer disbelief. "How did you find that out?"

"Let's just say maybe you're a little too trusting of the people you share your secret information with. And not that you'll heed my advice: But if I were you, I'd watch those I allow access into my inner circle. Again, take it however you like."

"Was it Andrew? Is he the one who told you?" Gabrielle asked. "He said I should tell you. He thought it would make you back away from this nonsense of you trying to take Jasmine from me when her mother *clearly* wanted her with me."

"You mean Jasmine's adoptive mother. Well, Gabrielle, maybe you should have taken the advice of your paid counsel. At least I hope you're paying him. We can always use more money. I have a penchant for expensive shoes." Paris looked down at Gabrielle's brown sandals. "Obviously you and I don't share that same penchant."

"Was it Andrew who told you?" Gabrielle asked again.

"I'll make a deal with you. Tell me the

father's name, and I'll tell you who you need to be careful of with your little secrets." Paris stared hard at Gabrielle.

"I can't. Please, Paris. I don't want Jasmine to end up getting hurt in all of this. She's a child, an innocent little girl."

"I suppose it *would* hurt her to learn that the woman who gave birth to her . . . the woman who didn't want her and simply gave her away, is the same woman trying to adopt her now, wouldn't it? That the woman is you."

"What?" a tiny voice boomed forth from the opening of the room as Jasmine stepped inside. "What?"

Gabrielle spun around. "Jasmine?"

"What does she mean you're my birth mother?" Jasmine stood at the entrance with a puzzled look. "It's you? You gave me away? You didn't want me?"

Gabrielle rushed over to Jasmine and kneeled down. "Honey, what are you doing listening in like that? I've told you it's impolite to eavesdrop on other people's conversations."

"I heard her. She just said that you're my mother."

"You must have misunderstood." Gabrielle looked to Paris for help. Paris held her nose even higher in the air, refusing to look back at Gabrielle.

"You didn't want me, so you gave me away?" Jasmine was crying now.

Gabrielle grabbed her and hugged her as tight as she would allow her.

Paris strolled past the two of them. "You don't have to bother seeing me to the door, Gabrielle. I'll let myself out." She gave Gabrielle a smug look, then left.

CHAPTER 36

For this cause I bow my knees unto the Father of our Lord Jesus Christ.

— Ephesians 3:14

Everything was in turmoil. Paris had come to Gabrielle's house and, with merely a few spoken words, turned her and Jasmine's world completely upside down. Not at all in the way that Gabrielle had planned it, Jasmine had just learned that Gabrielle was her birth mother. A mother she now believed never wanted her.

Tiffany had been the one who had called when the phone rang. Seeing the number on the caller ID, Jasmine had answered it when Gabrielle didn't. Tiffany had been worried that something may have happened to them. Jasmine told her that Gabrielle had company. She'd gone downstairs to tell Gabrielle about the call. She was also eager to go to Jade's house, having put on her new shorts outfit and the sandals Zachary had bought her.

That's when she heard the two women in the den talking. One of them, the one she later saw was Paris, said the words, "I suppose it *would* hurt her to learn that the woman who gave birth to her . . . the woman who didn't want her and gave her away, is the same woman trying to adopt her now."

Jasmine knew she'd been adopted. Gabrielle had told her that. She'd wondered about her real mother. She'd even talked about it with her friend Jade. But she had no idea that the woman she planned to look for and one day find would turn out to be Gabrielle, the same woman trying to adopt her now.

It was confusing and disorienting for an adult, let alone a nine-year-old child.

"If you didn't want me then, what makes you want me now?" Jasmine had asked.

Gabrielle tried to explain how much she did indeed want her. She told her it had been complicated. No matter what Gabrielle said, she couldn't seem to find the precise words to make things right again.

It was well after six o'clock when Andrew called. In all of the confusion and mayhem, she hadn't made it to his office and hadn't even *thought* to call him and advise him of what was going on at this point. There were so many emotions running through her. She could only *imagine* what little Jasmine was going through.

Crying, Gabrielle didn't feel like being cordial *or* polite. "Did you tell her?"

"Tell who what?" Andrew said.

"Paris. Did you tell her what we talked about? Did you tell her you were my lawyer? Did you tell her Jasmine was adopted? And did you tell her that I was Jasmine's birth mother? Did you, Andrew? Did you?"

"No. I mean yes. I mean —"

"Which is it, Andrew? Did you tell her or not? It's a straight-forward question with a straightforward answer. Is that why you wanted to represent me? So you could find out something and feed it to your wife. Did you give her my address so she could show up and shatter everything I've worked so hard to protect?"

"Okay, Gabrielle. I need you to take a breath here."

"Why? So you can get something else out of me and *further* destroy my life?" Gabrielle was working hard to control her sobs. "I trusted you, Andrew. I thought you were different from other people. But I suppose you proved me wrong."

"Gabrielle, let me come over there. I need to explain —"

"What's to explain? What did you want me to come to your office for?"

"To give you a heads-up," Andrew said.

"Well, thanks. Although, I would have preferred the heads-up *before* having my head handed to me on a silver platter. I trusted you. I . . . trusted . . . you! I even prayed about this. I guess I got it wrong, huh? Because I sure thought God was saying it was okay to work with you."

"It *was* okay. I *am* okay," Andrew said. "I was calling to tell you that I told Paris I was representing you because it felt like somehow she already knew. But that's all I told her. You have to believe me. All the other stuff, your address, that you were Jasmine's birth mother, that wasn't any of my doing. I swear to you, Gabrielle, it wasn't me."

"Then who was it?"

"I don't know. But I can't believe Paris came over there. Goodness!"

"Well, believe it." Gabrielle wiped her nose with a tissue. "She was here in living color. And I have a little girl upstairs who has cried her heart out. She cried so hard she ended up crying herself to sleep. And for what? Because Paris had to come here and *express* herself? She's asking me for the name of Jasmine's father, like that's any of her business *or* concern."

"Would you like me to come over?"

"No. There's nothing you can do now. The damage has already been done. Andrew, I need to know the truth. Are you *sure* you didn't tell her? Not even by accident. Or maybe you had some of my records at your house and she went through them."

"No. None of that. I went home during lunchtime today. I decided you were right about me telling Paris that you were my client. She's been acting weird since yesterday. Last night, she called me from some function she was attending, drunk as a skunk and talking all crazy. So when I saw her today, I told her. Naturally, she was upset. But there was nothing to indicate she'd act the way you've just described. Somebody else must have told her about the adoption and everything else between the time I left her and when she showed up at your doorstep. I'm definitely speaking to her about this though. Maybe her working like she's been doing is too much for her to handle. She sounds like someone who has fallen off the edge."

Gabrielle's doorbell rang. "Listen, someone's at my door. I have to go. Hopefully, it's not your wife back for round two. I tell you: She's really testing my relationship with the Lord today."

"I know. And I'm sorry. If you need me, you have my cell number. Call me."

Gabrielle hung up and answered the door. It was Johnnie Mae Landris. "I got your message and came over as soon as I could get here."

Gabrielle fell into her arms. "Thank you so much for coming."

Johnnie Mae hugged her. They went to the den and sat on the sofa together.

"Okay, so tell me what's going on."

Gabrielle filled Johnnie Mae in on everything that had happened, including her conversation with Andrew.

"So if *he* didn't tell her that you're Jasmine's birth mother, then who do you think did?" Johnnie Mae asked.

"I don't know. I've been racking my brain, going over in my mind all of the people who know about it. I've told you and Pastor Landris."

"Well, I can assure you that we didn't say anything. I feel confident that I can speak for Pastor Landris."

"Oh, I know that. I never even considered it was either of you. Then there's Zachary." Gabrielle was ticking off the names, using her fingers to keep count as she looked up at the ceiling on occasion.

Johnnie Mae laughed. "For certain Zachary didn't do it. That man loves him some you."

Gabrielle primped her mouth as she nodded. "I told my lawyer, Andrew Holyfield. Honest . . . he's tops on my suspect list. Andrew just happens to be married to the woman who's causing all of the trouble."

"Gabrielle, I don't want to seem harsh, but why would you hire someone as your lawyer that you *knew* might have an ulterior motive and possibly sabotage you?"

Gabrielle turned to Johnnie Mae. "I knew Andrew from a different time in my life. He was a good friend back then, a really good friend. And I trusted him now. I even prayed about it. I guess I was wrong on all accounts."

"Maybe not," Johnnie Mae said. "Anyone else on your list."

"Fatima and Tiffany from church. And other than her birth father and anyone he may have told, that's it. And I'm positive that he didn't do it."

Johnnie Mae twisted her mouth. "Fatima Adams Howard and Tiffany Connors from church and the dance ministry, huh?"

"Yes. But I only told them recently. It was the night of the slumber party I had here for Jasmine."

Johnnie Mae placed a hand over her mouth as though she was in deep thought.

"What?" Gabrielle said. "Do you know something? If you do, please tell me."

Johnnie Mae took her hand down and shook her head. "No. But I think you should talk to both of them and see if maybe somehow, not on purpose or maliciously, if one of them said something to someone else."

"But I asked them not to say anything to anyone about it. They promised."

Johnnie Mae smiled. "And they're both married. Sometimes married folks may discuss things with each other without even thinking that they're disclosing anything or betraying a confidence."

Gabrielle gave a quick nod. "You're right. I don't believe it was either of them, but I'll certainly ask them."

"Just be careful when you do it. You don't want anyone to be offended. People get defensive when they feel they're under attack — perceived or otherwise."

Gabrielle lowered her head, then raised it back. "Thank you. You're always so wonderful. You're just like a mother to me. I appreciate you *so* much."

Johnnie Mae patted her hand a few times.

"You were upset when you called. I had to come by and check on you. So where is Jasmine right now?"

"Upstairs . . . asleep. She didn't take hearing this in this way too well. She's literally heartbroken. I'm sure she's confused. I just hope this doesn't cause her to have a setback and get sick. Her immune system is still on the mends. Something like this could hurt her in more ways than one." Gabrielle began to cry again. "She wants to know why I didn't want her. She wants to know how I could just give her away without ever looking back. I tried explaining things. I tried to tell her that if there was any way I could have taken care of her myself, I would *never,* not in a million years, have given her up. I don't know if I'll ever be able to fully make her understand."

Johnnie Mae patted Gabrielle's hand again. "She will. Just keep at it. Show her all the love you have for her. You'll make her see. It's obvious you love her very much. Love has a way of breaking down walls. Love has its own way of speaking to the heart from the heart — heart to heart. You'll figure out a way to reach her."

"I'm sorry to have dragged you away from your family. Looks like whenever I have a crisis, I run to you."

Johnnie Mae smiled. "When I told Pastor Landris that I needed to come see about you, he literally shoved me out of the door. We care about you and what you're going through. And just between me and you: I think he and the children wanted me gone just so they could take the ground beef I was planning to make meatloaf out of and make hamburgers instead."

Gabrielle let out a short chuckle. "Please thank Pastor Landris for me. The two of you . . ." Gabrielle started crying again and covered her face with her hands.

Johnnie Mae pulled her into her arms and rocked her as she hugged her. Johnnie Mae began to pray. Gabrielle slid down on her knees as Johnnie Mae prayed, Johnnie Mae's hand then resting on Gabrielle's head.

Johnnie Mae prayed for guidance, wisdom, comfort, and healing. "Lord, I thank You for hearing me always," she said as she came to a close of her prayer. "And as always, we'll give You all the praises and all the glory, in Jesus's name, Amen."

Chapter 37

> Whom I have sent unto you for the same purpose, that ye might know our affairs, and that he might comfort your hearts.
>
> — Ephesians 6:22

The doorbell rang.

"It appears you have some more company," Johnnie Mae said. She stood to her feet and headed toward the front door. "You're going to be all right. You and I just went to the throne of God and kneeled at His feet. It's going to be all right. You just hold on." Johnnie Mae hugged her again. "I'll be in touch, okay? Now, if you need me, you know to just call me."

Gabrielle nodded, then hugged Johnnie Mae. She opened the door. Zachary was standing there.

"Hello, Zachary," Johnnie Mae said. She hugged Gabrielle once more and kissed her forehead. She then hugged Zachary and patted him on his hand.

Johnnie Mae stepped out the door, Zachary fully inside now. Gabrielle closed the door.

"You called the pastor's wife?" Zachary asked.

"She's more than the pastor's wife to me. She's like a mother."

Zachary nodded. "She's a good woman. She really is."

"Yes, she is."

"So where's Jasmine?"

"Upstairs. She's asleep." Gabrielle started to cry once more. "I'm sorry. I seem to be a regular water fountain today. She's hurt, Zachary. Jasmine is *so* hurt. You should have seen the look on her face when she was questioning me as the mother who didn't want her. It was awful."

"I'm going upstairs to check on her."

Gabrielle nodded as she wiped her eyes with her hands. Zachary hurried up the stairs. Gabrielle went to the den and balled up into a fetal position on the couch. Zachary came in the den ten minutes later and gathered her up in his arms.

"Tell me what happened," he said.

"I don't know. Somebody told Paris that Jasmine was adopted and that I was her birth mother. She came over here, throwing up everything she knew in my face. Jasmine heard her say that I was her mother who didn't want her in the beginning, and" — Gabrielle began to cry louder — "that . . . I . . . gave . . . her . . . away!"

Zachary rocked her in his arms. "I wish I'd been here. I'm so sorry you and Jasmine had to go through that alone."

"It's not your fault. You didn't tell anyone about me being her birth mother, did you?"

"Of course not. I just wish I'd been here so I could have thrown that woman out on her righteous —"

"Don't," Gabrielle said, holding her head up and looking into his eyes. "I know it's hard, but don't you *dare* let her take you there."

He guffawed. "I'm just so mad right now. You shouldn't have let her in the house. You should have thrown her out when she first started sounding like she was going to be trouble."

"She was accusing me of so much. How was I to know she knew all about me having given birth to Jasmine? I'd told Jasmine she was adopted, so that was no longer a secret. But only a handful of folks knew about me being her birth mother."

"So how do you think Paris found out?"

"I don't know. I've been racking my brain

trying to think of whom and how."

"Knowing Paris, she likely hired a private investigator. I wonder if she knows who the birth father is as well."

Gabrielle sat up completely and shook her head. "I don't think that she does. She kept asking . . . wanting to know Jasmine's birth father's name."

His voice escalated. "What business is *that* of hers?"

"That's what I said. She claims that someone I told is how she learned about me being Jasmine's birth mother. She was implying someone I trusted wasn't worth trusting."

"If that's true, then it likely wasn't a private investigator who told her," Zachary said.

"That's what I'm thinking. She said she would trade the name of the person I needed to watch in my circle for the name of the man who fathered my baby."

"Who do you think may have done it?"

"I have a short list of those who knew. You, of course —"

"Well, I hope you know I didn't do it. I would never do anything to hurt you."

She took his hand and squeezed it. "I know that." She released his hand. "There's Johnnie Mae and Pastor Landris."

"You can cross them off the list, too."

She smiled. "I already did."

"Of course, there's Lawrence and his friend William."

"I don't see Lawrence doing that since he's been trying so hard to shut his daughter down on this whole situation. He wouldn't dare do himself in like that."

"Trying hard, unsuccessfully, I might add. Although I believe her learning that Andrew was my lawyer may have effectively put a nail in *that* coffin."

"So she knows Andrew is representing you?"

"Yes. According to him, he told her today before she came over." Gabrielle began to play with her hands as she spoke.

"Then he must have also told her you're Jasmine's birth mother. Maybe that was his way of shutting her down before this court stuff went any further."

"I asked him. He said he didn't tell her that."

"So, do you believe him?"

Gabrielle pressed her hand to her chest. "In my heart, I do. But my head keeps trying to tell me that my heart could possibly be wrong."

Zachary laughed and placed his hand on her hand still over her heart. "Personally,

I'd say go with your heart. So far, your heart hasn't steered you wrong."

"So you don't think Andrew told her?"

Zachary shook his head. "I don't. I think he really sincerely wanted to help you. I don't see him stabbing you in the back like that. I don't."

Gabrielle forced a smile. "Thank you for that. I was starting to question my heart and to question whether I'd really heard from God."

He took her hand and gently caressed it. "Don't. Don't question your heart and don't question when you know God has told you something. Things don't always work the way we think. But if God speaks it, even when the devil tries to do us in, God will use it for our good. I truly believe that."

Gabrielle smiled and nodded. She wiped her eyes. "Now I just need to figure out who told Paris. I wouldn't put it past William Threadgill. He just might be a double-crossing snake in the grass. He has those shifty eyes. And he talks fast when he's trying to pull a fast one on you."

"I don't think it was William. If William was going to use it to double-cross Lawrence, he would likely use it purely for financial gain. He would leak it to the press or Lawrence's opponent." Zachary shook his head. "I don't see it being him."

"The only other people I've told are Fatima and Tiffany. That night when we had that slumber party for Jasmine, the three of us were talking about babies . . . more to the point, having babies. I became emotional. I told them what I'd done; they promised not to tell anyone."

"You know: The thing about a secret is the way people will tell that secret to someone else as *their* little secret. The best way to keep a secret from ever getting out is to keep the secret to one's self."

"So you're saying I shouldn't have told them?" Gabrielle stared into his eyes.

He took her hand and lovingly planted a kiss on it. "No, that's not what I'm saying. Everybody needs someone they can share things with. But that's my point. We all have a need to share something that bothers us or eats away at our insides. It's good to get it out, but then the person who has that information may have a need to share and get it out of them with someone else."

"So you think either Fatima or Tiffany may have told someone, only as a secret for them not to tell anyone?"

"Precisely. Not maliciously. Not to gossip. But let's say they're talking to their respective husbands and they happen to share that tidbit of information with them. They're not thinking that their husbands will tell anyone. Most wives I've spoken with wonder if their husbands are ever even listening."

"If Tiffany told Darius, I wouldn't put it past him to tell it or sell it. He was the one who was spreading the information about my past as an exotic dancer throughout our church last year. Do you think it might be him?"

"I don't know. But what I *would* do is ask both Fatima and Tiffany to see if they told anyone. But you just need to be careful in how you do it. Many great friendships have been broken up because of secrets shared among friends and the aftermath that arises when those secrets are breeched and the friends confronted."

"That's just what Johnnie Mae was telling me." Gabrielle looked at Zachary. "I'm so thankful that God sent you into my life. I really am."

He took her hand and kissed it, this time holding his lips to her hand. He then sheepishly looked at her. "When you marry me, I'll know that you really mean that."

She smiled. "Soon."

"Promise?"

"Cross my heart and hope to live with you for the rest of our lives here on this earth."

She pulled her hand away from his and made a cross sign with her index finger over her heart.

"Dr. Z?" Jasmine said in a quiet voice.

He quickly turned in the direction of Jasmine. She ran full-out into his arms and started crying. "It hurts, Dr. Z. It hurts so much." He stood up and rocked her. "Make it better. Please, make it better," she cried.

Gabrielle stood and placed her hand on Jasmine's back. She held it there without saying anything or doing anything to interfere with their moment together.

CHAPTER 38

> And your feet shod with the preparation of the gospel of peace.
>
> — Ephesians 6:15

Gabrielle called Fatima first. They'd become really close over the past year. She didn't want to do something like this over the phone, so she asked if she could come over.

Both Fatima and Trent owned a house when they married in May. Fatima talked Trent into selling his house and moving into hers, which was the bigger of the two. So she still resided at the same address. Fatima was in the kitchen cooking dinner when she arrived. They hugged and proceeded to perform all the usual niceties and courtesies.

Gabrielle sat at the kitchen counter in a tall metal-back chair while Fatima rinsed off broccoli in the sink. Fatima dried her hands and came over to the other side and sat in the chair right next to Gabrielle.

"Okay, Gabrielle. I can tell something is bothering you. Tell me what's up?"

Gabrielle smiled. "You know me *too* well."

"I know you well enough. So tell me what's going on."

"I need to ask you something, but I don't want you taking it the wrong way or thinking that I'm accusing you or anything like that."

"Okay."

"You remember at the slumber party when we were talking that night, girl talk?"

"Yeah." Fatima beamed. "That was a great time. And the talking helped me so much. It made me look differently at whether or not I wanted children this late in the game."

Gabrielle smiled. "I'm glad. I enjoyed it as well." Gabrielle swallowed hard.

"Gabrielle, whatever you want to ask or say, just say it. I promise I won't take whatever it is the wrong way."

Gabrielle gave a nod. "That night, we talked about Jasmine being adopted and I told you and Tiffany that I was, in truth, her birth mother."

Fatima nodded. "Yeah. Now that *really* took me by surprise. I didn't know exactly what to do with that information. I've never heard of such a thing. By that I mean: giving your child up for adoption and then years later being in a situation where you're about to adopt your own child back. That was mind-boggling."

"It is sort of mysterious, isn't it? But God works in mysterious ways. He has a way that will blow our minds, if we'll only allow Him the opportunity to do so."

"I know that's right. Okay, so you told us that. What's going on?"

"Paris came to my house yesterday afternoon."

"Paris? Paris? Who is Paris? Oh, wait, I know you're not talking about the woman trying to take Jasmine from you? *That* Paris?"

"Yes, *that* one."

"Why did she come see you? Is she ready to drop this whole nonsense?"

"I believe she is now."

"Well, praise the Lord! That's good news. Right? Why aren't you celebrating? You don't appear to be celebrating."

"That's because I'm not. Paris somehow found out that Jasmine is my biological child. There's other stuff to this story that I won't get into right now. But the end result is: She accused me of giving away my child because I didn't want her."

"What? You've *got* to be kidding me!"

"Nope. I wish I were. But that's not even

the worst part. The worst part is that Jasmine overheard her."

"Oh, my goodness! You poor thing." Fatima stood up and hugged Gabrielle. "I understand why you're so distraught. How is Jasmine?"

"Jasmine's not taking it well at all. She doesn't want to talk to me. She thinks I didn't want her. She's hurting." Gabrielle started crying even though she had vowed not to. "I'm sorry. I thought I was all cried out, but I guess I'm not." She fanned her face to stop the tears. Gabrielle reached over and tore off a sheet of paper towel, thankful that it was the good kind, soft enough to use to wipe away her spent tears.

Fatima sat back down. "How did she find out about you being Jasmine's birth mother and giving her up for adoption? Do you know?"

"That's why I'm here. I don't know. It's not in any records for her to find out that way. Not any she could get her hands on anyway. She told me she'd gotten the information from someone in my inner circle."

"She's claiming someone close to you told it?"

"Yes."

"Well, it wasn't me. I don't even know the lady. And if I did, after what she's done and put you through, there would be some words exchanged, and believe me: They wouldn't be 'God bless you' and 'Praise the Lord.' "

Gabrielle placed her hand over Fatima's. "I hate to do this, but I have to ask you. I'm not saying that *if* you did it, it was done intentionally to hurt me. But did you happen to tell anyone . . . anyone at all, about me being Jasmine's birth mother?"

Fatima recoiled from Gabrielle's words. "No. I'm telling you, whoever it was, it wasn't me." She leaned in closer to Gabrielle. "I value our friendship too much. You were there for me when my mother passed away. I'll never forget how wonderful you've been since we've become associates and then friends."

Gabrielle touched Fatima's hand. "And you are a good friend to me. But is it possible you may have mentioned it to Trent?"

"No. I didn't even mention it to him. I wouldn't do that. I wouldn't. You have to believe me, Gabrielle. If I had, I would tell you the truth. He's my husband, and if I had told him, I wouldn't have a problem telling you I'd done so." She shook her head. "But I didn't. I didn't."

"I didn't think that you would. But as you said, Trent is your husband. We all need someone to confide in. I can see a wife telling her husband something and not thinking she's divulging anything wrongly."

"If that were the case, I'd agree with you. But in my case, it didn't happen."

Gabrielle leaned over and hugged her. "Thank you. I hope you understand that I had to ask."

"So, have you talked to Tiffany about this yet?"

"No. She's the final person on my list. If it's not her, I have no clue where it could have come from because there are only about a handful of folks who know."

"I don't mean to start anything. And the Lord knows I don't want to be viewed as a gossiper or a talebearer. But that husband of hers, Darius . . . I wouldn't trust him with a ten-foot pole."

"I've kind of picked up that you don't care for him much. It almost borders on hate. After what he did last year by spreading what he did all over the congregation about me, I can understand if he's ever done something like that to you."

"Darius is a snake and a two-timing dog, that's all I have to say about the man."

"Wow, Fatima. You say that as though you truly know of which you speak."

Fatima stood up and paced around the

kitchen for about a minute without saying a word. She stopped and looked straight into Gabrielle's awaiting eyes. "Listen, I have something I need to get off of my chest. It's been eating away and eating away at me, and I need some release. I need to tell *somebody.*"

Gabrielle stood up and went to her. "Okay. Come and sit down." They sat down at the kitchen table. "I'm here if you'd like to talk to me about it."

"You have your own problems, Gabrielle. You don't need me dumping my garbage on you. Not at this point."

"Fatima, we're sisterfriends. Remember? So tell me."

"I don't know how you say something like this."

"You just open your mouth and say it. I promise: Whatever it is, I'm not going to judge you on it. I love you, Fatima. You really are like a sister to me."

Fatima was crying now. She snatched up a napkin out of the holder on the table. "Really? Because that's exactly how I feel about you."

Gabrielle nodded. "So please tell me. Get it out of you. I'm here."

Fatima sucked in a deep breath, then exhaled slowly as she said, "I had an affair with Darius Connors."

Gabrielle jerked back from Fatima.

"See, I knew I shouldn't have told you."

"When?" Gabrielle leaned closer and took her hand. "When was this?"

"Oh, it's been some years back. I broke it off for good in 2005. It was hard; I'm not going to lie. But God was with me every step of the way. Then God sent me Trent."

"I take it Tiffany doesn't know anything about this."

"Do I look like a fool to you?" Fatima said, then chuckled slightly. "Of course she doesn't know. I didn't even know her at the time. The affair lasted for about three years. After I broke it off with him, I met Tiffany. Because of the dance ministry, Tiffany and I ended up becoming friends. I certainly couldn't tell her something like that then. When is the right time to tell a woman you care about and you don't want to hurt that you once had an affair with her husband? Even if it was before we met."

Gabrielle shrugged. "Good question." But Gabrielle was thinking: *When is the right time to tell a one-time friend that you once slept with her father?*

"I know what kind of a person Darius is. He's a liar and a cheat. And those are his good qualities. Tiffany has no idea. She thinks he's a good man. But I know better."

"Well, he might have changed since you knew him," Gabrielle said. "People *do* change. Look at me: I changed."

"Yes, people do change. But I see the same slick guy, if not more so, that I knew back when. And he's *still* getting over on Tiffany. Sometimes, I just want to grab her up and shake her and tell her to wake up and see what's going on right before her eyes."

"She probably knows. On some level, she knows. My friend, Clarence Walker, busted Darius right in front of her once. It was last year, when Darius was spreading that information about me being an exotic dancer throughout the congregation. Clarence let her know that her husband had been hanging out at the strip club, paying his hard-earned money to see me and women like me."

"I'm sure Darius lied his way out of it." Fatima looked at Gabrielle with intensity. "So what do you think we should do? What can *I* do to help if anything? I don't want to accuse anyone of anything, but in my gut, I think Darius may be at the heart of this information getting out by way of Tiffany."

"First, I'm going to ask Tiffany because I don't want to indict her without giving her a fair hearing. Maybe she *did* tell him. And maybe he somehow found a way to tell Paris. That part I still can't quite figure out."

"While you're asking her things, ask her where her husband works. That's if he really *does* have a job, which I'm starting to question by the way she changes the subject if anyone asks her about it. That could be a clue. If he's really working, maybe there's a tie-in there somewhere. You never know. If not, maybe he found a way to sell the information either to this Paris directly or to someone close to her."

"You're right. You never know." Gabrielle stood up. "Well, I'm going to get going. Zachary is *so* great. He's with Jasmine. I think he's trying to get her to see things in a better light. I can't get her to talk to me at all. She's shut down on me completely. If I try to talk to her, she won't even look at me."

"You need to go on and marry that man before he ends up getting away."

Gabrielle smiled. "Trust me: I have every intention of marrying him. But I can only fight one battle at a time. And believe me: His mother is not going to be an easy battle. She says she likes me just fine, but she just doesn't want me marrying her son." Gabrielle shook her head. "Yep. Another battle for another day. For now, I have to settle things with my baby girl."

"At least you have your priorities in the right place. Jasmine needs you. Although, from the way Zachary acts when he's around you, that man needs you, too. He is *so* in love with you."

Gabrielle hugged Fatima. "Thanks for everything. Pray for me."

"Always. Let me know what you find out," Fatima said.

"Will do. Oh, and Fatima?"

"Yeah?"

"Your secret . . . the one you just shared . . . it's safe with me."

Fatima hugged *her* this time around. "Thank you." She released a loud sigh. "I feel so much lighter now that I've gotten that off my chest and out of my head. It can be heavy carrying around something like that and never feeling like you can tell it."

"That's the way the truth works, I suppose." Gabrielle walked over to the door. Fatima opened it. "The truth will make you free." She hugged her. "Bye now."

Chapter 39

> If any thing be revealed to another that sitteth by, let the first hold his peace.
>
> — 1 Corinthians 14:30

Gabrielle called Tiffany to see if she could stop by. She decided since she was already out, she might as well take care of everything all at one time.

"I've been worried *sick* about you," Tiffany said after she opened the door and led Gabrielle to the kitchen. "Come on in here and we can talk while I finish cooking. I'm trying to finish before Darius gets home." Tiffany frowned. "So what's going on?"

"I'm sorry about yesterday afternoon," Gabrielle said.

"You were bringing Jasmine over. I waited and waited, then after a while, I became concerned because you hadn't shown up or called. That's when I called and Jasmine told me you had company," Tiffany said.

"Jade's worried about Jasmine because she won't talk to her. Jade thinks she's done something to cause Jasmine to be mad at her. What is going *on*?"

Gabrielle was sitting at the glass table. She picked up a napkin and began dabbing her eyes.

Tiffany put her arm around Gabrielle's neck. "You're crying. Please tell me what's going on. Did you hear back from the court on your case? They're not taking Jasmine away from you, are they? Please tell me that's not it."

Gabrielle shook her head as she sniffled. "No. That's not it. I'm sorry. Tiffany, I need to ask you something."

Tiffany sat down at the table. "Okay. Whatever it is, if it's in my power to do it, you know I'm there." She took hold of Gabrielle's hand and squeezed it.

Gabrielle smiled. "It's a question really. Possibly two."

"All right. I'm listening."

"The night of the slumber party when I told you and Fatima the truth about Jasmine and me . . ."

Tiffany released Gabrielle's hand. "I have to admit: That was *truly* a shocker."

"Yeah." Gabrielle looked hard into Tiffany's face. "Did you happen to mention what I told you to anyone?"

"No. Of course not. You asked us not to."

"I know. But somehow it's come out."

Tiffany sat back, leaning slightly away from Gabrielle. "Well, it wasn't me, if that's what you're implying."

"I'm not implying or accusing you of doing anything . . . not on purpose anyway."

"Not on purpose or otherwise. Have you spoken with Fatima?" Tiffany sat up straighter.

"Yes. She said it wasn't her."

Tiffany twisted her mouth. "So why are you trying to find out about it? What exactly happened?"

"The woman who has been causing me problems in my efforts to adopt Jasmine came to my house yesterday. She blurted out the facts about Jasmine being my child that I'd given up for adoption."

Tiffany put her hand over her mouth. "Oh, my goodness, no," she said, taking her hand down from her mouth. "Please don't tell me —"

Gabrielle nodded and rocked slowly. "Yes. Jasmine overheard every word. And now she's devastated, absolutely devastated."

"That poor child. I can only imagine. So that's why she shut down."

"Yes. She won't talk to me. She just sits

and stares. About the only person she'll respond to much at all is Zachary. In fact, he's with her right now."

"I can't believe someone would be so evil as to put you through what you're telling me this woman is putting you through. That's just the devil there."

"She didn't *just* start doing things like this. I haven't said *too* much to many people. But she's been trying to stop me from getting Jasmine so she can adopt her."

"You've *got* to be kidding. I had no idea you were going through all of this. I knew you were having delays with the adoption going through, but I just figured it was how the process normally worked. I also knew you'd helped when they were searching for a bone marrow donor. I knew you'd taken the leave of absence to help them over the past months. And I knew after the mother died, you were in the process of trying to legally adopt Jasmine. But to have somebody do something like this . . ." Tiffany shook her head as she sneered.

"The woman's name is Paris. Ironically, I knew her long before all of this. I stayed at her apartment for about two and half months when I was eighteen."

Tiffany laughed. "There seems to be quite a *few* people around with the name Paris these days. Darius works with a woman named Paris."

"The name Paris isn't all that common," Gabrielle said.

"Yeah, I know."

"So where exactly does Darius work?"

"Excuse me?"

"I asked where does Darius work. I was here the day he came in and said he'd gotten a new job. I was wondering where he's working?" Gabrielle readjusted her body in the chair and clasped her hands together.

"He doesn't actually work for a company. It's more like service work."

"That sounds interesting. So who is he doing work for?"

Tiffany gave a short laugh. "Most likely nobody you'd know."

"Tiffany, why don't you want to tell me? Is it some kind of secret or something?"

"No. Darius just told me if I tell people they might think I'm bragging or something. I'm proud of where he works and what he's doing," Tiffany said.

"If it's not a secret, and you know I wouldn't dare think you were bragging, not the way you were praying for him to get a new job, then tell me." Gabrielle fixed her eyes on Tiffany's.

Tiffany grinned and became almost giddy.

"I've wanted to tell somebody this for the longest!" She continued grinning. "He's working on this campaign to get Lawrence Simmons reelected. You probably remember him; he did that bone marrow drive back when everybody was trying to find a donor match for Jasmine."

Gabrielle suddenly became sick to her stomach.

Tiffany frowned as she touched Gabrielle's hand. "Are you okay? You don't look so hot."

Gabrielle started fanning herself with her hands. "May I have some water?"

Tiffany hurried and got Gabrielle a glass of cold water. Gabrielle took sips, occasionally pressing the glass to her head.

"Are you all right? Should I call someone for you? Do you want me to call Zachary?"

Gabrielle waved her off. "I'm okay." She placed her hand over her heart. "Tiffany, this is important. Did you happen to mention to Darius about me giving my baby up for adoption? Please, Tiffany; this is important."

Tiffany took a deep breath and frowned.

"Please, Tiffany. I really need to know if you did."

"He's my husband," Tiffany said, now on the verge of tears. "He's hardly ever interested in things that have to do with me or the kids."

"Did you tell him?"

"I *may* have mentioned something to him along those lines." Tiffany put her hands up to her face and began to shake her head. "But he wouldn't have said anything." She took her hand down and looked at Gabrielle. "Why would he? He doesn't really care about you. I don't mean that to sound cruel or anything, but he *doesn't* care, not enough to tell your business to anyone. The woman who's been giving you troubles in adopting Jasmine . . . what's her last name?"

Gabrielle took Tiffany by the hand and squeezed it.

Tiffany shook her head slowly as tears fell. "No."

"Her name is Paris Simmons —"

"No," Tiffany said, her voice cracking.

"Holyfield."

Tiffany continued shaking her head in disbelief. "Darius told her? He was the one who told her? He was using me to get information to give to her? That's why he was always asking me how things were going with you. He was feeding her with information." She pressed her lips tight. "That's why he offered to keep the children, his children that he never volunteered to keep, whenever we were going to be doing something together. He wanted me to find out things so he could carry it back to her."

"Don't get *too* upset. I don't want to be the cause of any problems between you two."

"Oh, you're not the cause. You're merely the heat bringing the light that's being shed on this dark situation." Tiffany folded her arms. "Last year he lied about being the one spreading that information about you. He lies about other women." She unfolded her arms. "He thinks I'm stupid, but I'm not. I know for a *fact* he's had a least one affair while we've been married, even if I don't know the name of the woman. He's just a liar, plain and simple. But my part in this ruse ends today."

"I'm sorry, Tiffany. All I came here to do was to find out who may have told."

"And surprise, surprise, turns out it was *me.*"

"But you didn't do it on purpose. You didn't know."

"It doesn't matter. You told me something in confidence. And I was foolish enough to share it with the person I'm supposed to be one with, never thinking it would go any further than our bedroom pillow."

"I don't want to leave you like this, but I

really need to be getting home." Gabrielle stood up.

Tiffany stood as well. "I have one question for you. Has Darius ever come on to you? Has he ever hit on you?"

"Tiffany, don't do this to yourself."

Tiffany chuckled. "Just as I thought. You're too honest of a person to lie so you merely divert. What about Fatima? Do you know if he's ever come on to her?"

"I can't answer for anyone else."

Tiffany nodded. "Fair enough. Then I'll just ask her myself."

Gabrielle hugged Tiffany. "Pray before you do anything. Okay?"

"Sure," Tiffany said. "And I am *so* sorry for what my action has caused you."

"Well, I'm going to believe that what Satan meant for bad, God will use it for good. I have to believe and hold on to that. Otherwise, I'd probably lose my mind right about now." Gabrielle took Tiffany's hand and gave it one last quick squeeze. "I'll talk to you later. Keep us in your prayers."

"I will. And you do the same for us." Tiffany walked Gabrielle to the door.

Gabrielle stood on the other side of the door after it closed, placing her hand on it as she said a quick prayer.

CHAPTER 40

Hold fast the form of sound words, which thou hast heard of me, in faith and love which is in Christ Jesus.

— 2 Timothy 1:13

Gabrielle walked into the house tired, but determined to keep going no matter what. She could hear Jasmine and Zachary in the den playing checkers.

"Crown me. Crown me!" Jasmine said with a child's sinister laugh.

Gabrielle almost didn't want to go in and ruin what sounded like Jasmine being happy. She knew as soon as Jasmine saw her, she'd likely shut down as quickly as she'd done the last day and a half.

Gabrielle took a deep breath, put a smile on her face, and stepped into view. "Hi there."

Zachary looked up and smiled. "Hi. You came back, and not a minute too soon. I'm getting beat by this little nine-year-old genius."

"Yes, I'm back."

"I take it you were able to finish up all of your business?" Zachary said.

Jasmine got up from the checkerboard and started toward the entrance opening. Gabrielle was sure she was about to do what she'd done since hearing Paris's revelation — refuse to remain in the same room with her, if she could at all help it, any longer than she had to. Tears began to sting Gabrielle's eyes. This hurt so much. And no matter what she said or did, she didn't seem able to fix it. She wanted to reach out and pull Jasmine into her heart, to hug her so tightly that the ice enshrining her whole being now would simply melt.

Jasmine stopped as soon as she was close to Gabrielle. Gabrielle wasn't sure if she should attempt to reach out to her or stand to the side so she could walk by unimpeded.

Zachary stood up and looked their way. She could feel his heart reaching out to her . . . to Jasmine from where he stood.

Jasmine must have felt it, too, because she turned back and looked at Zachary. He smiled at her and nodded. Jasmine turned and took a step forward, then stopped.

"Miss G?"

Shocked that Jasmine had actually said anything to her without being prompted, Gabrielle struggled to find her voice. "Yes, baby."

Jasmine held her head higher, her face seemingly set like harden dough. Then all of a sudden, the most beautiful thing Gabrielle had seen since Gabrielle told Jasmine she could change into her new shorts outfit to wear to Jade's house yesterday: Jasmine smiled. "I love you," Jasmine said.

Gabrielle couldn't help it; she started crying, placing her hand up to her mouth as she dropped down to her knees. "Well, I love you more." She hugged Jasmine.

Jasmine wrapped her arms around Gabrielle tightly. "I'm sorry I hurt you."

Gabrielle continued to hold her. She nodded. "It's okay. It's okay. And I'm sorry you had to find that out in the way that you did. I would never do anything to *purposely* hurt you. I hope you know that. Never."

Jasmine pulled away from Gabrielle's embrace and looked into her eyes as she smiled. "I know. But when I first heard it, I thought you didn't want me."

"Oh, baby. I've always wanted you. Always! And I've always wanted you to have the best life has to offer. I wanted and want you more than words can say. That's why

I'm fighting so hard to make sure you and I are family — officially."

"We're already family," Jasmine said. "In here." She placed her hand over her heart. "Dr. Z and I had a nice long talk while you were gone. He told me how much you *really* love me. He told me how special I am. To have a mother who loved me enough that she gave me life. And when she felt like she couldn't do right by me, not because of anything she'd done, she . . . you . . . loved me enough to place me in the arms of someone who could and would."

"Dr. Z is right. You are . . . a *very* special little girl. And I thank God every day of my life for you."

Jasmine nodded. "Dr. Z said when I needed you, when my life depended upon it, that you were there for me. You didn't think about yourself; all you thought about was making sure I was all right."

Gabrielle was so overwhelmed with emotion she could only nod her head.

Jasmine continued. "I remember that first day I saw you . . . in the hospital. You came in and you just looked at me. I thought it was because I wasn't the prettiest looking child at the time. Dr. Z said you couldn't speak because of how beautiful you thought I was. He said I took your breath away."

She turned back and looked at him.

Gabrielle nodded. She forced out her words. "Dr. Z speaks the truth. When I look at you, you *always* take my breath away. Love can be hard to put into words."

Jasmine laughed. "That's exactly what Dr. Z said." She turned back and looked at him once more, then gave him a thumbs-up.

Gabrielle looked up at Zachary and smiled.

"Dr. Z said you've done more to show me how much you love me than words will ever say. You gave me life, you gave me parents who loved me . . . and, Miss G, they *did* love me. They were *so* good to me. They were."

Gabrielle nodded. "I know. I'm just glad to hear you say it was so."

"I know. Because some children end up with parents who don't love them or treat them right." Jasmine placed her hand on Gabrielle's shoulder. "Like *you* had to go through." Jasmine looked at Zachary again. "Dr. Z told me how your mother died when you were a little girl, younger than me. And that your father was sent away. How you had to go live with another family, and they didn't always treat you with love."

As hard as she was trying not to, Gabrielle

was *really* crying now. She nodded. "That's right."

"I don't mean to make you cry." Jasmine hugged her.

Gabrielle stood up. "It's okay. I'm fine."

Jasmine took Gabrielle by the hand and pulled her over to the couch, where they all sat down — Jasmine sandwiched in between Gabrielle and Zachary.

Jasmine turned to Gabrielle. "I know you didn't have any other choice at that time. I understand all of that now."

Gabrielle touched Jasmine's hand. "We always have choices. I just made the one I felt was the least about *me* and the most about *you.* If I had kept you —"

"You don't have to say it," Jasmine said. "Dr. Z told me how life works. He said you could have made a different choice and I might have been wishing my life was totally different. You just never know."

"Dr. Z lays too heavy of things that sweet little girls like you don't truly need to be bothered with sometimes." Gabrielle cut her eyes at Zachary.

"It's not too heavy. He just knows how smart I am and that I can handle real talk." Jasmine grinned up at Zachary, who winked back at her.

Gabrielle laughed. "Real talk, huh? Yeah.

Real talk."

"But I know you did the best you could *when* you could. I just thought you didn't want me, and that hurt. It did. It hurt."

Gabrielle hugged her. "People who give their children up for adoption don't always do it because they don't want them. In fact, sometimes it's because they want them so much. Knowing you were in this world somewhere gave me hope. I prayed you would someday want to find me and that we could have this talk. But —"

"But God had plans with an earlier timetable," Jasmine said, pulling out of Gabrielle's embrace and looking up at Gabrielle. "So we met now."

Gabrielle pulled Jasmine into her arms and held her. "I love you so much. I wish you only knew *just* how much. And there's nothing . . . *nothing* I wouldn't do to protect and take care of you. Nothing."

Jasmine pulled away and looked up at Gabrielle. "I know. I love you . . . Miss G."

Gabrielle broke down in tears, reeling Jasmine back into her arms. "I love you more, Miss Jazz."

CHAPTER 41

> Therefore thus saith the Lord God; An adversary there shall be even round about the land; and he shall bring down thy strength from thee, and thy palaces shall be spoiled.
>
> — Amos 3:11

Darius stepped lively in the house, having come from work where, for the second day in a row, Paris again hadn't shown up. It had been two days now since he'd last laid eyes on her. That was fine with him because he really didn't feel like dealing with any drama Paris might have from all that had recently transpired between them. He and Paris had both broken their marriage vows. Yes, they'd slept together. He'd done it a few times before, so it didn't bother him as much. But he knew that women weren't as adept to committing adultery as maybe men were. At least, that was his perspective on it. He hadn't found a woman yet who'd been with him and not regretted the act of having committed a sin after it was over, including those who *weren't* big-time Christians. They all seemed to wrestle with what they'd done.

But they generally got over it soon enough. And they were usually right back doing it again with seemingly less guilt, even though they promised him and themselves it would never happen again. He'd just never worked with a woman he'd cheated with. He didn't know how something like that might work out. So Paris's absence from work was giving him time to work things out in his head.

He found Tiffany sitting at the kitchen table.

"Hey, babe." He leaned down and kissed her on her cheek. "Something smells good in here. It's good to be home at this time of day for a change. So what's for dinner?"

"Nothing," she said, devoid of any feelings or emotion.

He walked over to the stove and lifted the top off the black iron skillet to find cooked spaghetti sauce. He then lifted the top off a pot only to find nothing but a pot of water. "You haven't cooked the spaghetti noodles yet?" He put the top back on the pot. "And it's eerily quiet around here. So where are the kids?"

"Fatima has them."

He quickly turned to Tiffany. "Fatima? You mean Fatima Adams?"

Tiffany was being robotic. "Fatima Howard."

"Yeah, yeah. That's right. She married that computer geek . . . the nerd and became Mrs. Howard," Darius said. "So how is it that our kids are with her? She's never kept them before, has she?"

Tiffany stood up. "Darius, we need to talk."

"About what?"

"About what you're doing," Tiffany said.

"I'm working and coming home to you, that's what I'm doing. I'm out there busting my tail pretty much seven days a week without a day off just to pay the bills and take care of my family, that's what I'm doing."

"You're working with a woman named Paris?"

"You already know that. I've told you that Paris and I are co-chairs over getting out the youth vote for Lawrence Simmons's reelection campaign."

"The same Paris that's trying to take Gabrielle's child from her," Tiffany said as though someone had turned on a tape and it was playing regardless of the present direction of the conversation.

"I don't know anything about her personal business. I'm just there trying to get a paycheck like anybody else working there." He stepped away from Tiffany and decided to head upstairs.

Tiffany followed behind him. "So are you sleeping with her?"

Darius stopped on the first step and turned toward Tiffany. "Am I sleeping with her? Am I sleeping with whom?"

"Paris Simmons-Holyfield. Are you sleeping with her?"

He chuckled. "Now you're tripping. Paris is married just like I am." He turned back around and continued up the stairs and into their bedroom.

Tiffany came in right behind him. "You haven't answered the question."

Darius turned to her. "Am I *sleeping* with her? That's your question?"

"Yes."

"Then the answer is no; I'm not *sleeping* with her." He didn't feel like he was lying. He wasn't *sleeping* with her.

"Have you been telling her things I've told you concerning Gabrielle?"

Darius chuckled again. "You're tripping for real now. Paris and I have no reason to talk about Gabrielle. We're professionals. Pro . . . fes . . . sion . . . als. I get paid to work in getting her father reelected. That's what I do."

Tiffany nodded. "Okay, then have you ever hit on Gabrielle?"

"Are you talking about the professional stripper whose sole job was to get men all excited so she could rake in more money? *That* Gabrielle?"

"That's not who she is now," Tiffany said.

Darius smiled. "You know what they say: Once a stripper, always a stripper."

"She's a Christian now. All of that is behind her."

"So says her. But then, I suppose people can believe folks like her have changed, but somebody like me, I get judged by my past all the time at every turn. Why is there such a double standard? Huh? I cheated on you one time." He held up his index finger to emphasize the number one. "We talked about it. I told you it was nothing, but here you are in my face accusing me of my past behavior *once* again."

"I'm still waiting on an answer to my question." Tiffany folded her arms.

"Have I ever hit on Gabrielle?" He rubbed his chin as he looked at the ceiling. "I guess that would be a yes. But that was when she was getting paid to have men throw themselves at her. I didn't mean anything seriously by it. I told you that I was merely going along with the other guys so they wouldn't think I wasn't interested in women. You know how men like to test other men just to be sure."

"And that's the only time you've hit on her? When she was working at that place? You haven't tried anything since she became a member of our church?"

Darius walked over and gently gathered Tiffany up by her shoulders. "Gabrielle is not my type. Trust me: I have all that I want right here. I don't know what she may have told you. But if you told her that I was working with Paris and she figured out it was the same person you say is trying to take that child from her, then wouldn't it stand to reason she'd say something to put doubt in your mind? Gabrielle is merely working you, baby. She was likely trying to get you so worked up you'd say something you might not normally say when your mind is not clouded with anger."

"What about Fatima?"

"What about her?"

"Have you ever hit on her? Have you ever had an affair with her?"

Darius laughed as he released her. "Okay.

Now this is getting crazy around here. How many more women do you have on your list? Are you going to ask me about every woman I've come in contact with on my job and at church?"

"No. Just the ones you've had an affair with in let's say, the past ten years."

He shook his head. "I'm not going to dignify that with an answer. I'm going to take a shower. And when I'm done, I hope you've taken off your head and screwed it back on right. My patience can only take so much." He headed for the bathroom.

"I've talked to Fatima," Tiffany said to his back.

He stopped and turned around. "I would hope so if you're going to take our children over there and leave them. What is she doing? Having some kind of a party and she needed our children to help make up the numbers or something?"

"I'm going to ask you this *one* more time, and I'd appreciate if you'd just tell the truth without us having to circle this mountain more than once."

He came close and tapped her on her nose. "You *do* have a way with words."

"Have you had an affair with Fatima at any time during our marriage?"

Darius twisted his mouth a few times,

then made a popping sound. "No."

Tiffany nodded her head nippily a few times. "So if I were to tell you that she says differently, you would contend to me that she's the one lying and not you?"

"Look, Tiffany. You need to stop this mess. Can't you see? Fatima and Gabrielle are friends. I don't know why, but it seems like the two of them have gotten together and decided to target me. Actually, it looks like they're targeting you, because what they're doing is trying to hurt you. They can't really hurt me. But going after you . . . well, all I can say is: With those kinds of friends, who needs enemies?"

"Okay. So you're telling me that if Fatima were to have said that you and she once had an affair . . . that would not be the truth?"

"Fatima would never tell you anything like that."

"Why? Because you think she loves you that much? Because she's married now and she wouldn't want something like that to get out at this point in her life?"

"Because you and Fatima are friends. And real friends wouldn't do something like that to hurt a friend. Not a real friend they cared about."

"Oh, but if this affair happened *before* we were friends, then that wouldn't count, now would it? I mean, it wouldn't count as a friend hurting another friend."

"What did Fatima tell you?"

"You're my husband. I'm asking you. And if you respect and love me as you claim to, you would come clean and tell me the truth. All of your tricky play on words has gotten real old."

Darius snickered. "Play on words, huh? I told you that you're tripping. How do I make a play on words?"

"I ask have you *slept* with this person, and you say that you're not *sleeping* with them. That to me means that you're not doing it right now at this exact moment, but it doesn't address whether you've ever done it."

Darius scratched his head. "Well, you do give me a whole lot of credit for seemingly being much smarter and way more clever than I really am."

"Okay, Darius: last time. Have you *ever* had an affair with Fatima? Have you ever *slept* with her? Have you ever broken your marriage vow between me and you with her?"

"And for the last time: no, no, and no. *No!* I don't know how to say it any plainer than that. The answer is no."

"Okay, Darius. If that's how you want to

play this, then I want you to leave."

Darius laughed. "You want me to do what?"

"I want you to pack your things and get out."

"Over somebody conspiring against me? You want me to leave *here*?" He pointed his finger at the floor. "You want *me* to leave my home."

"Yes."

"Well, that's too bad, because I'm not going anywhere." He stepped up close to her. "And you know what? You can't make me. This is *my* house. And if you don't want to be together, then you can pack up *your* stuff and get to stepping."

Tiffany nodded. "Did you have an affair with Fatima? That's all I'm asking. You're so tough. You're so big and bad. Why can't you stand up and be a man about what you've done? You did it. If you're man enough to sleep with other women, then you should be man enough to look me in my eyes and tell me the truth."

Darius was so mad, his top lip quivered. "All right. Since you can't leave well enough alone. Yes! I *did* have a brief affair with Fatima. It was before you ever met her. It was when you and I were having trouble in our marriage. Things haven't always been rosy around here; you know it and I know it. So are you happy now? Did I confirm what your little buddy apparently couldn't wait to tell you? She doesn't care about you, because if she did, she never would have told you this in the first place."

Tiffany started laughing, not in an amused way, but one of craze.

"What's so funny?"

Tiffany kept laughing.

He placed one hand on his hip. "What *is* so funny?"

"Fatima didn't tell me anything. But thank you. You just told me *everything.*"

"Well, if she didn't tell you, then why were you doing all of this?"

Tiffany stepped up to him. "I asked her if you had ever come on to her. She told me if I wanted to know the answer to that I should ask you myself. I asked her had the two of you ever had an affair. And again, she told me if I wanted to know the answer to that, I should talk to my husband. She didn't tell me because it's like you just said: She cares too much to want me hurt. She wasn't going to lie to me, but she wasn't going to tell me even though, to me, a real friend would tell it."

"And you don't have a problem with her? She had an affair with your husband, she became your friend, and she never told you what she'd done or asked for your forgiveness, but you don't have a problem with her. But you do, naturally, have a problem with me. Well, I'm asking for forgiveness. Although this happened years ago and has been over with for five, I'm asking you to forgive me now."

"Sure, Darius. I forgive you. But, dear husband of mine who needs to learn the true meaning of repent, I still want you out of this house."

Darius laughed. "Repent? So what does that mean? You want me to go before the church and confess my sin? You want me to go to the good Pastor Landris, who by the way, may or may not have something in his own closet . . . possibly the same problem as me. Who knows? But you want *me* to go and ask *him* for forgiveness."

"That's not what I want. Repent means to change your ways. It means to turn and go in a different direction. It means to recognize what you're doing is wrong and to stop doing it! Not just stop with the person you *had* been doing it with. It means those you're doing that same thing with right now." Tiffany took a step away from him. "All I know is: I'm not putting up with you treating me like this anymore. I deserve better, and I'm not going to allow you to do this and think that it's okay. I am *not* your doormat. From this day forward, you will *not* be wiping your feet on me!"

"Well, if you want me out of your life, then I suggest you be the one to pack your stuff and leave, because I'm not going anywhere. And the last thing I'm going to do is vacate this house, because do you know what happens then?" He chuckled. "It's called abandonment, and I lose my rights and claim to this place. So if you end up with *this* house, it won't be because I forfeited my rightful claim by leaving first."

Tiffany looked at him hard. "I'm going to Fatima's to pick up our kids." She grabbed her purse and walked out of the room.

"And I'll be here when you get back!" he yelled. "You can count on *that*!"

Chapter 42

For we can do nothing against the truth, but for the truth.

— 2 Corinthians 13:8

The next day when Darius got to work, he found a note laying on his desk telling him to see Lawrence as soon as he arrived. Darius thought Lawrence was out on the campaign trail. In fact, he'd almost not come in to work today, especially following the night he'd just had with Tiffany.

She'd gotten the kids from Fatima's and come home, bringing with her a plate of food Fatima had given her. When he'd asked what was he supposed to do for food since the children had eaten at Fatima's and she'd given Tiffany a plate for her, but apparently not one for him, Tiffany told him point blank, "What you do when you *don't* eat here."

That was the last words she spoke to him.

He didn't care. He preferred the silent treatment to her fussing any day of the week. There wasn't much on television. But there was never much during the end of July except for baseball games, cheap reality shows, and reruns. He'd sat down with a plate of spaghetti sauce and watched a baseball game. When he tried to go into his bedroom, the door was locked. So he slept in the den on the couch, which was also fine with him. That way he didn't have to deal with Tiffany's cold body language while in the same bed. He'd been here before. He knew it would pass shortly.

"You wanted to see me?" Darius said after knocking on Lawrence's door and being told to come in.

Lawrence stood and indicated for Darius to have a seat.

Darius was smiling. He knew he'd done a great job over the past few months. He was certain Lawrence realized now what a true asset he was to him. He might have blackmailed his way into the position, but his work had done the speaking as to who he was as an employee.

"I want to thank you for the work you've done on behalf of my reelection campaign," Lawrence said.

Darius grinned even bigger as he situated

his body better. "You're welcome. It's been a real joy. I never knew I'd be so good at something like this. But it's like I'm a natural. I was born to do this. What can I say?"

Lawrence nodded a few times, then held out a white envelope to him.

Darius leaned forward and took it. "What's this? A bonus or something? Because you know I can always use more money. Mo' money, mo' money. I'm not one of those who will dare turn down a blessing. Not Darius. No, sir."

"There *is* a check inside."

"Now we're talking." Darius began tearing open the sealed envelope. "He pulled out the check along with another piece of paper. He looked at the check. "What's this?"

"What does it say that it is?"

"It says, 'Final check for services rendered.' "

"Then it's correct," Lawrence said. "It should be completely up to date."

Darius stood up. "How is it a final check if I'm still working?"

"You're *not* still working. Today is your last day."

Darius began shaking his head. "Oh, no. I don't think so. I have a signed contract with four more months of pay left on it to be fulfilled."

"Your services are no longer needed."

"This is not going down like this. You're messing with the wrong one."

"Please close my door on your way out," Lawrence said, now also standing.

"Why are you doing this? Have I not delivered on what we agreed on? What kind of a man are you? Do you not know the kind of havoc I can wreak on you?"

Lawrence walked around to face Darius. "Let's see: Why am I doing this? For starters, I don't take kindly to being blackmailed. But I also have learned down through the years to never turn my back on a snake. The best way to know what a snake is up to is to put him in a glass aquarium, feed him while keeping a tight lid on where he's being held, and watch."

Darius laughed. "You're comparing me to a snake? You, Representative Copperhead, are calling *me* a snake?" Darius pointed at him. "That's funny right there. Yeah, that's a dump truckload of laughs right there."

"Have you delivered on what we agreed upon?" Lawrence said as though Darius's laugh wasn't fazing him in the least. "The answer to that question is a resounding no. You were supposed to keep my daughter occupied enough with this reelection effort to keep her nose out of my *other* affairs. Instead, you were out there adding gasoline to what could have been a smothered-out fire."

Darius was so mad now that his nose was flaring. He could feel it as it flared in and out.

Lawrence stared at him with equal resolve. "What kind of a man am I?" Lawrence gave a quick, short smile. "Hmmm, now let's see. I'm the kind of man who knows what he wants to happen and the power to make it so. I take care of my wife. I take care of my children. I take care of my business. And if anyone tries to cross me, I take care of them."

"Okay," Darius said. "What about my last question. Do you have any idea what kind of damage I can do to you?"

"Certainly. And that and four dollars might . . . *might,* mind you, get you a Happy Meal from McDonald's."

"You think this is all a joke, don't you?" Darius stepped up to him.

"I would advise you to back off."

"Or what, old man? What you gonna do if I don't? Huh?"

Lawrence leaned over to his desk and pressed the intercom button. "Mattie, send him in, please."

"Who you calling? Your lapdog, William. He can't take me any more than you can. You're both past your prime."

A tall heavy-set man dressed in a security uniform came in.

"Please escort Mr. Connors here out, will you? He is no longer welcome in our facilities."

"You heard him," the security guard said. "Let's go."

Darius leaned in close to Lawrence's face. "You just made the wrong call this time, Representative Simmons. You see: I've figured it out. I know the whole truth about you now."

Lawrence moved his face in to Darius's. "You don't know anything."

Darius turned to the guard. "My man, can you step out for a minute. It will just take a minute. I don't want you overhearing what I'm going to drop on your boss here."

The security guard looked at Lawrence.

Lawrence nodded his okay. "You can wait outside. He'll only be a minute."

After the guard left, Lawrence sat down. "Say what's on your mind, son, so you can get to stepping out of my office and permanently out of my life."

Darius sat down and leaned in closer to

Lawrence. "You and Gabrielle slept together when she was living with your daughter Paris. She got pregnant and gave the baby up for adoption. The child needed a transplant. You and Gabrielle teamed up, quite ingeniously if I may say so, and saved the child's life. How am I doing so far?"

Lawrence kept his facial expression the same. "Go on," Lawrence said. "You have thirty seconds left."

Darius sat back against his chair. "The adoptive mother dies. Gabrielle gets a chance to get her daughter back. Everything is going along smoothly. But then a hiccup comes along when Paris becomes convinced that you're Jasmine's birth father. Only thing: Paris gets it all wrong. Unbeknownst to Paris, she thinks you had an affair with Jessica, the adoptive mother. Jessica and Jasmine: J and J. Cute, huh? Anyway, Paris thinks the two of you had an affair because your youngest daughter is a perfect match for who Paris now believes is your youngest child. The two girls looking like sisters didn't hurt Paris's theory. Of course, Paris doesn't know at the time that Jasmine is adopted. She doesn't know that she's gotten that part wrong. She learns that Gabrielle had a baby and gave her up for adoption and this same baby just happens to be

Jasmine. Paris puts two and two together and comes up with three."

"Two and two is four," Lawrence said.

"Yeah. I know. That's the problem. She had the numbers right; she just came up with the wrong answer. Paris thinks that if Gabrielle had a baby around that time, then the father of Gabrielle's baby could be her husband, Andrew's, or some ex-boyfriend she's convinced Gabrielle slept with. The part she forgot to add into the equation is that Jasmine is somehow connected to you. I, being the smart man that I am, who by the way, excelled brilliantly in math, figured that you also had access to Gabrielle during that time. I figured out that you got Gabrielle pregnant and she gave the baby up for adoption. Miraculously, the child comes back into her life, but possibly causing major problems for you, the least being your political career. But let's face it, Lawrence: You're not going to win reelection. You and I know that."

"Is that so?"

"You know you're not. But" — Darius held his index finger in the air — "you *can* lose your wife. Your children can stop having anything to do with you. After they learn how you cheated on their mother and with a teenage girl to boot." Darius shook his head. "Tsk, tsk, tsk. Such a disgrace. So you see, Lawrence, you're going to give me my job back. And you and I are going to pretend that none of this *ever* happened."

"You make some good points," Lawrence said. "But I don't think so."

"Listen, I'm a man on the edge right now. My wife wants to leave me. Ironically, she found out about my affair with Fatima, the one you threw in my face once. You're trying to fire me from my job. My wife . . . I can handle. She'll come to her senses soon enough; she always does. But I don't need to be worrying about a job, not at this point." Darius stood up and held out his hand to shake Lawrence's. "So, we have an understanding here?"

Lawrence stood up and looked down at Darius's awaiting hand. "I have one question though. Well, maybe two."

Darius lowered his hand. "Okay. Hit me."

Lawrence chuckled. "Tempting choice of words. But I know what you mean. Okay, your wife wants you gone. I want you gone. Looks to me like you're going to have your hands full trying to convince your wife that she can trust you, learning of your affair with Fatima. And then there's my darling daughter, Paris, who probably won't be excited about having to explain to Andrew why she slept with you the other night. But do you know the best part?" Lawrence laughed as he lowered his head, then stopped laughing on a dime and stared hard at Darius. "The best part will be you trying to convince your wife why you slept with my daughter."

"Then it sounds like we'll all be busy, because your wife is not going to be happy about your extracurricular affair, either."

"True. But I have money put away so I'll be all right if I'm forced to start all over. Don't get me wrong now: I love my wife. I love her dearly. And if this comes out, I will fight hard to make sure she remains my wife. But the difference in my affair and yours is that mine was some ten years ago. Yours is not even a week old."

"But you have a lot more to lose than me," Darius said.

"If you go forward with this, we'll certainly find out." Lawrence sneered at him. "I told you from the start not to dare cross me. You didn't heed my warning back then. Now you find yourself on the other side of dare. What you do from this point on will determine whether or not I break you completely. I pray that you choose better than this last time."

"You're not going to get away with this. I

don't know how you managed to know so much about my personal life or how you set this all up, but you're going to get yours someday. I promise you that."

"You mean like you appear to be getting yours?" Lawrence held out an open hand. "Now, I need the keys to the company car."

"Then how am I supposed to get home?"

"Not my problem. I'm sure you can find someone to come and pick you up or give you a ride home. If not, there's always a taxi."

Darius took the keys to the car from his pocket and slammed them down on the desk. He stared hard at Lawrence, and with grit in his voice, said, "This isn't over. By no means is this over!"

"Yes, Mr. Connors. As far as you and I go, it is." He matched Darius's stare until Darius stood up straight. "Oh, and, Darius?"

Darius looked at him without saying a word.

"Close the door on your way out. Good day to you." He lowered his head, sat back down, and went back to writing in his notebook.

Chapter 43

> By honor and dishonor, by evil report and good report: as deceivers, and yet true.
>
> — 2 Corinthians 6:8

Darius went to his office to pack up his things. Without a way home now, he was planning to ask Paris to take him. She wasn't there. He called to see where she was, but didn't get an answer. He then called Tiffany, who wouldn't answer her phone or call him back. He called his friend Big Red, but his call went straight to voice mail. After calling a few other people, he finally just called for a taxi. Arriving home, he continued trying to reach Paris. He was worried about her now. This made three days straight she hadn't come in. It took two hours from the first time he'd called her number, but she finally answered. The way his life was going lately, he wasn't sure *what* to expect.

"What's going on?" Paris said. "Why are you blowing up my phone every five minutes? There were twenty-three missed calls, all from you."

"Where are you?" Darius asked.

"I'm at home. Where do you think?"

"What are you doing at home? And don't tell me you overslept. Nobody sleeps for three days straight; I don't care how tired you are."

"No one told you?"

"Told me what?"

"I was let go. Or as William and my father put it: downsized."

Darius paused a second. "They let you go?"

"Yes. Yesterday to be exact. They say the campaign is not going the way they were hoping. Campaign contributions are *way* down. Daddy said he'd have to let one of us go. So I told him he could cut me. I was tired of working anyway. And I miss my Ambrosia."

"Ambrosia?"

"You remember my baby . . . my puppy: Ambrosia. She's been over at my folks' house."

"Oh, yeah, your puppy, the Maltese. So they let you go and told you they were keeping me?" Darius said.

"That's what they said," Paris said.

"Well, they lied. They let me go today."

"No. Are you for real?"

"Yep. Just one more thing to add to the pile of things that are going wrong in my life."

"I'm sorry. But maybe it's all for the best. I mean the two of us not working together. I'm sure you'll find another job quick enough. With the work you did for my father, I'm certain he and William will give you a great recommendation."

"I don't know about either of them giving me a recommendation, great or otherwise."

"Listen, Darius. I want to thank you for everything. You were a good friend. I thank you for lending me your ear. And you were right: We did make a great team. But right now, my marriage is on the rocks. Seriously. At least, what was left of it."

"Sounds like trouble in paradise. Sounds like a lot of that's going around these days."

"Andrew is not happy right now. In fact, I've never seen him this upset about anything, not ever. I did something really dumb and completely insensitive."

"Yeah, I know."

"I'm not talking about what you and I did together the other night," Paris said. "And can we not ever bring that up again, please?

I'd really like to forget that ever happened. Okay?"

"Sure. Suits me just fine. But I wasn't talking about what you and I did. I was talking about your little trip to Gabrielle's place."

"How do you know about that? Who told you about that?"

"My wife is upset and, in fact, she blasted *me* big-time about it last night. She wants to leave me. It's a huge mess for sure."

"She wants to leave you over what *I* did? That makes no sense."

"She thinks I told you about Gabrielle being Jasmine's birth mother."

"That's ridiculous. She wants to leave you about something like *that*? And people have the nerve to call *me*a drama queen."

"Gabrielle is stirring up trouble. She's upset because you went over there and stirred up a whirlwind. She accused my wife of divulging that information to me. And knowing that you and I work together — correction, worked together — my dear wife came to the conclusion that I must have told you, which means I betrayed her confidence and the sanctimony of our marriage."

"Did you tell her you weren't the one who gave me that information?"

"I tried. She didn't believe me. It's funny:

Every time I tell her the absolute truth, she doesn't believe me. You were the one who told me. I only confirmed it."

"Would you like for me to call and talk to her?" Paris said. "I owe you that much."

"No. But thanks for the offer. I'll work it out somehow. I've been in the situation before, and we're still together. At heart, Tiffany is a real softie. She cares about family. In the beginning, she's always upset. But after a few days . . . tops, she'll settle down and come to her senses. She hates being mad at me. *She* knows it, and *I* know it."

"Okay. But if you change your mind, let me know. Otherwise, it's been nice working with you these past few months," Paris said. "Pray for me. Andrew is also really upset. I don't know how I'm going to make this right. I really messed things up. I wish I could have a do-over. I would definitely have left this part of it alone. But that's what happens when you go too far. Every relationship has a breaking point."

"As they say: live and learn," Darius said. "Good luck with everything. You say a prayer for me, and I'll say one for you."

"I believe in prayer, but I think it's going to take more than prayer to help me on this. I guess I just need a plan."

"If I'm not mistaken, that's what got you

into this."

"Maybe. But learning Andrew was representing my enemy, I'd say I wasn't the only double-dealing, double-crosser in our marriage."

After Paris said good-bye, he clicked off his phone only for it to ring before he could put it up. He looked down at the number and smiled.

"Big Red! What up?"

"I saw where you called." Big Red had a deep bass voice that rumbled.

Darius scratched his head. He didn't want to come out asking for anything right off the bat. If Tiffany stuck to her guns, he just might need a place to hang out until things blew over. "I was just checking on you. You and your old lady still having problems?"

"Naw, man. We good. She talked me into going down to that church where you and your old lady go and I talked to that pastor. He cool, man. Real cool. He speak straight up truth. And he ain't one of them religious nuts, either. You know how I feel about preachers now. DC" — he called him DC, short for Darius Connors — "man, some of them preachers turned me completely away from *ever* wanting to step foot in a church. But this one here . . . that Pastor Landris . . . he helped me see that I needed to grow up and get myself together. He pulled out this scripture and whipped it on me where it talked about when I was a child, I spoke as a child. But when I became a man, I put away childish things. It was like a lightbulb lit up in my head. I saw just as clearly that it was time for me to grow up and be a man."

"I hear you. So you're going to my church now with the wifey? Have you joined or are you planning on joining?"

"Yeah, man. I joined last week. I saw Tiff; I thought she told you."

"Nah, she didn't say a word. But that's cool, man. I guess that means we'll probably run into each other there sometimes."

"You know, DC, it's time for you to grow up, too," Big Red said.

Darius laughed. "Man, I'm good. My wife ain't complaining. No more than most wives typically do, you know what I'm saying?"

"That's not what I been hearing. Hey, man, you ate lunch yet?"

"No. I've been sort of taking care of business."

"Then let's meet for lunch. Can you get away now? My treat," Big Red said.

"What time?"

"It's lunchtime now. I'll see you when you get there."

Darius laughed. "And I don't *even* have to ask where."

"You know it. There ain't but one place I'll fork over my hard-earned money. I like to get what I pay for and then some."

"And Sadie's don't play!" they said in unison.

"I'll see you shortly." Darius hung up, looked at his phone, and smiled. Especially after the past two days he'd had, maybe things were about to start looking up. "Lord," he said, his head to the ceiling. "I pray so. A brother needs a break down here."

CHAPTER 44

> Be not deceived; God is not mocked: for whatsoever a man soweth, that shall he also reap.
>
> — Galatians 6:7

Darius walked into Sadie's and looked around. Big Red was easy enough to spot. He didn't get the name Big Red for nothing. Darius walked over to the booth, gave Big Red a manly hug, then they pounded fists, and both sat down.

"It's been a minute since I've been here," Darius said.

"I know I ain't seen you around here in a few moons."

"How's your mother?" Darius asked, sitting back comfortably in the seat.

"She all right. You know Mama."

"Yeah, Sadie hasn't slowed down since I've known her."

"She slowing down a bit these days. She

say she done did her part. Now it's our turn to step up and take over things. You know me. I love to eat, but I love fixing cars just as much. One of my older sisters quit her job, so she running things around here. I told them I'll do my part by bringing them my money and lots of hungry stomachs with plenty of money."

"Which sister is it?" Darius knew Big Red had four older sisters; he was the baby boy his mother called "the change baby" since she'd had him at age forty-seven while going through "the change."

"Clarice. Clarice can throw down in the kitchen just like Mama. Mama still come here, but she don't stay all day like she used to. She eighty-one years old now. I guess she really done did her stint. I told her it don't make no sense to be greedy. She draw Social Security and get paid from here. She say Social Security might go broke. But God blesses the chile who got his own."

"I heard that."

Big Red waved for the waitress.

She came over. "You finally ready to order now, Red?"

"Yeah. And put it all on my tab."

Darius and Big Red gave her their order. She smiled at Darius, then left.

Big Red leaned in closer to Darius. "Okay,

DC. Talk to me. What's going on? I heard you got this big-time important job now." He grinned, showing off the one tooth in the front of his mouth that was trimmed in gold.

"Had," Darius said. "I *had* a big time important job. I was let go today."

"You unemployed again? That was quick?" Big Red shook his head. "That sucks."

"Tell me about it. I was pulling in some major bucks, too. And I really liked what I was doing."

"Word on the street is you had a fine honey alongside you. They called her your ride-to-die-for chick. Say she was just that fine — a little bit of honey on the side."

"We were coworkers. And she wasn't any honey on the side, either."

"So you trying to tell me you didn't get with her? 'Cause I know you, DC. This your boy you talking to. This Big Red here sitting across from you."

"She was the boss's daughter," Darius said with a sheepish grin. "I might be a lot of things, but crazy isn't one of them."

"Ah, man, you know you love a challenge. Maybe that's why you lost your job. Her daddy found out and canned you."

"Nope. I was working on a political campaign. The money dried up. I also figured he didn't have a chance of winning, but like I said: The money was good. And loser money spends just as good as winner's money do."

A woman sashayed through the door. Darius recognized her immediately. Big Red started waving at her, which was a bit of a surprise to Darius. She smiled and came over to their table.

Big Red stood up and gave her a bear hug. "Hey there, pretty lady. You came to get your grub on, too, I see."

"Yes. You know after you introduced me to this place, I was hooked. I have to come get my fix at *least* once a week." She smiled, then looked at Darius.

"Where are my manners?" Big Red said. "Darius, this is —"

"Gigi Thornton," Darius said.

"Oh, so you two know each other. Well, I would imagine you might," Big Red said, still standing. "The Divine Gigi is a big-time PI. That's private investigator for all you common folks. She good, too."

Frowning, Darius stood up as not to be at a disadvantage. "You're a private investigator?"

Gigi nodded. "Yes, I am."

"She been one for years. How long you been doing this now, Divine Gigi?"

"Coming up on my tenth year anniversary next month," Gigi said.

"You here meeting somebody?" Big Red asked, scanning the restaurant. "Because you more than welcome to sit with us iffen you ain't."

"Yeah, I'm meeting somebody. But thanks for the offer, Big Red. You're always *such* a gentleman." Gigi looked at the door. "Well, it looks like my lunch date has arrived. It was good seeing you again . . . both of you." She smiled, nodded, then left to go to her table. Big Red sat back down.

Darius continued to look at the man she was greeting. He couldn't believe it; it was William Threadgill. Gigi must have mentioned to William that he was there, because William turned and looked his way, throwing up his hand to wave at him.

Darius didn't bother waving back. Suddenly, things were starting to come together. He sat down. "So how do you happen to know Gigi?" Darius asked.

"The Divine Gigi? She came to my shop looking for a good mechanic. It was something pretty simple with her car. She and I hit it off right off the bat. She would then stop by the shop from time to time just to say hello. She was hungry one day, said she was looking for a good place to get her grub on. I invited her here."

"How long ago was this? How long ago did she come to your shop?"

Big Red looked up as though the answer was written on the ceiling. He looked at Darius. "Sometime around the first of March of this year. You know I don't keep up with stuff like that. You're the one who was working for some big political head. I just fix cars."

"And you're good at it, so don't be saying you *just* fix cars."

"See, man, you always make a brother feel good. That's why I want to help you. I want you to get yourself on the right track though. You got a good woman in Tiffany. I don't want to see you lose her. You know they say you don't miss your water until your well runs dry. I'm trying to keep you from knowing what it feels like to be thirsty while in the ocean. I done been there; it ain't all it's cracked up to be."

Darius leaned in. "Big Red, I need to ask you something."

"Go ahead."

"Did Gigi ever ask you anything about me? Did my name ever come up or anything that would lead back to me?"

"Come to think of it, she did ask me something about you once. That was before

I knew she was a PI though. I didn't think nothing about it at the time." Big Red sat back against his seat. "You think somebody hired her to investigate you or something?"

"You see that man she's with right now?"

Big Red looked over where Gigi sat. "Yeah. The guy that's old enough to be her father. Is he her father?"

"That's the guy I was working for. Not exactly working for; he runs things for the guy I was working for. And, no, I don't think he's her father, although, it *is* possible."

Big Red nodded. "So they just probably hired her to check you out before they hired you. I can see that. I know a lot of these employers are doing stuff like that to make sure the people they're bringing in are on the up-and-up. They say they even check your credit scores now. I just wish I'd known that when she was cozying all up to me. I don't like being used. I should go over there and let her know as much."

"Don't, Big Red. It won't help. Don't worry about it."

"Yeah, you're right. I guess she was just doing her job. She just like the rest of us out here. She just a bird trying to find a worm so she'll have something to eat."

Darius looked Gigi's way again. She was laughing, throwing her head back. The waitress brought Darius and Big Red their food.

"This looks and smells so good it makes you want to slap your own self," Big Red said, rubbing his hands together.

"Yep. It makes you want to slap yourself," Darius said, still looking Gigi's way. It was all making sense now. Gigi was the person who'd likely done him in.

He finished eating and left ten minutes after Big Red did. Gigi walked up behind him. "I hope you know it was nothing personal," she said, almost whispering the words into his ear. "It was *strictly* business."

Darius didn't have anything to say to her. He continued to walk toward his vehicle. She'd deceived him on every turn. What was there left to say?

"Cat got your tongue? You're not going to say anything to me?"

He stopped and spun around. "What do you want?"

"I just wanted to come speak and to let you know it was only business."

"I've deceived others; you deceived me. I suppose it's true what they say: You reap what you sow."

"Galatians 6:7. 'Be not deceived; God is not mocked: for whatsoever a man soweth, that shall he also reap.' "

"Oh, so you know scriptures, too, huh? I guess the next thing you'll be telling me is that you're a preacher or something."

She smiled, then shook her head. "No. But I *am* a Christian."

"A Christian who lies. A Christian who'll pretend to be something that she's not. Hmmm, let's see now, what's the word for that? Oh, yeah: hypocrite."

"Before you waste time trying to get the speck out of my eye, maybe you should worry about the plank in your own," Gigi said.

"Let me ask you something. Is your real name even Gigi or was that all part of your elaborate scam?"

"I told you my birth name: Georgina Thornton. So, yes, my name really is Gigi. All of that was the truth."

"But all of that about looking for a job, needing some encouragement, you just happening to run into me at the coffeehouse, bumping into me at church . . . all of those things were merely fabricated lies to find out more about my life."

"The church part turned out to be a good thing. I *really* enjoyed Pastor Landris. And now that you know the truth about who I really am, I suppose I can feel free to come back to the church on a more regular basis.

I didn't want to run into you too often."

"Yeah. You wouldn't want to cause me to become suspicious or anything. I just might have figured out what you were up to." He smirked. "So how did all of this go down exactly?"

She shrugged.

"You owe me that much, Gigi, considering you may have destroyed my life and home."

"You can't blame that on me. You sow, and one day you're going to reap. It's a spiritual law. It might not be today, maybe not tomorrow. But in due time, in due season, you *will* reap what you've sown. Good or bad, it's coming up again, only multiplied."

"Please . . . spare me the moral lecture, will you?"

"I'm just trying to give you some godly advice."

"I'd prefer *you* not," Darius said.

"All right. You want to know how this went down. Originally, I was hired to find out who you were and if there were any damaging skeletons rattling around in your closet. I can't say what that was about; it's not for me to determine in order to take on a case. I learned quite quickly though of your proclivity for extra-marital affairs. One piece of advice if I may: If you don't want anyone to ever know about something, then don't disclose it to anyone else."

Darius nodded. "That's where Big Red came in."

"Don't blame him. He's a pretty nice guy. He didn't have a clue what I was doing or who I was."

"How did he find out you were a private investigator? He calls you the Divine Gigi, you know."

She smiled. "When he asked me to this restaurant. His sister, Clarice, recognized me. She'd hired me to check on something for her —"

"You mean her husband."

"That's none of your business," Gigi said.

"But *my* business was okay for you to disclose to other people. You didn't seem to have a problem with that at all."

"For that purpose, your business *became* my business."

"Ha-ha. You're just full of jokey-jokes."

Gigi shrugged. "Anyway, his sister told him I was a PI. But because of how Big Red and I met, he didn't think much of it."

"So he just told you all of my business? I guess he thought he was going to get with you or something?"

"You mean the same way you were thinking you were going to?"

"Just go on and finish telling me the rest of this so I can be on my way."

"I found out about folks like Fatima and Tracy —"

"Big Red told you about Tracy?" Darius shook his head. "There are times when Big Red really is one fry short of a Happy Meal, but he doesn't normally volunteer information like that. How did you get him to tell you things when he really didn't know you from Adam?"

"I'm really good at what I do. Think about how much you told me without you even thinking about it. You showed me a picture of your family, told me the names of your wife and children. You made comments about certain people like . . . what was that guy's name? Clarence Walker. Yes, Clarence Walker, when you were talking about Gabrielle and how she was fooling people about who she truly was. Clarence definitely had no problem telling me things about you. I take it there's some bad blood between the two you. I saw you with Paris that day at the coffeehouse, well, actually I kind of followed you there, and you told me —"

"Okay. I get your point." Darius held up his hand to make her be quiet. "But I don't know how you got Big Red to tell you the names of people I've had affairs with . . . both Fatima *and* Tracy."

"The same way you likely relayed it. You probably didn't come right out and *tell* Big Red all that you'd done. But if a person is smart enough to listen and read between the lines, it's easy enough to figure out the whole story," Gigi said. "And for some reason unbeknownst to me, people like talking about things like that with perfect strangers. I suppose it's because they don't think it will ever go anywhere. Oddly, people think that telling strangers things is safer than telling someone who may know that person. All I had to do was to get Big Red going on a particular subject. He gladly provided me with examples using one of his friends. I would press him further about it, reassuring him that I didn't know the person he was talking about anyway so it was safe to tell me what he otherwise wouldn't."

"So he thought he was helping you with *your* problem," Darius said. "The same way I did."

"There you go." Gigi moved her purse from one shoulder to the other. "Big Red thinks a lot of you. After you got that job with the representative's campaign, my job was pretty much finished as it pertained to you."

"Pretty much?"

Gigi smiled. "Yeah. There were a few other things I was asked to do. I probably shouldn't tell you that though."

"You owe me, Gigi."

She flashed him a smile. "Okay. What will it hurt now? I was asked to pass on some information to Paris. I was to get the information to her that Gabrielle was actually Jasmine's birth mother and that she'd given her daughter up for adoption."

"So you were the one who told Paris?"

"Not in person. I just made sure she got the information. I left it in an envelope on her desk in her office. I also let her know that her husband was representing Gabrielle against her."

"Oh, she got it all right; the day we had that event at the hotel ballroom. She was upset about it for sure. After her husband confirmed he was representing Gabrielle against her, thus believing everything else was true; she apparently confronted Gabrielle," Darius said. "But who? Who would put you up to doing something like that?"

"That" — she pointed her finger at him like it was the barrel of a gun — "I can't disclose. But what I *can* say is that I was paid *handsomely* to do it."

"So what's the deal with you and William Threadgill? Maybe he's not everything he's presenting himself to be. So are you working on another case?"

She started walking backward away from him. "I'm *always* working."

"Hold up. Don't go."

"Sorry," she said. "But this concludes our tête-à-tête." She turned and walked quickly to her car.

CHAPTER 45

> Can a man take fire in his bosom, and his clothes not be burned?
>
> — Proverbs 6:27

Darius was home alone. The children were both back in school and Junior at daycare. Tiffany was at work. It had been three weeks and a day since Tiffany learned the truth about him and Fatima and had asked him to leave (which he refused to do), three weeks since he'd lost his job, two days since he'd tried talking to Tiffany, who still uncharacteristically had nothing to say to him, one day since he'd thought about calling the church and possibly requesting someone to counsel him on what he should do to fix things with his wife, when his doorbell rang.

A man stood outside with an electronic handheld device. "Darius Connors?"

"Yes?"

"I have a package I need you to sign for."

"What is it?" Darius asked, looking at the large envelope the man held in his hand.

"I don't get paid to read them, just deliver them." He handed Darius the envelope, then held up the electronic device. "Sign on the line please."

Darius looked at the envelope and saw it was from a lawyer's office. He signed; the man left.

Walking back inside, he opened the envelope and couldn't believe his eyes.

He immediately called Tiffany at work. "You've filed for legal separation?"

"I see you got the papers," she said with a calmness that scared Darius a little.

"Yeah, I got them. What's this about?"

"It's about me asking you to leave and you refusing."

"That's because I want to work things out with you," Darius said.

"Listen, I can't talk right now. I don't want to lose my job," Tiffany said in almost a whisper. "I need this job, especially now."

"And I don't want to lose you; I don't want to lose my family."

"Well, maybe you should have thought about that when you were out there doing what you were doing."

"I made a mistake. Okay? And that was

years ago. It's over now. You can't convict me of something that's so far in the past it had to be dug up to be killed."

"Darius, it might be old for you, but it's new for me. I'm left to process a lot of things right now. You may have held that fire to your bosom years ago, but the clothes that were burned still show evidence of that fire. I'm hanging up now, Darius, because like I just said, I need my job. I have children to take care of."

"Please, Tiff —"

She hung up. He started to call back but knew it wouldn't do any good. He looked at the papers again. He was being ordered to leave his home? Legally, he was being forced out of his own house. *This was crazy!*

He hurled the stapled papers across the room toward the fireplace. "Where exactly am I supposed to go! Huh?" He looked up. "Where am I supposed to go?"

CHAPTER 46

> For it was not an enemy that reproached me; then I could have borne it: neither was it he that hated me that did magnify himself against me; then I would have hid myself from him.
>
> — Psalm 55:12

Lawrence arrived home a little after five o'clock that evening. A woman was there talking to his wife, Deidra. He'd seen the woman before but couldn't quite put his finger on when or where.

Deidra escorted the woman to the door. Lawrence listened for a second to see if something said might give him a clue as to who the woman was and from where he might know her. At least he could breathe a sigh of relief; it wasn't anyone he'd slept with.

"Thanks a lot, Gigi," Deidra said. "You've been *more* than helpful."

"Should you need me again, you know how to get in touch with me."

"Prayerfully, I won't need you again."

Deidra came into the den, where Lawrence sat holding the remote control as though he was just about to turn on the television. "Who was that?" Lawrence asked.

"Nobody important," Deidra said.

"She just looked familiar to me. I was trying to place where I may have met her."

"Oh, you know you, Lawrence. Out there on the campaign stump, you run into and see all kinds of folks. You surely can't remember everyone who crosses your path, now can you?"

"So what did she want?" Lawrence set the remote control on the sofa.

Deidra walked and stood over him. "Lawrence, I want you to quit the race."

He chuckled. "You want what?"

"I want you to get out of the race."

"Okay, you've officially lost your mind. In case you haven't heard, I'm up for reelection. If I quit the race, I *absolutely* lose."

"You've already lost," Deidra said.

"Sit down and tell me what's going on." He grabbed her hand and tried to pull her down beside him. She held her ground and refused to budge. Lawrence frowned. "Dee, what's your problem?"

"I want you to quit the race. Today. So call up whomever you need to call and tell them you're shutting things down. Now . . . today."

Lawrence stood up and looked into her eyes. "That's not going to happen."

She put her hand on her hip. "Yes . . . it is."

Lawrence twisted his mouth. "And what reason am I to cite for this change of heart?"

She shrugged. "It doesn't matter. One excuse is as good as another. Tell them it's family business that you need to deal with."

He grabbed her up lovingly by her shoulders. "Are you sick? Is something wrong?"

"No, I'm not sick. At least not in the way one might classify one as being sick." She pulled away from him and took a step back from him. "But I *am* sick of your lies. I'm sick of you doing things and thinking you're getting away with them. Do you really think I don't know about all of the women you've been with? Huh?"

"I'm not with any woman now . . . other than you, my lovely wife," Lawrence said. "So we can squash this talk about me getting out of the race. If I don't do this, then what am I supposed to do for a living to support us?"

She walked over and stood by the oak

built-in bookcase. "Find a job like everyone else."

"I'm good at what I do now. And I'm paid well to do it."

"Go and call William, and tell him you're shutting things down. Then I want you to decide what you're going to do about your daughter."

Lawrence nodded. "It's Paris again, isn't it? She's still upset about how things are going in her life, and she won't stop until she's ruined ours. Paris will be all right. Andrew is going to come around. I know they've been having problems. But it's no reason for our lives to be torn up because of what's going on with them. Besides, I've taken care of her; I let her go from her job working on my campaign so she can spend time at home with her own husband."

"I'm not talking about Paris," Deidra said in a quiet tone.

Lawrence frowned from concern. "Imani? Is something wrong with Imani? What's going on with her? Tell me."

"I'm not talking about Imani, either."

"All right," Lawrence said. "Then you've lost me, because we only have two daughters. And you'd better not be about to tell me that Malachi is going through some kind of an identity crisis or something. I'm not in the mood. Not today."

Deidra nodded. "Yes, we only have two daughters. But *you,* you, my dear husband, have another daughter."

Lawrence rushed over to her. "I don't know what you've heard, but I told you the last time this came up, whoever is saying something like this is just lying."

"Lawrence, cut it, okay. I'm not playing games anymore. I'm too old to be playing games with you. What I don't understand is how you could do something like that and continue to live with yourself."

"I'm telling you, Dee —"

"That little girl is your daughter, Lawrence. And you knew it the whole time you were manipulating us and making a fool out of me. She was sick. She could have died. And you were playing games, worrying about some *stupid* representative seat."

He grabbed her up by her shoulders. "I was worried about you. You have to believe me. I didn't want to lose you, Dee. You mean everything to me."

Deidra snatched herself out of his grip. "Poppycock! You were doing it to protect yourself and what meant the most to you. What if she had died, Lawrence? What if Imani hadn't pushed us to let her step up? Your daughter could have died! That eight-year-old little girl could have died last year!"

"But she didn't. And things worked out. I wanted to tell you." He grabbed Deidra up by her shoulders once more. "You have to believe me. I wanted so badly to tell you. You know you mean the world to me. You *are* my world, Deidra Jean Simmons. Don't you get that?"

Deidra nodded. "You slept with an eighteen-year-old girl, the exact same age your own daughter was at the time. And it didn't even bother you." She hunched her shoulders. "Didn't faze you one little bit. And to have a child out there for all of these years that you never acknowledged. You're a despicable man. And I never thought I'd be saying that about you." She shook her head as she primped her mouth.

"In the first place, I didn't know about her until close to the end of last year. I didn't even know I *had* another daughter out there. You have to believe that," Lawrence said, tears pooling up in his eyes.

"And why is that, Lawrence? Why didn't you know you had a daughter out there in the world somewhere? You knew she'd been given up for adoption, didn't you?"

"I didn't know that," Lawrence said.

"Why wouldn't you know that? Are you telling me that Gabrielle Booker never told you she was pregnant with your child? And don't lie to me, Lawrence. I'm telling you: Don't you *dare* lie to me!"

Tears began rolling down his face. He wiped them away and took in a deep breath. "I didn't know because she was supposed to have gotten rid of it. I thought she'd had an abortion. But she double-crossed me."

Deidra backed away from him. "Double-crossed you? You told her to get an abortion and she decided not to, and you think that's double-crossing you?" She backed away some more with her hands up. "You're more out of touch than I even suspected. Do you know how hard it is for a woman to terminate a pregnancy? Do you? Do you even know what goes through her mind when she has to think about doing something like that? Do you know that not everybody can live with doing something like that? And you think her decision — an eighteen-year-old girl who had no place to live, no real family to help her out — to go through nine months of pregnancy, pretty much alone, knowing in the end that she couldn't tell anyone, that she did it purely to double-cross *you*?" Deidra laughed . . . pain resonating all throughout it. She shook her head. "You are a *real* piece of work. My Lord, help me."

Lawrence hurried to her and gently pressed her face between his two hands to make her look at him as he spoke. "I was young and foolish. I wasn't thinking straight. I'm not *that* man anymore. I'm not."

She pulled her face from his grasp. "You were over forty. You were thinking straight enough to cover it up and keep it a secret. As for you not being *that* man anymore, you need to start being a real man." He grabbed her by the wrist; she jerked away. "Now call and let whoever needs to know that the campaign is officially over. You will *not* be seeking reelection. And you can tell them it's due to family matters that require your attention, if that helps you save face. But this is not up for discussion. The information about Jasmine being your daughter *will* be coming out. That's a given."

"But I've taken care of that. Gabrielle and I talked about it. She's not going to do anything, especially since I got Paris to back off from trying to take that child from her."

"You mean you got Paris to back off from taking your daughter . . . her half sister, from a person she felt had no right to her. Let's call it what it is, Lawrence."

"Does Paris know the whole truth now?" Lawrence asked.

"I called her to come over. She'll be here

any minute now, and *you're* going to tell her the whole truth. Apparently, she knew *something;* she was the only one fighting for your daughter." Deidra shook her head. "Your daughter."

Lawrence turned and rubbed his forehead. He then ran his hand over his head. "I don't know why we can't do this another way. We can weather this storm together, Dee. I know we can. I don't need to quit the race. This is manageable. It is."

"I'm not going through this publicly." Deidra shook her head. "I'm not going to have our dirty laundry aired in the public eye or, I should say, *your* dirty laundry. This is going to come out. And you're going to lose the reelection for sure when it does. Have some self-respect and decency, if not for you, then for your family."

"I'm sorry. I'm sorry that I'm making you have to go through this. Just please don't leave me. Please. I can't lose everything. Not now."

The doorbell rang. "That's Paris," Deidra said as she went to answer the door.

CHAPTER 47

The gates of the rivers shall be opened, and the palace shall be dissolved.

— Nahum 2:6

Paris stepped in the house. She could tell immediately that something wasn't right. Her father was standing in the den as though he was waiting on her. She wondered what she'd done now to cause her mother to call and ask her over like this. Maybe word had reached her mother about how she'd almost destroyed Gabrielle and her child. Andrew, most likely had told her, especially if she'd asked what was going on.

"Daddy," she said acknowledging him with a quick nod.

He didn't say anything back. Everybody seemed to have an attitude lately. It had been over three weeks, and Andrew still wasn't saying much to her. He hadn't quite forgiven her for what she'd done to Gabrielle and Jasmine. If only she could go back and do everything all over again, she definitely wouldn't have done what she had.

"Sit down," Deidra said. "Your father has something he needs to tell you."

Paris sat down slowly and angled her body to face her father, who continued to stand. Her mother sat down next to her and took her by the hand. She knew whatever this was, it *wasn't* going to be good.

Lawrence folded his hands into each other. "You know we love you, don't you?"

She looked to her mother first, then back to her father. "Of course."

Lawrence let his hands drop to his side. "Well, something has happened. Something we as a family need to deal with."

"You sound so serious; you're starting to scare me. Is everybody all right? Has somebody died?" Paris turned to her mother, squeezing her hand. "You don't have cancer do you? Please tell me you don't have —"

Deidra shook her head. "I don't have cancer."

Paris let out a sigh of relief. "Then what is it. Just say it. I hate when you string things out like this." Paris's thoughts immediately raced to a month ago when she'd slept with Darius. Had they somehow found out about that? Is that why they had called her here?

To give her a good tongue lashing? Did Andrew know and this was his way of breaking it to her that they were over and this was why? "Daddy, please, I can't take this. If you have something to say, just spit it out."

"You remember last year when Imani became the bone marrow donor for that little girl?" Lawrence said.

"You're talking about Jasmine Noble?" Paris frowned. Why was he bringing this up and in front of her mother, at that? He knew she had accused him of fathering Jasmine. He had denied it. And up until Paris had learned that Jessica wasn't Jasmine's birth mother, she was convinced Jasmine was her father's child. But she now knew that Gabrielle was Jasmine's birth mother, a child she'd given up for adoption.

"Paris . . . baby, I want to ask you to forgive me." Lawrence was saying that just at the time she knew what was coming next. "Jasmine Noble . . . that little girl is my daughter. That means she's your —"

"Oh, God," Paris said as she stood up and pressed her hands into her stomach. "Oh, God, I think I'm going to be sick!" She ran out of the den to the bathroom and threw up.

Her father had slept with Gabrielle. Her

father and Gabrielle had actually slept together. She threw up again.

CHAPTER 48

Behold, ye trust in lying words, that cannot profit.

— Jeremiah 7:8

Paris went home. She didn't want to hear any more. Her mother tried to make her stay until she felt better, but she had to get out of there. The walls were closing in on her. She wanted to yell at her father. *How could he do that?* How could he sleep with a girl the same age as his own daughter? How could he betray her and her mother in that way?

She always knew in her heart that Jasmine was her father's. She just never put it together like this. Not even after learning that Gabrielle was Jasmine's birth mother did she come to the right conclusion. She thought it could have been Cedric's child. Maybe, though unlikely, even could have been Andrew's. But never . . . never in a million years did she *ever* consider her father and Gabrielle having been together.

She raced to the bathroom again and threw up some more. She sat on the bathroom floor as she cried. How could her father be married to her beautiful mother and have so easily slept with someone else? It didn't make sense. Her father loved her mother; she knew that he did. She thought back to when Gabrielle was staying with her. Her parents weren't having marital problems, not that she knew of. Nothing more than what normal married couples dealt with. And if she was honest, most of their arguments tended to stem from things surrounding her.

When she was living in that apartment, her father wanted Gabrielle out of there. It was her mother who had argued that it was wrong for them to just throw Gabrielle out on the streets with nowhere else to go. Her mother had told her to give her time to get things together.

Paris held her head over the toilet and threw up again. She wiped her mouth with the wet face towel she now had with her. Her mother had advocated doing right by Gabrielle, and how had Gabrielle repaid her? By sleeping with her husband.

Paris looked up at the ceiling light in the

bathroom. "Daddy, how could you do that? How could you just sleep with someone like *her* without any regard to us?"

She threw up one more time, wiped her face, and got up off the floor. She dragged herself to her bedroom and laid across the bed. Thinking about her father and how he could so carelessly cheat on her mother — producing an illegitimate child, no less — it suddenly occurred to her that she was late having a cycle.

She got up and pulled out the calendar she kept with her circled days. She hadn't even thought about it before now. Counting back to the last time she'd circled days, she noted that she was two weeks late. But so much had been going on. Could she really possibly be pregnant?

The thought of it made her burst into a smile. She and Andrew had been trying for years now. Had she finally conceived after all her time of trying? She jumped up and rushed to the bathroom, happy that she'd bought an early pregnancy test kit in anticipation of this fateful day. She scanned the instructions, which were simple enough.

Five minutes later, she had her answer. She was pregnant! She was so excited; she couldn't wait for Andrew to get home so she could tell him the grand news. Just to be certain the results weren't a false positive, she used the second kit included in the box and took the test again. The second test confirmed what the first one had declared. She was definitely pregnant!

She did a happy dance, then picked up the phone to call her mother. With all of the bad news happening, it would be great to share something good at this juncture. She and Andrew were finally going to have a baby! Andrew was going to be the father he'd always dreamed of being. She began pressing the numbers to her mother's, when it hit her like a ton of bricks. She put the phone back in the holder.

What if this isn't Andrew's baby? She had, in fact, slept with Darius. She sat down on the bed and tried to think. How long ago and had she even slept with her husband during this time?

She and Andrew had been on the outs. Did the two of them even have sex during the time she would have conceived? Of course, they had. They had to have. Didn't they? How else could she be pregnant? And as for Darius, she was only with him that one time. Once, that's it. Surely she couldn't have gotten pregnant after only one time with him. *Even God wouldn't be that cruel to her.*

But she and Andrew had been trying for years now. And they hadn't produced a baby yet. Not until now. Surely, this baby *had* to be Andrew's. It *had* to be! It was, as far as she was concerned. This baby was hers and her husband's — the two of them.

Andrew cleared his throat. "I said hello."

Paris jumped, then looked up. "I'm sorry. I didn't hear you come in." Paris wiped her face with her hand to be sure she looked okay.

"Yeah. I could see you were in deep thought there." He walked to the bathroom, only to come back less than a minute later holding up a white plastic stick. "Honey, what's this?" He was grinning slightly.

Paris's eyes grew bigger. In her rush to call her mother, she'd left the pregnancy test sticks on the counter in the bathroom. Andrew held one of them now in his hand.

Andrew began to grin even bigger. "Is this saying what I *think* it's saying?"

Paris smiled, then nodded as though she were shy. "Yes."

"It says PREGNANT. We're pregnant? We're going to have a baby?"

She nodded quickly once more.

He set the stick down on the bed as he pulled her to her feet. "Oh, baby, that's wonderful!" He picked her up and spun her around. "We're going to have a baby! We're going to have a baby!" He suddenly stopped and gently set her back on her feet. "Doing that doesn't hurt you or the baby, does it?" She shook her head. He couldn't stop grinning. "I can't *wait* to tell my mother!" He kissed Paris while softly cupping her face. "I love you. I love you."

She forced out a smile. "I love you, too."

He picked her up again and gently spun around as he sang, "I'm going to be a daddy! I'm going to be a *daddy*!"

Chapter 49

So then because thou art lukewarm, and neither cold nor hot, I will spew thee out of my mouth.

— Revelation 3:16

Darius was confused as well as distraught. He couldn't believe his life had made such a harrowing dive in such a short amount of time. He'd been riding so high, and now he was slithering around like a snake on its belly. "I'm not going out like this," he said as he located the phone book and looked up a phone number. He called and was told to come right in.

He drove to the address he'd written down.

"What can I do for you?" Frank Johnson, Lawrence Simmons's Democratic opponent, said as the two men sat across from each other in Frank Johnson's campaign headquarters.

"It's not what *you* can do for me; it's what *I* can do for you," Darius said.

Frank leaned in. "Okay. You have my full attention."

"I realize that time is money," Darius said. "And I don't want to waste yours. I'm also hoping you'll find the value in what I have to offer. I'm presently out of work, and I have a lovely wife with three beautiful children to support."

"You don't have to say too much because I'm hearing you just fine." Frank locked his fingers together. "Let's hear what you got."

Darius smiled, swallowed hard, then nodded. "Up until a few weeks ago, I was working for your political opponent, Lawrence Simmons. I've come in possession of some information that I feel *sure* will help you cinch the win in November."

"Is that right now? Well, apparently you haven't heard the news today."

"What news?"

"Lawrence Simmons pulled out of the race. Had a news conference and announced it. That means he's no longer my opponent. The Republicans are left scrambling to find someone to fill the slot. But this is pretty much all over but the shouting." Frank locked his fingers behind his head and leaned back in his chair.

Darius pulled back. "He dropped out? Are you sure?"

"Yep. He made the announcement on TV a little while ago, citing family matters that required his attention. Says his family is more important than some election, so he's pulling up stakes and stepping aside. I'm sure it's more to it than that. It usually is. But he won't hear any complaints from me. I wish him well. Called him up and told him so myself." Frank sat forward, scooted his chair back, and stood up. "I appreciate you for coming by though. If you had shown up yesterday, I would have snapped you up in a hurry." Frank extended his hand to Darius. "That's the luck of the draw."

Darius stood up and shook his hand. "It was a pleasure to meet you. Listen" — Darius chuckled a little — "I can still use a job. I have experience working on a campaign. I was the co-chair in signing up and turning out the youth vote."

"I would love to help you out." Frank sucked his teeth twice. "But you see you're kind of tainted now. You were working for the other side. No offense, because I'm sure you're a decent enough man, but we can't trust somebody like you. It's like when it comes to your commitment, you're neither hot nor cold; you're just lukewarm. Nobody cares much for lukewarm anything. You understand. I need someone on fire, hot to make my winning this election a manifested reality. Not just someone looking for his next paycheck."

Darius twisted his mouth a few times. "Well, would you happen to know of anyone who *is* hiring? I really need a job. I'm about to be homeless." Darius didn't feel he was lying; he *was* being put out of his home, which would make him homeless when that happened.

"Not in this economy. But I'm sure you'll land on your feet. You look like the type who generally manages to land on his feet. Good luck to you." Frank sat back down, his red hair that hid his comb-over moving just slightly out of place. He took his hand and brushed it back to where it was supposed to be.

"At the church where I belong, Followers of Jesus Faith Worship Center with Pastor George Landris, that's a mega church you may have heard of it, we don't believe in luck." Darius was hoping Frank Johnson would be impressed with him mentioning the church, for one, and knowing that there were possible votes there.

"Whatever floats your boat. Now, if you *will,* close my door on your way out. I do appreciate it. And if you're in my district, I'd also appreciate your vote."

Darius gave a nod. "Of course." He left.

CHAPTER 50

> But ye have set at nought all my counsel, and would none of my reproof.
>
> — Proverbs 1:25

Darius couldn't believe his life had fallen so apart. He didn't know what to do at this point. Where would he stay now that he was being forced out of his home? What would he do for money now that he'd lost his job? Sure there was the familiar unemployment compensation. But Tiffany was surely set to get money for child support for their three children. He wouldn't have much left to do much of anything.

He had to talk to Tiffany and get her to see that she couldn't do this. They were meant to be together. Married people weren't supposed to so easily throw in the towel. They were supposed to work things out. When they married, the minister said for better or worse. Things couldn't be worse. And yet, Tiffany was taking her ball and running with it. Yes, he'd been wrong. And if he had to crawl on his knees over broken glass and beg for mercy and forgiveness, then that's what he would do.

But he couldn't do this alone. He needed some help. He made a U-turn and headed for the church, hoping Pastor Landris was still there. Pastor Landris would be able to help him. If anyone could help him turn things around, Pastor Landris could.

Thankfully, Pastor Landris was there, but he was in a meeting. Darius was told Pastor Landris wouldn't be able to see him, but that he could talk with another person on staff or make an appointment for later. Darius was telling the secretary that it was really important; he couldn't wait another day. It was a matter of life and death.

Johnnie Mae just happened to enter as he was saying that.

"I'm sorry," Johnnie Mae said. "Is there something I can help you with?"

"Sister Johnnie Mae." He gave her a hug. "I need to talk with Pastor Landris."

"And I just told him that Pastor Landris wouldn't be able to see him," the secretary said.

"But I desperately need to speak with someone," Darius said. "It's important."

"Well, I happen to have some time if you'd like to talk to me," Johnnie Mae said.

Darius looked back and forth between the two women. "No offense, but I don't know about talking to you about this," he said to Johnnie Mae. "I was hoping to possibly speak with a man, preferably my own pastor."

"Well, I don't mind talking with you. But you have to suit yourself," Johnnie Mae said.

"I can make you an appointment for tomorrow with one of the other counselors on staff," the secretary said.

"What's your name?" Darius asked her.

"Phyllis."

"Well, Phyllis, I appreciate your help," Darius said. "But I *really* need to see someone right now . . . today. Can you ask Pastor Landris if he might be able to speak with me for a few minutes? A few minutes, that's all I really need."

Phyllis looked up at Johnnie Mae.

Darius turned to look at Johnnie Mae, wondering if maybe she'd been shaking her head no to Phyllis behind his back. "Okay. If you have time," he said to Johnnie Mae.

"If you're sure about it," Johnnie Mae said. "I don't want you feeling uncomfortable talking to me."

"I'm sure."

"Phyllis, what conference room is available?"

Phyllis typed something on the computer. "Conference room L."

"Great. Right this way." Johnnie Mae led Darius to the conference room. She moved the sign on the door to state IN USE.

Johnnie Mae sat down at the rectangular table. "Please have a seat, Darius."

"I'm impressed. I see that you know my name," he said.

Johnnie Mae smiled. "Yes, I'm familiar with you, Darius Connors."

"You're probably a little *more* than just familiar with me. You likely know everything that's going on with me and mine. You know my wife, Tiffany."

"Yes."

"Well, did you know that she just served me papers for a legal separation?"

Johnnie Mae looked at him without giving anything she may or may not have known away. "Before we begin, I'd like to pray."

Darius nodded. Johnnie Mae prayed.

"Okay, Darius, now tell me what you consider to be a matter of life and death."

Darius stared straight ahead. "I'm about to lose my wife and family and I can't go on without them. I'll die without them in my life. Tiffany is like the air I breathe. One can't live without air."

"Sure you can live without her. If you have to, you can make it."

"No, I can't. Tiffany and my children are *everything* to me. They're my world. I know it's a cliché and everybody says it, but for me, it's true."

There was a sharp rap on the door. Johnnie Mae frowned. "Excuse me. I'm sorry. This must be important since the sign outside the door indicates that someone is in here in conference." She got up and answered the door.

"What are you doing here?" Johnnie Mae said with a jubilant lift in her voice.

"I came to lend my assistance," Pastor Landris said. "Do you mind if I come in?"

Johnnie Mae smiled as he strolled in and closed the door behind him.

"I heard you came by my office earlier," Pastor Landris said to Darius.

Darius stood up and shook Pastor Landris's outstretched hand. "Yes. I was told you were busy and wouldn't be able to see me today."

"You were told right. But God must have had other plans because here I am."

Darius sat back down.

Pastor Landris sat down across from Darius. "Go on, honey. I'm just here for support and assistance if you should need me," he said to Johnnie Mae, who was sitting at the head of the table.

She grinned as though the two of them had a secret between them.

"No, we were just getting started," Johnnie Mae said to her Pastor Landris. "We've already prayed and we were just about to talk about what's going on with Darius. He's married to Tiffany Connors. They have three children: Jade who is close to Princess Rose's age, Dana, and Junior. Correct?" Johnnie Mae said to Darius.

"Yes, that's right." Darius said to Johnnie Mae, then turned to Pastor Landris. "Tiffany is in the dance ministry."

"All right, Darius. Fill me in on what's going on with you."

Darius told Pastor Landris about him having worked for a politician's reelection campaign, how he'd lost that job about a month ago, how his wife had sent papers for a legal separation that just arrived today, and how there was now an order for him to leave his own house.

"And what are you leaving out of all this that you're *not* telling?" Pastor Landris asked.

"That's pretty much it," Darius said, playing with his hands.

"So you want me to believe that your wife just up and wants a separation for no good reason? You've done nothing to prompt any of this? She just decided she doesn't want to be married anymore and has papers delivered to just put you out?" Pastor Landris leaned forward toward Darius. "Come on, Darius. If you're going to come here for help, you need to confess the problem. Nobody can help you if you're going to present half-truths or hold back information. Either you want help or you don't. If you don't, there are plenty of folks out there who would love having this time and opportunity and would use it to be helped."

"I had an affair and my wife found out about it," Darius blurted out. "All right?"

"Okay," Pastor Landris said. "Well, you're not the first person to have an affair. It's not the best thing to be saying, but people have been able to put marriages back together after such a revelation. That's when the party who did the wrong repents and truly turns from that behavior. Nobody wants to forgive a serial adulterer."

"I told her I was sorry," Darius said. "And this affair was over five years ago. It's old news and, quite frankly, in my mind, irrelevant as this point in time."

"*When* it happens makes no difference; it's the fact that it happened that hurts and can be hard to get over," Pastor Landris said. "Is there anything else you think we should know?" Pastor Landris tilted his head slightly and waited.

"Just that the person I had the affair with is someone my wife has become friends with. I think that probably hurts her even more. But the two of them didn't even know each other back when me and her were together." Darius stood and began to walk around the room. "She's a member of this church, you know." He stopped and looked at Pastor Landris and Johnnie Mae. "The woman I had the affair with; she's a member here. She's also in the dance ministry with my wife."

"Does your wife know this woman is the person you had the affair with?" Pastor Landris asked.

He laughed. "Oh, she knows. She knows. It's Fatima Adams. Well, Fatima whatever her last name is now that she got married." Darius looked at Johnnie Mae, who didn't even flinch. "So I just need to fix all of this. I don't want to lose my house."

"Are you only really worried about losing your house?" Johnnie Mae asked.

"No, of course not," Darius said with a

slight chuckle. He came and sat back down. "I told you: I don't want to lose Tiffany . . . I don't want to lose my family." He turned to Pastor Landris. "So tell me: What do I do to fix it? Can you pray for me that I keep my family? Lay hands on me if you have to, so things will get back right. I can't lose everything. I've worked too hard for this stuff, Pastor Landris. I can't."

"I'm going to tell you what I think you should do," Pastor Landris said. "And then my wife and I are going to pray for you again."

Darius nodded with a smile. "Sounds good. I'm ready for things to get better. This has *not* been fun, you can believe that. I've learned *my* lesson."

"First, you need to move out as your wife requested," Pastor Landris said.

Darius jumped to his feet. "Hold up, playa! You apparently weren't listening to what I was saying. I can't leave; I have nowhere to go. I don't have a job. So if I leave my house, where incidentally I pay the note, where am I supposed to live?"

"Have a seat, Darius," Pastor Landris said.

"For what? So I can listen to this mumbo jumbo you're spouting? I didn't have to come here and spill my guts just to be told

I should leave like my wife is asking me to do."

Pastor Landris pointed to Darius's vacated chair. Darius eased down.

"Now," Pastor Landris said. "We have a program here that you can participate in. We work a lot with folks dealing with substance abuse who need help —"

"I don't have problems with alcohol *or* drugs," Darius said.

Pastor Landris leaned in, propping himself up on the table with his forearms. "If you'll just allow me to finish. We also deal with people who are going through marital troubles like you. There's a facility for women who are having problems or need a place to stay when their spouses have either put them out or they have left on their own, and we have a separate facility for the men. What I'd suggest is that you avail yourself of the men's facility. That will provide you with a place to stay. We have counselors on hand to work with you and who will help you work through the problems that caused the breakdown in your marriage. We encourage estranged spouses to participate during certain sessions as we tear down the old foundation and build up a stronger one. Our success rate is quite high for those who commit to working through the whole program. So what do you say?"

"If I do this, can you guarantee me my family back?" Darius asked.

"No one can guarantee that," Johnnie Mae said. "But if your wife sees you're making an effort, believe me, she'll be more likely to be receptive to reconciliation than not."

"Look, it's up to you," Pastor Landris said. "But if you're not serious or you don't really want this to work, then there's no reason for you to waste anyone's time, including yours."

"So you can't just talk to her and convince her to let me stay and we work this out that way?" Darius said. "I could still do the sessions. I just don't see how me leaving is going to make things better. My wife and I need to be there together in order to make things work. I still can't believe she had the nerve to see a lawyer. That's so not like her at all. I'm certain one of her little friends had something to do with her doing that. I wouldn't put it past Fatima or Gabrielle. We were doing fine until all of them hooked up and became friends."

"Darius, saying things like this won't help your cause any," Johnnie Mae said.

Darius began to chuckle. "Heck, I wouldn't doubt it if she hasn't talked to you and you just may have been the one encouraging her to do this," Darius said to Johnnie Mae.

"All right, now. Slow your roll. That's my wife you're talking to," Pastor Landris said. "And you *will* respect *my* wife. You might not have respected your own in the past, which is an indication as to why you're in the predicament you find yourself in in the first place. But you *will* respect mine. Do we have an understanding?"

"No problem," Darius said with a smirk. "I just wish instead of us going through all of this, you could slap me upside my head, knock me to the floor . . . what's that they call it? Slain in the Spirit? Anyway, put your hand to my head and pray, and when you're finished, everything is all right again."

"I'm sorry, but it doesn't quite work like that," Pastor Landris said. "So what's it going to be? Because if you're interested in the in-house facility, I need to let them know you're coming and get the ball rolling."

Darius stood up. "Let me think about it, and if I decide to move forward, I'll let you know. But right now, I'm leaning toward getting my wife back my own way, without having to go through all this. I *will* consider all that you've said, and I'll get back with you."

Pastor Landris and Johnnie Mae stood up as well. "Okay, then," Pastor Landris said. "You can call the church office here, ask for Phyllis. She'll get the information to me, and we will go from there if you decide that's what you want to do." Pastor Landris released a controlled quiet sigh.

Darius nodded and started toward the door.

"Wait up. We wanted to pray before you left. Remember?" Pastor Landris said, taking hold of Johnnie Mae's hand as they reached out for Darius's.

Darius looked down at Pastor Landris's hand as though Pastor Landris had just come out of the bathroom without washing his hand first, then back up to his face. "That's okay. I'm good." Darius walked to the door, opened it, and left without even so much as a thank you or a good-bye.

Chapter 51

For where two or three are gathered together in my name, there am I in the midst of them.

— Matthew 18:20

"Okay, so what just happened here?" Pastor Landris asked Johnnie Mae.

She shook her head. "Beats me. I was just so very pleasantly surprised when you showed up."

"You and I have talked about Darius Connors before. When Phyllis told me he'd come to my office pretty much demanding to see me, then told me you'd come along and offered to talk with him, I wasn't going to leave you alone with him."

"Jealous, are you?"

"Woman, please. I am *not* worried when it comes to you. I know the man that you love, the man to whom your whole heart belongs. And you love you some Him and

His name is Jesus. I know you're not going to do anything to hurt *or* disappoint Him."

Johnnie Mae laughed. "You're so cute. If it makes you feel better, after Jesus, I love me some George Edward Landris."

He blushed. "And I wouldn't want the order to be any other way," Pastor Landris said. "But back to Darius. Can you believe what he called himself doing?"

"You mean him sneakily telling us about Fatima and Gabrielle? Oh, yes, I caught that. Too bad he didn't know that he wasn't telling either of us anything that we didn't already know," Johnnie Mae said. "But had Fatima not informed me the other week all about her part with him, it *would* have caught me off guard. I remember the first time when I started helping out with counseling, Fatima came and talked with me. It was back when you preached on strongholds that time. She told me she was dealing with a married man and wanted to break completely from that stronghold. Who knew that some five years later, I would learn the name of that married man and it would turn out to be Darius Connors, of all people?"

"I just pray he's not still having affairs," Pastor Landris said. "I would very much like to help him. But I also feel in my spirit, he's headed for an even greater fall. Sadly, I don't believe he's hit rock bottom yet. He's too prideful. And the Bible says that pride goes before destruction. We can pray for him, but he has to want to change."

"Well, Tiffany came and talked with me a few weeks back. She was devastated about everything going on with Darius. She doesn't believe he's going to ever change unless he's confronted with the possibility that she won't be there taking his garbage any longer. She's fed up, and that's an understatement."

"Yeah, but we're Christians," Pastor Landris said. "We're not *supposed* to get fed up, right?" He grinned.

"It's like you've preached on a few times. Even Jesus got fed up enough that He turned over the tables of the money changers. Fed up is not always a bad thing."

"True. I just pray Darius comes to his senses before he really *does* lose everything. He needs to come completely clean with his wife, though. I still feel like he's not telling everything. The man needs heart surgery . . . a spiritual heart surgery." Pastor Landris was still holding Johnnie Mae's hand. "Well, it looks like it's just you and me. Whether he stayed for it or not, he still needs prayer."

"Let's do it, then. For Tiffany and those children. For Darius, even if he didn't care enough to stay and take part. For Fatima and Trent, because if Darius keeps running around telling this like he's doing, who knows what's going to happen. And for Gabrielle, Jasmine, and Zachary, who need all the help and covering they can get."

Pastor Landris and Johnnie Mae bowed their heads as they held both hands. Pastor Landris began to pray. "Father God, we come to You, humbly and with pure adoration. Thanking You for Your many blessings. Lord, I thank You for this blessing of a woman You have given me. Keep her in perfect peace. Be a lifter of her spirits, I pray. Bless those who have yoked themselves with this body, Followers of Jesus Faith Worship Center. Lord, You know what each is in need of. I feel Your presence right now. For Lord, You say where two or three are gathered together in *Your* name, You'll be in the midst.

"Lord, touch those who are sick in their bodies, sick in their minds, and sick in their hearts. We know You are a divine healer; You're a *rock* in a weary land. I ask a special blessing in the lives of Darius and Tiffany Connors. You know better than we. Send protection and a special touch of love into the Connors's household; into the lives of Fatima and Trent Howard; into the lives of

Gabrielle, Jasmine, and Zachary. Remove all anger, bitterness, and strife. Lord, I ask that You grant me the wisdom to lead Your people and to be a blessing to all I may come in contact with through whatever median You see fit. These blessings I ask in Jesus's name, amen."

Johnnie Mae squeezed his hand. "Amen."

Chapter 52

For with God nothing shall be impossible.
— Luke 1:37

It was mid-November 2010, a full year since Gabrielle first learned she wasn't a bone marrow match for the little girl she'd given birth to some eight years earlier. The doorbell rang. Gabrielle and Jasmine were in the kitchen mixing batter for brownies.

"It never fails, when I get really busy, something always interrupts me," Gabrielle said to Jasmine.

"You want me to get it for you?" Jasmine asked. "It's nobody but Dr. Z."

Gabrielle let the wooden spoon she was using rest inside the bowl. "No, I'll get it. I'm pretty sure it's *not* Dr. Z because he said he was working until six today."

"Well, maybe he got off early."

Gabrielle tapped Jasmine on her nose as the two of them headed for the door.

"You wish."

"What *I* wish is that we would hurry up and get married. Then he could just come home to us."

Gabrielle laughed. "We, huh?"

"Yes. You, Dr. Z, and me. *We.*" Jasmine put her thumb to her chest.

Gabrielle cracked the door open. "Andrew? What are you doing here?"

"Hi. I hope you don't mind me coming by without calling first," Andrew said.

"No, it's fine." Gabrielle opened the door a little wider.

"Hi, Gabrielle," Paris said.

"Paris."

"I hope you don't mind that I came with Andrew. If you'd rather, I'll go sit in the car and wait."

"It's okay." Gabrielle glanced down and saw Paris's definite baby bump. "I see that congratulations are in order." Gabrielle didn't say it with a lot of enthusiasm.

Paris placed her hand on her now showing stomach enhanced by the knit purple-print dress she was wearing. "Yes. Thank you."

"Come in," Gabrielle said, opening the door wide enough for them both to walk through together.

Andrew and Paris walked in and stood in

the marbled foyer.

Andrew looked at Jasmine, who was standing off to the side. "Hello, Jasmine."

Jasmine waved. "Hi there."

"Hi, Jasmine," Paris said, putting her hand over her mouth after saying Jasmine's name.

Jasmine merely gave a short flip of her hand.

Andrew turned back to Gabrielle. "We're not going to stay long. I just stopped by to bring you something." He held out a large gold-colored envelope to her.

Gabrielle took it. "What is it?"

"Open it and see," Andrew said.

Gabrielle looked at him and began opening it. She pulled the papers out.

"It's official," Andrew said. "They're your official papers. It's done, Gabrielle. It's all over." He smiled.

Gabrielle hurriedly scanned the papers. Jasmine was officially and legally her daughter. She hugged Andrew, then just as quickly stepped back. She then rushed over to Jasmine and hugged her. "You're my daughter now. It's official, Jasmine. It's official!"

Jasmine held on to Gabrielle tight. "I'm your daughter? We're officially a family now?"

Gabrielle pushed back and looked into her eyes. "Yes, baby! We are officially a family now." She hugged her again.

"Congratulations, Gabrielle," Paris said. "I'm so happy . . . for both of you."

Gabrielle stood up straight and turned to Paris. "Thank you, Paris. I appreciate that."

"I mean it," Paris said. "I really do." Paris looked at Jasmine and tears began to form in her eyes. "I'm happy for you both." She continued to look at Jasmine, tilting her head slightly as she smiled.

Gabrielle knew it was because she now knew that Jasmine was, in reality, her half sister. Lawrence had contacted her and told her everything that had gone down. Well, maybe not everything, but pretty much all she needed to know.

She thought when he first told her that his wife knew the whole truth about both her and Jasmine, that he was doing that to let her know any leverage she may have thought she had was pretty much gone. He sealed it by letting her know that he was no longer planning on staying in the race for reelection. He then went on to assure her that Paris would no longer be interfering with her and Jasmine. Gabrielle wasn't sure how exactly he could guarantee that, but she was taking what she could get.

Lawrence then shocked her by saying that one day he hoped she would tell Jasmine that he was her father and that she had other siblings. Gabrielle told him she wasn't ready to go there yet — not with him, not with his family, and most certainly not with Jasmine. She'd worked hard to repair the damage caused when Jasmine learned Gabrielle was her birth mother. She had originally planned on telling Jasmine that in her own time and her own way, but Paris had ruined all of that. Then there was fallout that came afterward. She didn't want to open up that wound right now.

For now, Jasmine wasn't asking about her father. But since Lawrence had told her he wanted a relationship with his daughter . . . that "they" wanted a relationship with Jasmine, mainly encouraged by his wife, who, it turned out, was instrumental in bringing all of this to fruition the way it had. She would tell Jasmine when she felt the time was right. Barring any more slipups, that information, she prayed, would go over a lot better than the information that had been revealed when it came to her.

"Would it be all right if I have a hug?" Paris asked Jasmine as they were getting ready to leave.

Jasmine looked at Gabrielle as though she was asking what she thought about it. Gabrielle smiled at Jasmine. Jasmine smiled back, then went to Paris, who promptly bent down and hugged her almost as though she didn't want to let go.

Andrew and Paris left. Gabrielle turned and looked at Jasmine. They both screamed at the same time while doing what they called "the happy dance" right there together in the foyer. The doorbell rang, prematurely interrupting their celebration.

"Wonder who that can be?" Gabrielle said, going to the door to answer it. "Maybe Mr. Andrew forgot something."

Gabrielle opened the door and her mouth literally hung open as she stared.

An older woman, dressed in the style of the Queen of England, cute little hat and all, stood at the door. "Hello, dearie," she said.

Gabrielle merely stood there, not knowing what to say, in complete shock. She suddenly began to cry, then began balling like a baby as she pulled the older woman inside the foyer and hugged her for dear life. "Miss Crowe! Miss Crowe!" That was all she could get out. "Miss Crowe."

Esther Crowe patted her on the back as they hugged, her hat falling to the floor.

Zachary stepped into view. Gabrielle let go of Miss Crowe, but only partially. She looked at Zachary and smiled.

"Surprise!" he said, stooping down and picking up Miss Crowe's blue hat.

Jasmine ran to the door and straight into Zachary's arms. "Dr. Z!"

Zachary scooped her up. "Miss Jazz!" He held her in the air as he stepped fully inside the house. He set Miss Crowe's hat on the round table in the foyer.

Gabrielle looked at Miss Crowe and hugged her again. "What are you doing here? Oh, Miss Crowe, I've missed you so much! I'm so glad you're here." She took Miss Crowe carefully by the arm. "Come. Come on in and let's sit down." She led her into the living room. Miss Crowe gently sat down alongside Gabrielle, who was still holding on to her, helping her with every movement.

They held hands as they sat closely next to each other. Gabrielle quietly laid her head on Miss Crowe's shoulder. Miss Crowe took her hand and brushed down Gabrielle's hair, straight now and not full of her usual rods of curls.

"You came back," Gabrielle said, looking into her face. "You came home."

"Yes, baby. I came back." Miss Crowe looked into her eyes and smiled. "I came back for you. They said I wouldn't make it. I'm not supposed to even be here. But guess what? I made it. I made it. With God, nothing shall be impossible to those who believe."

"You came back for me? For me?" Tears were streaming down Gabrielle's face.

Miss Crowe opened her purse and took out a handkerchief. She carefully began dabbing away Gabrielle's tears. "Yes. I came back for you. I came . . . so you and I can plan a wedding. That's right: I'm here for a wedding. And there will be no more stalling and no more excuses. Do you hear me? No devil is going to stop this from taking place. No devil or folks who think they know best. Miss Crowe is here."

Gabrielle nodded as she continued to cry. "You always know, don't you? You always know when I need you the most. And your speech . . . it's no longer slurred like it was last time I saw you."

Miss Crowe placed her feeble hands on each side of Gabrielle's face. "Yes, I *do* always know. And, no, my speech is no longer as slurred, praise the Lord from whom all blessings flow. I'm here now, Gabrielle. I'm here. And in spite of all that's going on, you and I are going to dance like nobody's business. You . . . and I —"

"And me!" Jasmine said, coming and flopping down on the other side of Gabrielle.

"Don't forget me. We're family now. She" — Jasmine pointed at Gabrielle — "is my mother. Isn't that right, Mama?"

Gabrielle cried out as she grabbed Jasmine and hugged her. For the first time, Jasmine had called her "Mama." Gabrielle nodded, unable to control her tears of joy. "Yes. We're *all* here, and we're *all* family. And I'm so proud that you're my daughter and that God allowed me to be your . . . mother." Gabrielle looked at Zachary.

He winked and blew her a kiss.

"So next stop," Miss Crowe said, "is the wedding. And we're going to have a *big* wedding, too. Cinderella ain't got nothing on what we're about to do down here in Birmingham, Alabama — home of the Magic City."

"Miss Crowe, I can't get over how much your speech is almost totally back to normal. It's simply amazing! Who would know that just last year about this time, you couldn't even say a word?"

"It's called the power of God. God's goodness and mercy. And there's nothing simple about our God and what He can do." Miss Crowe patted Gabrielle's hand. "Now, who's up to start planning for a wedding? Anybody? Anybody?"

"Meeeee!" Jasmine said, waving her hand

in the air. "I'm the flower girl!"

"Meeeee!" Zachary said, waving his hand like Jasmine. "I'm the groom!"

"Meeeee!" Miss Crowe said, also waving her hand, just not as high as Jasmine and Zachary. "I'm standing in for the mother or maybe the grandmother of the bride. Yeah, the grandmother of the bride and the aunt of the groom."

Gabrielle laid her head on Miss Crowe's shoulder as she continued to allow her tears to fall.

"Ahem," Jasmine said loudly, then patted Gabrielle on the leg. "Excuse me, but it seems that everyone present has raised their hand to be a part of this wedding except for one person in this room. Now *who* could that be? Let's see: One person has not raised her hand for anything yet. We're waiting." Jasmine tried to look mean at Gabrielle.

Gabrielle lifted her head off Miss Crowe's shoulder. "Meeeee!" she said, raising and waving her hand just as hard and as wild as Jasmine had done. "Let's see now, what can I do. Oh, I know. I'm going to be . . . the bride!" The weight of that word suddenly hit her. *She would be the bride.*

Jasmine leapt up off the couch and went over to Zachary. "Finally! It's a go! We're going to get married. So, Dr. Z. May I have this dance?" She curtsied.

He bowed from his waist. "Absolutely, my lady." He took her hand as they held a pose to begin a waltz.

Jasmine looked at Gabrielle and Miss Crowe. "Turn around, you two. Or close your eyes," Jasmine said.

"Close our eyes?" Gabrielle said. "For what?"

"Because Dr. Z and I are going to dance like no one's watching. How can we do that if both of you are watching?" Jasmine began to giggle.

Gabrielle laid her head back down on Miss Crowe's shoulder and closed her eyes. The wedding was on. The clock had officially begun. But in her heart, Gabrielle knew that yet another battle, most likely with Zachary's mother, and who knew who else, was now on a countdown to begin. For now, she would be happy. For now, all was right with the world.

Miss Crowe began humming a tune. Gabrielle lifted her feet off the floor and placed it on the couch as she laid her head in Miss Crowe's lap. Miss Crowe began brushing Gabrielle's hair down with her hand as she continued humming.

Gabrielle smiled. Jasmine was now officially and legally her daughter. Zachary and her daughter were laughing and dancing like nobody's business. Miss Crowe was once again back in her life and miraculously here with her. She and Zachary were moving toward the altar of holy matrimony.

Yes, for now, everything was right with the world. For *now,* everything was right with the world.

■ ■ ■ ■

A READING GROUP GUIDE THE OTHER SIDE OF DARE

VANESSA DAVIS GRIGGS

■ ■ ■ ■

ABOUT THIS GUIDE

The suggested questions that follow are included to enhance your group's reading of this book.

DISCUSSION QUESTIONS

1. Darius Connors is back big-time! What are your thoughts about him and Tiffany as a married couple?

2. Why do you feel Tiffany believes and trusts Darius even though he's proven that he doesn't always tell her everything or the truth? Do you really believe she was totally unaware of what Darius was up to when it came to his "extracurricular" activities?

3. Discuss your thoughts regarding Darius and Paris Simmons-Holyfield teaming up. Talk about their work relationship and the things that transpired, including the morning she woke up with him standing over her. What did you think about Gigi Thornton?

4. What were your feelings when it came to

Paris? By the end of the book, did your feelings change? Do you agree that she had valid reasons for the way she was and the things she did, including her pursuit to obtain custody of Jasmine?

5. Do you agree with the decisions Andrew made or were there things you think he should have done differently? What did you think about him and Gabrielle coming together in the way they did? If you were Gabrielle, would you have trusted him?

6. Lawrence was having a time trying to keep Paris under control. He did a lot when it came to her. Do you think he was right in the things he did? Discuss.

7. Talk about the slumber party at Gabrielle's house, including what happened later in the night. Also talk about the "girls' night out" the three women had at an earlier date.

8. When Paris showed up at Gabrielle's doorstep, what were your thoughts about that encounter? Would you have done anything differently than what Gabrielle did? Discuss.

9. When a cloud of suspicion came in Gabrielle's circle, she was forced to find out what happened. Do you agree with how she handled things? Discuss. If you had found yourself in the same situation, what would you have done? Discuss the problems that developed with Jasmine now knowing the truth, and talk about how things were handled.

10. Tiffany is fed up and now Darius is in a pickle. What are your thoughts on all that took place, including his new employment status? Discuss Darius and Big Red, as well as Gigi's apparent role in everything.

11. Discuss the meeting Darius had with Johnnie Mae Landris, including when Pastor Landris came in.

12. Deidra is laying things down for Lawrence. Discuss what transpired between them and give your thoughts on that entire situation.

13. Paris learns the truth about a lot of things, including the fact that Gabrielle is actually Jasmine's birth mother who gave her up for adoption and that her father slept with her (then roommate) close to

ten years ago. Discuss.

14. Paris also learns she's pregnant, but you know something her husband doesn't know. What are your thoughts about all that you know?

15. Paris and Gabrielle see each other on a day that Andrew delivers wonderful news to Gabrielle. What are your thoughts about everything that happened that day?

16. A dear friend comes back into Gabrielle's life. Discuss your thoughts and feelings about the woman who has made such a difference in Gabrielle's life and the reunion as well as the introduction of Jasmine to her that took place.

The employees of Thorndike Press hope you have enjoyed this Large Print book. All our Thorndike, Wheeler, and Kennebec Large Print titles are designed for easy reading, and all our books are made to last. Other Thorndike Press Large Print books are available at your library, through selected bookstores, or directly from us.

For information about titles, please call:
(800) 223-1244

or visit our Web site at:
http://gale.cengage.com/thorndike

To share your comments, please write:

Publisher
Thorndike Press
10 Water St., Suite 310
Waterville, ME 04901